EMERGENCY

MARION LENNOX
FIONA LOWE
LUCY CLARK

OUTBACK EMERGENCY © 2016 by Harlequin Books S.A.

THE DOCTOR'S RESCUE MISSION
© 2005 by Marion Lennox   First Published 2005
Australian Copyright 2005   Second Australian Paperback Edition 2016
New Zealand Copyright 2005   ISBN 9781760374006

PREGNANT ON ARRIVAL
© 2006 by Fiona Lowe   First Published 2006
Australian Copyright 2006   Second Australian Paperback Edition 2016
New Zealand Copyright 2006   ISBN 9781760374006

A BABY FOR THE FLYING DOCTOR
© 2010 by Anne and Peter Clark   First Published 2010
Australian Copyright 2010   Second Australian Paperback Edition 2016
New Zealand Copyright 2010   ISBN 9781760374006

Published by
Harlequin Mira
An imprint of Harlequin Enterprises (Australia) Pty Ltd.
Level 13, 201 Elizabeth St,
SYDNEY NSW 2000
AUSTRALIA

® and TM are trademarks of Harlequin Enterprises Limited or its corporate affiliates.
Trademarks indicated with ® are registered in Australia, New Zealand, the United
States Patent & Trademark Office and in other countries.

Printed and bound in Australia by Griffin Press

MIX
Paper from
responsible sources
FSC
www.fsc.org   FSC® C009448

CONTENTS

Marion Lennox was born on an Australian dairy farm. She moved on—mostly because the cows weren't interested in her stories! Marion writes Medical Romance™ as well as Tender Romance™. Initially she used different names, so if you're looking for past books, search also for author Trisha David. In her non-writing life Marion cares (haphazardly) for her husband, teenagers, dogs, cats, chickens and anyone else who lines up at her dinner table. She fights her rampant garden (she's losing) and her house dust (she's lost). She also travels, which she finds seriously addictive. As a teenager Marion was told she'd never get anywhere reading romance. Now romance is the basis of her stories, her stories allow her to travel, and if ever there was an advertisement for following your dream, she'd be it! Marion Lennox is an award-winning author. You can contact Marion at www.marionlennox.com

The Doctor's Rescue Mission

Marion Lennox

For Mum, who likes her romances dangerous.
With love.

CHAPTER ONE

THE CALL CAME as Morag prepared for dinner with the man she intended to share her life with. By the time he arrived, Dr Grady Reece was thrust right out of the picture.

The moment she opened the door, Grady guessed something was wrong. This man's career involved responding to disaster, and disaster was etched unmistakably on her face.

'What is it, Morag?'

That was almost her undoing. The way he said her name. She'd always disliked her name. It seemed harsh—a name suggestive of rough country, high crags and bleak weather—but the lilt in Grady's voice the first time he'd uttered it had made her think it was fine after all.

'We need to talk,' she managed. 'But...your family is expecting us.' Grady's brother was a prominent politician and they'd been invited to a family barbecue at his huge mansion on North Shore.

'Rod won't miss us,' Grady told her. 'You know I'm never tied down. My family expect me when they see me.'

That was the way he wanted it. She'd learned that about him early, and she not only expected it but she liked it. Loose ties, no clinging—it was the way to build a lasting relationship.

No ties? What was she about to do?

Dear heaven.

'You want to tell me now?' he asked, and she shook her head. She needed more time. A little more time. Just a few short minutes of the life she'd so carefully built.

'Hey.' He touched her face and smiled down into her eyes. 'I'll take you somewhere I know,' he told her. 'And don't look like that. Nothing's so bad that we can't face it together.'

Together...

There was to be no more together. She fought for control as she grabbed her coat. *Together.*

Not any more.

He didn't press her. He led her to the car and helped her in, knowing instinctively that she was fighting to maintain control.

He was so good in a crisis.

Grady was three years older than Morag, and he'd qualified young from medical school. He had years more experience than she did in dealing with crises.

His reaction to disaster was one of the things that had drawn her to him, she thought as she stared despairingly across the car at the man she loved—and wondered how she could bear to tell him what she must.

Patients talked to him when they were in trouble, she thought. So must she.

Grady was a trauma specialist with Air-Sea Rescue, a team that evacuated disaster victims from all over Australia. Wherever there was disaster, there was Grady, and he was one of the best.

He'd arrive in the emergency room with yet another appallingly injured patient, and the place would be calmer for his presence. Tall and muscular, with a shock of curly black hair and deep, brown, weather-crinkled eyes, Grady's presence seemed to radiate a reassurance that was as inexplicable as it was real. Trust me, those crinkling eyes said. You'll be OK with me.

And why wouldn't you trust him? The man was heart-warmingly gorgeous. Morag hadn't been able to believe her luck when he'd asked her out.

As a surgical registrar, Morag's job at Sydney Central included assessing patients pre-surgery. She'd first met Grady as he'd handed over a burns victim—an aging hippie who'd gone to sleep still smoking his joint. The man's burns had been appalling.

Morag had been impressed with Grady's concern then, and she'd been even more impressed when he'd appeared in the ward two weeks later—to drop in and say hello to someone no one in the world seemed to care about.

That had been the beginning. So far they'd only had four weeks of interrupted courtship, but she'd known from the start that this could work. They had so much in common.

They were both ambitious. They both loved working in critical care, and they intended to work in the fast lane for their entire medical careers. They laughed at the same things. They loved the same food, the same lifestyle, the same...everything.

And Grady had the ability to curl her toes. Just as he was doing now. She looked across at her with that quizzical half-smile she was beginning to love, and her heart did a crazy back somersault with pike. He looked gorgeous in his soft, lambswool sweater—a sweater that on anyone else but Grady might look effeminate, but on Grady it just looked fabulous—and it was all she could do not to burst into tears.

She didn't. Of course she didn't. Tears would achieve nothing. She turned away and stared straight ahead, into the darkness.

The restaurant he drove her to was a secluded little bistro where the food was great and the service better. Grady ordered, still sensing that Morag couldn't do anything other than focus on the catastrophe surrounding her. With wine poured and orders taken, the waiters let them be.

They must look a really romantic couple, Morag thought dully. She'd taken such care with her appearance tonight. Although dressed for a barbecue, there was little casual about her appearance. Her jeans were figure-hugging and brand-new. She wore great little designer shoes, high as high, stretching her legs to sexy-long. Her crop top was tiny, crimson, leaving little to the imagination, and she'd swept up her chestnut curls into a knot of wispy curls on top of her head. She'd applied make-up to her pale skin with care. She knew she looked sexy and seductive and expensive—and she knew that there was good reason why every man present had turned his head as Grady had ushered her into the restaurant.

This was how she loved to look. But after tonight there'd never be any call for her to look like this again.

'Hey, it can't be that bad.' Grady reached out and took her hand. He stroked the back of it with care. It was something she'd seen him do with patients.

Two weeks ago a small boy had come into Sydney Central after a tractor accident and Grady had sat with the parents and explained there was no way the little boy's arm could be saved. She'd seen him lift the burly farmer's hand and touch it just like this—an almost unheard-of gesture man to man, but so necessary when the father would be facing self-blame all his life.

She'd loved that gesture when she'd seen it then. And now, here he was, using the same gesture on her.

'What is it, Morag?'

'My sister.' She could hardly say it.

Don't say it at all! a little voice inside her head was screaming at her. If you don't say it out loud, then it won't be real.

But it was real. Horribly real.

'I didn't know you had a sister.' Grady was frowning, and Morag knew he was thinking of her mother, the brisk businesswoman to whom he'd been introduced.

'Beth's my half-sister,' Morag whispered. 'She's ten years older than I am. She lives on Petrel Island.'

'Petrel Island?'

'Off the coast of—'

'I know Petrel Island.' He was focused on her face, and his fingers were still doing the smoothing thing to the back of her hand. It was making her cringe inside. This man—he was who she wanted for ever. She knew that. But he—

'We evacuated a kid from Petrel Island twelve months back,' Grady said. 'It's a weird little community—Kooris and fishermen and a crazy doctor-cum-lighthouse-keeper keeping the whole community together.'

'That's Beth.'

'That's your sister?' His tone was incredulous and she knew why. There seemed no possible connection between the placid islander Beth and the sophisticated career doctor he was looking at.

But there was. Of course there was. You couldn't remove sisterhood by distance or by lifestyle.

Beth was her sister for ever.

'Beth's the island doctor,' she told him, finding the courage to meet his eyes. 'She's also the lighthouse caretaker. It's what our father did so she's taken right over.'

'Beth's the lighthouse-keeper? And the doctor as well?'

'Yes.'

'But…why?'

'It's a family thing,' she told him. Seeing his confusion deepen, she tried to explain. 'Dad was born on the island, and inherited the lighthouse-keeping from my grandad. He married an island girl and they had Beth. Then the lighthouse was upgraded to automatic—just as Dad's first wife died. She was seven months pregnant with their second baby, but she collapsed and died of eclampsia before Dad could get her to the mainland.'

Grady was frowning, taking it on board with deep concern. 'She had no warning?'

'There was no doctor on the island,' Morag said bleakly. 'And, no, he had no warning. Everything seemed normal. She was planning on leaving for the mainland at thirty-four weeks but she didn't make it. Anyway, her death meant that within a few weeks Dad lost his wife, his baby son and his job. All he had left was two-year-old Beth. But the waste of the deaths made him decide what to do. He brought Beth to the mainland, and managed to get a grant to go to medical school. That's where he met my mother. They married and had me, but the marriage was a disaster. Everyone was miserable. By time Dad finished med school, the government decided that leaving the lighthouse to look after itself— even if it was automatic—was also a disaster. The island was still desperate for a doctor, and the caretaker's cottage was still empty. So Dad and Beth went home.'

Grady's face was thoughtful. 'Leaving you behind with your mother?'

'Of course.' She shrugged. 'Can you see my mother living on Petrel Island? But I did spend lots of time there. Every holiday. Whenever I could. Mum didn't mind. As long as she wasn't seen as a deserting mother, anything I did was OK by her. She's not exactly a warm and fuzzy parent, my mother.'

'I have met her.'

He had. They'd moved fast in four weeks. Morag's eyes flickered again to his face. Maybe this could work. Maybe he...

But the eyes he was looking at her with were wrong, she thought, confused by the messages she was receiving. He was concerned as he'd be concerned for a patient. He was using a 'Let's get to the bottom of this' kind of voice. He was gentleness personified, but his gentleness was abstract. For Morag, who'd had a childhood of abstract affection, the concept was frightening.

'So you spent holidays with your father and Beth,' Grady was saying, and she forced herself to focus on the past rather than the terrifying future.

'Yes. They were... They loved me. Beth was everything to me.'

'Where's your father now?'

'He died three years ago. He's buried on the island. That's OK. He had a subarachnoid haemorrhage and died in his sleep, and it wasn't a bad way to go for a man in his seventies.'

'But Beth?'

'As I said, she's a doctor, like me.' Still she couldn't say what was wrong. How could she? How could she voice the unimaginable? 'My dad, and then Beth after him, provided the island's medical care. Because there's only about five hundred people living on the island, and the medical work is hardly arduous, they've kept on the lighthouse. too. Lighthouse-keeping's not the time consuming job it was.'

'I guess it's not.' Grady was watching her face. Waiting. Knowing that she was taking her time to say what had to be said, and knowing she needed that time. He lifted her hand again and gripped her fingers, looking down at them as if he was examining them for damage. It was a technical manoeuvre, she thought dully. Something he'd learned to do. 'So Beth's the island doctor...'

'She's great.' She was talking too fast, she thought, but she couldn't slow down. Her voice didn't seem to belong to her. 'She's ten years older than me, and she was almost a mother to me. She'd turn up unexpectedly whenever I most needed her. If I was in a school play and my mother couldn't make it—which she nearly always couldn't—I'd suddenly, miraculously, find Beth in the audience, cheering me on with an enthusiasm that was almost embarrassing. And when she decided to be a doctor, I thought I could be, too.'

'But not like Beth?'

'Beth wanted to go back to the island. It tore her apart to leave to do her medical training, and the moment she was qualified she returned. She fell in love with a local fisherman and the island's her home. She loves it.'

'And you?' he probed.

'The island's never been my home. I love it but I never thought of living anywhere but here.' She attempted a smile but it was a pretty shaky one. 'I guess I have more than a bit of my mother in me somewhere. I like excitement, cities, shopping...life.'

'Like me.'

'My excitement levels don't match your excitement levels,' she told him ruefully. 'I like being a surgeon in a bustling city hospital. I don't dangle out of helicopters in raging seas, plucking—'

But Grady wasn't to be distracted. The background had been covered. Now it was time to move on. 'Morag, what's wrong?' His deep voice cut through her misery, compelling. Doctor asking for facts, so he could treat what needed to be treated.

Her voice faltered. She looked up at him and then away. His hand tightened on hers—just as she'd seen him do with distressed patients. For some reason the action had her tugging away from him. She didn't want this man treating her as he'd treat a patient. This was supposed to be special.

This was supposed to be for ever.

For ever?

The prospect of for ever rose up, overwhelming her with dread. Somehow she had to explain and she had to do it before she broke down.

'Beth has renal cancer,' she whispered.

She'd shifted her hand back to her side of the table. Grady made a move to regain it, but she tucked it carefully under the table. It seemed stupidly important that she knew where her hand was.

He didn't say anything. She swallowed while he waited for her to go on. He was good, this man. His bedside manner was impeccable.

And suddenly, inexplicably, his bedside manner made her want to hit him.

Crazy. Anger—anger at Grady—was crazy. She had to force herself to be logical here. To make sense.

'I haven't been back to the island for over a year,' she managed. 'But last time I went Beth seemed terrific. She had a bad time for a while. She married a local fisherman, and he was drowned just after Dad died. But she was recovering. She's thirty-nine years old and she has a little boy, Robbie, who's five. She seemed settled and happy. Life was looking good.'

'But now she's been diagnosed with renal cancer?' His tone was carefully neutral, still extracting facts.

'Mmm.'

'What stage?'

'Advanced. Apparently she flew down to Melbourne last month and had scans without telling anyone. There's a massive tumour in the left kidney, with spread that's clear from the scans. It's totally inoperable.'

And totally anything else, she thought bleakly as she waited for Grady to absorb what she'd told him. He'd know the inevitable outcome just as clearly as she did. If renal cancer was caught while the tumour was still contained, then it could be surgically removed—removing the entire kidney—but once it had spread outside the kidney wall, chemotherapy or radiotherapy would make little difference.

'She's dying,' she whispered.

'I'm sorry.'

Her eyes flew up to his. He was watching her, his eyes gentle, but she wasn't imagining it. There was that tiny trace of removal. Distancing.

'I need to go to the island,' she told him. 'Now.'

'Of course you do.' He hesitated, and she could see him juggling appointments in his head. Thinking ahead to his frantic week. It was what she always did when something unexpected came up.

Until now.

'Do you want me to come with you?' he asked.

Did she? Of course she did. More than anything else in the world. But...

'I can call on Steve to cover for me for the next week,' he told her. 'If we could be back by next Sunday—'

'No.'

His face stilled. 'Sorry?'

And now it was time to say it. It couldn't be put off one moment longer.

'Grady, this isn't going to happen,' she said gently, as if this would hurt him as much as it hurt her. And maybe it would.

'My sister's dying. She has a little boy and she's a single mother. She has a community who depend on her.'

His face was almost expressionless. 'What are you saying?'

'That it'll be a lot…a lot longer than a week.'

'Can you take more than a week off?' His face changed back to the concerned, involved expression that was somehow turning her away from him. It was making her cringe inside. It was his doctor's face.

'I guess you must,' he said, thinking it through as he spoke. 'The hospital will organise compassionate leave for you for a few weeks.' He hesitated. 'I'll come for a week now, and then again for—'

'The funeral?' she finished for him, and watched him flinch.

'Morag…'

She shook her head. 'It's not going to happen.'

'I'm sorry. I shouldn't have said—'

'Oh, the funeral's going to happen,' she said, her anger directed squarely now against the appalling waste of cancer. 'Inevitably it'll happen. But as for taking compassionate leave…I can't.'

He frowned, confused. 'So you'll come back in a week or so?'

'I didn't say that.' She lifted her hands back onto the table and stared down at her fingers, as if she couldn't believe she was about to make the commitment that in truth she'd made the moment she'd heard her sister whisper, 'Renal cancer.' It was done. It was over. 'I'm not taking compassionate leave,' she said bluntly. 'I'm going to the island for ever.'

It shocked him. It shocked him right out of compassionate doctor, caring lover mode. All the things he was most good at. His brow snapped down in surprise, and his deep, dark eyes went still.

'You can't just quit.' Grady's job was his life, Morag thought hopelessly, and she could understand it. Until an hour ago she'd felt the same way. But she had no choice.

'Why can't I quit?' And then, despairingly, she added, 'How can I not?'

'Surely your sister wouldn't expect you to.'

'Beth expects nothing,' she said fiercely. 'She never has. She gives and she gives and she gives.' Their meal arrived at that moment and she stared down at it as if she didn't recognise it. Grady leaned across to place her knife and fork in her hands—back to being the caring doctor—but she didn't even notice. 'Petrel Island needs her so much,' she whispered.

'She's their only doctor?'

'My father and then Beth,' she told him. She stopped for a minute then, ostensibly to eat but really to gather her thoughts to continue. 'Because my father was a doctor, more young families have come to the island, and the community's grown. There's fishing and kelp farming and a great little specialist dairy. But without a doctor, the Petrel Island community will disintegrate.'

'They could get someone else.'

'Oh, sure.' It was almost a jeer. 'A doctor who wants to practise in such a place? I don't think so. After…after Beth dies, maybe…I'll try to find someone, but it's so unlikely. And Beth needs my promise—that the island can continue without her.

'So you see,' she told him, cutting her steak into tiny pieces that she had no intention of eating. It was so important to concentrate. It was important to concentrate on anything but Grady. 'You see why I need to leave?'

There was a reason she couldn't look at him. She knew what his reaction would be. And here it came.

'But…you're saying this might be for ever?' He sounded appalled. As well he might.

'I'm saying for as long as I'm needed. Do I have a choice?'

He had the answer to that one. 'Yes,' he said flatly. 'Bring your sister here. You can't tell me there aren't far better medical facilities in Sydney than on Petrel Island. And who's going to be treating physician? You? You know that's a recipe for disaster. Caring for your own family… I don't think so.'

'There's no one else.'

'There's no one else in Sydney?' he asked incredulously.

'No. On the island. Beth won't leave the island.'

'She doesn't have a choice,' Grady said, the gentleness returning to his voice. Gentle but right. Sympathetic but firm. 'You have a life, Morag, and your life is here.'

'And Robbie? Her little boy? What of his life?'

'Maybe he's going to have to move on. Plenty of kids have a city life. It won't hurt him to spend a couple of months in Sydney.'

'You mean I should bring them both here while Beth dies.'

'You have a life, too,' he told her. 'It sounds dreadful—I know it does—but if your sister is dying then you have to think past the event.'

'Take care of the living?'

'That's right,' he said, his face clearing a little. 'Your sister will see that. She sounds a pragmatic person. Not selfish...'

'No. Not selfish. Never selfish.'

'You need to think long term. She'll be thinking long term.'

'She is,' Morag said dully. 'That's why she rang me. She's been ill for months and she's been searching for some way not to ask me. But it's come to this. She doesn't have a choice and neither do I. Without Beth the community doesn't have a doctor. Robbie doesn't have a mother. And I'm it.'

Silence. Then... 'Your mother?'

'You've met my mother. Barbara take care of Robbie? He's not even her grandchild. Don't be stupid.'

He looked flatly at her, aghast. 'You're not seriously suggesting you throw everything up here?' he demanded. 'Take over the care of a dying sister? Take on the mothering of a child, and the medical needs of a tiny island hundreds of miles from the mainland? Morag, you have to be kidding!'

'Do you think I'd joke about something like this?'

'Look, don't make any decisions,' he said urgently. 'Not yet. Get compassionate leave for a week or two and take it from there. I'll come over and do some reorganisation—'

'Some reorganisation?'

'I'll talk to the flying doctor service. We'll see if we can get a clinic over there once a month or so to keep the locals happy. I can organise an apartment here that'd accommodate your sister. Maybe we can figure out a long-term carer for the kid on the island. He can go to day care here while his mum's alive, and then we'll find someone to take him over long term.'

Great. For the first time since Beth had telephoned, Morag felt an emotion that was so fierce it overrode her complete and utter devastation. She raised her face to his and met his look head on. He was doing what he was so good at. Crisis management. He was taking disaster and hauling it into manageable bits.

But this was Beth. Beth!

'Do you know what love is?' she whispered.

He looked confused. 'Sure I do, Morag.' He reached forward and would have taken her hand again but she snatched it back like he'd burn her. 'You and I—'

'You and I don't have a thing. Not any more. This is Beth we're talking about. Beth. My darling sister. The woman who cares for me and loves me and who put her own life on hold for me so many times I can't think about it. You'd have me repay that by taking a couple of weeks' leave?'

'Morag, this is your life.'

'Our lives. Mine and Beth's. They intertwine. As ours—yours and mine—don't any more.' She rose and stood, staring down at him, her sudden surge of anger replaced by unutterable sadness. Unutterable weariness. 'Grady, I can't stay here,' she whispered. 'I'm going home. I'm going back to Petrel Island and I won't be coming back.'

He stayed seated, emphasising the growing gulf between them. 'But you don't want—'

'What I want doesn't come into it.'

'And what I want?'

'What's that supposed to mean?'

'I want you, Morag.'

'No.' She shook her head. 'No, you don't. You want the part of me that I thought I could become. That I thought I was. Independent career doctor, city girl, partner while we had the best fun...'

He rose then but it was different. He put his hands on her shoulders and bent to kiss her lightly on the lips. It was a fleeting gesture but she knew exactly what he was doing, and the pain was building past the point where she could bear it. 'We did have fun,' he told her.

'We did.' She swallowed. It wasn't Grady's fault that she'd fallen hopelessly in love with him, she realised. Beth's illness wasn't his fault, and it wasn't his fault that their lives from now on would be totally incompatible.

It wasn't his fault that now he was letting her go.

For richer and for poorer. In sickness and in health. Whither thou goest, I will go...

Ha! It was never going to work. Beth needed her.

And Grady wasn't going to follow.

But his hand suddenly lifted to her face, as if he'd had second thoughts. He cupped her chin and forced her eyes to his. 'You can't go.' His voice was low, suddenly gruff and serious. The caring and competent young doctor had suddenly been replaced by someone who was unsure. 'Morag, these last few weeks... It's been fantastic. You know that I love you.'

Did he? Until this evening she'd thought—she'd hoped that he had. And she'd thought she loved him.

Whither thou goest, I will go.

No. It hadn't reached that stage yet. She looked into his uncertain eyes and she knew that the line hadn't been crossed. Which was just as well. It made the decision she was making now bearable. Just. Maybe.

'No,' she said softly. 'You don't love me. Not yet. But I do love Beth, and she needs me. The island needs me. It was wonderful, Grady, but I need to move on.'

Even then he could have stopped her. He could have come up with some sort of alternative. Come with her now, try the island for size, think of how it could work...

No. That was desperation talking and desperation had no foundation in solid, dreadful reality.

She didn't need to end this. It was already over.

'What can I do?' he asked, and she bit her lip.

'Nothing.' Nothing she could ever vocalise. 'Just say goodbye.'

And that was that.

She rose on tiptoe and kissed him again, hard this time, and fast, tasting him, savouring him for one last moment. One fleeting minute. And then, before he could respond, she'd straightened and backed away.

'I need to go, Grady,' she told him, trying desperately to keep the tears from her voice. 'It's been...fabulous. But I need...to follow my heart.'

CHAPTER TWO

MORAG FELT THE earth move while she was at Hubert Hamm's, and stupidly, after the first few frightening moments, she thought it mightn't matter.

Hubert was the oldest of the island's fisherman. His father had run sheep up on the ridge to the north of the island. That was where Hubert had been born and the tiny cottage was still much as Elsie Hamm had furnished it as a bride almost a hundred years before.

The cottage had two rooms. There was a tiny kitchen-living room where Robbie sat and fondled Hubert's old dog, and an even smaller bedroom where Hubert lay, approaching his death with stately dignity.

It'd be a while before he achieved his objective, Morag thought as she measured his blood pressure. Six months ago, Hubert had taken himself to bed, folded his hands across his chest and announced that the end was nigh. The only problem was that the neighbours kept dropping off wonderful casseroles and puddings, usually staying for a chat. His love of gossip was therefore thoroughly catered for. Hubert's bedroom window looked out over the whole island, and he was so eagle-eyed and interested that death seemed less and less enticing.

With Morag visiting every few days, his health did nothing but improve, to the extent that now Morag had no compunction in bringing Robbie with her as she took her weekly hike up the scree. There was a rough vehicle track round the back of the ridge but the scenery from the walking path was spectacular. She and Robbie enjoyed the hike, and they enjoyed Hubert.

Would that all deathbeds were this healthy, prolonged and cheerful.

'I'm worse?' Hubert asked—without much hope—and she grinned.

'Not so you'd notice. But you're certainly a week older and that has to count for something.'

'Death's coming. I can feel it,' he said in solemn tones, but a sea eagle chose that moment to glide past his window and his old eyes swung around to follow its soaring flight.

Death might be coming, but life was still looking good.

Consultation over.

'Have you finished? Is Mr Hamm OK?' Robbie looked up as she opened Hubert's bedroom door, and she smiled across at her nine-year-old nephew with affection.

'Mr Hamm's great. His blood pressure's fine. His heart rate's nice and steady. Our patient looks like living for at least another week—if not another decade. Are you ready to go home?'

'Yep.' Robbie gave Elspeth a final hug and rose, a freckled, skinny little redhead with a grin that reminded Morag achingly of Beth. 'When Mr Hamm dies, can I have Elspeth?'

Elspeth, an ancient golden retriever, pricked up her ears in hope, but back in the bedroom so did Hubert.

'She'll stay here until I'm gone,' the old man boomed.

'Of course she will,' Robbie said, with all the indignation of a nine-year-old who knew how the world worked. 'But you've put names on everything else.'

He had, too. In the last six months Hubert had catalogued his cottage. Everything had a name on now, right down to the battered teapot on the edge of the fire-stove. '*Iris Potter, niece in London*,' the sign said, and Morag hoped that Hubert's niece would be suitably grateful when the time came.

'There's no name on Elspeth,' Robbie said reasonably. 'And she's an ace dog.'

'Yeah, well, you're a good lad,' Hubert conceded from his bed. 'She'd have a good home with you.'

'I bet she could catch rabbits.'

'My oath,' Hubert told them, still from behind the bedroom door. 'You should see her go.'

'You know, you could get up and show Robbie,' Morag said, trying not to smile, and had a snort of indignation for her pains.

'What, me? A dying man? You know...'

But she never found out what she was supposed to know. Right at that moment the house gave a long, rolling shudder. The teapot, balanced precariously on the side of the stove, tipped slowly over and crashed to the floor.

For one long moment Morag didn't realise what was happening. Then she did. Unbelievably, she did. It seemed impossible but there was no time to wonder if she was right or not.

Earthquake?

'Robbie, out! Get away from the house.' She shoved Robbie out the door before he could utter a response. Elspeth gave a terrified whimper and bolted after him, and they were barely clear before Morag was back in the bedroom, hauling Hubert out of bed and of the house after Robbie and Elspeth.

'What the...?' For someone supposedly ready to meet his maker, Hubert clearly had a way to go. He was white with terror. Morag was practically carrying him across the cottage floor as his old feet tried their hardest to scuttle on a surface that was weirdly unstable.

'It must be an earthquake.' She had him clear of the doorway now. Robbie was crouched on the back lawn, holding onto Elspeth, and the dog was whimpering in terror.

'I don't believe it.' Hubert sank to his knees and grabbed his dog as well. 'We haven't had one of these on the island for eighty years.'

They were clear now of anything that could fall. The earth seemed to be steadying again and she had everyone well away from the house. Morag was hugging Robbie, and Robbie and Hubert were both hugging Elspeth, so they were crazily attached. It was a weird intimacy in the face of shared peril.

They didn't talk. Talking seemed impossible. They just knelt and waited for a catastrophe that...that suddenly seemed as if it might not happen.

More silence. It was almost eerie. They sat and waited some more but the tremors seemed to have stopped.

Then they sat up and unattached themselves. Sort of. A bit.

'Was it really an earthquake?' Robbie demanded, and when Morag nodded, he let out his breath in one long 'Cool...'

But his body was still pressed against Morag's and he was still holding on.

'We haven't had one of these for eighty years,' Hubert whispered.

'You've experienced this before?'

'We're on some sort of fault line,' Hubert told them, his colour and his bravado returning as the ground settled. 'A bunch of scientists came here years back and did some testing but no one took much notice.' He snorted, his courage building by the minute. 'It'll be the same as last time. A bit of a wobble and a fuss and then naught for another eighty years.'

'I hope you're right.' Morag grabbed Robbie around his middle and hugged, hard. Her little nephew was usually the bravest of kids but it didn't take much for him to remember that the world was inherently unsafe. His 'cool' had been decidedly shaky. Seven years ago his father had drowned, and four years back he'd lost his mother. Now he clung alternately to Morag and the dog, and Morag kissed his hair and hugged him tight and wondered where to go to from here.

The only damage up on the ridge seemed to be a dent in Hubert's teapot. But down below... She shaded her eyes, trying to see down to the little village built around the harbour. It was a gorgeous day. The sleepy fishing village was far below them, but from here it looked untouched.

Maybe a dented teapot was the worst of it.

Please...

'Maybe you'd better stay up here for a bit in case another shock comes,' Hubert told her, his voice showing that he was just as wobbly as Robbie.

But she had no choice. She was the island's only doctor and if there was trouble in the township...

'I need to head back to check the lighthouse and radio the mainland,' she told Hubert, but she was speaking to Robbie as well. There was a bit of a stacks-on-the-mill process happening here. Robbie was on her knees, Elspeth was sprawled over Robbie, and Morag had a feeling that if dignity hadn't been an issue then Hubert would be up here as well. Nothing like the earth trembling to make you unsure of your foundations.

Robbie sat even more firmly in her lap. 'I think we should all stay here,' he told her. 'What if it gets worse?'

'Aftershocks,' Hubert said wisely. He'd moved away a little in an attempt to regain his dignity. Now he clicked his fingers for Elspeth to come to him. Elspeth wriggled higher onto Robbie's lap and Hubert had to sidle closer himself to pat his dog.

They were depending on her, Morag thought despairingly. So what was new? The entire island depended on her—when often all she wanted to do was wail.

This was an earthquake. This was truly scary. Who did she get to tremble on?

No one. Ever. She swallowed and fought for calm and for sense.

'Hubert's right. Mild earth tremors are nothing to worry about.' She put Robbie gently aside and ruffled his hair. 'Robbie, you know I need to go.' She sent him a silent message with her eyes, saying she was depending on him.

And Robbie responded. He'd learned from birth what was expected of him as the doctor's kid, and he rose to the occasion now.

'Do you really have to go?' he asked.

'You know that I do.'

'Can I come with you?'

'It'd better if you stayed here for a bit.'

He took a deep breath. He really was the best kid. 'OK.' Elspeth got a hard hug. 'I'll look after Elspeth if Mr Hamm looks after me.'

'Is that OK with you, Mr Hamm?' she asked, and Hubert flashed her a worried look.

'It's fine by me, girl, but you—'

'I'll be fine.'

'You know, the first quake is usually the biggest,' Robbie volunteered. It really hadn't been a very big shake and it was already starting to recede to adventure rather than trouble. 'I read about them in my nature book. There's not likely to be another bigger one. Just little aftershocks.'

'That's a relief.'

'Maybe a bigger one'd be cool.'

'No,' Morag said definitely. 'It wouldn't be cool.'

'Or maybe this was a ginormous one out to sea and we just got the little sideways shocks a long way away,' he said, optimism returning minute by minute.

'Well, that'd be better,' Morag conceded, thinking about it. 'With the closest land mass being the mainland three hundred miles away, there's not much likelihood of any damage at all. Mind, a few dolphins might be feeling pretty seasick.'

Robbie chuckled.

And that was that.

The earthquake was over. Even Elspeth started to wag her tail again.

But she still had to check the village.

Robbie's chuckle was a good sound, Morag thought as she started down the scree. She'd worked hard on getting that sound back after his mother had died and now she treasured it. It was a major reason she was here, on this island.

Without a life.

Who was she kidding? She had a life. She had a community to care for. She had Robbie's chuckle. And she had flying teapots to check out.

But it didn't stop her mind from wandering.

Even though she lived in one of the most isolated places in the world, there was little enough time for her to be alone. She had so many demands made on her. If it wasn't her patients it was Robbie, and although she loved the little boy to bits, this time scrambling down the scree when she wasn't much worried about what she'd find below was a time to be treasured.

She liked being alone.

No, she thought. She didn't. Here she was seldom by herself, but *alone* was a concept that had little to do with people around her.

She liked being by herself for a while. But she didn't like *alone*.

Always at the back of her heart was Grady. The life she'd walked away from.

There was no turning back, but her loss of Grady was still an aching grief, shoved away and never allowed to surface. But it was always there.

He'd written her the loveliest letter when Beth had died, saying how much he missed her, offering to take her away for a holiday, offering to organise things in Sydney so she could return, offering everything but himself.

She'd taken the letter up to the top of the lighthouse. There she'd torn it into a thousand pieces and let it blow out to sea.

Enough. Enough of Grady. She hadn't heard from him for four years.

Concentrate on need.

Surely an earthquake was worth concentrating on.

Two hundred yards down the path she paused. The closer she came to the village the more it looked as if there was no damage at all.

Hubert really did treasure his isolation. The path up to his cottage was little more than a goat track on the side of a steep incline. She could stand here for a moment with the sun on her face, look out at the breathtaking beauty of the ocean beyond the island and wonder how she could ever dream of leaving such a place. It was just beautiful.

The sea wasn't where it was supposed to be.

She blinked for a moment, thinking her eyes were playing tricks. The tide's a long way out, she thought inconsequentially, and then she thought, No, it's a crazy way out. The beach was normally twenty or thirty yards wide but now...the water seemed to have been sucked...

Sucked.

A jangling, dreadful alarm sounded in her head as her eyes swept the horizon. She was suddenly frantic. Her feet were starting to move even as she searched, hoping desperately not to see...

But she saw.

There was a long line of silver, far out. She thought she was imagining it at first—thought it must be the product of dread. Maybe it was the horizon.

Only it wasn't. It was a faint line beneath the horizon, moving inexorably closer. If it hadn't been such a calm, still day she might not have seen it at all, for in deep water it was only marginally above the height of a biggish swell, but she was sure... There was a boat far out and she saw it bucket high—unbelievably high—and then disappear behind a wall of water.

No.

The villagers were out of their cottages. She could see them. They were gathering in the street beyond the harbour. They'd be comparing notes about damage from the tremor, fearing more. They wouldn't be turned toward the sea.

She was running now, racing up the goat path. She'd never moved so fast in her life.

At least she knew what needed to be done. This place had been the graveyard for scores of ships in the years since the first group of Scottish fishermen had built their homes here, and the islanders were geared for urgent warning. The track she was on overlooked the entire island. There were bells up here, set up to make the villagers aware that there was an urgent, life-threatening need. At every curve in the track—every couple of hundred yards—there was a bell, and every island child knew the way to be sent to Coventry for ever was to ring one needlessly.

Morag knew exactly where the closest one was, and her feet had never moved so fast as they did now. Seconds after she'd first heard her own mental alarm bell, she reached the closest warning place and the sound of the huge bell rang out across the island.

This wasn't a shipwreck. It was the islanders themselves who were in deadly peril.

They'd have to guess what she was warning of. 'Guess,' she pleaded. 'Guess.'

They heard. The islanders gathered in the street stilled. She saw them turn to face her as they registered the sound of the bell.

She was too far away to signal danger. She was too far away for her scream to be heard.

But there were fishermen among the villagers, old heads whose first thoughts went to the sea. They'd see a lone figure far up on the ridge ringing the bell. Surely they'd guess.

Maybe they'd guess?

She stood on the edge of the rocky outcrop and waved her arms, pointing out to sea, screaming soundlessly into the stillness. Guess. Guess.

And someone responded. She saw rather than heard the yell erupting—a scream of warning and of terror as someone figured out what she might be warning them about. Someone had put together the tremor and her warning and they knew what might happen.

Even from so far away, she heard the collective response.

People were yelling for their children. People were grabbing people.

People were running. A mass of bodies was hurling off the main street, scrabbling for the side streets that led steeply out of town.

She could see them but she could do nothing except go back to uselessly ringing her damned bell.

People were stumbling, stopping to help, to carry…

'No,' she was screaming, helpless in the face of the sheer distance between here and the town. 'Don't stop. Don't stop.'

She could see their terror. She felt it with them.

And she could see the smaller and smaller distance between the islanders and the great wash of water bearing down.

'Run. Run.'

The wall of water was building now as it approached land. It was sucking yet more water up before it. The shore was a barren wasteland of waterless emptiness.

And Morag could do nothing. She could only stand high on the hill and watch the tsunami smash toward the destruction of her people.

There was a soft, growing rumble. Louder…

Then it hit.

She watched in appalled, stupefied fascination as the water reached the shore. There were dull grating sounds as buildings ground together. Sharp reports as power poles snapped. It was a vast front of inrushing water, smashing all before it in a ghastly, slamming tide, the like of which Morag had never begun to imagine.

And there was nothing to do where she stood but watch.

Maybe she could have closed her eyes. She surely didn't want to see, but for the first awful seconds her eyes stayed open.

She saw the tiny harbour surge, boats pushed up onto the jetty, houses hit, the water almost to their eaves. Dear God, if people were inside…

She saw old Elias Cartwright open his front door just as the water hit—stubborn old Elias who'd consider it beneath his dignity to gather outside with the villagers just because of a mere earth tremor…

The water smashed and that was the last Morag saw of Elias.

It was then that she closed her eyes and she felt herself start to retch.

She kept her eyes closed.

Closed.

This was safe. Here in the dark she could tell herself she was retching for nothing. It was a dream—a nightmare—and soon she'd wake up.

But there was no line separating dream from reality.

The sun was still warm on her face. One of the island goats was nudging her arm in gentle enquiry. The world was just the same.

Only, of course, it wasn't. When she finally found the courage to open her eyes, the tiny Petrel Island settlement was changed for ever.

The houses nearest the harbour were gone. The harbour itself was a tangle of timber and mud and uprooted trees.

Devastation...

Her first thought flew to Robbie.

She looked upward to Hubert's place and the old man was staring down at her, her horror reflected in the stock-still stance of the old man. She was two hundred yards away but his yell echoed down the scree with the clarity of a man with twenty-year-old lungs.

'I'll take care of the lad. We'll watch the sea for more. Robbie and I'll stick with the bell and not leave it.'

She managed to listen. She managed to understand what he'd said.

Hubert and Robbie would watch to warn of another wave, she thought dully. And in offering to take care of Robbie, she knew what Hubert was saying she should do.

She was the island's only doctor. The islanders looked to her for help. For leadership.

She had to go down.

CHAPTER THREE

'NOTHING EVER HAPPENS in this place.'

Dr Grady Reece played with his mug of coffee and stared at the pieces on his chessboard. He'd beaten Dr Jaqui Ford three times and she'd beaten him five.

He was going out of his mind.

The weather was perfect, and that was half the trouble. Enough rain meant no bushfires. No wind meant no dramas at sea. They were out of the holiday season so people weren't doing damned fool holiday things. Which meant Air-Sea Rescue was having a very quiet time.

'Aren't you glad?' Jaqui enquired.

'Why should I be glad? I joined the service for excitement.'

'So you like people killing themselves?'

'I didn't mean that,' he growled. 'You know very well that I try my damnedest to stop people killing themselves. And you live on adrenaline just as much as I do.'

'Yes, but I have had a life,' Jaqui said mildly. 'Husband, kids, dogs. I come here for some peace. Yeah, I like the adrenaline rush of thinking we might be saving someone, but for the rest…work is my quiet time.'

Grady smiled at that. Jaqui was in her mid-fifties and was a very competent doctor. She'd only just undertaken the additional training to join Air-Sea Rescue, but already the tales of her tribe of hell-raising adult sons were legion. Everyone knew why Jaqui thought rescuing people in high drama was a quiet life.

'No, but you,' Jaqui said insistently. 'You can't depend on this for your excitement. Maybe you need kids of your own.'

'To provide me with drama? I don't think so.'

'So you're not into families?' Jaqui was probing past the point of politeness, but Grady's associate was no respecter of boundaries.

'Not interested,' Grady growled, hoping to shut her up.

It didn't.

'You're not gay?'

That got a grin. 'What do you think?'

'You never know these days,' Jaqui said, moving her bishop with a nonchalance that told Grady she was hoping he might not notice she was threatening his queen. 'Someone once told me you can detect gayness if a man wears one earring, but my sons wear one, two or sixteen, depending on how the mood takes them. As they also seem to have one, two or sixteen girlfriends, depending on how the mood takes them, who would know anything at all? So...' She sat back and subjected him to intense scrutiny. 'Not gay. Not seriously involved. There's never been a woman who looked like being long term?'

'Cut it out.'

'Max told me you were really smitten once. A lady called Morag.'

Max was their pilot. Max talked too much.

'Morag and I went out for about a month. Four years ago.'

'Was that all? I thought it was serious.'

Maybe it was, Grady thought ruefully. He'd hardly thought through the consequences at the time but after she'd gone...he'd missed her like hell. Not that there'd been any choice in the matter. She'd buried herself in some remote little settlement and that surely wasn't the life for him.

So what? Why was he thinking of Morag now? he asked himself. He'd moved on. He'd dated. Morag had been a one-month relationship followed up by a letter of sympathy after her sister had died. It had been an intense letter that had taken him a long time to draft, but she'd never answered. So...

So one of these days a lady would come on the scene who'd make him smile as Morag had made him smile. But with no attachments.

'You don't want kids?' Jaqui asked.

'Why would I want kids?'

'You want excitement. Kids equal excitement.'

'I'll get my excitement some other way,' he growled. He moved his queen, removed his hand from the board and then saw the danger. 'Whoops. Check.'

'Checkmate,' Jaqui said sweetly, and then looked up as Max came through the door. One look at their pilot's face and they knew there were to be no more chess matches that afternoon.

'What is it?'

'Code One,' Max said shortly. 'Huge. We're going in first, with back-up on the way. The army'll be in on this, but, Grady, you've been put in charge first off. Tsunami.'

'A tidal wave,' Jaqui said incredulously. 'Where?'

'Petrel Island. Contact to the island's completely cut. The first reports have come in from fishing boats that were out to sea when the wave hit. All we know is that there were five hundred inhabitants on the island when a wall of water twenty feet high swept through. God knows how many are left alive.'

It was ten minutes before Morag met anyone at all. She was climbing down as people were climbing up, but the shortest way to high ground wasn't the track she was on. So her path was deserted. At every step she took her dread increased.

Finally she reached the town's outskirts, and here she met Marcus. Marcus was the head of the town's volunteer fire brigade, a brilliant fisherman and a man who normally could be absolutely depended on in a crisis. He looked...lost.

'Marcus...'

He was at the top of the track she was taking into town, the road leading to the fire station. Or it was the track that *had* led to the fire station. Marcus was standing where the station had once stood. The flimsy shed had given way completely, and a pile of rubble covered the town's only fire engine.

Marcus was staring unseeingly at the mess, and he didn't turn as Morag touched his shoulder.

'I don't know where they are,' he whispered, turning to gaze down at the ruined township.

He was soaked. He'd been caught by the wave, Morag thought, stunned, which meant the water must have washed almost three hundred yards inland. A shallow gash ran down the side of his face, and he looked as sick as she felt.

But they weren't alone. Above the township was bushland and the bush seemed the extreme of the wave's reach. Morag turned and looked upward and here was the first good news. People were emerging. They were still obviously terrified, but they were slowly venturing out.

All eyes were still turned toward the sea.

'Marcus!' It was a cry of disbelief—of tremulous joy. A woman was running toward them, towing two seemingly scared-witless teenagers after her. Judy. Marcus's wife. Marcus's face went slack with relief, and so did Morag's.

This was Marcus's family. With Marcus behind her she might get something organised, and now he had his family safe she could start.

Something...

What?

First things first. She had to wait until Marcus had gathered Judy and the kids to him in the hug of a man who'd thought he'd lost everything.

Finally he released them and turned to Morag. 'S-sorry.'

'Don't be sorry,' Morag said unsteadily. 'I wouldn't mind if someone hugged me.'

Judy immediately obliged. Marcus added his mite. Teenage dignity forgotten, the kids joined in, too, until she was squeezed between the four of them. And suddenly she was sobbing like a child.

Two minutes were spent gathering herself, taking strength where she most needed it.

Then...as they finally, tentatively broke away from each other and turned to stare out to sea again, they found space to talk.

'There's not likely to be another, is there?' Marcus asked, and Morag tried to think clearly about the possibility.

'I don't know. Maybe. Hubert and Robbie are on lookout with the bell, and Robbie has the best eyes on the island.'

'Was it you who rang the bell?' Judy asked, and when Morag nodded she was hugged all over again.

'Thank God for you, girl. There we all were, like sitting ducks, huddled in the main street waiting to be washed away.'

'Who was left behind?'

'God knows,' Marcus said frankly. 'I was just climbing into the fire truck, thinking after the tremor I'd pull it clear in case it was needed. I heard your bell, but I was trying to get the engine started. It seemed… important. Then as the bell kept ringing I came out—just as the water surged up. I ran. Even so, I had to grab a fence or I'd have been washed away. Judy, you…'

'I was with most of them,' Judy told them. She was still clutching the kids—Wendy, aged fourteen, and Jake, who was sixteen. Normally they wouldn't be seen dead clutching their mother but they were clutching her just as much as she was clutching them. 'Most of us got to the bush. If we made it to safety, then I'd guess most people would have. Then I thought you'd be at the fire station, Marcus, so I came.' She hugged her husband again, and her teenagers hugged, too.

'There must be casualties,' Morag whispered, and Marcus nodded.

'Yeah. Thank God it's Sunday so the school's empty.'

The school was on the foreshore. The thought of what might have happened—and hadn't—was almost enough to steady her.

'OK.' Deep breath. Somehow she had to figure out a way forward, though the extent of the calamity was overpowering. But she had four able-bodied people—five, counting herself—and, by the sound of it, the bulk of the townsfolk were safe. She needed to gear up. She needed to think.

'Let's get everyone safe first,' she told them. 'The cricket ground is on high ground and we can set up the pavilion as a clearing house. Marcus, I want you and Jake to start a house-to-house search—get others involved if you can—and send everyone to the cricket ground. I want *everyone* settled on high ground as fast as possible. Judy, I want you to make a register so we can see who's missing. Every person has to report to you.'

She paused and gazed across the village where she could see the roof of her tiny, four-bed hospital. Thankfully it was on high ground but she knew at once that it'd be too small for what lay ahead. Plus, even though it was on high ground, it was low enough for a higher wave to do damage. It'd have to be evacuated.

'I'll set up a medical centre in the cricket pavilion,' she told them. 'On the way I'll go past the hospital and make sure everyone's out and safe. Judy, can you and Wendy come with me and help me carry things? I need supplies, plus the files holding every islander's records. Wendy, are you able to cross-match names with the list Judy's making?' She gave them all a tiny, watery smile. 'I know. I'm sounding bossy when all we want to do is hug each other. But we need to move. Marcus, that cut—'

'Can wait,' he said roughly. 'I've a feeling that's the least of our problems.'

As if on cue, there was a yell from below them. An elderly man—the village grocer—was running toward them, and his terror reached them before he did.

'Doc. Doc, thank God you're safe. Doc, Mavis got caught under water. She's so cold and limp... Oh, God, Doc... She looks awful. I've taken her to the clinic but there's no one there who can help. Can you come?'

Morag started work right then, and she didn't raise her head for hours.

So many injuries... She didn't know how many injuries. She could only focus on what was before her.

She worked first at the clinic, as that was where Mavis was. Morag worked over Mavis with fierce intensity, blotting out the sound of evacuation going on all around her, and blotting out the fact that another wave could come at any time.

But despite her best efforts, the outcome was tragedy. There'd been twenty minutes between immersion and the time Morag saw the elderly grocer's wife. When Morag reached her, one of the nurses had started CPR but it was no use. The ECG tracing showed idioventricular rhythm. Idioventricular rhythm was almost always irreversible—the last sigh of a dying heart—and this was no exception. Finally Morag stood back, defeated, and she put her arm around the grocer's shoulders in silent sympathy as he wept for his wife.

But there was no time for Morag to weep. The clinic was almost empty. Every patient and almost all the equipment was gone. They covered Mavis and left her there.

'This...this place can be the morgue,' she told one of the men who'd tried to help.

He nodded. 'We'll start bringing them in.'

Them? How many? She couldn't bear to ask. 'I need to see...to make sure...'

'If there's any doubt at all, we'll bring them to you,' he told her. 'But there's those...well, there's those where there's no doubt at all.'

Dear God.

Grim-faced, Morag made her way to the cricket pavilion. Here she found her surgery set up in miniature. Any villager not totally occupied with searching for survivors or helping the injured had been hauled in to help. Marcus and his family were working like a miniature army.

There was no time to wonder. Work was waiting everywhere.

Louise, a middle-aged nurse who usually acted as Morag's receptionist, had decreed herself triage sister and nothing got near Morag unless she said so. That meant Morag nearly missed seeing tiny Orlando Salmon. Her next tragedy.

Orlando had been held in his mother's arms when the water had slammed them from one side of the road to the other. Angie Salmon was left with bruising, but her tiny son was dead in her arms. Louise would have deflected her from Morag—Morag had so much on her hands that the clearly dead could no longer be her business—but Morag saw them out of the corner of her eye as she was treating a compound fracture, and the look on Angie's face had her move instinctively to help.

Once again, there was nothing constructive she could do. But Angie had to hear from a doctor that her little son was really dead. She had to watch as Morag took the time to examine the tiny child with love, and show Angie what had killed him. It had been fast. He'd died instantly in his mother's arms.

Explaining was all Morag could do, and it was all she had time for. There was no time for comfort. There were urgent cases waiting, but as Morag turned away she found herself choked again with tears. She and Angie had gone to school together. Angie had been the biggest tomboy on the island. She had four more kids, and each one was loved to bits.

Damn.

She needed Robbie, she thought bleakly. She desperately needed to hug her own little Robbie, but there was no time.

And she was depending on Robbie. They all were. He was the village eyes. Someone else had gone up on the ridge now, carrying the strongest field glasses they could find, but she knew that Robbie's sharp eyes would be behind those glasses.

Searching for another wave.

She couldn't think of another wave.

Morag worked and worked. Every time she turned around there was more need. Fractures, lacerations, grief…

Then about four hours after the water hit, they brought Sam Crane in, carrying him in on a brightly painted door that looked like it had once been entry point to one of the village's more substantial houses.

Louise saw Sam as the stretcher bearers reached the top of the stairs, and this time she had no hesitation in bringing him to Morag's immediate attention. Morag turned from the man she'd been treating and flinched. Dear heaven. So much blood.

'We found him round the back of the harbour,' Marcus told her. 'He was working on his boat when it hit. The boat ended up smashed on the harbour wall and we found him underneath. It's taken six of us to get the boat off him. As soon as we got the boat off, he started bleeding like a stuck pig. We've applied pressure but…'

But what? She was lifting the rough blanket way, searching for the source of the bleeding. And here it was.

'Boat crushed his leg,' Marcus told her. 'What'll we do?'

His leg was lost. That much was unmistakable. What was left was a mash of pulp and splintered bones. The only positive thing was that his leg had been crushed so thoroughly that the blood vessels themselves must have been crushed. With a wound like this she'd expect spurting blood and almost immediate death, but somehow, hours after the wave, he was still alive.

Not for long, though. Blood was oozing across the door and onto the pavilion floor.

'We need blood. Plasma. Saline.'

'We're just about out.' Irene, the island's midwife, turned from applying a pressure bandage to a small boy's thigh. 'I could use some here.'

'We need to set up a blood bank.' Morag was staring down at Sam's leg in dismay. She had two trained nurses: Louise and Irene. That meant there were three people with medical skills on the entire island. That was it. How could she cope with this? Sam needed his leg amputated right now if he was to live—but she had no anaesthetist. Her nurses would be needed to take blood. The sort of surgery she was envisaging was horrific, but if she didn't start now, Sam would die almost straight away.

Triage. Priorities. Someone else was calling out for her from below. The child Irene was working on really needed Morag's attention. Maybe Sam would have to be...

'Just cut it off, Doc,' Sam said weakly, reaching out and taking her hand. 'I know it's a mess. I can get by on one leg.'

'You can do anything, Sam,' she said in a voice that wasn't the least bit steady. She gripped Sam's hand and she wasn't sure who was gaining strength from who. 'Sam, I'm going to give you enough painkiller to block things out until we can sort out how best to cope with this.'

'But the leg has to come of?'

'Yes, Sam. The leg has to come off.'

'Let's get on with it, then.'

'Sure.' She loaded a syringe and injected morphine. She set up an IV line and watched as Sam drifted into sleep. Or unconsciousness. The combination of shock, blood loss and morphine meant he could no longer stay with them.

Irene was watching her. As Sam's hand loosened its grip and she stepped back, she found everyone was watching her.

The huddle of people in the pavilion were shocked past belief. Any islander who was fit and not needed to take care of their own family had been co-opted into helping with medical care. But in this tiny settlement everyone knew everyone, and the entire island was like an extended family.

So far the death count from this afternoon was ten and rising. They'd worked so far in numbed disbelief but suddenly that numbness had disappeared. Every single one of them knew what Morag was facing now.

She needed to turn away from Sam and give her attention to someone she could save.

She needed to give up on the impossible.

She couldn't. She just...couldn't.

'Irene, if I talk you through the anaesthetic...' she managed, and Irene nodded.

'I'll try.'

They both knew it was hopeless.

'Is this the medical centre?'

The voice from down on the cricket ground was strong and insistent, different to the frantic cries for help they'd been hearing. Morag turned, momentarily distracted, knowing she'd reached the end of her resources.

But this was no islander calling for help. They'd been so caught up in the appalling drama that no one had noticed the approach of a small group of yellow-overalled outsiders.

Outsiders.

Help.

Morag looked down at the cluster of people below her. They looked unreal. Like aliens from space. Every islander was mud-coated, battered and torn, either from their own meeting with the wave or from hauling others from the rubble. But these newcomers were clean, purposeful, dressed to work and work hard.

Where had they come from?

'The helicopter,' someone whispered. 'The fishing boats radioed the mainland for help. A helicopter landed ten minutes back.'

Morag hadn't heard any helicopter, but she had been so focused on urgent need that she'd heard nothing.

She stared down at the group of six. From this distance she couldn't tell what sex they were—who they were—but they were the first glimmer of the outside world. The first glimmer of sanity.

'Is anyone a doctor?' she called without much hope, but a tall, yellow-overalled figure separated from the bunch and strode up the stairs three at a time.

'I'm a doctor and so is Jaqui,' he called as he climbed. 'Ron and Elsey are paramedics and Doug's here to assess priorities so we can get the personnel we need from the mainland. Who's in charge?' His words were cutting through the confusion and the chaos, and his tone was measured to command.

'I guess I am,' Morag said unsteadily, glanced despairingly down at Sam. 'If you're a doctor…I need help. So much help…'

'You have it.' The man passed the group clustered round Sam's wife at the head of the stairs—and she looked up from Sam and saw who it was at almost exactly the moment he registered who it was he was talking to.

Morag saw shock—absolute stunned amazement. His amazement matched hers, and then she couldn't register any expression on his face at all.

Just for a moment her vision blurred. Just for a moment her knees sagged.

Then Grady was beside her. His arms were holding her against him, and just for a moment she let herself give way. The shock and horror and fear of the last three hours all culminated in this one moment of total weakness. This man was here where she'd never imagined. At such a moment.

Grady…

Enough. Of course it was Grady. Why should she be shocked? Grady was always dashing to Australia's disaster areas. That was what he did.

This was a disaster. He was here.

'Three deep breaths,' Grady was saying into her hair. 'Hell, Morag, I'd forgotten… But you're not by yourself. We're the forerunners, but there's massive help on the way. Tell me what needs to be done most urgently.'

She heard him. She took the three deep breaths he'd advised while she permitted herself the luxury of sagging against his chest. Feeling his strength. Feeling for this one moment that indeed she wasn't alone.

Then she regrouped. She hauled herself away. She looked up at him and searched his face and she saw the same implacable strength she'd seen in him four years before.

And his strength fed hers. The islanders were gazing at her with dismay. If she disintegrated they all could, their expressions said, and this one show of weakness had to be her last.

'We've set this up as command centre,' she managed. 'There are teams combing the island, trying to account for every islander. Ten confirmed deaths so far. Multiple casualties. But we can't cope. We've run out of every medical necessity. This is our last bag of saline. I'm out of morphine. Bandages. Everything.' She swallowed and turned to Sam. 'Priority here is Sam's leg.'

Grady had already seen. He moved her aside and checked the IV line. Lifted Sam's wrist.

Looked down at the mangled leg.

'I'm operating now,' Morag said, and he nodded, a half-smile twisting his craggy face.

'Of course you are. All by yourself.' Then he turned away to the yellow overalls following him up the stairs. 'We need operating facilities now,' he called. 'Urgent. Elsey, get saline, plasma, everything we need for major surgery right now. Bring it all up here from the chopper. Morag, don't worry about supplies. We came fully loaded for medical emergencies. Max, we need lighting. Jaqui, will you do the anaesthetic? I'll operate and Morag here will assist. Rod, can you help with the child's thigh, there? He looks like he needs an IV line and pain relief. Tell me what his blood pressure is. Morag, is there anything else that's as urgent as Sam?'

In one broad sweep he'd assessed the chaos. Leaving her speechless. 'No,' she managed. 'Not...not yet.'

He nodded. 'The first Chinook will be landing in the next half-hour,' he told her. 'The army's sending troops. We aim to have everyone accounted for by nightfall. Meanwhile, let's cope with this and face the rest of the mess afterwards.'

It was a dreadful operation, done in the most primitive of conditions. Removing a man's leg, even a leg as dreadfully injured as this, was nothing less than butchering. Morag had seen it done—had assisted before with patients with tumours or with complications from diabetes—and each time the operation had made her feel ill. How much more so now when her world was spinning out of control?

And yet...it was in control again—a little—because of this man. Grady was good. There was no one she'd rather have in this emergency than Grady. Once the emergency lights were set up, he went straight in.

They were using the door as an operating table. There was no screening from the rest of the people using the pavilion. Sterility of the environment was a joke. But it couldn't be allowed to matter. Grady moved with care, blocking out all else.

He took the leg off just above the knee. He tied off damaged blood vessels, working carefully, quickly and skilfully.

Finally the bleeding eased, and by the time the remains of the fisherman's leg could be removed and taken away for burial, everyone there knew that Sam had a fighting chance at life. And this had been no butchering job. The remains of the leg were viable. He'd have a stump which could be used as a basis for an artificial limb. The operation couldn't have been done much better if it had been done in a major city hospital.

For the first time, Morag felt the wash of hopelessness recede. Sam had suffered massive blood loss, but if he was going to go into cardiac arrest, surely it would have happened sooner. Now they had saline and plasma flowing at maximum rate, and Jaqui was watching his breathing like a hawk.

Jaqui might look an unlikely doctor—a middle-aged woman, almost six feet tall, skinny and shiny in her canary yellow overalls—but there was no doubting her skills as an anaesthetist. The bleeding had been stemmed and the otherwise healthy fisherman now had a chance to fight back.

Finally, as Grady worked over the dressing, Morag found herself with time to step away. For the first time since she'd seen that awful wall of water, she had time to assimilate what had happened.

Marcus was standing behind her. The big fisherman was waiting in the shadows, as if he, too, was taking a breather from the horror he'd been working with. She stepped back to him, taking in his shocked and haggard face. She knew her own face must mirror it.

'What's happening?'

'The world's arrived,' he told her in a voice that was barely audible. It was as if every ounce of strength had been sucked out of him with the shock. 'The chopper that these people came in on was a forerunner. Two Chinook helicopters full of army personnel are here now, using the paddock up the top of the fells as a landing base. Teams are searching the island. There's boats out to sea, still searching.'

'People are still missing?'

He lifted a piece of paper and stared down, unseeing. She followed his eyes and flicked through the names—and winced.

'The Koori community are missing about eight of their people,' he told her. 'They were on the beach. They saw the water being sucked out and went to get a closer look. They ended up being washed everywhere. Lots of lacerations but some of their kids… And some of ours…' His voice broke and Morag put her arms around him and hugged. Hard.

And tried not to think about a name she'd seen on the list.

'We can get through this, Marcus,' she said softly. 'But we can't break. Not you and I. Too much depends on us.'

'You're right.' He wiped his face on the back of his sleeve and his face tightened. 'You're bloody right, Doc. I'll be out again in a bit, but I just came to see how Sam was going.'

'He'll make it. Thanks to these people.'

'Yeah, it's a good thing there's an outside world,' Marcus said grimly. 'And maybe it's the only thing left to us. I've seen the town. The houses…'

'Don't think about it.' She glanced back at the table to where Jaqui and Grady were still working. They could do without her now. It was almost sunset. It was time to move on to her next priority. 'Marcus, I need to see to the lighthouse. What if the light's not working? And I need to see Robbie. He'll be frantic.'

'Yeah, you go, lass,' he told her. 'With two doctors here, they should be able to manage. You carrying your radio?'

She gestured to it on her belt. 'Always.'

'You'll need to walk,' he told her. 'Most of the roads are washed out.'

'Yeah, and I'd imagine my car is floating somewhere in the Pacific.' She shrugged. 'I can walk. I can even run. But…'

Marcus saw her hesitation and had no trouble identifying it.

'I've been on the line to some expert from Sydney. The Centre for Seismology or some such. She says the wave was from the shock caused by the earthquake. She also says the epicentre was miles from here. There were two smaller waves after the big one but they've settled. The scientists are on full alert for any more shocks, but she says more waves are incredibly unlikely—and even if they happen, we'll now get heaps of warning.'

'So we're safe?'

'Yeah. Sort of. Robbie's been watching all afternoon but he's off duty now.'

She managed a smile. 'The whole island's been dependent on a nine-

and a ninety-year-old. My guess is that Hubert won't choose to die this week.'

'I surely hope not. We've had enough deaths.' Marcus's smile matched hers—weak and with no life behind it. 'OK.' He shrugged. 'I need to go. I shouldn't have come, but I couldn't bear to leave Sam.'

'He stands every chance of recovering.' Morag glanced once more over her shoulder to where Grady was completing his work. He had no attention to spare for her, and she had none to spare for him.

But he was here. The thought was overwhelming in the measure of comfort it gave her. This afternoon had been her worst kind of nightmare, and she was taking any vestige of comfort wherever she could find it. So she let herself look at Grady for a moment longer, taking in the solid competency, his air of command, the presence he exuded without ever seeming aware of it.

Enough. She was being silly. His presence was a comfort but there was nothing more to be done here.

'Let's go,' she told Marcus—and she turned away from Grady to follow Marcus, out of the cricket pavilion and into the mess of the island that had once been their home.

CHAPTER FOUR

THE LIGHTHOUSE WAS a priority.

Morag had two jobs on the island. One was island doctor, the other was lighthouse-keeper, and who could say which was more important? They both saved lives.

Once, being lighthouse-keeper had been a full-time job, but now it was simply a matter of ensuring that the light was still functioning, and that was a vastly different task than in the days when kerosene had had to be carted up the tower every night. Now the light was powered by electricity, with solar back-up.

Normally an alarm would sound if the light was dimmed in any way, but the alarm was in the lighthouse-keeper's cottage. Morag's home. And the cottage was at the foot of the lighthouse, not high enough above sea level to avoid damage.

It had been early afternoon when the wave had struck. Now the last rays of sun were sinking over the horizon and the darkness caused more problems. The streets were a mess, the streetlights were history, and a walk that usually took five minutes took her half an hour.

She made her way along the devastated main street, skirting the massive build-up of clutter smashed there by the water, clambering over piles of what had been treasured possessions but were now sodden garbage, stopping occasionally to speak to people searching through the mess that had once been their homes.

People stopped her all the time. People were desperate to make contact, to talk through what had happened.

But there was no longer an urgent medical need for her. Grady and his people were coping with medical needs for now, and she had to move on.

She must. The light…

She came to the end of the street and turned from the shelter of the ruined buildings onto the tiny, wind-swept promontory that held the lighthouse.

The lighthouse itself was still standing. Of course. It was built of stone, built to withstand massive seas, built to cope with anything nature threw at it.

The cottage, though…

She stood and stared, seeing not the ruins of the whitewashed building that had been her home for the last four years but seeing what it had once held.

Robbie's memories. Photographs of Beth and her husband. Robbie's precious teddy, knitted for him by his mother when she'd been so ill she'd hardly been able to hold needles. The furniture carved by Morag's father, splintered, ruined…

The lighthouse. Concentrate on the lighthouse. She choked back tears and looked up to find the light blinking its warning into the dusk.

At least one thing in this dysfunctional world was still working to order.

She stared upward for a long time. Stay away from here, the light was saying. The light was supposed to be warning ships that here were rocks to be wary of, but this day the danger had come from the sea itself, and the wreck was inland.

Her home was ruined.

She'd have to find Robbie.

She turned away, blinded by tears, and someone was standing in her path.

Grady.

Grady was right…there.

'They told me you'd come here,' he said, in that serious voice she'd known and loved all those years ago. A lifetime ago. He was looking down at her in the half-dark and it was all she could do not to fall on his chest again. Only, of course, she couldn't. How could she? And why would she? Sure, this was a tragedy, but it was her tragedy. It had nothing to do with this man.

He was here because it was his job to be here, she thought bleakly. He had nothing to do with her.

'Aren't you needed back at the pavilion?' she asked, and his gaze didn't falter.

'I thought I might be needed here. With you.'

'There's nothing to do here. The light's still working.'

'You really are the lighthouse-keeper?'

'Like father, like daughter. Yes.'

'Morag, I'm sorry.'

She had no idea what he was sorry for. So many things... She had no idea where he intended to start.

'Don't be sorry,' she said. 'It doesn't help.'

'This is your house?' He gazed at the battered whitewashed buildings. The light was fading fast now, and the beam from the lighthouse was becoming more obvious, one brief, hard beam out over the waves each fifteen seconds. The waves were washing gently over the rocks, their soft lapping making a mockery of the wave that had come before.

From where they stood you couldn't see around the headland into the town. The ruins were hardly apparent—unless you stared into the smashed windows of the cottage and saw the chaos that had been her home.

'Do you need to do anything for the lighthouse?' he asked, and she shook her head.

'No. The electricity's cut but we have solar power back-up. The solar panels on the cottage roof seem to be just under the high-water mark, and the connections must still be intact. That was what I was most worried about. I needed to check that the light was OK.'

'To stop further tragedy?'

'Without the light...yes, there'd be further tragedy.' She gazed across the great white tower, following its lines down to where it was anchored on solid rock. 'It doesn't look harmed. One wave couldn't wash it away. Unlike...'

'Unlike the rest of the island.' He hesitated, watching her face as she turned again to face the wreckage of her home. 'It was some wave.'

'It was the most frightening thing I've ever seen,' she whispered. 'I thought everyone would be dead. I couldn't believe that so many would live. But still…there's so much…' She let herself think of the lists Marcus had held—and the name that among them all had her cringing the most. Doctors shouldn't get personal, she thought. Ha!

Somewhere there was a little boy called Hamish. Robbie's best friend.

Enough. The little boy had probably been found by now, and even if he hadn't, she couldn't let herself think past a point where madness seemed to beckon. She gathered herself tight, allowing anger to replace distress. 'Why aren't you back at the pavilion? I wouldn't have left if I thought you and Jaqui weren't staying.'

'We have things under control and I can get back fast if I'm needed,' he told her. He was still watching her face. 'There's two doctors on the Chinook—the helicopter we're using to evacuate the worst of the wounded. We're evacuating those now. Peter and Christine Rafferty. Iris Helgin. Ross Farr. You've done a great job, Morag, but multiple fractures and internal injuries need specialist facilities.'

She nodded. 'How about Lucy Rafferty?' she asked tightly. 'Did she go with her parents?' Peter and Christine had been badly hurt—Peter with a badly fractured leg and Christine with concussion as well as fractures, but their thirteen-year-old daughter hadn't seemed as badly hurt.

And their son? Hamish? She thought the question but she didn't add it out loud.

'We didn't have room for Lucy,' Grady was saying. 'And we thought—'

She nodded, cutting him off. She knew what he thought.

'And Sam?' she managed. He could hear how involved she was, she thought. He must do.

But so what? she demanded of herself. The medical imperative—not to get personally involved—how on earth could she ever manage that here?

'You can't act at peak professional level if your emotions get in the way,' she'd been taught in medical school, and she wondered what her examiners would think of the way she was reacting now.

Well, it was too late to fail her. They were welcome to try.

'We're making sure Sam's stable before we transfer him,' Grady was saying. 'But he'll make it. I'm sure he'll make it.'

'Without his leg,' she whispered. 'No more fishing.'

'But still a life.'

'Maybe.' She stared again at the ruins of her cottage. The water had smashed its way everywhere. Through gaps where once there'd been window-panes, she could see a mass of sand and mud and sludge a yard deep.

Where to start...

Robbie.

Hamish. Dear God.

'I need to find my nephew,' she said bleakly.

'Beth's child?'

'Yes.'

'Where is he?' Grady asked, and then added, more urgently, 'Morag, do you know where he is?'

What was he thinking? she thought incredulously. That she'd only now thought of the little boy's whereabouts?

'Of course I know where he is,' she snapped. 'I never would have left him if he hadn't been safe. I would have stayed. But I had to go. Sam... Hamish...the others. But Hubert will take care...'

She wasn't making sense, even to herself. Grady looked at her, his face intent and serious in the fading light.

'So he's with someone called Hubert. Where's Hubert?'

'Up on the ridge above the town. Hubert's cottage is the high point of the island. I was up there when...'

'When you saw the wave,' Grady said. 'You were very lucky. Marcus told me what happened. If it hadn't been for your quick thinking...'

'Yeah, if I hadn't been here,' she said, and it was impossible to keep the bitterness from her voice. 'If I hadn't been where I belonged, we'd all be dead. But I was. Now, if you'll excuse me, Grady, I need to find my nephew.'

'I'll come with you.'

'No.'

'Yes,' he said, and he took her hand, whether she liked it or not. 'You're as much a victim as anyone else on this island, Morag. Your home is in ruins. You possess only the clothes you stand up in. You're shocked and you're exhausted. I'm taking you in charge. We'll go up together and fetch Robbie and then I'll take you to the tents they're setting up on the cricket grounds to care for all of you. Learn to accept help, Morag. You'll have to take it over the next few weeks, like it or not.'

She stared at him. Helpless. Lost. And when he held her hand tighter, she didn't pull away.

She was going to need this man over the next few weeks? Right. She did need him.

The only problem was that it wasn't just for now. She'd needed him for four long years and that need had never faded.

She'd needed him then and she needed him desperately now.

Grady.

Her love.

It was all a mist, she thought. A delirious dream where horror and death and Grady and love—and sheer unmitigated hopelessness—all mingled.

They had to walk up the fells, scrambling up the scree to Hubert's cottage. The goat track was hard to find in the dim light. Grady had a flashlight and it picked out the path.

He held onto her hand all the way. To do otherwise seemed stupid. The fact that his touch made her sense of unreality deepen couldn't be allowed to matter.

Maybe she should release herself from his grip, she thought inconsequentially. She wasn't nervous of the dark. Brought up to know every nook and cranny on the island, Morag was as at home here as she was in the city on a well-lit street. Grady needed the flashlight but she let her feet move automatically.

Dear heaven, this was so dreadful...

The thought of Angie kept filling her vision. Angie's tiny cold baby. And Mavis. And so many dead...

And Hamish?

No.

She couldn't think. Somehow she blocked her thoughts until the only thing she was aware of was the presence of this man beside her.

It helped. It stopped her getting her head around what had happened this day.

So much had happened since she'd last walked up here that Morag was having trouble believing that any of this was real. This afternoon she'd strolled up the path with Robbie by her side, happy because it was a glorious Sunday afternoon and the island was the best place to be in the entire world. Robbie had kicked his soccer ball along in front of him, letting it roll down the scree, whooping and hollering and occasionally returning to her side to keep up his latest plea for a puppy.

'Please, Morag. We need a puppy. We need a dog. We need...'

Then there'd been the talk of Elspeth.

I wonder how many island dogs have survived? she thought, and then thought even more savagely, I wonder how many dogs need new owners?

Her head was right back into the tragedy. How could she escape it?

'It'll be OK.'

'How can it be all right?' she said into the night, not really talking to Grady. She was talking to herself. 'How can things be righted? So much destroyed...'

'The chopper pilot on the way over said there'd been talk of resettling the islanders,' Grady said cautiously. 'Making this an unpopulated island. With so much of the infrastructure damaged, maybe that'd be the way to go.'

Oh, right. Smash homes and then rip the island out from under them.

'Yeah, the government would like that,' she said bitterly. 'It costs them an arm and a leg in support—to have ships drop off supplies, to provide things like mail, telecommunications, health services...'

'You *are* the health services.'

'I know, and if I wasn't here they'd close the island in a minute,' she told him. 'They've decided again that the lighthouse can manage unmanned. They don't want to provide infrastructure and it drives the powers that be nuts that I agreed to stay here. I'm the only reason this island can function.' She shook herself, trying to lose the feeling of nightmarish unreality. 'And now there'll be more pressure. How the hell can we rebuild? All these people? There'll be so many problems. I can't cope...'

'Hey, Morag.' His hand tightened on hers, holding her, steadying her as she stumbled along a track which all of a sudden wasn't as familiar as she'd thought. And, dammit, she was too far gone to pull away. Sure, it was his bedside manner doing the comforting, but she needed any bedside manner she could get.

Liar. She needed Grady.

Whatever.

She'd deal with the consequences later, she told herself dully. For tonight—for now—she needed Grady.

He held on and she gripped him tight in return, and she sensed in the sudden, momentary stillness that her reciprocation had surprised him.

'Morag...'

'Shut up,' she told him. 'I don't want to think about tomorrow. I just need to see Robbie. I need to focus on now. That's all I can do.'

There was a candle in Hubert's cottage window, lit in welcome.

The electricity for the entire island was cut. The outside teams had brought emergency generators which they were using at the cricket ground, and the lighthouse had its solar power, but the rest of the island was in darkness.

But Hubert had never had need of electricity and, though the rest of the island was in darkness, here was light. As they walked up to the door, Morag felt a sudden surge of affection for the old man who'd surely surpassed himself this day.

She entered without knocking, ushering Grady with her. Hubert was sitting at the kitchen table, fully dressed.

He hadn't been fully dressed for months, Morag thought, stunned. In his fishermen's ancient jersey and overalls, he looked far younger than the Hubert she'd treated that afternoon. He looked tough and competent and extremely worried.

As they entered his face cleared, just a little.

'I thought you'd never come, girl. Thank God for it.'

'This is Dr Reece,' she told Hubert, and then moved to her first concern. 'Robbie...'

'He's fine,' Hubert told her. 'Or he's as well as he can be. We both saw what happened and he knew you were all right. Chris Bartner brought his telescope up to the ridge, and we've seen everything that's happened since. But Robbie's scared for his mates. For Hamish. And my...for all our friends.'

Morag swallowed. 'I haven't gone over the lists in full.'

'The lists...' Hubert watched her face and then rose stiffly and crossed to the stove. He lifted the kettle and filled his blackened teapot. His niece would be waiting a while longer for her inheritance, Morag thought dully. Hubert's teapot was still very definitely needed.

Then—teapot full—Hubert nodded gravely across at Grady.

'If you're a doctor, then you must be one of the people who came in by the first helicopter. Thank God for you. Chris's wife came up half an hour back to tell us we could leave our watching, and she said our Sam would live, thanks to you.' He hesitated. 'But, Morag, I need to know. Chris's wife couldn't speak for weeping. Elias is... Elias *was* her grandfather, and her grandmother needed her badly. So Christopher took her away before she could tell me more. Lists or not, tell me what the damage is.'

So she told him. It still seemed totally unreal. Sitting at the scrubbed wooden table, eating sandwiches that Hubert had magically produced— she hadn't realised how hungry she was but now she ate without tasting— sipping hot, sugared tea, with Grady sitting beside her, Morag outlined the damage as she knew it.

All the houses along the seafront were damaged, some irreparably. The flimsier structures, such as the shed that had served as a fire station, had never stood a chance. Even some of the stronger-built houses had been smashed to firewood. There were twelve confirmed deaths now, mostly from those first awful minutes. Death by sheer smashing force or by drowning as people had been caught in rubble, unable to escape the water. Another six had been reported missing. So far. Not including the Koori population, and the initial reports from the settlement were disastrous. She needed to go out there.

She needed to do so much. So many missing...

Maybe the missing were still alive, she told herself. But maybe not. The more time passed, the more unlikely it was that anyone would be found.

But all the local boats were assisting in the search—boats that had, thankfully, been out at sea when the wave had struck. The local fishermen were now combing the coast, trying to find anyone or anything swept away.

That was the appalling news. That was the news that made Hubert's face grow grey, and Morag put out a hand, ostensibly to give him comfort but also to check his pulse...

There was more. Little things she'd learned without realising it came to her now as she sat between these very different men. The loss of Robbie's teddy. Pets. William Cray's border collie. William was a writer, who had made the island his solitary home. He considered himself an intellectual—a cut above the islanders. He kept to himself. Yet as she'd walked to the lighthouse, Morag had seen him sitting on the debris-strewn beach, sobbing in appalled disbelief.

His dog was nowhere.

And the injured and the missing... Among them...

No. She wasn't going down that road. She wouldn't say it unless she knew for sure.

'What'll we do?' Hubert whispered as Morag's voice finally trailed off. Grady had stayed silent, seeming to know that she needed to talk. By making it real, maybe she could take it out of the realms of nightmare. Maybe it could be something that was over.

But, of course, it wasn't.

'I don't know,' she told him. 'But... Thank you for caring for Robbie. I had to trust you.'

Her voice faltered and Grady's hand came across the table to touch her. One day four years ago she'd pulled away from this comfort. Not now. Now when she needed him so much.

His touch was light. Intuitively, he was letting her focus still on Hubert.

'You knew I wouldn't let you down,' Hubert told her, his voice becoming all at once fierce. He glanced across the table at Grady, and his old eyes were suddenly defiant. 'That's what this island is all about. We depend on each other. We're tight-knit. And we're not done yet. No blasted wave is going to smash away our community.'

He had realised the situation well before her, Morag thought. While she'd been down at sea level tending to medical imperatives, Hubert had sat up here caring for Robbie, watching for more waves and thinking through what this meant long term.

'It's not the first time Petrel Island's faced tragedy,' he told Grady, still fiercely, as if in Grady he saw the threat of the outside world. The threat of the end of this lifestyle. 'When I was a kid they were still re-membering the *Bertha* that ran aground on the far point. My dad swam out that night and brought four souls ashore, but a hundred and sixty-eight drowned. Then, fifty years back, the diphtheria came through. We didn't have a doctor—no one on the island was vaccinated against anything—and there are twenty-five more in the graveyard who died before their time.' He glanced from Grady, who he wasn't quite sure of, to Morag, who he was.

'You're a doctor and you try and save us all,' he told her. 'But there's always fate, girl and you can't rail about it. You take what comes.'

'You fight,' Morag said.

'Yeah, you fight, and that's what you've been doing today while I've cared for the bairn.' He shrugged and cradled his teacup some more. 'He's a good kid, Morag. He knew he couldn't go down. He knew he'd have to wait up here with me. Waiting's the hardest but we did it together. He's in my bed.' A crooked smile crossed his face. 'With Elspeth. The two of them are worn out with worrying. I reckon I just might have to put Robbie's name on Elspeth.'

'Elspeth is Hubert's golden retriever,' Morag told Grady. 'And here he is promising to leave her to Robbie when he dies. But…don't die to-night, will you, Hubert?'

'Can't,' Hubert said bluntly. 'Someone else is in my bed. You want to join him? It's a big bed.'

Morag flashed an unsure glance at Grady. 'I…'

'You look stuffed to me,' Hubert told her. 'What do you reckon, fella?' He jabbed Grady in the chest. 'You agree you're capable of seeing that our girl is done in?'

'She is,' Grady said seriously. 'There's beds being set up in tents on the cricket ground.'

'Do they need her there now?'

Grady glanced at his watch. 'Maybe not,' he conceded. 'The urgent medical cases have been seen, the worst have been evacuated and Jaqui's there now in case more problems arise. We'll take it in turns to sleep and she'll call us if she needs us.'

'Then, barring complications, you can both get some shut-eye up here,' Hubert said in satisfaction.

Morag gazed across the table in wonder at this dying old man who suddenly wasn't anywhere near dying. He seemed like a man in charge. 'Hubert, you're the one who's sick.'

'I'm still dying,' Hubert said morosely. 'But I'm not sick. There's a difference.'

'Why are you dying?' Grady asked, startled, and Hubert snorted.

''Cos I'm ninety-two and it's time. They've taken my craypot licences off me. But, as Morag says, not tonight. Now...there's a couple of them camp stretcher things in the shed and there's a heap of bedding and it's not a cold night. Morag, you slide into bed with the little fella. He'll be real glad to see you when he wakes—that wave was the stuff of nightmares. Me and the mainland doc will settle down here unless you're needed. You both have your radios on?'

'We do.' Morag was struggling to think, though in truth she couldn't. Her mind was so addled she was past thinking. The idea of sliding into bed with Robbie and holding him close was overwhelming.

Staying up here had much more appeal over going down to the huge tents they were setting up on the cricket ground—trying to sleep where everyone would be wanting to talk to her. And to sleep knowing that Grady was nearby...that the responsibility had been lifted from her shoulders... It was an unlooked-for blessing and she could no sooner refuse it than fly. She glanced uncertainly across the table at Grady, and the hand touching hers moved so he was covering her hand entirely.

'I can't take your bed,' she told Hubert, forcing herself to concentrate on something other than the feel of Grady's hand.

'It's already taken,' Hubert told her. 'Don't be daft. I've spent half my life sleeping in fishing boats, sometimes on bare deck. The bairn's already asleep. Don't argue.'

But... 'Can we stay here?' she asked.

Grady was watching her, his face calm. He saw what she was thinking, this man. Of course. He'd always been able to see.

'I think we can,' he said gently. 'Hubert's idea is excellent. I'll radio in and let my team know what's happening. If we're wanted, they'll call us. But you're exhausted, close to dropping. We all need to sleep. There's nothing else to be done until dawn.'

'How can I sleep in Hubert's bed?'

'Hey, I put clean sheets on,' Hubert growled. 'Elspeth's even warmed your side up. Why can't you?'

Because he was her patient, she thought, torn between tears of exhaustion and a sudden inexplicable need to laugh. This afternoon she'd been treating him. To have him suddenly rise from his deathbed and say, Here, I've put clean sheets on the bed; you take a turn...

'Hey, and deathbed or not, you're not allowed to die in it either,' Hubert told her, and he grinned. It was the first time she'd seen a smile since the wave had struck, and it felt good. Like the world was finally starting to settle.

Grady was smiling too, the smile she remembered so well from all those years ago, a smile that twisted her heart.

'Go and find Robbie, Morag,' he said, in the gentle tone she remembered him using with her once before. But this time was different. This time she grasped the comfort of his tone and she held on. It was warmth in a world where there wasn't warmth. It was hope.

'Go and sleep,' he said gently. 'Hubert and I will be right here, watching over you. You've done the work of a small army today. Now let someone else take care of you for a change.'

'But—'

'Goodnight, Morag. Go to sleep.'

Grady lay on the camp stretcher beside Hubert, but sleep wouldn't come.

The camp bed with no mattress was as hard as nails but he didn't mind that. It wasn't discomfort that was keeping him awake. There'd been one mattress, which he'd insisted the old man have. 'For heaven's sake, man, I'm trained to sleep in a harness hanging off a cliff face if I must,' he'd told him, and it was the truth.

He'd trained himself over the years to snatch any sleep that was available. He needed sleep now. Jaqui knew what he was doing up here was important, and he'd organised that he take first break. He'd relieve her at three a.m., they'd decided, and then he'd be back here by six when the cottage occupants woke up.

He needed to sleep now.

Hubert snored softly beside him, and Elspeth wuffled and moaned.

That wasn't disturbing Grady. Grady could sleep in a force-ten gale. He'd done it often.

He'd never done it while thinking of Morag.

The sight of her today had knocked him sideways.

He'd known she was here. Always in the back of his mind he'd known Morag was on Petrel Island. For a while he'd toyed with the idea of staying in contact, but...

But it was an exercise in futility. Morag was beautiful and intelligent and funny and she was fully, absolutely committed.

And it wasn't just commitment to her nephew. It was the commitment to a community that he found so incomprehensible. For Grady, whose life had been spent moving from parent to parent as they'd shifted from one dysfunctional marriage to another, the idea of ties was abhorrent. Ties hurt. His parents had wealth and influence and if there was a problem they paid to have it sorted. They never got involved. He'd learned early that detachment was a way of survival. You showed care and concern when it was appropriate, and then you moved on.

And Morag... She'd excited him four years ago. In Morag he'd recognised the same hunger for excitement. The same ambition. She had been one of the youngest surgical registrars ever to qualify at Sydney Central. She'd thrived on the adrenaline of demanding cases, life-threatening events. When he'd first met her, he'd thought she was gorgeous.

She was still gorgeous.

But she was very different now, he conceded as he stared up at the moonlit ceiling. Her smart little designer suits and jeans, her perfectly shaped curls, they were all things of the past.

In the shock of the news of the tsunami he hadn't thought of Morag. And when he'd seen her...

She'd been wearing ancient jeans that must have been ragged even before the shattering events of the afternoon. She'd worn an oversized man's shirt, and her tangled curls had been bunched back with a piece of crimson ribbon, like a child's. He tried to remember the last time he'd seen her four years ago, the way every curl had known its place. He remembered her sophistication. Her sureness.

She didn't look so much worse now, he conceded. Maybe...maybe even better.

But sophistication? Purpose? Ambition?

Hell, what was he doing, lying in the dark thinking about what a woman looked like? Where a woman was going in life?

Morag...

She was nothing to him, he told himself as he tossed on the hard little bed and tried to force himself into sleep. He needed to sleep. There were still huge medical needs on the island, and the way to operate at less than his best was to allow his mind to wander when it should shut down in sleep.

Morag...

She was just the other side of the wall.

Yeah. In bed with a nine-year-old. Shouldering the responsibilities of a shattered community. Treading a path he knew they could never share.

But...

The briefing he'd had before leaving played over in his head. It had been harsh, fast and to the point.

'Petrel Island is a logistical nightmare, even without the tidal wave,' he'd been told. 'We've offered the locals reimbursement if they'll resettle on the mainland. It's too early to say but let's not focus on rebuilding too early. Let's see what happens.'

If Morag could be persuaded to leave the island... If the community dispersed, there'd be no real choice.

Maybe then...

Maybe he needed to go to sleep.

Finally he succeeded. Finally he fell asleep—but Morag was in his dreams.

He'd dreamed of Morag before.

But this was the Morag of now. Not the Morag of yesterday.

CHAPTER FIVE

SHE WOKE WITH the first glimmer of dawn.

For a moment Morag didn't know where she was. She only knew that she was warm, the first rays of sun were falling across her face and Robbie's small body was curved into hers.

And then another thought. Somewhere close was Grady.

Grady.

The whole nightmare of yesterday was ready to slam back into place, but as reality hit there were two small comforts holding her steady. Or, if she was honest with herself, they weren't small comforts. They were huge comforts.

Robbie was here. Robbie was safe.

And out in the front room was Grady.

Why should that be a comfort?

Grady's life was disaster management. Grady's life had nothing to do with hers. But now that she was in the midst of the worst kind of disaster, at least Grady could be here. For a tiny while.

And then what?

Reality.

Hamish?

Comfort faded. She felt Robbie stir. The sun had just caught the sill and flooded the bed, disturbing them both. Robbie rolled over and found her, his expression changing from one of panic to relief in a moment.

'Morag. You're here.'

'I'm here.' She'd hugged him in the night as she'd replaced Elspeth and climbed into bed beside him, but she was unsure how awake he'd been. He'd hugged her back but he'd hardly woken. Now she saw consciousness return. And with it relief—but also the enormity of what he'd been through the day before.

'Morag,' he said again, and buried his small face against her breast and burst into tears.

She held him. It was all she could think of to do. She'd held him like this too often, she thought drearily. There'd been too many times in this small boy's life when fate had slapped him hard. And now there'd be more people he knew, more people he loved, who he wouldn't see again.

Hamish. Please, God, not Hamish.

Thank God Robbie had been up here with her, she thought. Thank God they both had. If they'd been on the flat and she'd been hurt... If he'd had to cope without her...

No. She was here for him and she wasn't going away.

She had to get up. There was so much to do. A priority had to be a trip out the Koori settlement, she thought, but then... There was so much.

But for this minute there could only be Robbie.

There was a tentative knock and Grady was peering around the door as if he didn't want to intrude. He flinched at the sound of Robbie's sobbing.

'I'm sorry.'

'It's OK.' She gave Robbie a hard hug, ran her fingers through his hair, then lifted his tear-drenched face so she could see him. 'Robbie's having the cry that everyone else had last night. Sometimes the only thing to do is cry. Don't you think so, Dr Reece?'

'I surely do.' He smiled and crossed to the bed, then stood looking down at them. It was a weirdly intimate moment, Morag thought, still dazed by sleep. Grady was standing over Hubert's big bed while she and Robbie lay in a huddle of aunt-nephew sogginess and tried to recover their mutual composure.

At least Grady was composed. He was in his yellow overalls. Dressed and ready for the day, he looked cool and competent and...dangerous?

Where had that word come from? Ridiculous.

'Hi,' Grady was saying, holding his hand out to Robbie. 'I'm Grady

Reece. I've heard about you. I'm a friend of your aunt's—a doctor—and I've come to help.'

Robbie sniffed. He sniffed again but Grady's hand was still outstretched and finally he took it.

'Did you come in the helicopter?' Robbie asked, a trifle warily but seemingly willing to be distracted from his misery.

'That's right.'

'You guys in the yellow overalls were the first to arrive. We saw you land through the field glasses.'

'We're the emergency Air-Sea Rescue team.'

'You came to rescue us?'

'It seems,' Grady said, smiling but with a depth of seriousness behind the smile, 'that you've done a fine job rescuing yourselves already.'

'Some people are dead.'

There was only one answer to that, and Grady had the sense to give it. 'Yes.'

Robbie seemed to think about it. He gazed up at Grady but his small body was still curved into Morag's. And here came the question she'd been dreading. 'What about Hamish?'

'Hamish?' Grady looked questioningly at Morag.

'Hamish is Robbie's cousin and his best friend,' Morag told him, feeling more and more unreal. She was lying in bed discussing the outside world with a man above her, for all the world as if she was a patient and he was her doctor. It was completely alien. It was as if somehow she'd been placed in the position where it was someone else who did the caring. Not her.

Which was ridiculous. Ever since she'd returned to the island the weight of the world had rested firmly on her shoulders, and that weight was never lifted. To think that Grady was somehow going to alleviate that burden was a nonsense.

And there was so much to do...

Grady was still talking to Robbie. Taking his concerns seriously. Let him respond to his query about Hamish, she thought dully. She couldn't.

'I don't know who the islanders are yet.' He raised his brows at Morag. 'Do you know anything about Robbie's friend?'

'I didn't see Hamish yesterday,' Morag admitted. 'I know that his parents—Peter and Christine—were injured. They were the couple you evacuated last night.' She turned back to Robbie. 'Peter and Christine had broken limbs that need to be set by experts in Sydney, but we think they should be OK. As for the kids...one of the nurses told me Lucy had scratches down her leg and they were treating her, but I didn't see her and I haven't seen Hamish. But I've been so busy...'

And that was all she could think of to say. It was all there was to say.

Hamish hadn't been brought into the cricket pavilion with his parents or Lucy. And his name—she was sure Hamish had been on the list as a query. She hadn't had a chance to ask questions.

No. She hadn't been brave enough to ask questions, she conceded. And maybe by now he'd been found. Maybe...

She glanced up at Grady and found his face closed. Uh-oh.

Did he know something she didn't?

She still wasn't going to ask. Not now. Not with Robbie listening to every word.

How much grief could one child stand?

'Can I go and look for him?' Robbie asked.

'The professionals are looking for everyone,' Grady said gravely. 'We have people searching everywhere, trying to sort out where everyone is. Meanwhile, your friends are gathering down in one of the big tents. I'm about to go down there and I'll check for myself. Give me Hamish's details and I'll let you know.'

Robbie considered and seemed to find that satisfactory, at least in the short term.

'Is that why you're here?' he asked curiously. 'Do you go round the country rescuing people?'

'We do. I'm a doctor. Our team helps the injured.'

'But there's more people looking than just the guys in yellow overalls.'

'We have the army here as well. They'll keep searching until every-one's found.'

'And then what?'

'What do you mean?' Grady asked. Morag might as well not be there. Robbie was intent on inquisition and Grady, it seemed, was accepting being grilled.

'Will you take us all to the mainland 'cos our island's smashed?'

Whew. What a question. How had Robbie figured that one out?

At least one of them was focused, Morag decided. But it wasn't her. She was feeling more and more disorientated. She was still stunned that somehow she'd ended up in Hubert's bed and she was here, holding Robbie, while this man stood above them...

His yellow overalls looked tough and businesslike, his professionalism accentuated even more by the Air-Sea Rescue insignia on his arm. His hair hadn't been combed this morning—it sort of flopped sideways, looking as if it had been raked by his long fingers over and over. His skin was tanned and weathered, and his eyes crinkled down at them, and he made her feel...

Stop it. Oh, for heaven's sake, stop it, she told herself. Of all the times—and of all the places!—for her to feel the stirring of unashamed lust...

It was totally inappropriate. She turned away from him and gazed at Robbie, who was gazing straight at Grady. He'd clearly decided Grady was hero material, worthy of closer inspection.

'Tell me some of the things you've done,' he was demanding. 'I've read about Air-Sea Rescue. That yacht race last year, was that you? When they had to winch all those people out of the water and the waves were sixty feet high and one of them got his ribs all smashed against the side of the boat...'

'It was me,' Grady said, grinning. He sank down on the bed as if he was a familiar relative rather than a man Robbie had never met. 'Well, it wasn't me who got his ribs smashed, but I was the one who winched him up. Robbie, I hope there'll be time in the next few days for me to sit down and tell you everything about me,' he confided. 'But for now... Hubert says you know pretty much exactly what happened on the island yesterday.'

'We watched through field glasses and then Chris's telescope,' Robbie admitted. 'It was awful. Mr Hamm said if he was younger he'd be out there in his boat to get the people who were swept away, but he couldn't go, so we figured that we'd stay up here and just watch the sea and stay close to the bell. We didn't stop watching until dark.'

'I think you were fantastic,' Grady said gravely. 'But the scientists tell us that the danger's over.'

'Another wave won't come?'

'It's a really long shot, Robbie, and we have seismologists checking for earth tremors all the time now. If there's another wave, there'll be heaps of warning.'

Robbie thought about that and nodded. 'I guess it's not much use watching, then.'

'No. But there's other things we need to do.'

'Like what?' He was still very close to Morag.

'Well, your aunt and I are needed at the medical centre. There are people who were hurt yesterday who need your aunt's care. We have three doctors on the island now and we're all needed.'

'Might people still die?' Robbie asked, and Grady looked gravely down at him.

'They might, Robbie, but not if Morag and I can help it. But while Morag and I are working, I wondered whether you and Hubert would do something that would help Air-Sea Rescue enormously.'

Morag was feeling more and more dazed. This was so like being a hospital patient, she thought, lying in bed while the doctor stood over her, telling her the best course of action for her illness.

And maybe it wasn't a bad thing. The events of the day before had left her shattered, and for her to stay in control now—to take on the responsibility for the entire medical mess—was surely too much. She could operate but only in a subservient capacity, she decided. The normally wilful and decisive Morag was more than content to lie here hugging Robbie while Grady took control.

'What do you want us to do?' Robbie asked.

And Morag thought, Yeah, me too. Count me in on that question.

'We have media arriving,' Grady told Robbie, professional to professional, without a trace of patronage. 'There are reporters from all over the world headed here right this minute. Camera crews, photographers, reporters—you name it. Now, we can't let them down near the harbour. It's too great a mess and it's going to upset everyone to have reporters close. So what we thought was that we'd direct them up here. They'll be coming by helicopter so they can land like we did on the plateau behind this place. I'll have someone rostered to direct them here. You and Hubert can give them a first-hand account of what happened—you

realise you're the only ones who had a bird's-eye view of the whole thing?
You can point out the whole island from here, and they can take long-
range photographs.'

'You mean…you want me to stay up here with Mr Hamm?'

'If you would,' Grady said diffidently, still as if he were asking a colleague for help and not a child. 'If you can keep the reporters happy and
out of our hair, it would be enormously appreciated.' He lifted a radio
from his belt and laid it on the coverlet beside Robbie. Morag blinked.
This was a pretty impressive piece of equipment.

'If you listen in on this, you'll hear everything that's going on with the
emergency services all over the island,' he told Robbie. 'You'll be able
to keep the reporters up to date. We'll keep you informed as to what's
happening.' Then he hesitated, as if suddenly unsure. 'Robbie, Hubert's
offered to do this for us, but he's very old and his heart's not so good.
I'm hoping you can help.'

But Robbie didn't need persuading. He was already pushing back the
covers, the horrors of yesterday receding as he lifted the amazing radio
to his ear and started fiddling with buttons.

'I'll be able to hear all over the island?'

'All over the island.'

'You don't need me, do you, Morag?'

'No.' Not true. She missed him already. She missed the warmth of his
little body against hers. Grady might be able to deflect Robbie's horrors
but he couldn't deflect hers.

But it was time to move on.

'I'm going to talk to Mr Hamm,' Robbie said importantly. 'We have
to get organised. You go with Dr Reece, Morag. I'll look after everything up here.'

Morag was left alone with Grady. She wanted to get up—she must
get up—but she'd gone to bed in knickers and bra. Her clothes were on
the far dresser.

She was a bit stuck.

As for Grady… She'd checked him out by now, and discovered that
he'd already been out. His big black boots were wet. He'd already been
down into the village, she thought, and she knew she had to make herself ask the hard questions.

'What's the latest?' she asked, and Grady nodded as though this was the question he'd been expecting.

'Fifteen confirmed dead. Three from the Koori settlement to add to the list from last night and some missing. But in the meantime, there's some good news. We brought in three fishermen during the night. They were coming into harbour when the wave struck. Their boat was smashed but they were wearing lifejackets. One has a broken arm. The other two only copped lacerations and shock. We found them floating half a mile out to sea—there was no way they could fight the currents. Luckily the sea's relatively mild at this time of year so we don't have hypothermia to contend with.'

'Lucky us,' she muttered.

'You have been lucky,' Grady said seriously. 'It could have been so much worse. If you hadn't seen—'

'I did see,' she snapped. 'And fifteen of my people are dead. Don't call me lucky. Do you have a list of the dead?'

'I have a list.'

She caught her breath, suddenly remembering the way he'd backed off a little at Robbie's question.

'Is Hamish still on the list as missing?'

'Yes.' He hesitated. 'Hamish is listed as definitely missing. No one's seen him.'

'Oh, no.'

'Morag, I have no more information than that,' he told her. 'But we're still searching.'

'How many are missing?'

'Three now from the Koori settlement. Only Hamish here.'

She swallowed.

'OK.' She closed her eyes. Taking a grip. Moving forward. When she opened her eyes again she was in business mode.

'You've been up for a while?'

'I slept for four hours. I don't need more. I've been organising.'

'Finding spare radios?'

'That, too.'

'To keep Robbie happy?'

'He'll be useful.'

'You could easily have sent someone else up here to cope with the press contingent.'

'Hubert and Robbie together are more than capable.' He smiled, that slow lazy smile that had the power to unsettle her world. Then. In the past. A long time ago. Now a smile couldn't unsettle her. A wave had done that pretty decisively already. 'I've done a fast examination of Hubert,' he told her. 'He's pretty solid. What makes him think he's dying?'

'I revoked his fishing licence,' Morag confessed. 'He hit the jetty at full tilt and pushed a full day's catch by the entire fleet into the bottom of the harbour.'

'So he decided he'd die?'

'Why not? Dying's interesting, as long as you can stretch it out a long, long time.' She managed a fleeting smile. 'And today you've made life even more interesting, for both of them. Thank you.'

'It's self-interest,' he confessed. 'I have need of the island doctor.'

Her smile faded. 'Of course. I'm sorry. I should be up.'

'You needed to sleep. There's a lot to cope with, Morag,' he told her seriously. 'As you said, these are your people. We're coping with major trauma—major physical damage—but as well as that there's also shocking emotional damage. If you're strong enough to work through this, you'll be our most valuable medic.'

'You mean…you're being nice to me so that I can cope mentally with what's coming?'

'Something like that.' He smiled down at her, his eyes crinkling at the corners. 'Hey, Morag, it's really good to see you again.'

'It's good to see you, too,' she whispered. He didn't know how much. 'What do you want me to do?'

'Cope. Not collapse. My job is to support you. I can do hands-on physical stuff but this community needs you if it's going to be viable.'

'You're thinking it's still viable?'

'I don't know what the decision will be.'

'I want to be in on that decision-making.' She eyed her clothes on the dresser and thought about making a grab for them. To be sitting in bed…

'Of course you do,' he agreed. 'And one of my tasks is to make sure you're capable of that.' He smiled again. 'Now, I'm going to make us some toast. Do you want some space to get dressed or do you want some help?'

Help her with dressing? He had to be kidding. 'I can cope.'

'I'm sure you can.' His smile faded. 'You seem to have coped so far. Alone.'

'I haven't had much choice.'

'No.'

Silence. It was a tangible thing, this silence. It was loaded with history and with pain.

Loaded with emptiness.

'Get dressed, love,' he said at last, almost roughly. 'I'll make you breakfast, but we need to move fast. For today we need each other.' Then he grinned and reached for her pile of clothes. 'Here's your modesty. You know, you really do remind me of you.'

They both knew what he meant by that. Once upon a time he'd thought he'd fallen in love.

With someone who was no longer her.

CHAPTER SIX

SHE MIGHT FLEETINGLY remind Grady of the Morag she'd once been, she thought bitterly as the morning progressed, but the old Morag was long gone. The sophisticated career-woman who'd only cared for herself... Ha!

Even that thought hardly had time to surface. Everywhere Morag looked there was need. Aching, tearing need that she had no hope of meeting. The walk back down to the ruined township had her stopping time and time again as people wept on her, people hugged her, people tried to talk through their fears.

But at least she wasn't the town's only doctor. At least she had help. They all had help.

It seemed the Petrel Island tsunami had caught the sympathy of the world, and resources were pouring in. Huge Chinook helicopters were ferrying in resources as fast as they could, and already there was order emerging from the catastrophe.

Last night the cricket ground had looked like a massive disaster area. Now huge tents held dormitory-style bunks for everyone. Apparently even those whose homes were undamaged were being advised to stay here. The huge wash of water had caused more than direct problems, with landslips and flooding leading to sewerage and plumbing nightmares.

But engineering problems, thankfully, weren't Morag's worry. She had enough to face without that.

The place Grady took Morag to—finally—was another huge white tent. It turned out to be a stunningly set-up field hospital.

People had worked all through the night, Morag realised, dazed and washed with guilt that she'd slept through such an effort.

'You needed to sleep,' Grady said gently as they stood at the entrance to the big tent. Damn, how could he guess what she was thinking almost before she knew she was thinking it? 'You were so shocked and exhausted that you were past operating. Do you want to see Sam?'

'He's not been evacuated?'

'We're taking him out this morning.' He grimaced. 'There was the small matter of his cat.'

'Sam's cat.' Morag thought about Sam's cat while she stared around her.

The tent had a foyer, just like a real hospital. A woman clad in emergency-services yellow was seated at a desk, directing traffic. Two corridors led off—one labelled EMERGENCY and the other WARDS. Wards? How could they have done this in such a short space of time?

It looked unreal. If it hadn't been for the grass underfoot, the building could have been a city clinic.

Her head was spinning. She had to focus on one thing at a time. Hamish. The Kooris.

Sam's cat. That was easiest.

'I know Oscar,' she said. The vast, overfed tom was almost an institution on the island. He was fiercely protective of his master, and most of the islanders actively disliked him. He hissed and spat at anyone who came near Sam's boat. If anyone threatened his Sam—and that might be by saying hello and holding out a hand to be shaken—then Oscar knew what to do. He ruled the island cats with well-sharpened claws, and he wore each of his many battle scars like the tattoos on the toughest of bikie gangsters.

'He would have been on the boat with Sam,' Morag said, dismayed. Oscar was definitely not her favourite cat, but she knew how heartbroken Sam would be without him.

'That's right,' Grady told her, smiling. 'He was washed out of the boat with Sam, and Sam's wife assumed he was dead. But Sam wasn't having a bar of it and insisted on staying until he found out. Anyway, about an hour ago Heather came marching into the hospital with the most bedraggled cat you've ever seen. She dumped it on Sam's coverlet and said, "Here, here's your damned cat, now you can get yourself fixed up properly." The cat's fine. Elsey, our chief nurse, tried to be nice and approached Oscar with a towel. Oscar put two fang marks in her hand and she'll have to have a course of antibiotics. Despite losing his leg, suddenly all's almost OK with Sam's world.'

Grady was smiling. And suddenly so was Morag.

This was normal. These were her people, responding as they must to extraordinary circumstances. For the first time she thought there might be a tomorrow.

And this was the worst. From here, it could only move forward.

'What do you want me to do about it?' she asked.

'Explain to Sam why he can't take his cat to the mainland?'

'I can do that.'

'Find someone to offer to look after it?'

'Harder,' she admitted. 'But Oscar hangs around the lighthouse. I can put cat food out. Not that he'll deign to eat it. He steals food from every kitchen in the island. Then what?'

His smile faded. 'Morag...' He hesitated but she knew as soon as he looked at her—as soon as his smile faded—what he was going to ask.

'Morag, the injuries we've got are substantial. The worst have been evacuated but we've got twenty beds filled. Sadly, the injured people are mostly those who were in the worst places, and because it was a Sunday they tended to be in family groups. So we have injured people where there's often a matching death. We'll bring in trained counsellors, but these people need to talk straight away and you're their family doctor. We've decided that unless there's further immediate trauma, your most urgent need is to check the lists, get yourself up to speed, then go from bed to bed and talk people through what's happened. As you have been on the way here. These people need you, Morag, and that need is more for talk than for action.'

She nodded. She'd expected no less.

It was odd, she thought dully. Four years ago she'd wanted desperately to be a surgeon. She hadn't wanted one bit of personal medicine. The sooner patients were anaesthetised and she could concentrate on technical skills rather than interpersonal stuff, the better she'd liked it.

But now... Interpersonal stuff was medicine just as surely as surgery. She knew what Grady was asking was just as necessary as hands-on trauma stuff, and every bit as important. Maybe even more so.

'Check injuries yourself as you go,' Grady was saying. 'Yesterday was chaos. Look for things that may have been missed. There are still people coming in. My team and I can cope with front-line stuff, but you need to do the personal. Can you do that?'

'Of course I can.'

'Good.' He hesitated and then shook his head. 'No. I'm sorry. Of course it's not good. But it's what you're here for, Morag. Four years ago it was your decision to be a part of this. For now I'm afraid you have to live with it.'

She did. And maybe she needed to start thinking for herself. 'I need to go out to the Koori settlement before I do anything else,' she told him. 'They'll need me.'

'Jaqui's gone out there now.'

She frowned. That was a waste. If they'd asked her... 'They won't let her help.'

'Why not?'

'They hardly let me.'

'She'll be able to give us an overview at least,' Grady told her. 'Surely. But you're needed here. With only three doctors I can't afford for you both to be there, and she's already gone. She's good, Morag. I think you'll find she can help. You work here for this morning and if there's a need you can go out there yourself this afternoon.'

'There will be a need.'

'There's need here, Morag. There's need everywhere.'

'Grady, I need to prioritise. The Kooris—'

But Angie Salmon had been standing in the shadows, waiting for them to finish. As Morag caught her eye, the woman stepped forward. She looked distraught to the point of despair.

'Morag,' she faltered. 'I just wanted... I just...I didn't sleep and the kids are hysterical and Don's blaming himself and all he can do is cry and...I need...'

Priorities. How could she choose?

She just had to trust that Jaqui could pull off a miracle out in the Koori settlement.

She had to trust in Grady.

So for the rest of the morning she moved from one personal tragedy to the next. Listening.

She listened to Angie, then tucked her firmly into bed and gave her something to make her sleep. 'You're no use to anyone if you collapse,' she told her. 'Get yourself strong. Others are looking after your kids. I'll see Don and we'll work something out so you can both have time out.'

It was no solution—there *was* no solution—but it was all she could do.

Grady and his team worked a surgery, assessing, treating, assigning beds, organising evacuations. The rest was left to Morag. It was too much for one doctor to handle, but she was the only one who could do it.

And it was mind-numbing work. Dreadful. They didn't teach you this at medical school, Morag thought as she cradled old Hazel Cartwright against her breast and listened to her sobs. Elias Cartwright had been slightly demented and hugely demanding. When the wave had hit, Hazel had been out walking, taking a breather from her heavy role of carer. The wave had killed Elias instantly. Even though Hazel had expected her husband's death any time these past ten years, shock had her in a grief as deep as that felt by Angie.

There was little Morag could do but listen to Hazel. There was little she could do for anyone but listen.

Over and over she heard the stories. Where people had been. How they'd felt as the wave had hit. How they couldn't do anything. The feeling of sheer absolute helplessness, of lives suddenly out of control in the face of this catastrophe.

That was the deepest feeling. Being out of control.

Like Hazel... Death in bed at the end of a long life, death by misadventure, even death by disease—these things could be explained. Somehow. But to have the island decimated like this...to lose faith in their very foundations...

All Morag could do was listen.

But sometimes there were practicalities. Sometimes there was pain she could alleviate.

Like thirteen-year-old Lucy, huddled in bed, miserable and alone and frantically fearful because both her parents had been airlifted to Sydney and her brother was missing. She'd been treated for gravel rash—she'd been swept along a road in the same motion as being dumped by a wave, only this time the beach had been the gravel road outside her home. Her parents had been badly injured, and Lucy had been the one to run for help, so her injuries had been only cursorily inspected by one of the nurses in the first hours when Morag had been so occupied. She needed to be reassessed now.

She didn't want to be reassessed. Morag reached her bed and the teenager's face closed, almost in anger. But as she turned away from Morag, she winced.

The gravel rash was on her left. She'd turned to her right. What was wrong with her right side?

Morag put her hand on the girl's left shoulder and let it lie. Softly. As if she had all the time in the world.

'Your arm's hurting?'

'No.'

'I think it is.'

'Everything hurts.'

They should have evacuated Lucy as well, Morag thought, but even if she had gone to Sydney, her parents were in no condition to comfort her. And someone had thought, What if Hamish was found, injured?

But it wasn't fair on Lucy. She should be with her parents.

'Where's your grandmother?' she asked. May wasn't on any list. Was the sprightly elderly lady out looking for her grandson?

'She came in before,' Lucy muttered. 'I told her to go away.'

'To look for Hamish?'

'Hamish is dead.'

'We don't know that.'

'Yeah, we do,' Lucy spat. 'Where else would he be?'

Morag closed her eyes. Deep breath.

'Your grandma will need you as much as you need her,' she said, but had a fierce head-shake in return.

'I don't want anyone.'

'Lucy?'

'What?'

'Let me see your arm.'

'My arm doesn't matter. I want to know what's happened to my parents.'

Before she saw each patient, Morag did her homework, finding out as much as she could about what had happened to each of their families and discovering, if she could, the extent of the damage to their homes. She'd treated Peter and Christine last night and she'd read the report on the family house. Plus, she'd checked. So now she was able to give as much reassurance as there was to give.

'I radioed Sydney fifteen minutes ago,' she told her. 'Your dad has a fractured thigh and the doctors in Sydney are operating on him right now. Your mum hurt one of her legs as well. It's a simple fracture that only needs a plaster, but she also hit her head. That's why she was drifting in and out of consciousness when you last saw her. But she's conscious now. The Sydney doctors will be doing all sorts of tests in Sydney and we'll tell you the minute we know.'

'What are they testing for?'

'For insurance,' a man's voice said behind Morag, and it was Grady. Grady.

Morag had been working solidly for about four hours. She hadn't realised how exhausted she was, but when she turned and saw him she felt the pressure lift—just like that. He was dressed in a green theatre gown, with his mask pushed down as if he'd just emerged from surgery. She'd guess that he'd been working as hard as she had, if not harder.

So there was no reason for her to look to him for support. Was there? But as he pushed aside the curtain dividing Lucy's bed from the rest of the tent, it was all she could do not to stand up and hug him.

He saw it. He gave her a small, reassuring smile, which should have been nothing but it gave her the strength to take another deep breath and carry on.

Grady's smile had moved to Lucy. Good. The girl needed more reassurance than Morag could give.

'I was the one who assessed your mother before she left,' Grady was telling her. 'She was drifting in and out of consciousness then, but I think shock might have been having an effect, as well as the pain from her broken leg. There didn't seem to be any intracranial swelling.'

'Intracranial swelling?'

'Sometimes when people hit their heads they bleed into their brains,' Grady told the girl. 'Pressure can cause major problems. But usually when that happens you can tell. You open people's eyes and check their pupils. I checked your mum's eyes and her pupils looked fine.'

'What would they look like if they weren't fine?' Lucy demanded, almost belligerently.

'When you shine a light in people's eyes, a normal, undamaged brain makes the pupils get smaller,' Grady told her. 'I shone a light into your mother's eyes and her pupils reacted just as they should. Also, her pupils stayed exactly the same as each other. That's a really good sign.'

'So why did you send her to Sydney?'

'Just as a precaution,' Grady told her. 'So if things change or if I was wrong and she does need an operation to relieve pressure, then she'll be in the right spot. And your dad was going anyway.'

'Why couldn't I go?'

'No room on the helicopter,' Grady told her ybluntly.

Lucy hesitated. 'What about Hamish?'

'We're still looking for Hamish.'

Lucy hesitated. Her face closed in what almost seemed teenage rebellion. 'I don't want to stay on this island any more,' she whispered. The teenager's eyes were determinedly defiant, but there was more than a hint of moisture behind them now. It was as much as Morag could do not to gather her in for a hug—but she knew instinctively that it wouldn't help. It was a fine line—when a kid turned into an adolescent and when a hug from an adult became patronising and claustrophobic.

It was only for a few short years that teenagers became untouchable and it was dreadful that this had happened right in the midst of it. But if it got worse...

Grady flicked a questioning look at Morag, colleague asking permission, and he got an imperceptible nod in return. It was fine by Morag. This was no time for being precious about patient boundaries. She wanted all the help she could get.

'If Dr Morag is worried about your arm, maybe we could look at it together,' Grady suggested.

'My arm's OK.'

'There's no medals for heroes in this game,' Grady said gently. 'Lucy, I've been treating grown men this morning with lesser injuries than you, and some of them have been crying. You don't need to pretend, and no one will tell anyone if you have a really good howl. Now...let us look at your arm.'

Lucy stared at Grady for a long moment. Grady gazed calmly back.

And Lucy cracked first.

'OK,' she conceded.

'Sensible decision,' Grady told her, without a flicker of relief that the girl had agreed.

Then, as Morag watched from the sidelines, he sat on the bed and carefully lifted Lucy's arm.

'Can you move your fingers?'

'Yeah.'

'Try.'

He got a belligerent look, but he met Lucy's gaze calmly and dispassionately. He was a fine doctor, Morag thought. He had so many skills. But, then, she'd known that about him all along.

'Who's looking for Hamish?' she whispered, and Grady met that with calmness as well.

'We have every fit islander, plus a team of almost fifty army personnel, combing the island.'

'He was swept away with the wave?'

'I guess he must have been,' Grady told her, feeling each finger and watching her face. 'The wave hit you and your parents with such force—'

'But Hamish wasn't with us.'

Morag stilled. The search for the small boy—for Robbie's best mate—was centring around the fact that he'd been swept out from his parents' front yard. His parents had been too dazed to do any more than ask for news of their son, and Lucy hadn't been questioned. The searchers were working in the assumption that he'd been with his parents when the wave had struck.

Dangerous assumption. She saw Grady focus, and his hand came out to take the girl's good one.

'Lucy, we've been searching for Hamish around your house. Are you saying he could be somewhere else on the island?'

'He went over to Morag's.'

'To the lighthouse?' Morag's heart sank. The promontory that held the lighthouse had been swept clean by the force of the wave. If Hamish had been out there... 'Did he come over to see Robbie?'

'Yeah. Mum said he should do his school project but Dad said he it was too good a day to keep a kid inside.' Her face crumpled and she gave a despairing whimper. 'It's not fair. He shouldn't have gone. Where is he? I want my mum.'

'I tell you what we'll do,' Grady told her, as, like it or not, Morag moved to hug the girl close. Lucy was so distressed that she suddenly almost seemed to welcome it, her body curving into Morag's like she belonged there. Only for a moment. Only for a second. Then she re-grouped and pulled away. But somehow...her hand stayed just within contact with Morag's.

'We'll X-ray your arm. If, as I think, you've fractured your forearm, we'll put it into plaster so it doesn't move and it stops hurting,' Grady told her. 'And then we'll organise a helicopter flight for you to the mainland so you can be with your dad while you wait for your mother to get better.'

'But Hamish...'

'We're doing all we can, Lucy.'

'Can I ask your Grandma to come in?' Morag asked, and the girl's face closed again.

'No,' she muttered. 'I don't want to see her again. Grandma started crying. Grandma never cries. I don't know what to tell her. Hamish...'

'Can you remember,' Morag said carefully, trying to make it sound as if it was important but not too important, 'how long it was between Hamish leaving home and the wave hitting?'

'He left home just after lunch and we have lunch at one,' Lucy said fretfully. 'I remember 'cos Dad said he couldn't go until we'd done the washing-up.'

'We left the lighthouse just before two,' Morag told Grady. 'He must have just missed us.'

'Mum said if Robbie wasn't home he had to come straight back,' Lucy told them. 'He had loads of homework to do. It was Dad's idea to let him go but I think Mum was a bit pissed off.'

'Where else would Hamish have gone?' Grady asked her. 'If Robbie wasn't home, were there any other friends he'd contact?'

'I don't know.' The teenager seemed to realise Morag was still in contact with her hand, and she pulled back some more, whimpering a little as her arm jarred. She hauled up her bedcovers as if they could protect her from impending pain. 'I don't know.'

'We'll look,' Morag promised, but she couldn't promise that they'd find him.

They knew the odds.

The odds were dreadful.

Lucy's arm had a simple greenstick fracture. Morag assisted while Grady carefully prepped the arm, wrapped it and then put a backslab on the forearm. There was considerable swelling around the wrist. Given that it had happened over twelve hours ago, it was probably as swollen as it was going to be. It'd have to be checked in a few days.

In a few days Lucy would be in Sydney, Morag thought. Hopefully with her recovering mother and father.

And her brother?

The impending tragedy stayed with them while they worked. Lucy was white-faced and silent, and they knew her silence wasn't caused by her own pain. She was terrified for her parents and for her brother— and she had every right to be.

'I'll contact Sydney,' Grady said, grim-faced, as they left Lucy with a nurse and came out again into the little reception area. 'Maybe the father might know where Hamish might be?'

'I'll contact him,' Morag told him. 'Peter's my friend.' She grimaced. 'And Christine is Robbie's aunt. Christine's brother was Beth's husband— Robbie's father. He drowned when Robbie was tiny, so they know already what tragedy is.'

That hurt. 'Oh, hell...'

'It is,' she said bleakly. 'Hamish is Robbie's cousin and they've been extraordinarily close all their lives. If I hadn't come back when I did, Robbie would be part of their family.'

'They would have taken him in?'

'Of course.'

He frowned. 'So why did you come back?'

Why had she come back? Did he understand nothing?

'That's a great question,' she snapped. 'Very empathetic. Look around you at this community and use your head. Is Jaqui back from the Koori settlement?'

'She's been back for a while.'

Morag stilled. 'So they didn't let her help.'

'I gather not. They said there were no problems.'

'Oh, sure. No problems? They'd hide them.'

'Why would they hide them?'

'They just would.' She raked her hair in distress. 'I should have gone.' None of the Koori people would admit to Jaqui that they needed help, she thought grimly. She'd been stupid to hope that they would.

'If Jaqui can't help, how can you?' Grady asked.

'They trust me.'

'But—'

'There's no but,' she snapped. 'Of course they won't let Jaqui near them. I should have been out there this morning. Or last night! It's taken my family two generations to get their trust, and I have it. So I'm needed. Ask me again why I came home, Dr Reece.'

'I never meant—'

'I know you never meant,' she said softly, almost under her breath. 'You never meant anything.'

First she had to make the phone call to Peter—Hamish's father—and it was dreadful. For this little family, the drowning of Beth's husband—Christine's brother—followed by Beth's death, was still real and dreadful, and Morag could hear the horror of past pain as well as terror for the future in the way Peter spoke to her. Peter was badly injured himself, just coming around from anaesthesia. His wife was still not out of danger. And...where was his son?

'I was sure he'd be with Robbie,' he told her. 'I was sure. When they said he was still missing... I just said find Robbie and he'll be there. They said Robbie was up with Hubert so I just assumed...' His voice broke. 'I can't believe I left the island not knowing. I was just so worried about Christine. And I couldn't find May.'

May was Peter's mother. At least she could reassure him there. 'I've seen May and she's OK. She's worried to death about Hamish, of course, but she was out of range when the wave hit and her house is undamaged.' She was worried to death about Lucy as well, but Lucy still wouldn't let her close and she wasn't about to burden Peter with his mother's distress. 'She'll be here for Hamish when we find him. And you were so badly hurt yourself,' Morag said gently. 'Peter, we're doing all we can.'

'He must have followed you up to Hubert's.' Peter's voice cracked with desperation. 'Maybe he'd guess that you'd be up there. Maybe...'

'I'll check everything,' Morag told him. 'Meanwhile, we're sending Lucy over to be with you.'

'But if Hamish needs her... If May needs her...'

'I'll be here for Hamish and for May, I promise.'

Distressed beyond measure, she put the phone down and turned to find Grady watching her. His face was etched deep with concern.

'Dreadful?'

'Dreadful,' she agreed. 'That little family's lost so much already. I'm worried Peter might crack up completely.'

'He can't,' Grady said bluntly. 'His wife and daughter depend on him.'

'Yeah.' She shrugged, still cringing inside from the pain she'd heard in Peter's voice. 'It does hold you up. This feeling that if you fall over it'll have a domino effect.' She took a deep breath. 'Maybe I need to speak to Robbie. He and Hamish were planning to spend the afternoon together before Hamish's mum said he had to spend the afternoon on homework. I wonder what were they planning to do?'

'Homework together?' Grady queried, and she managed a smile.

'Or not.' Her smile faded. 'I need to phone Robbie before I go out to the settlement.'

'I've cleared the way to come with you.'

'You don't want—'

'I need. As you say, there may well be medical imperatives out there. If I'm assisting you, will that be OK?'

'Maybe. If you're seen as the junior partner with no authority.' Her worry receded for a whole split second while she thought of the impossibility of Grady being the junior partner in anything.

'I'll be the junior partner,' he said, with a meekness that had her glancing at him with suspicion, but his face was impassive. 'Phone Robbie. I'll start loading gear.'

Robbie knew nothing.

'I dunno where he'd be.' Robbie had held up so well, but the thought of losing Hamish had him almost incoherent with anguish. 'We were just going to do...stuff.'

'What sort of stuff?'

'I dunno.' There was an audible sniff on the end of the line. 'Morag, can you come and get me? Now?'

'I need to go out to the aboriginal settlement,' she told him, almost twisting inside with pain. He needed her. He needed her so much, but she was stuck. To take her with him when she didn't know what she'd find...she couldn't. But she had to go.

He had to see it.

'Robbie, the Koori people...many of them may well be hurt and they won't let anyone near except me.'

He gulped and she heard him fight back tears. 'Do you...do you want me to stay another night with Hubert?'

'If you can, Robbie,' she said gently. 'I know it's a lot to ask, but so many people here need me. I'll come up later and share Hubert's bed again.'

Then she was forced to listen while he fought panic. But finally he managed to do the right thing. The adult thing. The thing that a nine-year-old shouldn't have to do when he was faced with what Robbie had faced in the past, and what he was facing in the future.

'I'll be OK,' he quavered.

'You're a good kid, Robbie.'

'Sometimes I get sick of being a good kid,' he said rebelliously, and she winced.

'You know something, Robbie?'

'What?'

'Sometimes I get sick of being a good adult, too,' she confessed. 'You reckon one day you and I might run away from home?'

He thought about it, but only for a moment.

'If they close down the island, we won't have to run away. They'll chuck us off.'

'There could be a good side to that. Maybe we wouldn't have to be good any more.'

'Yeah, but you'd just get a job somewhere else and we'd have to be good all over again,' he told her. 'We'd better stay here.'

'OK.'

'But, Morag...'

'Mmm?'

'I'll stay here and be good,' he told her. 'But you find Hamish.'

CHAPTER SEVEN

'ROBBIE'S TAKING IT hard?'

Grady hadn't said a word until they had one of the few undamaged four-wheel-drives loaded and were headed south toward the Koori settlement. He produced sandwiches and handed them to her piece by piece as she drove. She knew the way and it seemed suddenly important that she keep the illusion that she was in control. But Grady was glancing across at her as she drove, and she knew that he saw that her knuckles were white on the steering-wheel.

And one sandwich seemed enough to choke her.

'Morag?' he prodded gently, and she had to force herself to respond. What had he asked? Was Robbie taking it hard? Stupid, stupid question.

'You don't know how much.'

'You've really dug yourself deep here, haven't you?'

'No,' she said tightly. 'I haven't dug myself anywhere. The hole's been dug for me.'

'You elected to come.'

'Yeah,' she said tightly. 'I did.'

'Were you happy here?' he asked. 'Before the wave struck.'

'Of course I was happy. Why wouldn't I be happy?'

'You don't miss Sydney?'

Oh, for heaven's sake. What a time for an inquisition.

'Why should I miss Sydney?' she snapped.

'I just thought——'

'Well, don't think.' She hesitated. And then thought, No, why not say it? All these things that had built up for so long...

'Why would I ever want to be somewhere other than here?' she told him, her anger suddenly threatening almost to overwhelm her. 'I like there being only three shops on the island. I like always drinking instant coffee and wearing the same clothes everyone else wears, and I like it that everyone on the island knows every single thing about my life. I like having dated the island's only two eligible men—and deciding they weren't so eligible after all. I like cooking our own dinner every damned night except once a month when Robbie and I treat ourselves to dinner at the pub where we have a choice of steak and chips, fish and chips or sausages and chips. I like being on call twenty-four hours a day, seven days a week and fifty-two weeks of the year. And I like it that Robbie will have to go to Sydney to board for the last few years of secondary school and he'll probably never come back and I'll be stuck here for ever...'

Her voice broke and she dashed an angry hand across her face. Tears? When had she last cried? Before yesterday, she couldn't remember.

'So if the island is declared unfit for habitation,' Grady said cautiously into the stillness, 'you won't be too upset?'

She swivelled. They hit a bump on the dirt track and the truck lurched, but she didn't notice.

'What the hell are you talking about?'

'The infrastructure's been smashed. It'll cost a bomb to fix the power and sewerage and the buildings. It'd be much cheaper for the government to pay for resettlement on the mainland.'

'Oh, great.'

'You don't want to be here.'

'I didn't say that.'

'I think you just did.'

'Well, I didn't!' She was so angry now she was almost spitting. 'I know. I miss things from the mainland. Of course I do. And I feel trapped. But these people... A tiny group of highlanders settled here two hundred years ago and their descendants still live here. Most of the kids now leave the island when they're about fourteen to go to secondary school and a lot of them don't come back. But the ones that do…they come because they want to.'

'Maybe they feel obligated. Like you.'

'So you'd say let's not give them the choice?'

'If it costs a bomb…maybe not.'

'And the true islanders?' she snapped. 'The Koori? They've been here for thousands of years. They keep apart from the rest of the island. They speak their own language. They're the most extraordinary artists and craftsmen. Magical. But their way of life hasn't changed in generations. Except that they get emergency health care and inoculations.'

'Thanks to you, and you don't want to be here.'

'I didn't say that.'

'You did.'

'No,' she snapped. 'I said I missed things. I do. Of course I do. But if I truly wanted to leave, you wouldn't see me for dust.'

'And if you and I…'

'What?' She turned and faced him and the truck hit a stump in the road. The truck jerked sideways and she swore and pulled the car to a halt. Maybe driving when she was white hot with rage wasn't such a good idea.

'There's still something between us, Morag,' Grady told her. He was watching her face. Carefully. Choosing his words. 'You know, I haven't forgotten you. All these years… If you came back…'

It needed only that.

'You're saying we could take up where we left off four years ago?'

'I didn't realise how much I'd miss you,' he said softly. 'Until you left.'

She closed her eyes. After all these years. At such a time…

'I'm sorry,' he said gently. 'This isn't the time.'

'No.' Her eyes flew wide and she stared straight ahead at the road. Carefully she steered back from the verge, keeping careful rein on her fury. 'No, it's not.' Then, very carefully, thinking it through, she said, 'Grady, when you came here, were you told to start preparing us for full evacuation?'

'I—'

'I know it's early,' she said. 'The focus is on searching. But there's a huge number of troops on the island now, yet the main road's still blocked. And I was talking to one of the men who's been working on the gas main. He was telling me that they'd succeeded in blocking it completely. Now, that might just be temporary, for safety…'

'It is.'

'So you know that for sure?' she said carefully. 'You seem to be taking care of me, but people are deferring to you. You're some sort of leader in all this. Can you tell me for sure that there are no plans to declare this island unfit for habitation?'

She waited. She kept driving.

There was no answer from beside her.

She'd expected none.

'I'm right, aren't I?' she said grimly. 'Well, it's not going to happen. We won't all leave.'

'If there are no services…'

'If there's no services, most of the townspeople will leave,' she told him. 'Of course they will. They have no choice. Even the people like Hubert. I dare say if you removed his pension and took away all support, then maybe he'd be forced to go, too. But not the Kooris.'

'Do the Koori need our intervention?'

'No,' she snapped. 'Of course they don't. They don't want us helping in any way, shape or form. They'll tell you that over and over. So do you believe them? You'd leave them to fend for themselves.'

'If that's what they want.'

'You don't know anything about what they want,' she said dully. 'You know nothing at all. Just shut up, Grady. Help me if you can, but shut up about the future. I need to focus on putting one foot in front of the other and that's all I want to do. And as for you and me… Ha!'

He said nothing.

It was like he was stepping on eggshells, he thought. Try as he may, he was about to crush things he had no wish to crush.

And he wasn't at all sure what it was he was crushing.

He didn't understand. He knew nothing. That was what she'd accused him of, and she was right. He had no understanding of this small community, of the dynamics that held it together and why its hold on Morag was so strong.

And behind everything… The thought nagged.

There'd been an alternative for Robbie. Robbie had an Uncle Peter and an Aunt Christine and a cousin Lucy, and maybe even still a cousin Hamish. Four years ago Morag had implied there was no one for the boy. That was why he'd let her go.

No. No one let Morag go anywhere, he thought as he watched her heave her gear from the back of the truck and turn to welcome the two old Koori men who'd appeared to greet her as the truck had drawn to a halt. She was her own woman. She did what she wanted.

She hadn't wanted him.

Of course she had, he told himself. She'd wanted him as much as he'd wanted her, but she'd wanted this community more. And it wasn't just her wishes that were holding her here. She was tied by the community's needs.

For Grady, who'd been raised with immense wealth but with no commitment to anyone, this was a concept he found almost impossible to comprehend. Commitment to people. Love, not for just one person but for five hundred...

Hell. He was too confused to think this through any further. All he could do was watch.

The cove where they'd parked the truck was as far from the township as it was possible to be. There were no visible buildings. A band of palms surrounded a broad sweep of beach. Wide strips of rock ribboned the sides of the cove, and even from two hundred yards away he could see white crusting that spoke of generation upon generation of oysters, building on the remains of their past.

The cove itself... It must have been beautiful yesterday, he thought, but the wave had ripped it apart. Some of the smaller palms had been uprooted and a mass of mud, leaf litter and assorted debris coated everything. In the shadows of the palms he could make out the flitting figures of dark-skinned people, fading back behind the trees as if scared of these people appearing from another world.

Morag was ignoring him. She was speaking to the two men, urgently, in a dialect he didn't recognise. Their language? It must be.

The men were elderly, white-haired, with deep, brown skin that was covered only between their waist and their knees. One of the men had a jagged wound running down the side of his shoulder. He put a hand to it occasionally, as if it hurt.

Morag looked as if she hadn't noticed.

They spoke for a good five minutes, the old men softly spoken but obviously hugely distressed. As they spoke they paused every so often to glance across at him with a look that said they were deeply distrustful.

Distrustful. Great. He tried very hard to merge into the pile of medical supplies and look harmless.

How did you look harmless?

But finally they broke apart, and Morag led the men across to where Grady stood.

'Dr Reece, this is Yndilla and Nargal. Yndilla, Nargal, this is Dr Reece.' She was speaking slowly, giving the men time to understand a language they were clearly not comfortable with. 'We want to start work now,' she told the men. 'Will you bring us those you believe we can help?' She hesitated. 'But, please…remember that wounds from coral or oyster shells get infected fast, and remember that we can help stop that infection.' Then, as their expressions again became uncertain, she reverted again to their language.

Once again, Grady could do nothing but wait.

Finally the two white heads inclined ever so slightly. It seemed permission had been given.

'What's happening?' Grady asked, as the men disappeared into the shadows to talk to their people.

'They've lost seven of their own,' she told him, gazing after the elders with a worried look. 'A lot of the kids ran to the beach when the water was sucked out, and they were hit hard. But most of them survived. These people live in the water. They knew enough to let themselves be washed out and then swim in after the first rush. The deaths will have been caused by injury. Two elderly men. One woman, two babies and two little girls.'

He winced. And then he moved to organisational mode. This was, after all, work he was trained for. 'OK. We need to transport the bodies to town. Can I call someone?'

She shook her head. 'They're already buried.'

'But the coroner—'

'The coroner accepts the judgment of the tribe elders,' she told him. 'So do I. Yndilla and Nargal have agreed to let us see the urgent medical cases, and for that I'm grateful.'

'Yndilla has a gash that needs stitching.'

'No.' Once more she shook her head. 'He won't let us stitch it. He says he hit it on a rock, and he's cleaned it.'

'It'll scar.'

She smiled. 'Yeah. Right. Did you see his chest?'

He had. The old man's chest was crossed with scars that were obviously part of some tribal ritual, and there was no doubt that the scars were worn with pride. A slash across the old man's shoulder was hardly likely to have him cringe with self-consciousness.

She was still smiling and the corners of his mouth curved involuntarily in response. He liked it when she smiled, he thought. He...

He nothing.

Hell. Back to work.

'What else?'

'There's a couple of suspected fractures that probably need setting,' she told him. 'Kids. We're permitted to give pain relief while we set them.'

'But X-rays...'

'No X-rays unless there's a real call for it.'

'Like if we think it's broken?'

'No. These people live rough. There are fractures all the time. They won't tolerate me taking kids into hospital for a greenstick fracture.'

He stared. 'Hell, Morag...'

'We do what we can,' she said simply. Then she shrugged. 'I know you don't like it but it's the way it is. If there's a major problem, if it's clear that a leg's going to end up shorter than the other or not heal at all, then I'll push hard, and because they know I don't push unless it's imperative, usually they'll agree. But it needs huge persuasion, Grady, so I don't try unless I think it's really, really dire.' She hesitated, giving him a searching glance. 'So...can you start on the fractures? The elders will stay with you all the time. They have a little English if you speak slowly, and they'll translate as best they can.'

'And you?'

'There's an old lady I need to see. She's with the women.' She hesitated. 'Just don't ask me about her, Grady. Can I leave you to the rest?'

'Sure.'

'Right.' But still she hesitated. 'Grady...please, remember that these people don't want intervention. No dressings unless they're really necessary. Same with stitches. Stitches get infected. Scars will become part of the legend of this tsunami. They'll be shown with pride to grandchildren. So we're not interested in cosmetic results, right?'

'Right.'

'Fine,' she said, and cast him an uncertain smile. Then a woman called out from the shadows. Morag hesitated, but there was nothing left to say. She was being forced to trust him, he thought, watching her face, and he knew that it was a weird sensation.

He watched in silence as she collected her doctor's bag and strode into a mass of palms at the back of the clearing. Leaving him with the shadows fading in and out of the cover of the palms.

Leaving him...confused.

There wasn't time for confusion, however. He had things to do.

Nargal emerged first from the backdrop of palms. The old man had a child by his side, a little girl of about six or seven. She was holding one arm with the other, and was big-eyed with pain and fear.

Nargal looked almost as terrified.

Morag had persuaded these people to trust him, he thought, and suddenly the responsibility of what he was facing seemed enormous. One bad move and these people would disappear into their shadows, he knew, and then...and then there'd only be Morag who'd be allowed near.

She was desperately alone. This was all he could do for her.

He watched the man and the child walk falteringly across the clearing and he made no move toward them. As they came close he squatted so he was at eye level with the child. He didn't smile, but kept his eyes focused on her arm.

'Is it broken?' he asked, and the old man grunted assent from above.

'She said...it cracked.'

'I can help with the pain. If you'll allow.'

The old man spoke to the child in murmured dialect and the child listened. She hadn't taken her eyes from Grady.

'I need to give an injection,' Grady said softly, and the man inter-preted to the child.

The little girl whimpered and backed away a little, but she didn't run.

'The injection will hurt a little,' Grady said. 'But then it won't hurt while I examine the arm. I can make sure the arm is straight and I can wrap it tightly so it won't hurt as much while it heals.'

More interpretation. He repeated himself a couple of times, a word at a time. And then he waited.

Silence.

He was very aware of the shadows. Scores of people watching from the shadows.

He waited, as if he had all the time in the world.

He waited.

Then there was a frightened whisper from the child to the old man and a one-syllable response, before the old man again addressed Reece.

'She wants that you are friend of Dr Morag. I told her yes.'

Grady nodded gravely. 'Thank you.'

'You can give her...injection,' the old man said. 'She knows a friend of Morag will not harm her.'

It went against everything Grady had ever been taught. To not X-ray...

He gave an injection of morphine and gently felt the fracture site. Then he held the child's arms out, measuring reach. He carefully tested each finger, each part of the arm, searching for nerve damage, searching for any sign that the bone had splintered.

It seemed OK. It was probably a greenstick fracture, but not to take an X-ray...

He had no choice.

He splinted the arm still and carefully strapped the arm to keep it immobile.

A cast would be better, but he couldn't apply plaster here. Besides, the arm was badly scratched and he was acutely aware of Morag's warn-ing about infection. If there was infection under a cast and there weren't constant checks, she could well lose the arm.

Enough. He fashioned a sling and finally dared a smile at the little girl.

'You're very brave.'

The old man translated and the little girl's face broke into a grin. And what a grin! It was like the sun had suddenly come out.

'Than' you,' she whispered and Grady felt his gut give a solid wrench—a wrench he hadn't known he was capable of feeling.

'You're welcome.' He smiled at her, and then looked up to find his interpreter was also smiling. 'She must keep this on for six weeks. I'll come and check it.'

'Six weeks?' the old man repeated, and Grady nodded.

'She will keep it with care. But...Morag will check it. Not you.'

Right. Of course. This was Morag's place.

Not his.

After that he saw an ankle that he hoped—where was the X-ray?—was just sprained. Then there were two nasty cuts that needed careful cleaning and debridement. Amazingly, he was able to convince the children to accept tetanus shots and an initial shot of antibiotics. They'd need a ten-day course, but he left it to Morag to explain about the medication. Hell, if he explained it wrong...

He didn't stitch either of the cuts. He pulled them together with steristrips as best he could, and told his interpreter that the strips could come off after a week. He hoped like hell that Morag would approve.

'How's it going?' She was suddenly behind him and he almost jumped. She was like a cat, moving among her own with a sureness that had him disconcerted.

'Fine,' he managed. 'Can you explain a course of antibiotics for these kids?'

'I can do that. One of the women's very good at dispensing medication. Nargal will explain it for me.'

'Nargal can't do it himself?'

'The tablets are food. That's women's work. Asking Nargal to make sure a child has a tablet twice a day would demean him.'

'I see.' He adjusted the dressing and smiled a farewell to the little boy, and looked uncertainly at Morag. He felt all of about six, asking, 'Please miss, have I done OK?'

'I had to use dressings,' he confessed.

'Sure you did,' she said, and then grinned. 'Heck, you look like I'm about to slap you.'

'You're not?'

'Argrel—the little boy with the first cut you treated—came to show his mother his bandage while I was with the women. He said the big doctor—I guess that's you—said he couldn't get it wet for three days. He explained to his mother that he wasn't allowed to get it dirty and in three days he could take the dressing off and he'd have a wonderful man scar.' Her smile widened. 'You certainly know the way to a small boy's heart.'

'Promising him scars.'

'Out here they're better than a jelly bean.'

They were smiling at each other—like fools. Which was really stupid.

'What next?' he asked.

'I'm finished.'

'Finished?' He frowned. 'Two lacerations, a broken arm and a sprained ankle?'

'I've strapped two fractures.'

'Nothing else?'

She hesitated. 'They did lose some of their people. There's nothing we can do there.'

'But there's no serious injuries.'

'Once again, not...not that we can do anything about.'

'What do you mean?'

'Two of the old people are badly injured,' she told him. 'One of the elderly men has a compressed skull fracture. He's deeply unconscious and his breathing's starting to weaken already. And there's an old woman with a fractured hip.'

He stared. 'So what are you going to do about it?'

'Nothing,' she said simply. She was collecting gear and tossing it into the back of the truck. Then she relented. 'No. I have been allowed to do something. I've left enough painkillers so Zai will drift toward death in peace.'

'For a broken hip?' he asked incredulously. 'We can take her back. Set it. And the compressed fracture—we could alleviate pressure—'

'You know as well as I do that if there's been pressure on the brain for twenty-four hours, the damage will be irreversible. And Zai...yeah, you're right, we could operate. But that means a trip to Sydney. She'd be in hospital for weeks, facing rehabilitation. She can't do that.'

'How fragile is she?'

'Not very.'

'Then why can't she do it?'

'She'd die,' Morag said simply. 'You put Zai in a Western hospital ward and she'd die of shock and terror.'

'So she'll die anyway?'

'Yes,' she said flatly. Dully. 'Of course she will. She knows that. But at least she'll die out here, surrounded by her people and the way of life that's been hers for ever. It's the way she wants it, Grady, and I'm not about to argue.'

'You can't just——'

But he wasn't allowed to continue. 'Yes, I can,' she snapped. 'Of course I can. These people have a way of life that I respect, and that way of life has nothing to do with the customs we hold dear. If this island's deemed uninhabitable...'

'They'll be resettled. Maybe they'd be better off on the mainland.'

'I don't think so.'

'Why not? At least they'd have medical facilities.'

'They have medical facilities now,' she said in a savage undertone that was laced with pain. It hadn't been easy, he guessed. To walk away from a patient she could have helped. 'They have me. I've worked so hard to get their trust, and I'm succeeding. OK, it's a tiny bit at a time, but I'm allowed to help the children. They call me now if a mother gets into major trouble during childbirth, and that's a huge concession. Even though I've no specific obstetric training, I can often help. And I'm certainly better than nothing.'

She gazed up at him, her eyes troubled, trying to make him see. 'They can't be isolated from our world for ever,' she admitted. 'But they can be assimilated ever so carefully, ever so gently, so they can preserve the values and traditions they value while taking the best of ours.'

'But to leave her to die... Morag, surely you don't believe——'

'Oh, for heaven's sake. Leave me be!' He was suddenly aware that there were tears welling up in her eyes and she swiped them away with an angry gasp. 'Do you think I like not being allowed to treat Zai? Don't you think I mind that an old lady I've known and respected since my father brought me out here twenty years ago is dying out there among the palms? And do you think I haven't thought these issues through again and again? Of course I have. But you...you're going to hold a public meeting in the next few days. I know you are. Marcus told me that's what the plan is. Give us a day or so to appreciate how deeply we're in trouble, and then you and the rest of the bureaucrats you work with are going to say close down that island, take these people to the mainland—they'll be better off. As if you know anything at all...'

She broke off. She gave an angry sniff and then another, but as he made a move to touch her she backed away as if his touch would burn.

'Don't touch me. We have to get back to town.'

'Morag—'

'Just...leave it. I've just said goodbye to two people I love. Leave me alone to get over it. You wouldn't know what that's like, Grady Reece. You fly to the rescue, you do your dramatic thing and then you leave everyone else to pick up the pieces.'

'Morag...'

She gulped. 'I'm...I'm sorry,' she managed. 'That's not fair. You've been...you've been an enormous help and I'm incredibly grateful. But can you imagine what sort of lives these people will lead if they're transplanted to the mainland? Can you?' She shook her head. 'No. I'm sorry. You can't have thought... And why would you? This isn't your business, Grady. Just leave me be to come to terms with it.'

CHAPTER EIGHT

THEY DROVE BACK to the village in unbroken silence. There were egg-shells everywhere, Grady thought ruefully, and he wasn't sure where to tread. Where to go to from here?

Back to Sydney? Of course. In a couple of days. When the disaster was over.

Or when the disaster was just beginning...

He couldn't afford to think like that, he told himself. Could he?

In the meantime, silence seemed the only option.

They arrived back at the field hospital just as Lucy was being prepared for the helicopter flight to the mainland. Jaqui had been looking after her, and as Morag appeared in the hospital entrance, Jaqui looked up in relief.

'Lucy was hoping you'd be back before she left.'

'I've been out at the settlement,' Morag told the teenager.

'Are there more deaths out there?' Lucy whispered, and Morag took her hand and squeezed. Grady stood back with Jaqui, watching in still more silence. He was starting to feel impotent. There was nothing he could do. Nothing!

'There are,' Morag told her.

'My dad'll hate it.' Lucy hesitated. 'Nargal?'

'Nargal's fine.' She smiled, and turned to include Jaqui and Grady. 'Nargal shows Lucy's father the best place to fish. Lucy's dad found Nargal after his canoe was upended in a storm twenty years ago. Peter spent the night out searching when everyone else had given up. By the time he found him, Nargal had almost reached the end—he was far gone with hypothermia. But Peter brought him back and Nargal's been good to him ever since.' She hesitated and then turned back to Lucy. 'Nargal says his men are out looking for Hamish.'

'Everyone's looking for Hamish.' The girl's voice broke on a sob. 'I should be.'

'No. You shouldn't.' Morag ran her fingers down Lucy's face. 'You've lost skin all down your chest, your arm's broken and you're in no fit state to do anything but recuperate.' She motioned back to Grady and Jaqui. 'You know these two are part of the country's top Air-Sea Rescue team. If they can't find Hamish, no one can. We have hundreds of people combing the island and the sea.'

'He'll be drowned.'

'If he is,' Morag said gently, 'then it's even more important that you be with your parents. They'll be going out of their minds, Lucy. I know you can't do anything here, but you can be with them and, believe me, it's the most important thing. When you can't do anything else, you give yourself.'

Hell.

Grown men weren't supposed to cry.

Grady sniffed.

Jaqui cast him a suspicious glance and offered him an out. 'Dr Reece, Doug wants you in the control room,' she told him. And then, as he turned to leave, she pressed something into his hand. 'Don't forget your hanky.'

'So where the hell is he?'

'There's nothing else we can do, Grady.' Doug, their search and rescue chief, was looking grim as Grady emerged from his encounter with Lucy. 'We have to assume all the missing are drowned. The Kooris were all on the beach when the wave hit and we can assume Hamish was on the beach as well. There's been bodies washed in but if they were caught in currents, we need to accept the fact that we're never going to find them.'

'You're still searching?'

'It's been twenty-four hours. Surviving in the water for that long...'

'It's possible. Especially if they caught hold of debris.'

'Grady, it's been a really calm day. The water's like a pond. Our visibility is great. We're checking every piece of debris in a twenty-mile radius—'

'Make it thirty.'

'Grady...'

'These are kids,' Grady said. 'Kids.'

'Grady, let's keep the emotion out of it,' Doug told him, giving him a curious glance. 'We're doing the best we can.'

'And long term?' he asked dully.

'Services are non-existent,' Doug told him. 'No power, no water, no sewerage. No money and no political clout. There's no long term for this island.'

That was blunt. Grady dug his hands in his pockets and stared out into the late afternoon light. From this point high on the cricket ground, he could see the devastation the wave had caused. There was so much destruction. To rebuild...

Morag would have to leave.

It was personal. He found his hands were clenched into fists deep in his pockets and Doug was staring at him as if he didn't recognise him.

'You OK?'

'Yeah.' He grunted an assent. 'Yeah, I am.'

'The powers that be want a health statement from you,' Doug told him. 'No water, no sewerage... You know the risks.'

'And the answers I give will mean this island goes under.'

'This island went under yesterday,' Doug said bluntly, and then looked skyward as a helicopter appeared on the horizon and started its descent. 'Here's the chopper for the girl. Maybe we could move some more people out on the same flight. The evacuation has to start some time.'

'Not yet,' Grady growled. A group of men were making there way up from the township and he recognised Marcus, the unofficial spokesmen for the townspeople. He was walking slowly, his shoulders slumped. Like a man defeated, Grady thought. Hell.

'Let's get everyone out who's medically unfit at least,' Doug urged, and Grady thought back to the old lady dying slowly and unnecessarily back at the Koori settlement.

'Let's not,' he muttered. 'Not yet.'

* * *

He paced.

The helicopter landed and took off again, half-empty. From where Grady stood he had watched as Jaqui and Morag had seen Lucy on board, handed her medical notes over to the flight team and then stood back while the chopper had roared off toward the mainland.

He watched as Jaqui turned and gave Morag a hug.

He wasn't the only one this situation was getting to, he figured. His team was trained to be dispassionate. Trained to get in hard, do what had to be done and get out again.

In two or three more days they'd have made a decision about evacuating the island. The place would be empty and he'd have moved on.

And Morag?

She'd have moved on, too. Back to Sydney?

He couldn't see it.

Did he want to see it?

It didn't matter, he thought heavily. It wasn't going to happen. He and Morag… No and no and no…

Jaqui was down there, hugging her. Damn, why wasn't he down there, hugging her?

Because he knew that if he touched her, he'd commit himself.

Hell, Reece! He gave himself a sharp mental kick. He didn't do commitment. At least, not to women who were caught up with small boys and islanders and who were going to blame him for every decision that was made about this island and…

This was really deep water.

He dug his hands still further into his pockets. Morag was walking back to the tents. There might not be a medical need back in the hospital beds, but there was certainly an emotional need. From the moment she'd appeared back from the settlement the rest of the med team had been telling Morag who desperately needed to talk to her. She was burdened as no woman should be, he thought savagely. How dared the islanders put such a load on her shoulders?

'She's quite a woman,' Jaqui said softly, and he jumped. He'd been watching Morag, and hadn't noticed his partner come up behind him.

'She's devastated,' he said, almost to himself. 'This island's finished.'

'It'd take a huge commitment to keep it going. One doctor's not going to cut it.'

'Not only one doctor. The infrastructure...'

'I know.' Like him, Jaqui was looking down at the ruined town. 'Did you know my husband's head of the Public Works Department in Sydney West? I've been talking to him about the vast effort it'd take to rebuild this place.'

'Huge.'

'It'd be such a project...' She cast him a look that was as curious as the one Doug had given him. 'How did you go with the Kooris?'

'They're...' He hesitated and then shrugged. Why not say it? 'They're fantastic. They take our medicine on their terms.'

'They wouldn't let me near,' Jaqui told him. 'But, oh, I wish...' Her voice trailed off and he knew exactly what she wished. He was wishing it himself.

'It's not going to happen,' he said roughly. 'They'll be relocated.'

'I'd imagine they'll refuse to be relocated,' Jaqui said. 'They'll stay here with no medical facilities at all, and all the good Morag's done will be undone.'

'It's none of our business.'

'No,' Jaqui said, with another curious sideways glance. 'Of course it's not. How can it be?'

There were still a couple of hours of daylight left. He could go back into the hospital and help Morag—but for most of the things she was doing she didn't need help. She'd be adjusting pain medication, talking through terrors, facing the future.

With her people...

The thought was unsettling and Grady wasn't sure how to handle it.

At least there was other work to be done. He took himself down the hill to where an army of people was sifting through sodden belongings, searching for some trace of a past that had been washed away.

Doug overtook him there and together they checked the smashed infrastructure as Doug talked him through the impossibility of rebuilding.

'OK, it's not possible,' Grady said at last. He gazed at an elderly woman in the ruins of what had obviously been the village church. The wave had gone straight through, leaving only a shell. Pews and fittings had been shattered into a pile of jumbled ruins. The nave, though, with its vast, east-facing window, was still almost intact. The window was without glass, but from where Grady stood he could see right to the ocean beyond.

The woman was staring outward, looking at the sea. Just…looking. In the midst of all this confusion, it was an incredibly peaceful scene, and Grady thought suddenly that there was little need for fittings. It was breathtakingly lovely, just as it was.

The woman turned and saw the two men, she gave them a faltering smile.

'The doctor. Just who I need. I have a splinter that's stopping me working.'

Grady crossed the ruins to meet her. She was none too steady on her feet, he noticed, and she let him take her arm and help her out to the remains of the church-ground. While Doug watched, he lifted her hand and saw a shard of wood had been driven right under the nail.

'I'll take you to the medical centre.'

'No.' She shook her head. 'I have too much to do to bother. But if you could pull it out…'

'It's in deep.'

'Just…pull.'

'I need to cut the nail.'

'Then cut it,' she said, and there was desperation in her voice. 'Now. Please. The pain's driving me crazy and I need to concentrate. Please, will you help me?'

He looked down at her, trying to figure how to argue, but what he saw in her face gave him pause. There was no argument. She wouldn't go to a medical centre. And the light here was good enough…

OK. He could do this. He always carried a fully equipped medical kit in his backpack, and in a way he welcomed something practical to do. At least this was something medical rather than medical administration.

The questions he and Doug were trying to find answers to were impossibly difficult. How long could villagers survive without a viable water source? What were the risks of disease if sewerage contaminated the groundwater?

Or maybe they weren't impossibly difficult. Maybe they were questions to which he knew the answers, but he didn't like facing them. The thought of Morag's reaction when she heard was dreadful.

Morag. He couldn't think of what she was facing. He didn't understand her fierce love for this little community but now at least he knew that her love was for real, and the dispersing of the islanders would break her heart.

Hell! He'd much rather face a splinter, complicated or not.

So, as Doug excused himself, he found himself perched on a low stone wall, carefully extricating a splinter from an elderly lady's finger.

Working with care, with her hand spread on the sun-warmed stones, he blocked her ring finger with local anaesthetic. Then he carefully sliced a wedge from her nail, lifting it free so he could reach the sliver underneath.

The woman—she said her name was May Rafferty but that was all she was saying—stared straight ahead as he worked and she didn't speak until he applied antiseptic and dressing and asked her about tetanus shots.

'They're up to date,' she said shortly. 'Morag sees to that.'

'I'd imagine she would.' He hesitated. The woman, in her late sixties or early seventies, lean and weathered, with the look of someone who'd seen a lifetime of hard work, was staring again through the ruins of the church toward the sea.

'I'm sorry about your church,' he told her.

'It'll be OK. We'll rebuild.'

Would they? Grady thought of the report he was preparing and he winced. But now wasn't the time to talk of that.

'My husband was buried from this church,' May said softly. 'And my baby daughter. That's how I got the splinter. There's a plaque somewhere that my husband carved when our baby died. I thought...I thought I might be able to find it.'

'Would you like me to help you look?' he heard himself say, and she nodded as if she'd expected no less.

'I'd be very grateful.'

So with all the work to be done—with the momentous decisions still hanging in the balance as to the fate of this island—Grady found himself hauling aside splintered timber and ruined furnishings, trying to reach the base of the west wall, trying to locate one tiny carving...

Like the technical medicine of removing the splinter, it was work that he welcomed. It let him stop thinking of Morag's face as she read the report.

Morag...

Enough. Stop thinking now!

He had thick leather gloves to work with, and the task was simple enough. From the sidelines the woman watched, still in silence. Without gloves, and with her injured hand, he wouldn't let her haul things aside, but her eyes still searched the ruins. Ceaselessly.

And when he hauled aside a section of what looked like a door, she saw what she was looking for. She gave a soft moan of relief and darted forward to lift a plaque.

It was a battered piece of wood, a little less than a foot square, and it looked as if it had once been highly polished. The wave had battered it with force, marring the carving, but the lettering was still clear.

Morag Louise Rafferty
29 July 1970–20 January 1971
Precious infant daughter of May and Richard.
Died of diphtheria, aged six months.
A tiny life; a jewel;
a love that will live for ever.

May was cleaning the lettering with her sleeve, smiling down at it as if she'd found the child herself. And for the second time that day Grady found himself swallowing. Hard. Hell! He didn't do emotion. He didn't!

'Morag,' he managed after a while. 'Your little girl was called Morag?'

'Mmm.' She smiled mistily up at him. 'Your Morag was named after her.'

'My Morag?'

'The Morag you've been working with,' she explained. 'Your Morag's father was my second cousin. He was best man at our wedding, and he was our Morag's godfather. We're so intertwined, the two families. My son...' She clasped the plaque closer. 'My son Peter—my Morag's brother—married Christine. Christine's brother was David, the fisherman who married Beth, your Morag's sister. So Christine is Robbie's aunt.'

He thought it through. He was confused. Very confused. Genealogy wasn't his strong point, and the complexities of this island's relationships had his head spinning. But he finally thought he had it. 'So your son and his wife are Peter and Christine Rafferty, the couple we've evacuated to Sydney?'

'Yes.'

'Then Lucy—Lucy and Hamish...'

'Lucy and Hamish are my grandchildren.'

That had him even more confused. 'Then why...?'

'Why haven't I been with Lucy?' She shrugged and hugged the plaque against her, as if suddenly cold. 'Lucy didn't want me. She's so angry. So distressed. She said I should be out here searching for Hamish, and, of course, I have been. But there's nowhere else to search and your people are so much more competent, and suddenly...' She shivered again. 'I just wanted...'

She just wanted contact with her daughter, Grady thought with sudden insight. Her little one. This plaque was a tangible link with the past, a link to hold onto when the future looked dreadful. Grady could see it in her face and he let her be for a moment, waiting until she turned again to the east window. She gazed out to sea for a long moment, and finally her face regained a little of its serenity.

'You're all so intertwined,' he said softly. 'I'd thought...I'd thought when Beth died that Robbie had no one.'

'Robbie never had no one,' May said simply. 'Robbie has every single islander. There's no one here who wouldn't give the boy a home and be glad to do it. But Beth and Morag were sisters. They were very close. You don't mess with closeness like that.' It was said with such flat simplicity that there was no argument.

He tried to take it all in. He tried. 'This island's one big family.'

'It is,' May told him, and attempted a faltering smile. 'In a while...in a little while, when everyone who can be saved has been saved, then this church will be cleared and the funerals will start. When my Morag died, when Beth died, when Beth's husband David was drowned...every single islander was here to bid them farewell. It'll be no different this time. As long...' She faltered and then attempted to recover. She didn't quite make it. 'As long as they find Hamish,' she whispered. 'If he's drowned... They must find his body. They can bury him next to my Morag. I...'

But the thought of the loss of her grandson was suddenly overwhelming. She put a hand to her face and turned away. 'Enough. If there's any news, let me know. I'll be up at the tent place that everyone's calling home. Thank you for tending my hand.' She hugged the plaque again. 'And thank you for finding my...for finding my Morag. If I can't find Hamish...' She faltered again and closed her eyes, but when she opened them there was a calmness there. A strength. Generations of tragedy had touched this woman and would touch her further, but she was here, here with her people, and life would go on.

'Take care of your Morag,' she whispered. 'She needs it most.'

Doug was waiting in the background with more of his damned facts.

'It's impossible,' he said. 'There's no infrastructure. We'd have to pull in really top people from Sydney. This needs an engineer who really knows what he's doing to supervise, huge manpower to pull it off, tradesmen of all descriptions... Then there's the medical side. We have a situation where the entire island's been traumatised, including the local doctor. She's a single mum. She can't cope with this long term. The money...the commitment...'

'The islanders won't leave.'

'They won't have a choice,' Doug said bluntly. 'It's either abandon the island or be cut off from all services. You'll never get political support for the sort of funding this place needs. And you'll never get the personnel.'

He should go back to the medical centre. There was still an hour or so before dusk and Jaqui might need him. But Grady's radio was on his belt and he knew he could be contacted, so he found himself picking his way through the debris until he came to the promontory where the lighthouse stood.

Morag was there. As he'd hoped. He rounded the cliffs that separated the promontory from the township and he saw her, standing at the foot of the lighthouse, staring up at the whitewashed tower.

David and Goliath.

That was what she looked like, he thought. A tiny figure, facing immeasurable odds.

He called and she turned, but she didn't smile. She simply watched as he made his way down the cobbled walkway that reached out to where the lighthouse tipped the promontory.

'I hoped I might find you here,' he said, but there still wasn't a smile.

'I need to put out some food for Oscar.'

Oscar. Of course. Sam's cat.

'He comes here?'

'He likes here,' Morag told him. 'Oscar's the most independent cat we know. He lives on Sam's boat but for some reason he thinks this is his territory, so he visits us each night.'

'Maybe he likes you,' Grady said gently, but he still didn't get a smile.

'Maybe.'

'You're exhausted.'

She nodded. 'And...defeated. So much death.'

'You need to go back to Robbie.'

'I just phoned him. He's OK. He understands. I just wish...I just wish he didn't have to.'

'Let me help you here and I'll walk you up to Hubert's'

'No.'

'No?'

'It doesn't help,' she whispered. 'If I learn to lean on you.'

There was nothing to say to that. He watched as she scooped a can of cat food out into a crevice beside the lighthouse walkway, out of sight of watchful seagulls but certainly in smelling distance of the tomcat if he cruised past later in the night.

She straightened and looked at him as if she couldn't quite figure out why he was there. 'I need to check the light,' she told him, and it was a dismissal.

'I want to see.'

'Grady—'

'I know.' He held up his hands in mock surrender. 'I'm not helping. But I'm curious. I've never been in a lighthouse before.'

'It's not as good as it used to be.'

'Why not?'

She hesitated then shrugged, as if she didn't have the energy to tell him to get lost. Though her shrug said she'd certainly like to. 'The light used to be fantastic,' she told him. 'It was a huge Fresnel lens that once filled the lantern room.'

'Tell me about it.' More than anything, he ached to take that look of utter defeat from her face. He could think of no way to deflect her. But she must love this lighthouse.

And it seemed that she did.

'It was vast,' she told him. 'Wonderful. It had about a thousand individual glass prisms mounted in brass. It stood almost twenty feet tall and six feet wide, and was large enough for a man to stand inside. But now... Now we have a small green DCB-24 Aerobeacon. It's about a hundredth of the size, even though it can still be seen for almost eighteen miles.'

'Can we go up?'

'I guess...I guess we can,' she told him. 'At least, I can. I usually go up and check the light every couple of days. The globes change automatically—it's fully automated—but things still go wrong. Once I went up and a sea eagle had somehow smashed through the glass and was beating itself to death trying to get out again. I managed to get it out—amazingly it flew off and even looked like it might survive—but it had damaged the beacon.'

'You coped with a sea eagle alone?' he asked, stunned, and she looked at him as if he was stupid.

'Of course I did. What else was I to do?'

Scream and run? he thought. Call for Air-Sea Rescue?

That'd be him.

Call for him?

'I can go up now because the lamp's not burning,' she told him. 'After dusk you'll blind yourself.'

'I'd like to come.'

She gave him a dubious look. 'Aren't you supposed to be busy writing down all the reasons why the island should be declared uninhabitable?'

'Morag…'

'It's what you're doing, isn't it?'

And there was no answer but the truth. 'Yes.'

'Creep!'

'Don't shoot the messenger,' he said mildly, and got an angry glare for his pains.

'If people would support us—if the politicians realised how wonderful this place is…'

'You're too far from the mainland. Even the lighthouse doesn't need maintenance any more. It's been through a tidal wave without a blink.'

'Go jump, Grady.'

'Show me your lighthouse,' he told her. 'Please.'

'Fine,' she snapped. 'And then will you get out of my life?' She stomped forward and walked up the three huge stone steps to the lighthouse door, produced a key that was almost as big as her hand—and then paused. Instead of inserting the key in the lock, she simply pushed.

The lighthouse door swung wide.

'It's unlocked,' she said, and added, staring down at the lock, 'It's smashed.'

'The wave…'

'I checked yesterday. It was still locked and firm. This door's been built to survive battering rams.'

'It can't have been locked.' Grady wasn't really thinking of locks. He was thinking of Morag. Only of Morag. Of the way she looked…tired and defeated, yet still with shoulders squared and with the flash of fire in her words. Pure courage…

He'd thought it took courage to do what he did. Rescuing people from high seas, from burning buildings, from all sorts of peril.

But maybe Morag had needed a different kind of courage to do what she'd done over the past few years—and she'd certainly found it. In spades.

'It looks like someone's attacked the lock with an axe,' she was saying, and he hauled himself out of his preoccupation and moved forward to see.

She was right. The vast wooden door was intact, except for one slash, splintering deep into the lock.

Grady frowned and pushed the door further inward.

There was an axe propped against the wall where the spiral staircase started its long swirl upward.

'Who...?' Morag moved to the stair, but Grady stopped her.

'Let me go first.'

'The axe is down here,' Morag said reasonably. 'We're not about to get attacked.'

But Grady was already climbing, his face turned upward and his ears tuned to danger.

'If you're thinking it's a house burglar, there's not a lot of call for used aerobeacons,' Morag told him.

'Hush.'

'They're a bit strong for spotlighting rabbits.'

He smiled at that, but schooled his features to seriousness, turned and frowned her down. She was wonderful, he thought. Her humour shone through no matter how black things were. How could he have let her go four years ago?

But he needed to focus on other things beside Morag. 'Will you shut up, woman?'

'I only thought—'

'You didn't think enough. Hitting lighthouse doors with axes isn't a reasonable thing to do. So someone's acting unreasonably. Let's find out why before we treat this as a joke. We don't know if someone's here, but let's assume there is.'

And a hundred and twenty-nine steps later they had part of their answer. The trapdoor up into the lantern room was securely bolted. From the other side.

Behind Grady, Morag had grown obediently silent. Her spurt of laughter had been as fleeting as any joy on this island this day.

Grady pushed the trapdoor upward but it didn't move. Frowning in concern, Morag edged him aside and knocked. Hard.

'Hello,' she called into the stillness. 'It's Morag. Dr Morag. Who's up there?'

The voice from above them responded immediately—a male voice, deep and gruff, with the hint of an educated English accent.

'Can you go away, please?' The man sounded distracted, almost panicked.

'William.' Morag seemed confused.

'Yeah, it's William,' the voice said. 'But, Morag, please…go away. I hadn't intended anyone to be here. I'm sorry, Morag. I'm sorry you have to…cope with this. Cope with me. But, please, let me be. I need to jump.'

CHAPTER NINE

THERE WAS A moment's deathly silence.

'Why?' Morag called sharply and urgently, as if William might jump at any minute. Which he might well do, Grady thought grimly. The pressure of onlookers could form an impetus to push a man hesitating on a death urge straight over the edge. 'William, tell us why.'

There was a moment's loaded silence. Dreadful silence.

'*Us?* Who's with you?'

Grady let his breath out. Contact established. The first hurdle crossed. He'd been involved in rescue efforts for intending suicides often in his career—taking people from ledges, rescuing them after they changed their minds, bringing them medical attention when a serious attempt didn't work—and he knew this first contact was vital.

Hauling people back from the abyss.

Often it didn't work. Too damned often. The hardest part of medicine was the life you couldn't save.

Morag had done the same training as he had, he thought grimly. She knew how important it was to establish empathy.

'Dr Reece is with me,' she called. 'Grady Reece. He's part of the rescue team.'

'William, I'm here to check out the lighthouse,' Grady said, interjecting just as strongly as Morag had. They needed to establish his presence was non-threatening. No one was going to burst in and haul him away from the edge. 'There's only the two of us. I persuaded Morag to bring me up to show me the light.'

'Grady, this is William Cray,' Morag told him loudly, as if she was performing an introduction. The last thing they wanted was for William to think they were whispering behind his back. '*The* William Cray. William is the island literary celebrity. He wrote *Bleak Cradle* and…and…'

'And *Dog's Night* and *Evil Incarnate*.' Grady's mind was working fast as he made his voice sound excited. 'I know who William Cray is. Hey, I loved those books.'

'No one here reads them,' William said, softly now so they were struggling to hear.

'I read *Bleak Cradle*,' Morag told him.

'Did you like it?' William demanded, and Grady held his breath again.

'No,' Morag said honestly. 'You killed the heroine.'

Good answer. Honest answer. It was the sort of reply that engendered trust even further. William would know Morag wouldn't soft-soap him down.

But they could take this further.

'Hey, I liked it,' Grady told them, slightly indignant. 'I thought the heroine asked for what she got. What a dimwit. But the hero—what was his name? Demszel. Boy, you put him through some hoops.'

'You have read it.' William sounded disbelieving and Grady thought maybe he could play the affronted card.

'Hell, yes. Of course I have. Why would anyone not have? I've read everything you've written.'

'No one reads every one of mine.'

'I have.'

There was a moment's stunned disbelief. 'Tell me why Lucinda died.' A test.

He racked his brains. In truth, William's books were hardly his books of choice, but there were long, boring waits between rescues and a man couldn't play chess all the time.

'She made it with her sister's husband, and her kid was also her brother-in-law's kid, and the kid found out and…heck, it was really convoluted.'

Silence.

'Yeah, well, you'll be the only one who's read them.'

'Is that why you're planning on jumping?' Morag asked softly. 'Because you're depressed about your writing?'

'I'm not depressed about my writing.'

'Then what?'

'I'm not depressed.'

'You're not happy,' Morag said softly. 'Happy people don't think about suicide. Even in times like these. Can you tell us? William, will you explain?'

Keep him talking, Grady thought. Great going, Morag. If they could get him engaged...keep his mind off the jump...

'I'm just... Hell, it's all such an effort,' William was muttering. 'I've been fighting this for months now. Over and over. I can't think. I can't make myself do anything any more. Everything's just a huge effort. You know, just figuring out the commitment to ring my agent takes me days, and often I just can't do it. It's just...like living in black sludge. I can't move. And now my dog is dead.'

'You don't know your dog is dead,' Morag said sharply. 'They're still searching.'

'Yeah.' William's voice was a jeer. 'One dog. Twenty-four hours in the sea. You know, I would have killed myself months ago but for Mutt. He... Hell, he keeps me sane.'

'So if you jump now and Mutt's found, what are we going to do with him?' Morag asked.

'Get your nephew to keep him. And his friend. Hamish and Robbie, they're always pestering me to take him for walks.'

'You really think your Mutt would want to live with a nine-year-old rather than live with you?' Morag asked incredulously, and there was a moment's pause.

But then there was the sound of dragging—a door being opened above them—and Grady saw Morag wince. He guessed that William was opening the door to the ledge outside.

'William, you know we're both doctors,' he called, and there was another moment's silence, as though William was considering whether to answer them or not.

But finally he did.

'I know that. So you can help Morag with...with the mess. I need to—'

'You know you're suffering from depression.'

'I'm not suffering—'

'You are, mate,' Grady called urgently, knowing that time here was horribly limited. 'What you're describing sounds like real, dark and appalling depression. If I'm right, what you have is not just a bit of temporary sadness but a medically treatable, chemical imbalance. It's not just a bleak mood. It's depression as in a major clinical illness. Depression with a capital D—as in an illness that can be cured.'

'Cured…' There was a harsh laugh. 'Don't be funny. Cured. What a joke. It's been months. The times I've told myself to snap out of it…'

'It doesn't work, does it?'

'Of course it doesn't.'

'Treating yourself for this sort of depression is impossible,' Grady called. 'You can't do it. The more you try to tell yourself to snap out of it, the more you can't and the worse it gets. You feel a failure because you can't make yourself operate. You can't make the most minor decisions. You can't think forward with any glimmer of hope at all.'

'Yeah.' The door dragged again.

'But we can help,' Grady called strongly and urgently. 'It's not something you can cope with alone, but you can move forward. There's new antidepressants…'

'Yeah.' William's voice was a mocking cry. 'I've read about 'em. They knock you right out. You smile and wave but there's no one at home.'

'The old ones were like that,' Grady told him. 'Not any more. I swear. There's all sorts of people operating normal, optimistic lives while they're on antidepressants. While they're being cured. People you can't believe would ever need them. Depression's insidious and everywhere. They call it the black dog. William, believe me, it's treatable, and we can help you.'

Silence.

'It'd be an awful shame,' Morag said softly into the stillness, 'if we found Mutt tonight and you weren't here to welcome him home.'

Another silence. And then a rasping sob, choked back.

'If I go away,' Grady said, casting an urgent look at Morag. 'William, if I go downstairs, will you open the hatch to Morag?' He hesitated. 'It's over to you, mate. We're here to help. I swear we can help.'

'You can't.'

'Will you give us the chance? For Mutt's sake at least?'

'I...'

'Look, I'm going down,' Grady called, with a silent, urgent message to Morag. They had to act fast while William was hovering in indecision. Endless talk wouldn't help—not when there was no eye contact. The longer he stayed up there... Well, it was over to Morag. 'I'll stay down below,' he called. 'Either to scrape what's left of you off the rocks or to welcome you down when you come down with Morag. Your call. Over to you, Morag. See you below, mate.'

He turned and deliberately started the long climb down the stairs, allowing his boots to scrap on the worn steps so William could hear him going.

Please...

And before he'd gone twenty steps he heard the trapdoor being dragged back.

Morag was being allowed to enter.

He was brilliant.

With Grady present, William might have maintained a front. He might have played the man. But with Grady gone, all pretence disappeared and as Morag climbed the last few steps into the lightwell, he crumpled against her.

William had been one of the two men Morag had dated in the years she'd been back on the island. For a while things had looked possible, but in the end... He was trying really hard not to be gay, William had told her, and she'd decided pretty fast that this wasn't a strong basis for a relationship.

Plus, there was the fact that he hadn't made her heart flip as Grady had. No one had. Ever.

But now...Morag knew William enough to hug him and to smooth his hair and hold him close until the ragged sobs subsided. This had been a serious attempt at suicide. She was under no illusion that if she and Grady had arrived ten minutes later they would have found a body at the base of the lighthouse.

But now...thanks to Grady...

She couldn't think about Grady. She needed to focus on William.

How much of his isolation had been caused by undiagnosed depression? she wondered. He held himself aloof and most of the islanders thought he was an intellectual snob. Once she had him started on antidepressants, would it be possible to pull him more into island life? Have him help in the planning for the rebuilding? Run a course for islanders interested in creative writing? Maybe...

Maybe nothing. There wasn't going to be an island, she told herself.

It was finished.

But now wasn't the time to say that. She held him for as long as he needed her. Finally William hauled back and looked at her with a smile that was half-ashamed. 'I've been a fool.'

'You've been ill,' she told him. 'You are ill. I should have seen it. I should—'

'You'd blame yourself?'

'Heck, William...'

'I'm a grown man. It's up to me to ask for help.'

'Are you asking for help now?' she asked, and there was a long silence. She met his look square on and waited—for however long it took.

And finally it came.

'Yes,' he said. 'Yes, I am.'

Marcus was waiting with Grady when they emerged from the lighthouse. They walked out the door and William put up a hand as if to shield his eyes from daylight. He'd walked up these stairs expecting never to climb down, Morag thought, and it must be quite a challenge to start again.

And here were Grady and Marcus. Marcus had been a tower of strength over the last twenty-four hours. The big fisherman seemed to be everywhere, organising, helping, planning. As Morag led William out the door, the two men she'd leaned on most were sitting on the stone coping, soaking the last rays of the day's sun.

What had Grady told Marcus about William? she wondered. Whatever it was, there was no judgement on Marcus's face. He peeled his long body off the stones and gave William a smile.

'I've been looking for you.'

'Is it Mutt?' William asked hoarsely, and Marcus's smile faded. There were islanders frantic about their loved ones, but for many, especially those who lived alone, the fate of their pets was just as important.

'No, mate,' he said gently. 'We haven't found your dog. But we're still looking. The reason I've been searching for you is that we're trying to sort out a bit of privacy for those who are in urgent need of it. Your cottage is one of the few that are undamaged. You have a water tank, a septic tank for sewerage and you have two bedrooms. We're wondering if you could take in old Hazel Cartwright. You know Elias was killed and her home is shattered. She's in the dormitory tent, just…just sitting. Your place is just up the hill from hers and she could still see the harbour. She can go to her daughter in Sydney if you refuse, but she's desperate to stay for as long as she can.'

Had Grady done this? Morag flashed him an uncertain look. One look at his impassive face made her sure that he had. Of all the… This was perfect. To give William a need…

For the next few days, until antidepressants could take effect, William needed constant supervision. In a city, Morag would recommend that he become a voluntary patient in a clinic specifically designed for those at risk of self-harm. Here there could be no such supervision.

But caring for Hazel… It might work. She could even talk to Hazel about William's needs, and they could care for each other.

Would he do it?

He was having trouble taking it in, she thought. She let her hand lie in his, aware that he was in need of support himself. To ask him to support another…

Would his black depression make him too self-absorbed?

'Hazel plays the piano,' William said softly. 'I've heard her. Mutt and I walk past her place on the way to the beach, and there's always music.'

'They said she could have been a concert pianist if she'd stayed in the city,' Morag told him. 'But she chose a life with Elias, a life on the island.'

'I have a piano,' William said, and Morag cast a fleeting glance at Marcus and guessed he'd already thought this out.

'Would you do it, mate?' Marcus said, ignoring the fact that Morag was still holding William's hand.

William stared at Marcus. Then he turned and stared up at the lighthouse. Finally he released Morag's hand and gave himself a shake, as if he was shaking off a cloak. A cloak of fog and darkness and despair...

'Of course I will,' he said. 'I'll come with you now, shall I, and ask her if she'll be my guest.'

Grady promised to call at William's in an hour with medication and for a talk. To check on Hazel, he said, but they both knew it was more than that. Marcus and William started back to the makeshift township, and Morag and Grady were free to talk.

But for a while there was silence. Morag stared after them as if she couldn't believe her eyes. Finally she turned and asked the question that was slamming through her mind.

'Was that you?'

'Sorry?'

'Was that chance—or did you play a hand?'

'I might have,' he acknowledged, with the hint of a rueful smile.

'How?'

'Marcus came here at a run,' he told her. 'Apparently William left a note saying what he wanted done with his possessions. It was pinned to his front door. The nextdoor neighbour was curious and took a look. She panicked and gave the note to Marcus.'

'So Marcus knew William intended suicide. He never let on.'

'Do you think he should have?'

'No.'

'We're agreed the note blew off in the wind and no one ever saw it,' Grady told her. 'Marcus will square it with the neighbour.'

'And Hazel?'

'Once Marcus calmed down about William—there wasn't much either of us could do with the pair of you locked in the tower—he sat down and talked to me about the worst of his concerns. Hazel was top of the list.'

Morag sighed. So many things...so many worries...'Hazel's a wonderful old lady,' she told him. 'She's played the church organ for ever. Whenever anyone's in trouble there's always been Hazel. We all love her.'

'Including William?'

'He might. Our William might just learn to love. He might just figure out there's different forms of loving and they don't all have to do with sex. I'll start him on antidepressants tonight. I guessed a while back that he was depressed but until now he hasn't let me close.'

Enough. She sat down beside Grady on the stones and turned her face to the setting sun. Her shoulders slumped. She'd been so afraid...

'This island's all about loving,' Grady said softly, and she closed her eyes.

'It is.'

'I've been talking to May.'

'She's another wonderful lady.'

'This island breeds their women wonderful,' he murmured, and she grimaced. Then she opened her eyes again. She took a deep breath and faced what was coming.

'Yeah, right.' She stared down at her feet, as if her rough walking shoes could provide an answer. 'What will happen to the islanders?'

'I'm sure the spirit of the place will go on,' he said uneasily.

'What—in five hundred different locations, wherever we're dispersed?'

'The tentative plan is to relocate the bulk of the population to Port Shelba,' he told her. 'There's a big migrant centre there that's not being used. We can take that over as temporary accommodation until permanent housing's organised. The harbour there is under-utilised. The government would be prepared to give land grants, building grants, fishing licences—basically anything it takes to get families resettled.'

'You must really want this island evacuated.'

'They,' he said heavily. 'Not me.'

'You work for them.'

'I'm just an emergency services doctor, Morag.'

'You're a spokesperson for the government.'

'OK,' he said, gazing out into the fading light at the greyness of the sea and not at her. 'You tell me what's wrong with the plan. It sounds good to me.'

'It's terrible.'

'Why?'

'We're islanders,' she told him. 'We have our own heritage. Port Shelba's big. We'd be integrated into the broader population and our sense of community would be lost.'

'Is that important?'

'You've seen the damage depression can do,' she told him. 'Look what just happened here. Depression... You know, I've been working on this island for four years now and William's will be the first antidepressant I've prescribed. And that's only because he's a relative newcomer and he's held himself so aloof.'

'You've been lucky.'

He didn't have a clue, she thought bleakly. Not a clue. 'No,' she snapped. 'I haven't been lucky. I've been part of a community, but you don't know what that means, do you, Grady Reece? You can't possibly see how important that is. Without the community Hubert would be dead by now. The community keeps him alive and interested and in-volved. And what about the Kooris? How is the government planning on resettling them?'

'They're not.' This was the hard part and Grady stared out to sea some more. 'The Kooris won't move. We know that. But...maybe they don't want what's being offered even now in the way of health services. They're fiercely independent.'

'Oh, right.' Her anger was building to the point where she felt like kicking someone. Kicking Grady? Maybe. 'So because they're indepen-dent, you'd abandon them completely.'

'Of course not. We'd make provisions.' He met her look, her anger meeting his calm, placid response. As if he was really making sense. 'Morag, if you came to Sydney with me...'

Her breath stopped right there. 'What?'

'I love you, Morag,' he told her, so softly that she had to strain to hear what he was saying. And then he said it again, louder. 'I love you. I've fought against it all this time. Hell, if I knew how much it'd hurt four years back, I'd never have let you walk away.'

There was a deathly silence. 'You didn't have a choice,' she whispered at last, her anger sucked right out of her. 'You didn't let me go. I came all by myself.'

'But you didn't want to come,' he told her. 'Not really. Oh, you had no choice, I accept that. You loved Beth and you love Robbie and you care for this damned community.' He reached out and gripped her hands, ur-gently, as if he could somehow impart his message through touch.

'But, Morag, it's finished,' he told her. 'You've done a fine job. A wonderful job. These people...what you've built... I'm so proud of you.'

'Gee, thanks.'

He wasn't listening. 'Morag, we could build a life back in Sydney. I know you want to keep up with your medicine. And I'd be blind not to see your commitment to the Koori people. So what I suggest is—'

'What do you suggest?'

He caught her anger then, and frowned. 'Don't you want hear?'

'Of course I want to hear.'

'You'd bring Robbie with you,' he told her. 'That's understood. He's a great kid. He loves you and I'm sure...' He hesitated a little, but only just. 'I'm sure that I could be...more than a friend to him. I'm willing to try, Morag. For you.'

Her anger wasn't dissipating a bit. 'That's big of you.'

'Just listen. Morag... The Kooris...' He was trying so hard to make her see. She was listening to him and hearing his urgency, knowing that he was trying to make a case but not recognising that her heart was closed. It had to be closed. 'You could be the remote medical officer for them,' he told her. 'There'd be ample funding. With what the government saves in providing the infrastructure for this settlement, they'd be more than happy to spend in employing you. You could fly out here once every couple of weeks and do clinics at need. They'd still be in contact.'

'Every two weeks?'

'We think that's workable.'

'And if a woman goes into labour? You'd say she should wait two weeks for attention?'

'She'd have to come to Sydney before she was due.'

'She wouldn't.' She hauled her hands back and stared at him as if he was someone she'd never seen before. Someone she could never, ever understand.

Someone she could never love?

'Then maybe...' He hesitated. 'Morag, the Kooris chose this lifestyle. Maybe the risks come with the territory.'

Love didn't come into this, she thought bleakly. How could she think about loving this man when he was speaking such nonsense?

'They didn't choose this lifestyle,' she snapped. 'And now we've introduced them to a different one. We—my father and then Beth and now me—have taught them to trust. They bring the worst of their illnesses in their young to me now. The major traumas. And in childbirth, if there's a need, they come to me now. You'd take that away?'

'There's no choice, Morag,' he said flatly. 'Do you think you could get political support to rebuild this place?'

'Not without help.' She knew that. But that was all she knew.

And what help? She didn't even know who she needed.

The bleakness in her heart was growing by the minute.

'You don't have help,' he told her. 'Morag, you're so alone. It's crazy.'

'I'm not alone. I have all these people. Marcus. May. Hazel. Five hundred people who are part of me.'

'Those people are leaving.'

'But not the Kooris.'

'That's their choice.'

'And you think I have a choice?' she whispered. 'You want me to leave?'

'Yes,' he said, sure of his ground in this most important question. 'Yes, I do.'

'Why?'

'Because it's impossible here. And more...' He was standing before her now, and he was suddenly closer, his body language urgent. She'd also risen, glaring at him against a backdrop of setting sun. He reached out to take her by the waist but she stepped back.

'Morag, we've lost so much time,' he said. 'You've given this community four years and they can't expect any more. It's time to move on. Time to come back to me. Morag, I love you.'

It needed only this. Grady loved her? Still? And he was offering her a life.

So... She could walk away from her islanders, she thought dully. She could leave right now. She and Robbie could leave this island, go back to the life she thought she'd chosen all those years before.

How could she tell Robbie that they were leaving?

She might not have a choice. If the island truly was evacuated... If his best friend was dead...

But these were *her* people. If the island was evacuated, how damaged would they be? How much more would they need the doctor they'd leaned on for years? It wasn't just her. She was part of a dynasty of trust. Her father and then Beth and now her.

Take away their homes? Take her away as well?

No. She couldn't leave them.

'Grady, this isn't going to work,' she said softly. 'Not now.' She glanced around at the mess the wave had made of the shoreline and she shuddered. 'Look, we're talking about the future here—and the present's such a catastrophe that we can't even think straight. Can we just get on with it?'

'But you and I—'

'There's no you and me.'

'There is.'

'Grady...'

'Morag, I was mad to ever let you go,' he said strongly. 'I can't imagine why I did.'

'I didn't give you a choice.'

'You're saying you didn't regret it?'

'No. I...'

'You're saying you don't love me?'

She stared at him. He was so...capable, she thought desperately. Strong, competent and a little bit...dangerous? Ruthless?

He had all the answers, she thought, anger surfacing as it had four years ago. He'd take over her life and he'd put it back on track. Organise. Order.

Her life would be great. Robbie's life would be great. He'd care for them and make them laugh and make love to her and make her toes curl and the world would be a funny, happy, busy...

Her community would be without her. May. Hazel. Marcus and Judy and the kids. Angie Salmon, who'd hardly started to grieve.

'No.'

'Morag...'

'Grady, please. Don't ask.'

'I must.' His hands came out and caught hers. 'Morag, what's between us...it's irreplaceable. Four years ago I thought it was...not all that important. I thought I'd meet someone else. But there's only you. Morag, I can't bear to let you go again. We'll get the island evacuated—'

'No!' She was almost yelling at him now. Fear was surfacing behind the anger. Fear that she was losing control. She was losing her direction and it was desperately important that she find it again.

'Why not?' he said, his voice gentling.

'I can't. How can you not see?'

'I see what's between us.'

'There's nothing between us.'

'Don't be so...'

'So what?' She was close to tears. She was close to breaking and it must be obvious. Grady's face changed and suddenly instead of urgency there was tenderness. Compassion.

Love.

'Morag...'

There it was again. The way he said her name. It had the capacity to shift her off her bearings. It had the capacity to...

To weaken?

For suddenly she felt herself being drawn into him. Against her better judgement—against any sort of judgement—she was allowing those big, capable hands to pull her against him. Her breasts were pressing against the strength of him. His hand was cupping her chin and tilting her face.

And then...

He smiled down at her, a rueful, searching smile that asked more questions than it answered. And she couldn't reply. How could she reply as his mouth lowered onto hers?

She could drown in this kiss.

Four long years...

She'd thought she was over it. No. No, she'd never thought she was over it, she thought desperately, but she'd pushed away the feel of him. The scent of him. The pure animal magnetism...

Her love for this man was so real. It was an aching need that had had her crying out in her sleep for the first twelve months of her stay on the island. Her dreams of her dead sister had been crazily mixed with her need for this man.

Loss. She'd lost so much. Her loss was real and dreadful, and the sudden lessening of it, the sudden glimmer of hope that her loss wasn't irrevocable, had her responding now as if her body had known all along that this was her rightful place.

This was her home. This man was her man, and the only place in the world that she could ever be at peace was right here.

Within the arms of the man she truly loved.

So for one long moment she melted into his kiss. For one glorious moment she let herself surrender to the promise of his body. To the feel of his hands, pulling her into him. To the feeling that here in his arms anything was possible. With Grady beside her, she could take on the world. Save her island. Find Hamish safe and well. Care for the Kooris.

With Grady she could do anything. She could fly!

Above her head the light from the lighthouse shimmered on, automatically powered to light up with the gathering dusk. The flash of light across her face was hardly enough to haul her back from insanity—it didn't—but it was enough to make her catch a trace of reason. To haul back. To gasp and push back with both hands. To stand and stare with eyes that were wild with want and hope and aching, tearing need.

And above all…despair?

'Grady, don't…'

'You want—' he started in a voice that was far from steady.

'What I want doesn't come into it,' she whispered. 'This is crazy. A tidal wave washes away the foundations of my community and you're saying I should leave them? I can't. Grady, don't ask me.'

'Morag—'

'Leave it,' she said, roughly and despairingly. 'Go back from where you came, Grady. You're needed in a crisis. Medical emergencies. But what I do…I don't do emergencies, Grady. I do for ever.'

She stared at him for one long moment, as though taking in everything she could about him. One long, last look…

'I need to go home,' she whispered. 'I'm sorry, Grady. I have to go back to Robbie.'

And before he could say another word she'd turned and fled, back to where the track started its winding way up toward Hubert's cottage.

Back to the community where she belonged.

CHAPTER TEN

GRADY WALKED BACK to the hospital and met Jaqui about to organise a search party. He'd turned his radio off during the conversation with William and hadn't turned it on again—a transgression that had every member of their team concerned. Briefly he outlined what had happened, but halfway through she interrupted.

'You mean he jumped?'

'No.'

Her eyes narrowed. 'But you look like something dreadful's happened.'

'It hasn't.' He gave a rueful smile. 'Morag wouldn't let him jump. She's better than any psychiatrist.'

'She's a damned fine doctor,' Jaqui told him. 'The islanders think the world of her.' She hesitated, and eyed him sideways. He knew she could see there was still something badly askew in his world—but she didn't press further.

'The reason we were trying to find you was that the politicians want to fly in tomorrow for a public announcement.'

'That the island's to be evacuated?'

'You helped Doug make his report.'

'I did,' he said heavily.

'There's health risks in not doing it fast,' Jaqui told him. 'You know it. The water source is contaminated. If we're not careful we could have a great little epidemic of typhoid. Just what we all need—I don't think.'

'If we could get the resources——'

'They aren't available.' She hesitated, and gave him that questioning look again. And obviously decided to push it. 'And, besides, this way you'll get your girl.'

'What the hell is that supposed to mean?'

'I mean you're nuts on your Dr Morag,' she told him bluntly. 'Any fool can see that. If the island's evacuated, it means she'll have to leave, too.'

'She won't *have* to do anything.'

'Is that what you were doing?' Jaqui asked slowly. 'Is that why you look like you do? Because you were asking?'

'Jaqui…'

'Just enquiring,' she said thoughtfully, throwing her hands up in defence. 'OK, moving right on…' She gave him a grin that contained real affection. 'Do you have time to assist in removing an appendix?'

'An appendix?' He stared.

'You wouldn't read about it.' Her grin widened. 'After all we've gone through. Mary Garidon is fifteen years old, and she's been clutching her stomach since the wave hit. Her parents assumed it was stress and maybe I'd have agreed with them if I'd seen her earlier. But her mum came in to get the haematoma on her thigh checked. She was caught by the end of the wave. Anyway, Mary was waiting with her father, and her dad was telling her to pull herself together. But she looked sweaty and was clutching her stomach so I checked. She's got rebound, Grady.'

'Rebound…' He stared. 'You mean the appendix has ruptured?'

'That's what it looks like. I think we should go in now. Can you help?'

'Of course.' If the appendix really had burst, the time taken to evacuate her to Sydney could well mean the infection would be much worse.

'I was hoping you'd be back,' she confessed. 'You've got the best fingers I know.'

'Gee, thanks.'

'You don't want to call Morag? She's Morag's patient.'

'The whole island is Morag's patient,' Grady growled. 'Everyone needs her.'

'Including you?'

'Butt out, Ford.'

She grinned. 'When have I ever? But we don't contact Morag?'

'She's had a hell of a day. She's just talked someone out of jumping, and her kid must be going nuts without her. Let her be.'

'There's a real load on her shoulders,' Jaqui said seriously. 'Do you think she'll be happier without it?'

'When it's hauled out from under her?' Grady grimaced. 'No.'

'Even with you?'

'I said butt out. Her future's none of our concern.'

But as they scrubbed and prepared the teenager for surgery—as Grady reassured the frightened parents and promised them Morag would come if there was the slightest hint of trouble—as he performed the procedure with his trained anaesthetist and his two trained nursing staff and thought how Morag would have had to do this alone—somehow—if he and his team hadn't been here—he thought, How could her future be none of his concern?

He was going to worry about her for ever.

Morag made her way slowly up the scree. She flicked her radio transmitter back on to check in with Jaqui, who briefly outlined what was happening to Mary.

'Do you want me to come?' Morag had paused at a bend in the track and was involuntarily turning.

'We're fine. Two doctors, two nurses, one appendix. We have it under control.' There was a moment's hesitation and then Jaqui asked, 'How do you cope with something like this when you're on your own?'

'I talk one of the nurses through the anaesthetic,' she told her. 'I have no choice.'

'It's real bush medicine.'

'It's better than no medicine at all.'

'Do you enjoy it?' Jaqui asked curiously.

Morag hesitated. 'Yes,' she said at last. 'Yes, I do. To go back to ordinary medicine...'

'Like our Dr Reece stopping swinging on rescue harnesses.' Jaqui chuckled. 'A life lived on the edge. You two suit so well.'

'We don't,' Morag said quietly, and clicked off the receiver before she could hear Jaqui's next comment.

We don't.

* * *

Robbie would be desperate for her.

The little boy had been so good. To ask a nine-year-old to stay calmly up at Hubert's cottage while there was so much going on below—and when there was still no word of Hamish—must have been unbearable. She'd radioed him constantly during the day and each time his voice had sounded more and more strained.

'When will you come? Where's Hamish? Can't I come down?'

He and Hubert had done a wonderful job. The media circus was confined to the hills and she'd heard indirectly that Robbie had given the same interview over and over.

'The old man gives a nice artistic embellishment or two,' one of the reporters for the national broadcaster had told her when she'd finally agreed to a fast telephone link. 'But the kid...he's amazing. He'll be on the national news tonight.'

And he wouldn't be able to watch it, Morag thought ruefully. If she'd had time, maybe she could have phoned her mother on the mainland and had Barbara tape it for her.

Her mother... She hadn't heard from her mother, she thought bleakly. Would Barbara even know there'd been a tidal wave on Petrel Island?

Would Barbara care?

She trudged on upward. Once upon a time she'd thought she could lead the sort of life her mother led, where career and appearance were everything. She'd changed so much. She'd changed and Grady had stayed the same.

But she loved him...

She couldn't think of Grady. The moon wasn't yet over the horizon and it was deeply dark. She needed to concentrate on her footing.

The candle wasn't in Hubert's window.

Frowning, she quickened her steps, and suddenly a wavering flashlight appeared from the cottage door. The beam circled wildly and found her. It was a cameraman, his bulky equipment draped round his neck. There were a score of reporters and cameramen camped out near the helicopter landing pad. What was this man doing here?

Why wasn't the candle lit?

'Who are you?' she demanded, more sharply than she'd intended, and he blinked as if he was trying to adjust to reality.

'Dave Barnes. National Reporting.'

'What are you doing here?'

He peered at her, trying to see in the light from the flash, and she hauled her backpack from her shoulders and found her own torch.

'I'm Dr Lacy,' she told him. 'Morag Lacy. Where's my nephew?'

'You're a doctor?'

'Yes.'

'Thank God for that.' He grabbed her arm and practically hauled her into the cottage. 'We're camped behind the ridge but the old man said earlier that we could take a shower here if we wanted. I came down and the old guy and the kid were arguing. I went for a walk along the ridge to catch the last of the sunset, and when I came back he was like this.'

Like what? Who? But Morag was inside the cottage and through to the bedroom, and what she saw made her stop in dismay. 'Hubert!'

'I found him on the floor and for a minute I didn't think he was breathing,' Dave told her. 'I was just thinking I'd have to do CPR and then he groaned. Hell, I was glad to hear it. I've got him on the bed but he looks awful.'

He did. Hubert's gaunt face was staring up in terror as he clutched his left arm. He was sweating profusely. Morag placed her fingers on the pulse in his neck, and his skin was cold to the touch.

At least she had equipment. Morag's doctor's bag was huge. Vast. It was twice the size of most doctor's bags but it hardly ever left her back and she had never been more glad of it than she was now.

'It's…it's a heart attack?' Hubert whispered. Behind them the cameraman was doing his best to hold the flashlight steady, but his hands were shaking. The beam was erratic, a wavering and eerie light across the bed of the sick man.

'Maybe it is.' She undid Hubert's shirt and placed her stethoscope on the old man's chest. His heartbeat was reasonably stable, she decided thankfully, though every four or five beats were slightly irregular— maybe ectopic? She hauled more equipment out of her bag, searching for aspirin. 'Put the flashlight on the dresser,' she told the cameraman.

'See if you can aim it so it's pointing at this arm. I need a glass of water. And there are candles somewhere in the kitchen.'

'First cupboard on the left,' Hubert quavered. 'And matches. I was just about to light them when...when...'

'Hush,' she told him. But this was good. If he had the strength to think about candles...

'Hell, it hurts,' he whispered, and reached out and clutched her arm. 'It hurts to breathe. Morag, I don't... I don't want to die. Not yet.'

'How about that?'

She even smiled as she adjusted the blood-pressure cuff and then had to force herself to stay smiling as the results told her that dying was a possibility. Eighty on fifty. There was definitely something nasty going on.

The cameraman returned with a large glass of water. She tipped three quarters of it out the open window and broke her soluble aspirin into what was left, swirled the water until the aspirin had dissolved and then held Hubert so he could swallow.

'Let's get it into you,' she told him. 'If you really don't want to shuffle off this mortal coil, drink this.'

'What is it?' He peered into the glass in deep suspicion.

'Really high-tech medicine. Otherwise known as aspirin. It acts as an anticoagulant, letting the blood flow a bit more easily. Maybe there's a slight blockage...'

'Slight? How can this be slight?' He sounded affronted and she smiled again.

'If it wasn't slight, you'd be dead.'

'Gee, thanks.' He grimaced but his lips managed to twitch. 'That's a real comfort.'

'I'll give you something for the pain.' Five milligrams, she decided, and then looked at the sheen of sweat on his forehead and thought, No, he was cracking hardy. Seven.

Behind her, the cameraman was setting up candles, working quietly and efficiently. His hands appeared to have steadied and Morag blessed him for it. You never knew with onlookers. Sometimes you got calm, intelligent help, as this man was providing, and sometimes you got panic.

She'd learned early not to expect anything of anyone. A flighty teenager might be far more help than her sensible middle-aged father.

'Will I live?' Hubert faltered, and she rested her fingers on his pulse again.

'You've lived through a darned sight more than a mild heart attack,' she told him. 'But I need a cardiograph to tell any more than we already know. Hubert, we're going to have to take you to the pavilion.'

'To that makeshift hospital you've set up?'

'Yes. We have everything there we need.'

She even had Grady.

'I can't be sick. There's the public meeting tomorrow about the fate of the island,' he said fretfully. 'I gotta be there for that.'

'Let's just concentrate on tonight,' she said softly. 'For the moment, more than anything else you need to relax. Please. There are others who will worry about the island for you.'

'You'll fight for it?'

'Of course I will.'

'But Robbie...' His eyes widened, as if remembering something the pain and the shock had driven from his mind. 'I forgot Robbie. Hell, Morag, I shoulda been taking care of him. I need to...' He struggled to rise but she pressed him back.

'No. You're not to fret about Robbie. I'll take over his care now.' She bit her lip. Where was he? 'I've left him alone too long,' she said softly. 'He's been so good. But, Hubert, you've been wonderful, too. Now it's time to hand over the care to others.'

She passed her radio to the cameraman behind her. 'This is set to contact the medical team at the pavilion,' she told him. 'The hospital's commandeered about the only two workable vehicles on the island and I need one. Tell them we need transport to take Hubert down to the hospital. Tell them it's a suspected coronary.'

'Can do.' The man backed into the kitchen, obviously grateful for the chance to escape from the sickroom.

'I need to tell you about Robbie,' Hubert whispered, but there was a weariness in his voice that told Morag he was past worrying about anything but the beating of his own heart.

'Don't worry.' Robbie had been here a few minutes ago, Morag thought. The cameraman had seen him arguing with Hubert. If he'd seen Hubert collapse, he'd be dreadfully upset. Maybe he'd run to try and find her.

Damn, she couldn't do anything about Robbie. Not now. Not yet. The medical imperative...

She had to get Hubert stabilised. Hubert's life was under threat and the fact that her small nephew was distraught couldn't be allowed to interfere. But it hurt.

Grady. She needed Grady—now!

But she also needed to concentrate. Somehow Morag worked on, adjusting drips, monitoring, waiting. Often pain like this was a precursor to a main event. The aspirin would help—maybe.

Please...

Not another death, she found herself begging. Not Hubert. OK, he was ninety-two, but she wasn't ready to say goodbye to him yet.

And if Robbie thought he was somehow responsible... For him to carry that on his shoulders...

No!

Finally, with the drip steady and the old man drifting toward sleep as the morphine took hold, she was able to focus on something other than imperative need. She stepped back into the kitchen and found the cameraman putting down her radio.

'Dr Reece is busy,' he told her. 'Apparently there's been an emergency appendicectomy. But they're sending a truck.'

Her heart sank. Of course. The appendix.

No Grady.

Well, what was so unusual about that? she asked herself harshly. She'd been used to it for four years. She needed to get used to it again.

Robbie...

'The child who was here,' she ventured. 'Do you know where he is?'

The man smiled. 'He's a great kid, isn't he? He gave us some fantastic footage.'

'But...'

He got her worry then, and his smile died. 'I'm sorry. They were arguing as I arrived.'

That was what she didn't understand. Robbie didn't argue. At least, not with Hubert.

'I overheard it as I walked up the scree,' the man said apologetically. 'Do you want to know what about?'

'Yes.' Then, because her voice had been a little bit desperate, a little bit raw, she repeated herself. 'Yes, please.'

Still there was a tremor in her voice and the cameraman gave her an odd look before continuing. He couldn't understand her fear. And maybe...please...the fear was illogical.

'I heard Robbie say he'd guessed a place where someone called Hamish might be,' the man told her. 'He wanted to go there but Hubert was saying he had to wait for you. As I came within sight, the kid seemed to lose it. He yelled that he'd waited and waited and he had to go now, because Hamish would be stuck. When Hubert said he couldn't go by himself he said he'd take Elspeth. Would that be the dog?'

'Right.' She bit her lip. Where...?

'Will you go search for Robbie straight away?' The cameraman cast an uneasy glance at Hubert, and Morag shook her head. An appendicectomy meant that both Grady and Jaqui would be fully occupied. She'd have to stay with Hubert until one of them could take over.

But Robbie needed her. He needed her so much.

He'd needed her all day and she'd left him alone.

'Hey, it'll be fine,' the cameraman said gently, and she caught herself and managed a faltering smile. She was scaring him. She was the doctor. She was in charge. So she had to get on with it.

'I... Of course it'll be fine.

'We'll take the old man down to the hospital and then we'll find your kid.'

'Thank you.'

'It makes good copy,' he told her.

'I didn't think you were supposed to be involved in breaking news,' she told him, striving for lightness. 'If you're not careful, you'll be on the front page of your paper as a hero.'

'It's you who's the hero,' he told her. 'And there's not a man, woman or child on this island who'd disagree with me.'

CHAPTER ELEVEN

DOWN AT THE hospital tent, the cardiograph showed no significant change. No significant damage. Morag read the tracing and breathed a little easier.

Maybe Hubert would be lucky. At ninety-two he could hardly complain that he hadn't had a good innings, but the old man was part of the fabric of this island. If he died...

The island was going to die anyway, she told herself bleakly as she adjusted his intravenous line and wrote up his medication.

Louise was normally a beaming, bright-faced nurse who saw the world through often infuriatingly rose-coloured glasses, but the woman who helped settle Hubert was white-faced and silent.

'They're saying we have to leave the island,' she whispered.

'Hush,' Morag told her, but Hubert had drifted into a drug-induced sleep and seemed unaware of their presence. For a moment Morag was stung by a pang of pure envy. To just close her eyes...

'It'll be OK,' she told the nurse, and Louise hiccuped on a sob.

'No, it won't. My Bill...he set his little goat cheese dairy up from scratch. Do you know not a goat was killed? Not a single one? They're the cleverest creatures. Bill went up to the dairy last night and they were all there. We wanted to expand, and to say we have to leave...'

But Morag had no comfort to give. She had her own anguish, and her own desperate need.

'Louise, have you seen Robbie?'

'Robbie?'

'He had an argument with Hubert. I imagine he'll have come down here to find me.'

'I haven't seen him,' Louise told her. 'I've been on the front desk, so I'd have noticed.'

Damn, where was he? She couldn't leave until she had back-up for Hubert, she thought desperately, and Grady and Jaqui were totally occupied. 'The appendix is messy?'

'It's burst and it's awful,' Louise told her. 'Dr Reece has been working in there for well over an hour.'

So here it was again. The medical imperative. She needed Grady—or Jaqui—but Grady and Jaqui were both totally occupied.

She had to find Robbie, but if Hubert suffered cardiac arrest...

She couldn't leave.

'I need to find Robbie.'

'You said he's coming here...'

'No. I assumed he was here.' Morag was trying hard not to panic. 'If he was coming here, he'd be here now. He said he was going to find Hamish.'

'But Hamish drowned,' Louise said blankly, and Morag winced.

'We don't know that.'

'It's...it's a reasonable assumption. By now.'

'No.' Morag bit her lip. 'It's not a reasonable assumption. Nothing's reasonable.'

Help! She felt like kicking something, she thought desperately. Or weeping. Or yelling in sheer frustration.

Or all three.

Robbie, she thought frantically. Grady. Dear heaven, she needed Grady.

She couldn't have him. He had his life and she had hers.

'Will you sit with Hubert?' she asked Louise, and the nurse searched her face and gave her a swift hug. These first hours after a coronary event were vital and they both knew it. In a normal intensive care unit, there'd be monitors set to a central desk. Here everything had to be done the old way.

'Of course. But you'll stay within call? Oh, Morag, what are we going to do?'

'I don't know,' Morag told her. 'I don't have a clue.'

She couldn't leave. Not until Jaqui or Grady were free to leave the operating theatre could she go out of call of the old man. Even with Louise sitting by his bed, with Hubert in the early stages of coronary trouble, there had to be a doctor right there.

But Robbie... Robbie...

Someone else would have to search.

She'd call Marcus, she thought, but no sooner had she thought it than the man himself walked through the entrance of the tent. Marcus looked grim. But, then, the whole island looked grim.

'Morag.' He must have been looking for her, as his face changed as she emerged from Hubert's canvas cubicle. But it didn't grow lighter. 'Thank God you're here.'

More problems? She wasn't sure she could cope with anything else. She glanced across in the direction of Grady's makeshift theatre. The lights they'd set up were brilliant, oozing through the canvas and telling her that Grady and Jaqui were still a hundred per cent occupied.

She could hear a man's low, gravelly voice giving orders. Grady. If Grady wasn't here, it'd be she who was trying to cope with Mary's appendix, she thought grimly. She should be thankful for that at least.

'What's wrong?' she asked, forcing herself to turn back to Marcus. To the next problem.

Marcus hesitated. 'Maybe it's nothing.'

'Tell me.' She knew he didn't want to. They knew they were both carrying intolerable burdens, and to place more on each other seemed impossible. But if something else dreadful had happened then she had to hear it, and Marcus knew it. The lines round his eyes grew tighter. There were dark shadows underneath them.

'May's just been with me,' he told her. 'She asked if I could set up a radio link so she could contact the Sydney hospital where her family is.'

Of course. That made sense, Morag thought. Peter and Christine and Lucy were May's family. She'd be desperate about them, as they'd be desperate about Hamish. 'Did she get through?'

'Mmm. That's why I came to find you.'

'Christine?' The head injury. Dear God...

'No. Christine's not worse.' Marcus could see where her thoughts were headed and moved fast to reassure her. 'She's fully conscious and she's been given the all-clear. But Lucy's with her parents now. That's why I'm here. You know Lucy wouldn't speak to May?'

'She'd hardly speak to anyone.'

'That's right. But now her mother's made her talk. It seems she thinks she knows where her brother might have gone.'

'She knows where Hamish went?'

'She's guessing. Apparently he's been doing...what he's been doing for a while. Lucy knew she should tell her parents, but she didn't, and then when the wave came she realised he must have been killed and she felt like it was all her fault. And she couldn't tell you either because... well, it's Robbie.'

Robbie. Her heart seemed to stand still.

'What about Robbie?'

'She thought...she assumed they were together.'

'Doing what?'

There were small trickles of terror inching down Morag's spine. There was something about the way Marcus was speaking. It was as if he was giving really, really bad news. He was giving her bad news about Hamish, but where was Robbie?

The vision of Hamish's cheeky face was suddenly before her. Hamish and Robbie. The two little boys treated this island as their own personal adventure playground.

Where...?

'It seems they've been robbing petrel nests,' Marcus told her.

'Petrel nests?' She forced her panic to the backburner. Panic was useless. She had to think. The petrels were big seabirds, twice the size of gulls and many times more fierce. They nested on the far side of the island, on rugged, crumbling cliffs that dropped straight to the western shore. The sea there was a mass of jagged rocks and savage breakers. This was the place where the *Bertha* had gone aground all those years before, with the loss of a hundred and sixty-eight lives. A dreadful place.

'They've been climbing the cliffs?' she whispered, appalled.

'Lucy said Hamish boasted about it one day when she'd called him a baby,' Marcus told her. 'It's a game. One of them climbs up and grabs an egg, then he has to bring it down without smashing it, holding it in his hand to keep it warm. The other has to get it back to its original nest. Then he chooses another egg and it starts again. They push themselves to reach harder and harder places. When he told Lucy what they were doing and she threatened to tell Christine, Hamish said it wasn't really dangerous because there were rocks at the bottom and they could climb around from the beach on the south side. It was only the birds that worried them.'

'Only the birds?' Morag drew in her breath in horror, thinking of the birds with their razor-sharp beaks and fierce claws, attacking the little boys as they defended their young. 'Only the birds? Marcus, they... How...? When...?'

'Apparently they've been telling you and Christine that they've been going to the school playground,' he said ruefully. 'With their skateboards.'

She closed her eyes. A nine-year-old, to be putting himself in this sort of danger. What sort of a guardian was she? What sort of a—?

'Hey, Morag, I did it,' Marcus said ruefully, eyeing her with concern. 'My dad caught me and my brother at it when I was their age and we got what-for. I'd forgotten about it. But apparently they've thought of it again all by themselves. And maybe... If Hamish's alternative was to spend his Sunday afternoon doing homework or practising his new skill by himself—well, I know what I'd have done.'

She looked at him as if he were mad. There was even a hint of admiration in his eyes. He had to be kidding! Admiration at such a time. When a little boy could be stuck... Could be washed off.

One little boy?

Or two?

Where was Robbie? On that awful cliff?

For one awful moment she thought she might faint. The world wavered, but just as she started to sway a man's hand gripped on her shoulder.

Grady. It was Grady, still in his theatre gown. He held her, steadied her and waited for the dizziness to pass.

'What's happening, love?' he asked gently, and she winced. But somehow the feel of him was enough. Somehow she collected herself. Love... What on earth did he think he was doing, calling her *love*?

'Don't call me love,' she whispered, and it was all she could do not to burst into tears. She turned her attention frantically back to Marcus. 'Marcus, surely those cliffs have been searched?'

'Maybe not,' he admitted. 'I mean…hell, Morag, you know how rough they are. Why would we look there? But now…I was just coming to find you. I thought—if you didn't mind—we'd take Robbie out in one of the fishing boats and get him to show us exactly where they climbed.'

'But Robbie's gone,' Morag said blankly. 'He's gone to find Hamish. He ran away from Hubert about an hour ago. Dear God, if he guessed where Hamish might be, he'll have gone to the cliffs.'

'He can't have,' Marcus told her, while Grady watched in concern.

'Why not?' he asked.

'The base of the cliffs, where they'd usually scramble around…the force of the wave knocked it into the sea,' Marcus told them. 'I've noticed the collapse on our way in and out of the harbour as we've been searching. That's what makes me think, if Hamish was up on those cliffs when the wave struck—if he was high enough to be safe from the wave—there's a possibility that he might not have been able to get back. He might be stuck. It's just a small hope but it's worth a look.'

'Well worth a look,' Grady said firmly. He put his arm around Morag and pulled her hard against him. She couldn't pull away. She'd have fallen over if she had. 'I overheard what Marcus has been saying,' he told her. 'So we have two missing boys—one of whom might be on the cliff face.'

'But Robbie?' She was past thinking coherently. 'If he was trying to reach Hamish…'

'He'd see pretty fast that he couldn't get round from the bottom,' Marcus said.

'He wouldn't try and climb down from the top?' Grady demanded, and his hold on her firmed as she winced in disbelief.

'He'd be a damned fool to try,' Marcus said bleakly.

'But if he thought he knew exactly where his friend might be…'

'I'm taking the boat around now,' Marcus told them. He hesitated, looking at Morag's bleached face in concern. 'The fastest way to look is from the sea. Maybe…maybe I can take you—or Grady—in case.'

'OK.' Grady moved straight to operational mode now. This was what he was trained for, and it showed. 'Marcus, can you send a team of locals overland to check the clifftops, then organise your boat to play floodlights over the cliff face? I'll bring the chopper from overhead. It's hard to search cliff faces from the air, but we can do it. I'll scramble the team now.'

'Not with Hubert…'

Too much was happening too fast, but there was still the medical imperative. Briefly Morag outlined what was happening to Hubert, and Grady's face grew more grim.

'OK,' he conceded. 'Morag, you stay here.'

But that was too much. 'I'm going.'

'But—'

'I'm going!' Enough was enough. Medical imperatives had just been overtaken by the personal. 'If it's Robbie… You must see that I need to.'

Grady searched her face and came to a decision. 'OK. Maybe that's for the best anyway. Jaqui will only be minutes while she's reversing Mary's anaesthetic. Then she can take over Hubert's care. Marcus, you take Morag on the boat—with a decent complement of competent people. With life jackets. I'll check Hubert and hand over to Jaqui as soon as I can. Tell me who I can take in the chopper to direct us.'

'May's outside, waiting,' Marcus told him. 'She's Hamish's grandmother. There's not a lot of people know the island better than May, and she's desperate to help.'

He'll refuse, Morag thought wildly. May was an elderly lady. To take her in the helicopter in the dark on such a mission as this…

But Grady was made of sterner stuff. 'Tell her to be ready in five minutes,' he told them. 'Meanwhile, you two go. We'll be right behind you.'

Then, before Morag could react, before she could begin to guess what he intended, he bent and he kissed her.

Her world stilled. The panic inside her froze. For these few short seconds… Everything else disappeared.

For this was no light kiss of reassurance. This was the kiss of a man who was giving a message to his woman. *His* woman. It lasted for long seconds, communicating information that was as unmistakable as it was real.

I love you. You're mine. I'll be with you in this, my heart.

The words were unspoken yet unmistakable, and for those few seconds, Morag felt herself surrendering to his kiss. Surrendering to her own desperate need. She was taking as well as receiving. Laying a claim of her own.

I need you, now and for always. Stay with me?

There could be no such claim—no such question. This man was here only as part of a medical team, to save lives and then use his medical knowledge to declare this island unfit for human habitation. The tough decisions would be made and he'd move on to the next crisis. To the next need.

But for now that need was hers. She clung and took her strength here, where it was offered. She melted into him for this one harsh kiss, this kiss that must end...

They knew it.

It tore Morag apart. It seemed in this overwhelming chaos that all she had between her and madness was the touch of Grady's mouth.

He'd stay with her whatever it took, the kiss said, but she knew it wasn't true.

He'd stay with her only until tomorrow.

Reality was all around them. Someone pushed back the canvas divider between Reception and the makeshift operating theatre, and somehow she reacted. She pulled back from Grady's arms and gazed at him with eyes that mirrored his own gravity, his own uncertainty—maybe even his own fears? Competent and tough as he was, maybe Grady had no answers.

Answers...

She needed so many answers. Somewhere out there in the dark was her own little Robbie. Maybe he'd walk in the door at any minute, frightened about his friend but safe. But Morag no longer believed he was making his way to her.

Not now she knew where Hamish might be.

Robbie was dependable—far too dependable for one small boy. But he'd been brought up to be self-sufficient, to make a judgement call when needed. He could decide if a phone call was something he should interrupt his aunt for when she was talking earnestly to someone who was crying on their doorstep. If someone appeared at their back door, bleeding, Robbie would find a towel and tell them to press hard before he ran to find Morag. If Morag wasn't home when he got back from school—if she'd been called away on an emergency and hadn't had time to make provision for him—then he'd take himself off to his Aunt Christine's.

Normal kids—normal nine-year-olds with milk-and-cookie mums—

would never be asked to make decisions such as these, but with a doctor-mother and then a doctor-aunt, Robbie had been asked to make them almost from birth.

So now Morag knew instinctively the decision Robbie would have made. He was worried sick about his best friend. Morag hadn't appeared before dark to help him, and he hadn't been able to ask Hubert to go with him.

So he'd gone alone.

Grady was still watching her. His calm eyes were a caress in themselves, and she accepted it because she needed it so much.

She gave him a faltering smile in return.

'Take care of Hubert for me,' she whispered. 'And, Grady, come as soon as you can.' She reached out and touched him, lightly on the hand. It was a fleeting gesture that meant nothing—and everything.

'Thank you, Grady,' she whispered. 'My love...'

CHAPTER TWELVE

IT WAS NOT a good night to be out of the harbour mouth.

The sea, as flat as a millpond during the chaos of the tidal wave, had started to stir. A building sou'westerly was driving a strong, erratic swell in against the cliffs. As soon as the *Minnow-Eater* emerged from the harbour, the fishing boat started an erratic bucketing.

'You do that life jacket up tight, lass,' Marcus called, and she nodded and hauled the straps tighter as she huddled into her oversized waterproofs.

Marcus's boat was one of the best equipped available. They were very lucky it hadn't been in the harbour when the wave had come, but, then, most of the boats had been out. Thankfully. Otherwise they'd have been destroyed.

Marcus headed a crew of four, usually rostered down to three. The town had been lucky it had been Marcus who had been rostered off the day before, but Morag was grateful he hadn't rostered himself off now. The big fisherman was calmly competent, and in this sea they needed every trace of competence they could get. It was a sea that would have an inexperienced fisherman running for cover.

Marcus and Grady were alike, she thought inconsequentially. The two men were separated in age by twenty years but they were really similar. Grady could be just like this in twenty years. But then...

Grady would never look as Marcus did, she thought bleakly. Marcus loved his wife and his kids and his island. He looked at life through calm eyes, with a placid acceptance and muted pleasure with his chosen lot in life.

Whereas Grady... Grady had been here for less than two days and already he was thinking about moving on.

The boat swung south. The moon was lifting over the horizon—thankfully the sky was clear so they'd have moonlight to search. As they rounded the headland Morag could see the brilliant beam from the lighthouse.

Her lighthouse.

If she moved away from the island, if she wasn't here and something happened—another sea-eagle crashed into the lantern room, anything...

Stop it, she thought fiercely. Stop it.

Robbie...

Robbie. Grady. Her island. Her people.

So much to care about. So much to think about. So much, she felt ill.

They were moving fast. The boat was crashing over the cresting swells. Marcus took the boat wide of the rocks that jutted from the southern tip of the island, and then curved in again. Suddenly the sea seemed calmer, but that was an illusion. It was only because they were moving with the same motion as the swell.

'You feeling OK?' Marcus yelled over the noise of the big diesel engine, and she nodded.

'Fine,' she yelled back. Not seasick at least. Just sick with fear.

'There's the boyfriend.' Marcus jabbed a finger skyward and she saw a faint light lifting off from the ridge. Grady had moved fast. It had been twenty minutes since they'd left and already he had his crew mobilised for take-off.

What had Marcus called him? Her boyfriend?

That was a joke.

'We're going in close now,' Marcus told her, and one of the men came toward her with a clip and harness.

'Lifelines,' he told her. 'We lay craypots in here, but not normally in weather as rough as this. It's safe enough if you know what you're doing—and we know what we're doing—but we put the lifelines on anyway.'

'Fine.'

They were nearing the cliffs. Morag had been out here during the day many times as she and her father and sister had fished the waters. She knew these cliffs. In the daytime they were steep and jagged and alive with a mass of seabirds. Now they were dark and forbidding. The sound of the waves crashing on the jagged rocks all but drowned the sound of the boat's big engine.

Robbie. Hamish. The man who'd clipped her lifeline switched on the floodlights.

Where were they?

Their light swept up and down the cliff face in long searching runs. Over and over. Over and over.

Was this stupid? Morag was straining to see along the rockface. Had Hamish been washed out to sea long before this? Was Robbie even now searching somewhere on the island for a friend he'd never find? Alone— as he'd been alone for too long.

She wouldn't cry. She hadn't cried when she'd left Grady or when Beth had died. She mustn't cry now.

But the thought of Robbie alone… Searching for Hamish as they were now doing, but with no one to hold onto him….

Her eyes were still desperately following the line of the floodlights, but she was becoming more afraid by the minute.

The helicopter had reached the cliff face now. Grady. His machine was hovering above them at the far end of the breeding grounds. The helicopter's floodlights scanned to the cliff face and joined the raking, searching lines of light.

At least if the boys were somewhere here they'd know people were looking, Morag thought desperately. Everyone was looking.

Grady was looking. The thought gave her an indefinable comfort, though how one man could make a difference…

He couldn't. Block out Grady.

Search.

Her eyes were straining upward until they hurt. They were only about fifty yards from the base of the cliffs now, as close as Marcus dared to go. Between the boat and the cliffs were rocks, freshly tumbled into the sea as the tsunami had smashed the cliff face and the ledge at the base of the cliffs had crumbled. Above the tumbled rocks in the sea there were jagged crevices filled with sleepy birds staring outward, indignant as the floodlight interrupted their sleep.

The floodlights raked on. The rockface curved in, out, in…Morag was holding the rail, leaning forward, her body swaying with the movement of the sea. Her father had spent so much of his time on the sea and she with him. And Beth. Her family.

Robbie…

The boat jerked, bows downward, as a breaker foamed over the stern and water rushed over the deck. Morag's hold on the rail tightened but her eyes didn't leave the cliff.

Please…

'We'll have to go further out,' Marcus called, and Morag half turned toward him.

But as she did so, the man who'd adjusted her lifeline gave a hoarse shout, filled with disbelieving hope.

'There. Two thirds of the way up. Shift the flood to the right. No. Hell, I thought I saw—I thought…'

The beam shifted. Shifted some more.

And then Marcus was hauling the wheel round and someone was lunging for the radio. For there on the ledge…

'It's Hamish.' Morag was staring, as if at any minute the sight would disappear. But it wasn't imagination. A little boy waving wildly, screaming, as if they could hear over the sound of the wind and the waves and the engine.

'It's Hamish.' There were tears suddenly cascading down her cheeks. Here at last there was one happy ending. Hamish. She could tell Robbie… He couldn't have found his friend yet, she thought wildly. Here was Hamish, and the land party would find Robbie as they searched the clifftops. They'd be able to tell him…

'The chopper will be able to get him off,' Marcus was calling. 'They'll lower someone by harness.'

Of course. Morag didn't dare to take her eyes from the child—as if in losing sight of him she might lose him for ever—but she was aware that the helicopter had already changed course. Now it was zooming downward with its own lights. Grady was up there, she thought wildly, almost dizzy with relief. She'd be able to ring Christine and Peter with such good news. Grady would come down and swoop the child up and he'd be safe...

'Is that a dog?' Marcus asked, narrowing his eyes against the spray.

Hamish was standing on a ledge, half-hidden by a boulder that must be protecting him from the worst of the elements. He was still yelling and waving, as though he hadn't realised they'd seen him, though it must have been obvious.

'I reckon I can see two dogs,' the man beside her said. He had a pair of field glasses in his hand and he wiped them clean and handed them to Morag. 'Two bloody dogs. Where did they come from? Isn't one that the dopey mutt of William Cray's?'

William's border collie. Of course. The big dog often got bored with William's solitary writing, and he'd been known to take off with the boys on their adventures.

So here was another blessing. Morag lifted the glasses and saw the big black dog slink behind Hamish's legs as if terrified of the noise and light. As well he might be.

'I can only see one dog,' she said. 'I'm sure it's William's. He'll be so pleased.'

But...

Something caught her suddenly. A jarring note amidst the joy.

Morag stared on through the salt-sprayed glasses. Hamish was still yelling. Screaming. He still looked terrified, Morag thought.

But why? Why terrified? Hamish wasn't a kid who'd be afraid of a helicopter. The ledge he was standing on looked wide enough. Solid enough. He'd be hungry and thirsty and cold, but...terrified?

They were coming in to rescue him. Surely he should be starting to be reassured?

She took the glasses from her eyes and wiped the salt mist again. Refocused.

And then she froze. The man beside her had been right. From out behind the boulder came a second dog. A golden retriever.

Dear God.

'It's Elspeth,' she whispered, almost to herself. 'It's Hubert's dog.'

Her mind shifted to overdrive and then moved up another notch. Elspeth was with Robbie. Elspeth had left Hubert's place with Robbie, and Elspeth would only have left Robbie to go back to Hubert.

Hubert was in hospital.

If Elspeth was down on that ledge, she'd have come down with Robbie.

Robbie must have tried to climb down from the top.

Her glasses swung back to the child's face. To the unmistakable terror on Hamish's face. To his frantically waving arms. The little boy was staring out at them, but every other second he was glancing down at the water.

Down...

'Robbie's in the water,' she screamed. She lunged for the floodlight but the men were there before her, hauling the light away from the child on the ledge and down to the blackness and foam around the rocks.

'Where...?'

They saw him together in a wash of water. A flash of carrot hair among the foam. An arm waved in a feeble call for help. Marcus yelled a warning, and so did the man beside her.

Morag didn't yell.

He must have tumbled from above, she thought. The sea right at the base of the cliff was relatively free from rocks, or he'd already be dead. He'd fallen and been washed out to where the remnants of the original ledge formed a vicious circle of jagged rocks, holding him enclosed.

Not that there was anywhere for him to go. If he tried to reach the cliffs, he'd be smashed against the cliff. The surf was surging in through gaps in the rocks between him and the boat. There was no way he could swim out to where the water was clearer.

The floodlight was washing the water now in brilliant white and Morag caught a glimpse of a face...

Of terror.

The next wave slammed into him. Dear God, how long had he been there? He was going under.

'Get me a lifeline,' she screamed. She was unhooking herself from the lines set up round the boat and dragging off her waterproofs, kicking off her shoes as she ran along the deck to the bow of the boat. The closest point.

'Grady will come down,' Marcus yelled. He reached out and grabbed her arm. 'We're in radio contact. He's in a harness.'

'It'll take time. Robbie's going under now. I'm going in.'

'You can't. You'll be smashed on the rocks.'

'Then we'll be smashed together. But I can do this. Clip a line on me now or I'm going in without.'

He was staring at her in horror. 'I'll go.'

'I can swim better than you can, and you know it.' It was a skill she'd gloried in as a kid—trained in a city squad, she'd been able to beat any kid on the island.

Marcus knew it. And he'd seen that tiny face washed by the wave. He knew it'd take minutes to get the lines down from the helicopter—minutes Robbie didn't have.

He wasted no more time. He barked a command for someone to take the wheel, then hauled a line free to clip it to her harness.

'Go,' he muttered.

She'd rid herself of the last of her waterproofs. Now she straightened. She focused one more time on exactly where Robbie was—there was a tiny flash of colour and that was all.

She dived deep into the mess of rocks and surf and the darkness.

Grady had moved fast. As soon as Jaqui was free to take over Hubert's care, he had May and the crew into the helicopter, and the chopper was rising almost before they'd hauled their gear out.

Kids...

Rescue missions were always fraught, always emotional, but when it was kids it seemed a thousand times worse. 'There might be a kid on the cliffs,' he told the crew, and it took just one look at May's drawn face as he helped her into Jaqui's usual seat for the crew to know how serious the situation was.

And Grady wasn't expecting a happy ending here. After all, what were the odds? That a kid had been caught high enough to escape the wave but still be safe almost a day and a half later?

It didn't stop them moving fast. The boat below had beaten them to the cliff face, but only just. They started the long raking of the cliffs with their searchlight with an intensity that said if the child wasn't found, it wouldn't be for want of trying.

And then the boat's light found Hamish… It was a magic moment. A miracle moment.

May cried out with shock and joy—but it was too much for her to take in. She was so shocked that her stomach reacted.

Doug handed her a sick-bag but she was left to fend for herself as they started to fasten Grady into his harness.

'You reckon you can get in close enough to be safe?' Grady demanded of his pilot, and Max nodded.

'I think so. What I'll do is go above the level of the cliff. We'll lower you from there so if the wind gusts up, we won't get slammed into the rockface.'

'Thanks very much,' Grady told him, knowing it was he who'd hit rock. But that was OK. He knew enough to ward off rock with his boots—hell, he'd practised this manoeuvre a hundred times.

'I guess we could land and lower someone from dry land,' Doug said, and Grady looked out, considering.

'We'll get the dogs off that way in the morning. But the land up there's too rocky to get close and I want the kid up now.'

They all did. The boy looked fine—wonderful, even—standing yelling at the helicopter for all he was worth—but he'd been alone for too long already.

The way he was yelling spoke of hysteria.

'You'll get him,' May whispered from the reaches of her sick-bag, and Grady put a hand on her shoulder and gripped, hard.

'I'll have him with you in minutes. The dogs will have to wait…'

'Dogs?'

But she didn't get further. The radio crackled into life. 'Robbie's in the water,' a man snapped.

What?

The boat's floodlights had suddenly veered downward. Max hauled the chopper outward. 'Get me beams below,' he yelled.

'Who…?' May was almost incoherent.

But Grady wasn't listening. He was lying on his stomach on the chopper floor, staring straight down. A tiny copper-coloured head.

And then...

'She's going in,' Doug yelled.

Grady turned toward the boat.

And Morag was in the water.

Morag surfaced, spluttering for air in the foam. She was being washed against the rocks, and she had to get clear, through the gap to where she'd last seen Robbie.

At least the floodlights let her see, in the tiny fractions of time when the surf receded.

To her left...a gap in the rocks.

She turned and a breaker bore down on her. She duck-dived, then surfaced again.

Now.

With every ounce of strength she possessed, she swam for the gap. Let her get to mid-gap before the next breaker struck...

It struck and she was washed forward, tumbled into the cauldron of foam.

Somehow she surfaced, hoping desperately she was where she'd aimed to be.

There was no reason in the surge of the water. There was no gap between breakers. The surf was like a giant washing machine—worse, a washing machine with jagged rocks and no bottom to hope to find a footing.

And somewhere here... Robbie?

'Robbie?' She was screaming into the dark and the terror of the unknown. 'Robbie!'

The lights were focusing—from both boat and helicopter. She was suddenly in a flood of brilliant light, but she couldn't see.

'Robbie?'

A wall of water smashed against her, driving her back against the rocks she'd just surged past. She felt her leg buckle and a shard of pain shot through her leg.

She'd thought she'd had room for no more sensation. Wrong.

'Robbie!'

She struck out, forward, into the centre of the cauldron. Away from the rocks.

'Robbie…'

A hand clutched her hair.

She was jerked sideways, but she didn't hesitate. All the times of her childhood, with her father on the beach where they'd practised surf life-saving drill, came to the fore. When grabbed, grab back. Hard. Under the arm, lift, break, turn. Face the victim away from you, and move with force. You're no help to anyone if you drown.

Over and over her father had practised the manoeuvre with both Beth and Morag. Even aged seven or eight, she could break away from a grown man.

So now the hand gripping her head was struck upward but seized at the same time. Robbie? It had to be Robbie.

She hauled him round so he was facing away from her. And, gloriously, she felt him respond to her hold. She felt him curve into her.

Then, for the first time, she could accept that she'd found him.

'It's Morag,' she screamed. 'Don't fight me. Robbie, don't fight.'

He didn't. The hand that had reached for her must have contained the last ounce of strength he possessed.

He slumped.

She clung on.

Another wave smashed her forward. Her right leg wouldn't work—wouldn't move. The pain… She was treading water with one leg—that was all she could do. Her lifejacket was holding her up, sort of, but the tumult of water was making it almost impossible to breathe.

She still had a line holding her, and the line was attached to the boat, but a lot of use that was. If they tried to drag her back through the gap…

They couldn't. They'd know it.

She had to stay out of the range of the rocks.

Another wave jarred her forward. A submerged rock struck her leg, and she heard herself crying out again.

In her arms Robbie stirred and whimpered.

He was still OK, she thought. He was still alive. All she had to do was hold on.

Grady would come.

Please...

'Two lines.' Grady was out on the skids already. 'Just hand me two lines.'

'I'll come in with you.' Doug was clipping a harness in place at Grady's front so all he had to do was find someone, pull them into the harness and be dragged back up. Simple...

'Yeah, and who'll operate the line?' Grady was feeling sick. Of all the times for them to be flying without their full complement... All Max's attention had to be on the helicopter, maintaining its hover, and he needed Ron on the spotlight. Elsey had gone with Hazel to make sure she was settled in William's cottage—and also to surreptitiously check on William—and there'd been no time to wait.

Usually, if there were two in the water they'd both go in. But that was in open seas. Two people in that maelstrom below them would be no use at all. It'd only add to the confusion and double the risk.

Doug knew it. He held Grady by the shoulder for a fraction of a moment and gripped, hard.

'Go.'

Her leg was dragging her down.

How could a leg drag her down? She was wearing a life jacket. She had Robbie securely under his arms, clutched against her breast. If only the water would stop smashing her...

If only her leg would stop dragging...

'Morag!'

The yell seemed to come from a long way away, but in this white water even a foot was vast distance.

But she'd heard him through her fog of pain and fear. Grady was coming. She knew he was coming.

There was a knife in her thigh.

'Morag...' She felt a sharp jerk sideways. And then another.

He was coming. He must.

Once Grady had touched the water there was no chance of finding them by sight. He'd been lucky when he'd been lowered to find a line right under him. He guessed what it was straight away—the line linking Morag to the boat—and he sent a silent blessing to whatever fates might be helping him.

Help him some more.

She had to be at the end of the line. Just pray the line didn't catch on a rock and snap.

Just pray.

Hand over hand...

Morag.

She was here! His hand reached out and touched her, and she was his! He reeled her in and held her tight as the next surge of water threatened to carry her away from him. He was clipping himself to her, clipping himself to the harness she thankfully already wore, but his hands still held her. The power of these waves could rip them apart at any minute.

'I'm here,' he told her, pulling her strongly into him. As he did he felt what she held.

She had the boy.

The three of them were linked.

'Morag...'

'Take him,' she managed. She twisted around so that Robbie was between them, so he could slip his spare blue and orange harness around the little boy's midriff and click the metal links into place. Then, with the attachment complete, she gave him a shove that should have sent him away from her.

It didn't.

'Take him. Please... Lift him out of here.' She was screaming but he could barely hear her.

The child seemed unconscious. Normally he'd be turning him, seeing if he was breathing, trying to give a few short breaths. But to try and assess him here was impossible.

To stay longer was risking all their lives.

'I'll be all right,' Morag was screaming. 'Go.'

He'd attached the spare line to her. It wasn't a lift harness—he couldn't take her up without breaking her arms. He'd have to be lowered again to retrieve her.

But to let her go...

There was no choice. Move, Reece, he told himself. The sooner you get him up, the sooner you can come back for her.

Morag.

He caught her with the arm that wasn't holding Robbie and somehow, crazily, he managed to kiss her. Kiss? Sort of a kiss. Certainly not the best kiss he'd ever given a woman. But maybe it was the most important. His lips just managed to brush her face, and then with a wrench that cut like a knife he let her push him away.

He gathered the child tighter against him. Then he raised his arm in the air. Above their heads Doug saw the signal for Max to lift.

They wouldn't waste time trying to winch Grady and Robbie into the helicopter. They'd land him on the clifftop, Grady thought as he swung upward, over the mass of surging water. May could help then. May must help. If the clifftop searchers weren't there yet, then they'd put May out to care for the child while he returned for Morag.

Unless Robbie needed resuscitating, he thought desperately. Why wasn't the child stirring? If there was a medical imperative for him to stay...

Jaqui wasn't with them.

Dear God, no.

Please...

Morag waited.

The pain in her leg had taken her so far to the edge that she had no strength left to fight the water. Somehow she managed to breathe. Somehow she managed to struggle enough to gasp for breath as the life jacket stopped her sinking.

Robbie was gone.

Grady was gone.

They were safe?

A wave slapped her face. Another. She choked and choked again, and struggled to turn away from the wash of water. The pain jabbed through her leg with an intensity she hadn't believed possible.

Grady...

Help me.

She didn't know whether she said it. She had no way of telling. What was reality and what was nightmare? Who could say?

Grady...

The water smashed her against the rock again. Her leg... Robbie...

Grady.

It was too much. She'd done all she could do and more.

She let herself slip away into the dark.

CHAPTER THIRTEEN

SHE WAS LYING in the sun.

Morag let her eyes open—just a little—and the rays of the early morning sun were playing over her face.

Heaven?

It was unbelievable but for the moment she asked no questions. She was warm and dry and there was sunlight.

Robbie.

The thought jarred her eyes wide. The light hurt and she closed them again, but as she did so, a strong hand caught hers. And held.

'Morag.'

It was Grady. Grady was holding her.

She risked the sunlight again and there he was, right in front of her.

She was in bed. In a sea of white. White coverlet, white canvas around her...

But Grady was in green. Theatre garb? She gazed up at him, trying to bring him into focus, trying to make him real.

Not a dream. Please...

'Robbie,' she whispered, and her voice didn't seem to belong to her. Her throat hurt.

Her leg. What was wrong with her leg? It seemed heavy. Unbearably heavy.

'Robbie,' she croaked again, and then Grady was gathering her into his arms, tenderly so as not to disturb the mass of lines that seemed to be attached to her at every angle.

'Robbie's fine,' he said, and his voice didn't seem normal either. 'He's asleep. Look.' He moved her gently so she could see across to the next bed. Robbie's hair was a splash of colour against his pillows, and his freckles stood out on his too-pale face. 'He was awake in the night, asking for you,' he told her. 'But he was content to wait until you woke.'

'In the night?' She stared wonderingly out into the sunlight.

She was in the field hospital. She and Robbie seemed to have a 'room' to themselves.

Someone—Grady?—had lifted a flap of canvas, hooking it high so she could see the sun rising over the horizon.

Dawn...

'I've been asleep?'

'For long enough.' He held her as he'd hold a piece of Dresden china— as if she might crack at any minute. 'We operated on your leg last night. Compound fracture. Hell, Morag, you might have lost your leg.'

She let that sink in. It was like a story about someone else. 'So you and Jaqui operated—as you operated on Sam.'

'Not quite like Sam,' he told her, and his hold on her tightened. 'Your leg's going to be OK. We would have sent you to Sydney but the blood supply was compromised. You'll need another operation before you're through, but for now...for now you're safe.'

That was enough for the moment. He held her in silence while she absorbed what she'd been told.

Safe...

They were good words, she thought dreamily. 'You're safe.' She wasn't dead. She wasn't in heaven. She was alive, in Grady's arms.

And Robbie? She still had questions.

'You're sure Robbie's OK?' Her voice still seemed to be coming from a long way away.

'He ate eggs and bacon at midnight. He's suffered a couple of nasty lacerations and some bruising, and he's had a huge fright, but as soon as he realised you and Hamish were OK, the whole thing started fading to an adventure.'

Good. That was good.

Why wouldn't her sluggish mind think?

'Hamish?' she managed.

'He ate eggs and bacon at midnight, toasted sandwiches at five and I think he's complaining that he's hungry again now. He was a little dehydrated, but he drank so much lemonade after we dragged him up that we didn't bother putting a drip up.'

'Oh, Grady...'

'And the dogs are fine, too,' he told her in a voice that was decidedly shaky. 'The team decided they wouldn't leave them there overnight, so Doug and Max lowered themselves over the cliff face and brought them up in harnesses. Doug took Mutt home, and William's decided he's going to wait a bit before he starts the antidepressants. The first couple of days' medication can bring drowsiness, and William has too much to do to be drowsy.'

Then, at the look of sheer confusion on her face, he smiled down at her with a gentleness that turned her heart right over. 'That's all,' he told her. 'You're barely with me, my heart. But you are with me. That's all that matters. For now...you need to sleep.'

Sleep.

It seemed a good option to her. Even a great option. Her eyes were so tired.

But still she clung, and still he held. She could feel the beating of his heart, she thought dreamily. Her Grady...

Her heart was beating with his. What more could she ask?

Nothing.

She woke again and Grady wasn't there. Robbie was gone from the next bed, but Louise was watching. The nurse fussed and clucked and went and heated some soup. She helped Morag drink a little then she adjusted her pillows, checked her drip and told her not to worry.

'Robbie's with Hamish. He's fine. Can you believe that child? He's scratched to pieces and an adult would be groaning for days, but William's brought Hamish down.'

She looked confused. Why wouldn't she look confused?

'William's brought Hamish down?'

'Hamish and May are staying with William because of the dogs, and also because Hazel was so pleased. You know Hazel and May are cousins? After losing Elias, finding Hamish has cheered Hazel up like nothing else could. It's cheered everyone up. Now the two boys and the dogs are sitting out in the sun, comparing adventures.'

Adventures... There'd been too many adventures. 'They won't go back onto the cliff?'

'Are you kidding? I don't think they ever want to see that cliff again in their lives. William's told them if they wander from sight he'll scalp the pair of them, and they've promised. You know they're kids who keep their promises.'

They were, too. But...

'Grady.' She was thinking aloud. 'Where's Grady?'

'He's at the town meeting. Like everyone else except Irene and me—we're keeping the hospital running.' She gave a tight, distracted smile, and her pleasure in talking of the little boys faded a little. 'Which is just as well. Someone has to.'

'The meeting.' Morag's mind focused sharply. 'Oh, no, the meeting... Louise, I need to be there.'

'Right, so you can just pick up your bed and leave? I don't think so.' The nurse smiled and started to fit a blood-pressure cuff. 'Stop your worrying, girl,' she told her. 'You've been doing too much worrying. About everyone. And now Grady's worrying about you, and William's worrying about you, and Marcus and May and Hazel and just about everyone else on the island.'

'But—'

'You know you've got a really nasty fracture of your leg?' Louise sounded as if she was scolding. 'Jaqui and Grady worked like fury to try and re-establish a blood supply, and you're dead lucky your leg didn't to go the way of Sam's. So if you think you can just get up and keep going, you're gravely mistaken.'

'I must,' she said in distress. 'The island... If I'm out of action they'll evacuate the island and we'll never return.'

Louise's kindly face clouded. 'I don't know about that,' she said stolidly. 'But there's nothing you and I can do about it, and worrying won't help. So how about I call Irene to double-check the drugs, and we'll give you the injection Dr Reece ordered? That'll stop the pain and let you settle back to sleep. I'd imagine when you wake up, everything will be decided.'

'Everything will be over.'

Louise pursed her lips and turned to call Irene. 'Wait and see.'

Morag did sleep. Her body gave her no choice. She drifted in and out of a drug-induced stupor all through that long afternoon.

When she woke, the flap of the tent was closed. She could no longer see the sea, and the light was starting to fade.

She winced and groaned a little as the pain in her leg caught. But that wasn't what was worrying her. The effects of the morphine had receded, her mind was clear and she was faced with the overwhelming realisation that she'd missed the meeting.

And she was injured. She understood enough of the injury to her leg to know she'd be off work for many weeks. The island would have no medical officer, and that'd be the death knell to the island. The decision about the island's future was a foregone conclusion.

'It's about time you woke up.'

She twisted and Grady was at the entrance to her makeshift ward.

'Hi, Morag,' he told her, and he was smiling. What a smile. It was a smile to make her catch her breath. 'We've been waiting for you to wake up for ages. Welcome to your future.'

Her future. What on earth was he talking about? She tried hard to focus, tried to see...

We've been waiting for you to wake up?

Who?

Robbie.

Robbie was beside him, clutching his hand as if he belonged there. Robbie and Grady. The two men in her life. Her love for them both was so intertwined, the fact that they stood hand in hand hardly took any explaining. It felt...right.

But Robbie was looking desperately anxious. He mustn't be anxious.

'Robbie,' she whispered, and the little redhead darted toward her like an arrow to its target. She gathered her to him with her free arm and she held him close.

But over his head she looked at Grady.

'What...? What...?'

But there was more to understand. *We*, Grady had said, and he'd meant *we*. It wasn't just Grady and Robbie. There were people behind Grady.

Lots of people.

And they were all smiling.

'Your island's safe,' Grady told her.

'Safe?'

Grady opened his mouth to continue, but he was interrupted.

'We've got a plan.' Jaqui was pushing her way past Grady, elbowing him aside as if he were an annoying obstacle. She was dressed in her yellow overalls—so was Grady. And there was Doug in his overalls and... more...

'Grady wanted to tell you by himself,' Jaqui was saying, 'but I said no way. He said you're not ready for any more than one visitor at a time, but what would he know? He's too close to be your treating physician, so I've elected myself. And joy's not going to kill you, girl. Now, is it?'

'Joy?'

'The meeting,' she said in some satisfaction. 'We knew you'd want to be there. But we couldn't wait. It was far too soon for anyone to be level-headed. Only two days after something as massive as a tsunami, there's been so little time to think. But decisions had to be made immediately. Either everyone needs to work like crazy and get some sort of drainage and water system in place, or we all get out of here now. The infrastructure's so damaged there's a real health risk.'

'She knows that. Don't waffle,' Grady said darkly, trying to edge her aside again, but Jaqui refused to be edged.

'Who's waffling? Who had the best idea?'

'Grady did.' It was Marcus, pushing in past Jaqui. The burly fisherman was in front now, and likely to stay that way. After all, he was the biggest. 'It seems Grady's brother's a politician in Sydney, with more clout than we know what to do with. So he's pulled strings like you wouldn't believe.'

'But it's my husband who clinched it,' Jaqui retorted. 'My Craig is the head of a big public works department on the mainland and he's bored. We're both bored. And we have four adult sons living with us who are driving us crazy. Craig's been talking of retirement, but who wants to retire and do nothing? Anyway, we've been thinking about getting away—doing something completely different—and now I've met the island goats...'

'What are you talking about?' It was as much as Morag could do to whisper, and Robbie pulled away from her to stare into her face in concern. Like he was worried she might have bumped her head.

Like she was being adult-obtuse.

'It's easy,' the little boy told her. 'Hubert explained it to me and Grady told me again. Dr Jaqui's husband is an engineer and he's going to come over and start digging drains so we can stay on the island. And Dr Jaqui wants to help with the goats.'

'Craig doesn't exactly dig,' Jaqui conceded. 'But he's really good at organising. And Robbie's right about the goats. Anyway, with Grady's politician brother pulling strings to keep the army lads over here to help, and William's friends moving mountains...'

'William's friends?' Maybe Robbie was right. Maybe she had been hit on her head. Her head was certainly spinning.

William was there, too, she saw, stunned. He was standing at the back, grinning like he'd won the lottery.

'William has the arts community in the palm of his hand,' Grady told her. He was one of ten or so people crowding around her bed now, but suddenly they may as well have been alone. He was smiling and smiling at her, his eyes locked on hers. Promising the world.

But still talking practicalities.

'From the time William got Mutt back, he's been on the end of a phone, contacting every land council—every human rights group—every arts board—to the end that if we take anything away from the Koori people that's been given to them already—like twenty-four-hour medical support—there'll be a national uproar.' Grady turned to smile at William—who was blushing, for heaven's sake. 'It seems the Koori artwork here is known worldwide, and that's given us even more leverage. The elders worked with William on this, Morag, and Yndilla and Nargal even consented to use our radio to confirm their needs with the mainland Koori organisations. You've gained the Koori people's trust, Morag. They want you.'

'But…' She was too dazed to take it in but it wasn't making sense. 'They can't…I have to leave…'

'That's the best bit.' It was Hubert, piping up from the other side of the canvas, and Morag's flimsy side wall was twitched aside to reveal the old man lying in the next cubicle. Like Morag, he was attached to IV lines, but his colour had returned and his voice had a strength that said he might well be good for a few years yet. 'Tell her the best. Tell her.'

'I'm trying to,' Grady said, half laughing.

'He's trying to tell you we're staying,' Jaqui told her. 'Craig and I are staying. I just looked at this place and I knew…'

'You and Craig are staying?'

'I told you,' Jaqui said with exaggerated patience. 'I've fallen for the goats. One licked me on the face when I was trying to sleep in the sun and I was hooked. Craig will oversee rebuilding and I'll be a medical partner. With goats on the side.'

'Me, too,' Grady told her, and the whole world seemed to hold its breath.

'You…you, too?'

'You haven't asked her,' Jaqui told him. 'Bill and Louise can't share their goats with everyone—and Morag might not want a medical partner.'

'That cuts you out, then,' he retorted.

'Well…'

'Jaqui, shut up.'

'Only if you tell her, stupid.'

'Jaqui and I have been talking,' he said a little bit desperately, and she gazed up at him in disbelief.

She was still cuddling Robbie. The little boy was curled against her, but he was gazing up at the crowd around his aunt's bed as if this were a theatre spectacular. And he had the best seat in the house.

'You and Jaqui have been talking?' Morag prodded, and Grady cast a despairing glance around at his audience.

'I don't suppose there's any chance you lot will go away,' he said, and got unanimous grins.

'Not a snowball's chance in a bushfire,' Marcus said calmly. 'Tell her.'

'OK.' He took a deep breath, obviously a man caught between a rock and a hard place. 'Um… I thought I might stay here, too,' he told her.

She thought about it. Her leg should be hurting, she thought dazedly, but she couldn't feel her leg. She couldn't feel anything. Was she floating?

Who needed morphine when this was happening?

But... 'What on earth would you do here? she managed.

'I wouldn't mind a bit of privacy,' Grady tried again.

'It's not going to happen,' Jaqui told him. 'Tell the lady.'

'Yeah, well, Jaqui and I have been talking. And we think—'

'We think this makes a really fantastic base for Air-Sea Rescue, from here to New Zealand,' Jaqui said. 'There's so much sea traffic...'

'You have to be kidding,' Morag whispered. 'You're crazy.'

'We are a bit,' Grady admitted. 'But we have the government interested in setting up a medical base to service all the remote islands north and east of here. Individually each has tiny populations but when you put them together—'

'It makes economic sense to service them from here rather than send everyone to the mainland.' Jaqui's voice was triumphant.

'And when you add the indigenous populations...' Grady managed.

'The education needs,' William added. 'Health education for the Kooris has to be a priority.'

'Then there's the fact that the lighthouse needs protecting from marauding sea eagles,' Marcus added. 'So we need you and Jaqui and Grady. Plus, I'm going to teach Grady to fish.'

'Me, too,' said Jaqui.

'I can fish already,' Robbie told her. 'I'll help teach you.'

'But—'

'And we're going to run remote training sessions,' Grady added with a flourish, as if it was his trump card. 'Jaqui and William and Marcus and I started work at dawn, planning this. After Jaqui and I sorted your leg out we were too high to sleep, and no one else was sleeping either. There's such potential. We have everything here. We have such expertise.'

'We're the best,' Jaqui said modestly, and everyone laughed.

And then the laughter died.

They were all looking at her, Morag realised. They were all waiting for her reaction.

She couldn't react. She didn't know how to. There was so much to take in...

'The island must remain viable for everyone,' Grady said softly. 'And it can. You know, Angie Salmon stood up at the public meeting today and told everyone that Orlando would be buried here because this was where he belonged. It was where everyone belonged. She said she was staying here and so were her family, and if they took the doctor away then the world would be inflicting another disaster on the island as big as the tidal wave. The cameraman who helped Hubert has resurrected a damaged photograph of Orlando, and the world's press is splashing his picture all over the world's newspapers right now. We're safe, Morag. We're all safe. We're home.'

'You're home? You?' She could hardly take it in.

'I will need to go to Sydney from time to time,' Grady told her, as if he needed to lay all his cards out on the table right now. 'So will Jaqui. We'll still be part of the emergency services network, which is run from the mainland. But we thought—'

'We thought we could go, too.' Robbie was almost gleeful. 'Grady talked about it to me like I was a grown-up. He said you really liked shopping and he bet me that I'd like it, too. He said Sydney has cool stuff. And he said that when I go to school in Sydney, you guys could all come over a lot to visit me. He said you'll have three doctors on the island, so you'll all be able to take turns.'

'You have it all worked out.'

'Yup,' said Grady. 'And this way I get to be assistant lighthouse-keeper. How cool is that?'

'You've already talked Robbie into it.'

'Yup,' said Jaqui. 'And I'm going to be assistant to the assistant of the lighthouse-keeper.'

'Is there anything you haven't planned?'

'The wedding,' Grady said, and the whole world stilled.

'The...'

'Right.' Enough was enough. Grady squared his shoulders. He turned to face the assembled congregation.

'I'm doing this by myself,' he decreed.

'Hey, don't mind us,' Hubert said.

'You can't keep all the good bits for yourself,' Jaqui added.

'Out,' said Grady. He plucked Robbie from Morag's arms and swung him round to William. 'Find the kid a dog,' he said. 'Robbie, I need to organise your future.'

'It's already organised,' Robbie told him.

'No, it's not. Your Aunty Morag hasn't agreed to marry me.'

'You will, though,' Robbie said. 'Won't you, Morag?'

Morag was laughing. Joy was bubbling up so fast it threatened to overwhelm her. They were all looking at her now—seemingly the whole island. This was a proposal from Grady, but it was also a proposal from all of them.

They'd taken Grady to their hearts. He was part of them. Part of this community.

Part of her heart.

Why should she wait until the room was clear? she thought, dazed beyond belief. Why should she wait another moment?

'Of course I'll marry you,' she told Grady. 'Of course I will, my love. That is...' She grinned with pure mischief. 'That is, if you ever get around to asking me.'

Grady groaned. But he was smiling down at her, and suddenly he realised that this wasn't the way it was supposed to be. With a despairing glance around the room at his unmoving audience, he finally shrugged and dropped to his knees next to the bed.

'Morag—'

'That's better,' Hubert said approvingly.

'Ooh, I like this,' said Louise.

'Shut up,' said Grady. 'Morag—'

'Have you got a ring?' Robbie said anxiously from William's arms. 'He has to have a ring.'

'Have one of mine.' It was Hazel, who'd been squishing in at the back between May and Hamish. Now she held out a ring—one of many that adorned her work-worn hands. 'Elias gave me a ring every wedding anniversary so I have sixty-two rings. I can't think of a better way to recycle one of them.'

'Thank you,' Grady said with as much dignity as he could muster. 'Until I have time to buy my own...'

'Diamond solitaire,' Hubert advised. 'Girls like diamond solitaires.'

'Will you all shut up?' It was a roar that almost lifted the tent.

It shut them up.

'Well!' Louise ventured, inclined to be indignant. 'In a sickroom.'

'Louise...'

'Just joking.' She held up her hands as if to ward off his anger. 'Don't mind me. Everyone, hush.'

Everyone hushed.

'Morag Lacy,' Grady said finally, catching her hands and holding them—and holding her eyes with his, with all the love in his heart. 'Morag, I've loved you for four long years and I love you now more than I ever believed possible. You're the woman I want to spend the rest of my life with. I love you and I need you, Morag, now and for ever. Will you do me the honour of becoming my wife?'

'Ooh,' said Hazel, and sniffed.

'Is that how it's supposed to be done?' Robbie asked, and William hugged him.

'Yes, my boy, that's exactly how it should be done.'

But Morag wasn't listening. Her hands were holding Grady. He was looking up at her and he...he looked anxious. Anxious? How could he possibly doubt her reply?

He was waiting.

The whole island was waiting.

And there was only one answer to give.

'Of course I'll marry you,' she whispered, and then, as he gathered her into his arms and held her, she repeated herself. 'Of course I'll marry you, my heart.'

And with those words, fractured leg or not, Morag Lacy stepped forward into her future.

With love.

* * * * *

Always an avid reader, **Fiona Lowe** decided to combine her love of romance with her interest in all things medical, so writing medical romance was an obvious choice! She lives in a seaside town in southern Australia, where she juggles writing, reading, working and raising two gorgeous sons with the support of her own real-life hero. Fiona would be delighted to hear from readers so please write to her at www.fionalowe.com

Pregnant On
Arrival

Fiona Lowe

To Jude, Melissa, Serena and Nic:
inspirational women and critique partners extraordinaire.

CHAPTER ONE

BRONTE GRABBED THE handle of her suitcase and tugged. The old leather case stayed put on the trolley, refusing to budge. She tried again, this time pulling really hard.

The case moved quickly and suddenly, knocking her backwards. She found herself sprawled on the terminal floor, in a sea of assorted underwear and toiletries.

Great. Just great. It looked liked things were going true to form even though she was a thousand kilometres from home. She picked up some lacy underwear that had landed on her chest. The scattered clothes and broken case pretty much represented her life at the moment.

She stood up and hastily collected her belongings and shoved them back into the case as a few people looked on, amused.

'Dr Hawkins?'

A wave of embarrassment raced through her. *Oh, no, please no.* But she knew the score. This *would* be her new boss. And his first view of her had been with her bottom up in the air. She wanted to crawl inside the recalcitrant suitcase and hide.

Bronte glanced up very slowly from her kneeling position. A pair of moleskin-clad legs came into view. Very long legs wearing workboots caked with red clay.

She followed his line of leg up across a broad chest to his face. Tanned brown by the outback sun, he had the tell-tale lines of a man in his thirties. High cheekbones defined a strong face, and the day-old stubble outlined a solid jaw.

Glossy magazine handsome he wasn't, but he had an attractive ruggedness about him. A man who lived life to the full. The type of man her sister dated. The type of man she now knew never dated her.

Except his sky-blue eyes seemed to be appreciating her behind. She must be imagining things. Travel fatigue must have got to her.

'Dr Morrison?' Bronte forced her voice to sound light and friendly rather than nervous and embarrassed. Without thinking she stuck out her hand to greet him, forgetting she was still kneeling.

His hand grasped hers firmly and a tingling sensation raced up her arm. He quickly pulled her to her feet, the strength of the pull propelling her straight into his chest. His very solid chest.

The warmth of his body mixed with hers. She stepped back quickly, heat flooding her face. 'Ah, sorry. Thank you.'

For a brief moment his lips widened into a grin, exposing straight, white teeth and he nodded. 'Yes, I'm Huon Morrison.' His gaze rested on Bronte, intense and vivid blue. Then his eyes flicked over the dilapidated case and he smiled. Dimples appeared, giving him a mischievous look.

Butterflies took flight in her stomach.

'By the looks of you and your case, this final leg of your trip to Muttawindi is about all you're both up to.'

'There's no hope for the case, but I'm fine.' She tried to smile but her face felt stiff. Why was her heart hammering? She was flustered, as well as giving the impression of being a total klutz.

She hauled in a calming breath. Time to take charge. After all, this was her new life. Taking in a deep breath, she flicked her head up, looked Dr Morrison straight in the face and noticed shadows of fatigue lingering under his eyes. The country had trouble attracting doctors and doctors already in the field worked long hours. Hopefully her arrival would ease his workload. And those shadows.

She forced her attention back to what she wanted to do. 'Please, call me Bronte.'

He took her proffered hand and shook it. This time his fingers wrapped around her hand gently, sending a delicious tingling along her arm.

'Welcome to the outback, Bronte. Call me Huon.' His fingers lingered for a moment on her hand. Warmth spread through her. Was he flirting with her? Men didn't usually flirt with a plain Jane like her, not unless they were trying to get closer to her gorgeous sister, Stephanie. It was a shame she'd taken so long to work that out.

Damien had been the last man to flirt with her and she was still dealing with the fallout from that disaster. Professionally she'd always stood up for herself. Outside work she didn't always have the same self-assurance. But the debacle with Damien had made her determined to transfer that work confidence into her personal life. She wouldn't allow herself to be used again.

She had no intention of dating again for a long time.

Unfortunately, that insight didn't stop the sensation of disappointment snaking through her when Huon finished the handshake.

'Muttawindi's been short a doctor for a while now, and we've been counting the days to your arrival.' He grinned again. 'It's great you're finally here and joining our community.'

She smiled back. His enthusiasm and welcome were infectious. 'I'm really looking forward to joining the team and settling in Muttawindi.'

'Excellent.' Huon picked up her case, securing it shut by splaying his first two fingers against the lid. With a businesslike sweep of his free arm, he indicated the double doors back to the tarmac. 'We need to leave now.'

She stifled a sigh. Definitely not flirting. Just her new boss welcoming his subordinate. Just good manners shining through.

'Follow me.' Huon strode off through the doors, out into the wall of heat, and headed towards a waiting plane.

Grabbing her handbag, Bronte ran to keep up with his long stride.

Halfway across the tarmac he turned and paused, waiting for her to catch up.

'Sorry to rush you, but we're taking advantage of the plane being free in between clinic runs. The workload's pretty steep out here, and we're often working against the clock, not to mention the heat.' His gaze raked over Bronte's petite body.

She recognised the analytical look that so many colleagues gave her, thinking she would not be physically up to the demands of medicine.

A spark of anger fizzed inside her.

For a moment his outback-blue eyes clouded with discomfort. 'You're very slight and this job is very physical.'

Bronte tossed her head back to hide the pain that always slugged her when people judged her by her physical appearance. 'Ah, looks can be deceiving, Doctor. I'm fit as a Mallee bull.'

'Good. You'll need to be.' He moved again towards the plane and at the steps he stood to the side. 'After you.'

The deep timbre of his voice sent a quiver through her and a tiny thrill flared at his courtesy. How could her body betray her like that? Had she learned nothing over the last two months? Couldn't her body work out that the man just had exceptional manners?

Huon ushered her up the steps into the plane and she ducked her head as she stepped inside. She looked around excitedly, pinching herself that she really was in a flying doctor's plane. Fitted out with two stretchers and a lot of medical equipment, the plane also had three normal passenger seats.

The pilot turned around from his controls as Bronte entered the plane.

'Bronte, I'd like you to meet Brendan, one of our pilots.' Huon's voice sounded in her ear over the dull roar of the engines, making her jump slightly.

'G'day, Bronte. Welcome to Broken Hill.' Brendan gave her a cheeky smile. 'Sorry I didn't come into the terminal but we're on a quick turnaround today.'

'That's OK, Brendan, I understand.' At least she'd only embarrassed herself in front of one man instead of two. She had to be thankful for that.

Brendan picked up his headphones. 'Huon will show you how to buckle up the harness and we'll get going. It's about thirty minutes to Muttawindi.' He smiled again and turned back to his controls.

'Sit here.' Huon directed her to a seat and pulled the harness over her shoulders, his fingers briefly brushing the tops of her arms. Warm tingles washed through her and she struggled to concentrate on his explanation of how the harness connected. But as she watched him click the buckle pieces together all she could think of was how his fingers had gently wrapped round her hand when they'd met.

Bronte wanted to shake herself. She was losing it. She didn't daydream about men and their hands. Especially a colleague's hands, her new boss's hands.

Time to focus and clear her head. This was the first day of her new job. Her new life. She leaned back in her seat and closed her eyes. She was tired, bone weary, in fact, which wasn't like her. But, then, with all the recent upheaval she had a right to be tired. Coming to Muttawindi was a complete change and a new start.

A new start she desperately needed after her foolish lapse of judgement. And a job that put a thousand kilometres between her and Damien. Thank goodness she'd never have to clap eyes on him again. Her cheeks blazed with embarrassed heat at the thought of her naïve stupidity. She'd believed every lie he'd told her and he'd reeled her in, then dumped her like a fish floundering on a pier. How could she have missed the warning signs?

This position was just what she needed. Muttawindi would give her a job she could sink her teeth into. A place where she could shine and be valued. A place to belong.

Now she just needed to make a good first impression in Muttawindi and wow Huon with her medical skills. Prove she had the stamina he thought she might lack.

She opened her eyes to find Huon scanning her face intensely.

'You OK? You look pale but your cheeks are fire-engine red. Do you have a temp?'

She forced her voice to sound light and cheerful. 'I'm fine.' Actually, she was feeling queasy but there was no way she was going to tell him that.

Huon buckled his harness. 'It's not far now. Muttawindi's only two hundred kilometres from Broken Hill. You'll soon see your new home.' His smile radiated hospitality and reaffirmed her decision to leave Melbourne and start again.

The engines roared and the King Air raced down the runway, quickly rising up into the cloudless sky. For a moment Broken Hill lay below them, defined by a seven-kilometre mullock heap. It quickly disappeared and the red dust of the outback, tied down with occasional clumps of saltbush, stretched out before them.

The throbbing sounds of the engine, combined with her fatigue, lulled Bronte into a relaxed state and her heavy eyelids drooped closed.

The plane hit an air pocket. Bronte's stomach lurched. Airsick? She'd never been motion-sick before, but she was definitely experiencing it now.

She pulled in a long, slow deep breath as another wave of nausea hit her. Bile scalded her throat. She gulped in air. She couldn't be sick, she wouldn't be sick.

'Are you *sure* you're all right?' Huon leaned over, concern etched on his face.

'I...I think I need...' Bronte's hands flew to her face as she began to heave. Huon quickly grabbed a sick bag and handed it to Bronte just in time for her to vomit. Mortified, the heat of her embarrassment scalded Bronte's cheeks. 'Oh, God, I'm so sorry.'

His body stiffened for a moment and then he relaxed and gave her a wry grin. 'Obviously you're not all right. Perhaps it was something you ate on the flight from Melbourne. Airline food can do that to you.' He reached out and grabbed a towel and a water bottle. 'Here, drink this.'

Bronte took a sip of water, trying to banish the acidic taste from her mouth. The pervading, acrid odour of vomit permeated the plane, making her feel ill again.

Vomiting in front of anyone was embarrassing enough, but chucking up in the company of her new boss wouldn't win anyone brownie points. 'I'm so sorry. I never get motion sickness. I don't understand.'

'Don't look so horrified. We're doctors, people vomit. It goes with the territory.'

Slowly, she leaned back in her seat. Another wave of nausea hit her.

'Here. Hold this.' Huon handed her another bag. 'We're going to start descending in a minute, which might stir things up again.' He gave her a penetrating look. 'And as soon as we're at the clinic, you're having a thorough check-up.'

She didn't have the energy to argue, she was too busy concentrating on not throwing up again.

The King Air touched down on the outback strip with a slight bump. As soon as the plane came to a halt Brendan released the door, and Bronte clambered out of the plane into the fresh but hot air, her hand gripping the stair rail. At first her legs seemed rubbery but they soon steadied and the nausea started to recede.

She glanced around. A low-roofed, utilitarian, rectangular building stood one hundred metres away with the obligatory rainwater tank standing at one end. A large, evaporative air-conditioning unit balanced on the roof, testimony to the oppressive summer heat of the outback.

'Come on inside the clinic, Bronte. You need to get out of this heat. Brendan will bring your bag.' Huon placed his hand gently under her elbow and propelled her forward.

His supportive hand at her elbow made her feel like a fraud. This wasn't the best way to start her new job. She was a colleague, not a patient. She stepped forward, away from his touch, putting a slight distance between them.

He opened the door for her. 'Have a seat in the waiting room.' Huon directed her to a row of moulded plastic chairs. 'I won't be long.' And he disappeared down a long corridor.

Feeling much better now she was on terra firma, Bronte didn't sit but took in her surroundings. Health promotion posters for Sunsmart and Quit Smoking programmes plastered the walls, many with peeling corners. The occasional piece of artwork hung haphazardly, interspersed with the posters.

Bronte noticed that all the artwork was original. She stepped closer to examine a couple of the paintings. Their colours reflected the outback perfectly—brown, orange, red and yellow with occasional flashes of green. They were good, worthy of their own display wall.

'Bronte, come on through.'

She turned from the painting to see Huon at the entrance to the long corridor. A white polo shirt with the clinic's logo and navy blue shorts had replaced his other clothes. The blue of his eyes and the tan of his skin seemed more vivid against the white shirt.

She swallowed and shook her head. She needed sleep and she needed food. Then she would be back to her old self, and her cast-iron stomach.

Bronte walked towards Huon. 'Look, I'm fine now. I think it was just fatigue. The last few weeks have been really hectic. All I need is a good sleep. So we can skip the check-up.'

'No, we can't.' He spoke firmly. 'You've looked peaky since Broken Hill. I need a doctor who is fit, well and on deck so let's just make sure you're not harbouring some nasty bug.'

'Really, Huon, I'm a doctor, too, and—'

'No arguments. I'm the doctor in charge and I'm pulling rank.' He ushered her into an examination room, sat her down and put a thermometer in her mouth.

She automatically rolled up her sleeve as he wrapped the blood-pressure cuff around her arm. She glanced at the sphygmomanometer as the mercury fell, feeling the blood pounding through her arm and working out a rough BP based on that.

'Fine,' Huon commented as he unwrapped the cuff, with the tell-tale sound of ripping Velcro. He removed the thermometer from her mouth and read it. 'Normal.'

'See? I said I was just tired.' Bronte went to stand up.

'Not so fast. I said a check-up so I need to test your urine.' He gave her a grin and handed her a small container. 'Why is it that doctors detest submitting themselves to a routine check-up?'

She threw him a look she hoped spelt out her displeasure at the process he seemed to find entertaining and stomped off to the bathroom. Fortunately, she was quickly able to fill the container. She didn't need any more embarrassing situations that day.

Returning to the office, she handed over her specimen. Huon took it over to a bench and stood with his back to her. She heard him unscrew a jar, which she assumed contained the Multistixs, to test the urine.

'Any headaches lately?' Huon walked back to his desk and sat down.

'No.'

He checked her eyes using his ophthalmoscope and then checked her ears with his auriscope.

'That's all fine as well.'

Bronte rolled her eyes. 'Just like I said, all I need is a good sleep.'

'Just humour me, Bronte. After all, I was the one who witnessed you being sick earlier.'

Heat burned her cheeks. 'Sorry about that. It's never happened before.'

Huon checked the lymph nodes in her neck and tapped her knees with his white plessor. 'No sign of infection so that's good. Perhaps your self-diagnosis was close to the mark.'

'Great. So now if I can just be taken to my house, I can get that catch-up sleep I really need.'

'I'll just check your urine test.' Huon stood up and walked back to the workbench. He checked the Multistix against the bottle's colour chart.

'All OK?' Bronte asked with a hint of self-righteousness. She noticed him pick up something else from the bench.

His shoulders stiffened and he turned slowly to face her. His smile had gone, his dimpled cheeks suddenly stark with tension. A deep furrow lined his brow and his expression was a mixture of disbelief and aggravation. 'You're pregnant.'

The two words hit her like a shot from a gun. The shock sent her blood rushing to her feet and her head swirled. This couldn't be.

Could not be.

She gripped the edge of the chair, struggling to think. She'd only slept with Damien twice and both times they'd used contraception. *The condom broke.* But she'd taken emergency contraception.

Oh, no! Surely she wasn't one of the twelve per cent of cases where it didn't work. Surely the gods wouldn't let that happen.

Huon pushed the white pregnancy stick into her hand. Two stark pink lines stared back at her.

Apparently they would.

'Oh, God.' She slumped in her chair and dropped her head into her hands. Of all the things she could have imagined happening to her, this wasn't one of them. This was not in her plan for her new life.

CHAPTER TWO

FRUSTRATION ALMOST MADE Huon vibrate. Bronte was pregnant. He couldn't believe it. When Head Office had rung him two weeks ago with the news they finally had a doctor to share his workload, he'd been sure his whoop of joy had been heard in the Barcoo. Now his plans of working with a colleague committed to Muttawindi for the long haul, and all the professional advantages that spun off from that, lay in a heap at his feet.

Why was it so hard to get a good doctor to come to the outback and stay? He was so tired of working alone. It had been a tough couple of years. After a string of locums they'd had 'Dr Disaster'. Muttawindi was still recovering from placing their trust in a man who had turned out to have fake medical qualifications.

How someone hadn't died in his care was a miracle, but his legacy had scarred and scared the people of the town. A new doctor was going to have to work really hard to regain their trust.

And he'd been convinced that the extra vigilance applied to the interview process and the quadruple checking of all the paperwork and referees would pay off. But now he had a pregnant doctor.

A pregnant doctor was just what he *didn't* need. Especially one that looked like a stiff breeze would blow her over.

Anger curled in his gut at her betrayal. By withholding this information she'd just snatched away his dream of some real help. 'I would have appreciated you telling me you were pregnant *before* you arrived. I would have told you not to bother coming.'

Bronte raised her head and looked at him, shock and bewilderment playing across her face. 'I had no idea I was pregnant.'

'Yeah, well, you do now.' His words sounded harsh and he regretted them the moment they'd left his mouth. Hell, she probably was telling the truth if the whiteness of her face was anything to go by. She looked as if she was about to faint. He pushed a glass of water over to her. 'Here, drink this.'

Her long, thick eyelashes caressed her cheeks as she blinked back tears. 'Thank you.'

A strange ripple of sensation flicked along his veins. He squashed the feeling immediately. Since Ellen's death his body had been dormant. He planned to keep it that way. The safe way.

She gripped the glass. Slowly a slight hint of colour returned to her face but she was still very pale. Determination sparked in her eyes, shards of blue shimmering across the grey. She pulled her shoulders back. 'This doesn't change anything. I'm still the doctor you need, Muttawindi needs.'

'Really? I need a doctor who doesn't vomit in a plane.' Sarcasm dripped off his tongue and his stomach clenched as the whole messy situation swirled in his gut. He let it take hold, pushing away the unsettling heat that had been part of him since he'd first seen her bent over that ridiculous excuse of a suitcase at the airport.

'You're pregnant—of course it's going to change things.' Aggravation made his voice rise. 'You won't even be able to commit to the full length of your contract. At best you'll be a temporary doctor, a fill-in. I don't need *another* locum. It's probably better that you don't even start.'

Pain and shock slashed her face, bringing him up short. Damn. He hadn't meant to be so blunt. He sat down next to her. 'Look, we've both had a shock but I think the best thing for you would be to head back to Melbourne, talk to the father of your baby and pick up your old job. At least you'll get maternity leave.'

'I don't want to go back to Melbourne. I—'

The radio crackled, drowning out her words. Mary Callahan's voice from the Broken Hill base sounded in the room. He turned away from

Bronte's outraged face and picked up the handpiece. 'Huon Morrison at Muttawindi, Mary. What can I do for you? Over.'

Out of the corner of his eye he noticed Bronte move towards the radio, her expression serious and intense.

'Huon, there's been a fire at Gaadunga Station and a jackaroo is badly burnt. You're the closest doctor so Brendan is circling back to collect you. Over.'

'Right, Mary. I'll head out to the airstrip. Over.'

'Take Dr Hawkins with you. Over.'

'That won't be necessary, Mary.' He ignored Bronte's sharp intake of breath.

'Huon, there's no flight nurse on board so Dr Hawkins must attend with you. Brendan's ETA is three minutes. Over.'

His stomach churned. He had no choice. Without a flight nurse his hands were tied. Bronte Hawkins would have to come.

Well, she could have her one emergency run out of Muttawindi, just so she could see for herself the sort of work she'd be expected to do. The sort of work she was not physically capable of at the moment. It might just make her see sense. Then she, with her slate-grey eyes and lush mouth, would head south and he'd find himself another doctor.

But right now she looked like hell and he didn't need a sick doctor as well as a patient. He grabbed an unopened bag of jellybeans from his desk. He always had a stash for his young patients. 'Catch, Bronte.' He tossed the bag at her. 'Get some sugar into you, you're going to need it.'

The King Air's engines sounded. 'Let's go.' He ushered her out the door, back into the heat.

Fifteen minutes later Brendan's voice came through his headset. 'ETA ten minutes.'

Huon passed Bronte an intravenous set. 'Set this up, please, we're going to need a couple of lines.'

He checked the equipment. Burns cases were always unpredictable and he wanted everything organised. They'd have enough concerns with an unstable patient without equipment problems.

He glanced up to see Bronte efficiently priming two IV lines. The paleness of her face made her grey eyes seem even larger. She'd pulled her long chestnut hair back with a standard-issue rubber band, which made her look about sixteen. She had an aura of fragility that tugged at him.

He swallowed against the feeling. He didn't want his emotions tugged. He'd locked them down when Ellen had died and he didn't want them waking up now. Not ever. There was too much risk of pain down that road.

As the plane circled Gaadunga's airstrip, Bronte pointed to a ute tearing along the strip, a plume of dust raised behind it. 'What's he doing?'

''Roo run.'

'Pardon?'

'They scare off any kangaroos with the noise of the ute. We don't want to crash into a 'roo when we land.'

'Oh...right.' Her expression was a classic city-girl look.

The intercom crackled. 'Prepare to land, Huon.'

'Thanks, Brendan.' He nodded at Bronte as she buckled the harness correctly. Often it took a few tries before new staff managed it.

The landing on the baked dirt strip was straightforward with minimal bumps. Huon grabbed the resuscitation equipment and medical kits, which from the outside looked like fishing-tackle boxes. He passed one to Bronte.

They exited the plane into a wall of heat and a squad of flies.

Huon recognised Lachlan Phillips, the station manager, as he ran over to them, looking extremely worried.

'Doc, thank goodness. He's pretty bad.' He pointed to the very dusty Holden utility. 'I've got the ute.'

'Thanks, Lachlan.' Huon started to jog over to the ute. 'This is Dr Bronte Hawkins.'

Lachlan acknowledged Bronte with a bushman's silent nod of his head. He lent forward and took the resuscitation box from her. 'I'll grab that for you.'

'No, really, I'm fine,' Bronte protested.

'Pass it over, you'll run faster without it.'

She shrugged her shoulders as if in the presence of a foreign culture and handed over the large box. 'Thanks, Lachlan.'

The track down to the homestead had more potholes than road and Huon was worried how Bronte would cope with the rough track.

It was just another reminder that having her stay wouldn't work. He needed to worry about his patients, not his colleague. 'Hold on to the overhead handle so you don't bounce around too much.'

Bronte nodded and surreptitiously shoved several jellybeans into her mouth.

He turned away and looked at Lachlan. His brow was creased in concentration as he negotiated the track.

'So what happened, Lachlan?'

'Ben was priming the pump with diesel and, I dunno, there must have been a spark. The whole thing went up in a fireball.' His voice went very quiet. 'He's burned pretty bad.'

'What first-aid did he get?' Bronte leaned forward.

'We put him in the bath for a bit until he started to shiver and now he's on a bed with clean linen.'

'Well done. Cooling down a burn victim is the best thing you can do.' She gave Lachlan a warm, reassuring smile.

It was the first smile Huon had seen on her face since he'd met her. It totally changed her, lit her up, and the permanent slightly worried frown she wore disappeared.

His breath shuddered into his lungs. That smile could warm the protective ice he'd nurtured around his heart since Ellen's death.

The ute pulled up and they ran into the house. Ben, the jackaroo, lay on a bed surrounded by three very worried people.

'Come on, you lot, move out and give the docs some space.' Lachlan's voice echoed around the room.

'Hey, Ben.' Huon infused some lightness into his voice, knowing how scared Ben would be. 'How's it going?'

'I've been better, Doc.' The young man grimaced.

Miraculously his face was clear of any burns but his arms and torso were in a bad way.

'Pulse one hundred and twenty, resps forty.' Bronte pulled the stethoscope out of her ears.

He was reluctantly impressed. Bronte hadn't waited for him—she'd proactively taken a set of observations.

She pulled out the oxygen and unravelled the mask and green tubing. 'Ben, I'm Bronte and along with Huon we're going to get you stable and safely back to Broken Hill.' She touched Ben's cheek. 'I'm going to put this mask on you to help your breathing.'

Ben nodded and bit his lip. 'Can't feel me arms.'

Huon wanted to bite his own lip. Ben's black and yellow arms meant full-thickness burns. 'The burns on your arms are pretty deep, mate, which is why you can't feel them. We're going to put two drips into your legs so we can get some fluid into you. Your body will be going into shock.'

The station workers had done a good job of cutting off his clothing. Huon continued to examine Ben, using the rule of nines to work out what percentage burns he had sustained. With both of Ben's arms burned and his chest, he estimated he had burns to about thirty-six per cent of his body.

Bronte wrapped the blood-pressure cuff around Ben's leg to get a reading. 'Huon.'

The tone in her voice made him look up. A deep furrow marked her brow.

'BP is eighty-five on fifty.'

'Right, he needs fluids, *now.*' He opened up the medical bag and withdrew two large-bore cannulae. 'You put the drip in the left leg and I'll do the right.'

He rested his hand on Ben's leg. 'Ben, this is going to sting a bit.'

'Doc…it can't…hurt more…than my…chest.' Ben squeezed the words out.

Huon almost flinched for the young man. 'As soon as we get the drips in, we can give you something for the pain.'

Ben moved his head slightly as if a nod was too difficult. He closed his eyes, blocking out anything that would tax his preciously needed energy.

Bronte wrapped the tourniquet around Ben's calf and, using her fingers, deftly probed for a vein. 'Got one.'

Huon opened the cannula packet for her. She took it, flicked off the plastic covering and cleanly inserted the silver needle into the vein.

'Well done.' He passed her the IV tubing and some tape. 'Open it up full tilt, we need to hydrate him stat.'

'Litre of saline and a litre of Hartmann's.' Her firm voice stated a fact rather than asked a question. Her actions so far demonstrated a doctor confident in her craft.

'Good idea. I'll put the Hartmann's up on my line.' He swabbed the other leg ready to insert the drip.

Bronte returned the favour of opening the packet and the drip went in quickly.

He was struck by how they anticipated each other. But this one example of her work wasn't enough to change his mind. He didn't need a pregnant doctor to worry about on top of all his other commitments.

'Thank goodness Ben's legs were spared or getting a drip into him would have been a nightmare,' he murmured to Bronte, taking advantage of the rare opportunity to share his thoughts with a colleague.

'Absolutely. But I'm worried about his breathing. Before we give him pethidine I'll recheck for stridor.'

He nodded. 'He could have an inhalation burn. Although the men did the right thing with the bath, I think he's hypothermic. We need to warm him up, but first let's get these burns covered.'

'Right. I'll check his air entry and you cover the burns?' She raised her brows as if requesting confirmation.

She'd worked calmly and solidly since arriving, working through the ABC of triage, not waiting for instructions like many new associates did. Her actions belied the fact that she felt unwell. He had to give her that.

Huon passed her the stethoscope. 'Go for it.'

He started to cover the burns with sterile non-stick dressings. He worked quickly, wanting to wrap Ben up in the space blanket as soon as possible. The medical mantra for burns sounded in his head—Airway, Breathing, Circulation, Disability and Exposure.

Bronte touched his arm and drew him aside. 'He's got a stridor that's getting worse. If we give him peth, that will compromise his breathing. But we can't have him in pain either, because that will exacerbate his shock.'

'Let's intubate him. I want him out of here a.s.a.p., but we need him stable for the flight. He needs to go to Adelaide, which is over an hour away.'

'So we tube him and sedate him. What about his hands?'

Bronte's question echoed Huon's own thoughts. The badly burnt, oedematous hands meant Ben's circulation could be impaired. He didn't need gangrene on top of burns.

'We'll watch them and do a fasciotomy if we need to.' Huon picked up the laryngoscope, the metal cool in his hands. 'How long since you last tubed a patient?'

'About a month ago.' Bronte met his gaze, her eyes almost saying, *Throw what you like at me, I'll catch it.*

'Right, then.' He passed over the laryngoscope. 'You're up and I'll assist.' He wanted to see how she handled the tricky procedure.

Bronte took in a deep breath, accepted the proffered equipment and walked over to Ben. Huon had to hand it to her. The only emotions being expressed were for their patient. Professional and empathetic.

Bronte touched Ben's cheek and his eyes fluttered open. 'Ben, remember when I told you we might need to put a tube in your throat to help you breathe?'

'Yeah, Doc, I do. Is it time?' His voice came out in a hoarse whisper.

'Yes, Ben, it's time.' She bit her lip at the stoic bushman's attitude.

Huon injected some pethidine into the IV bung. A minute later, Bronte inserted the 'scope, located the vocal cords and slid the number eight endotracheal tube down Ben's throat. She deftly attached the air-viva and began to squeeze the bag, providing the jackaroo with much-needed oxygen and bypassing his constricted trachea. She hadn't hesitated for a moment. She was completely up to speed with emergency medicine.

'Lachlan.' Huon called out for the station manager. 'Get Brendan to bring in the stretcher, we're almost ready.'

'What about catheterisation?' Bronte asked.

He smiled. This woman had all bases covered and pre-empted his thoughts. 'That's why we're almost ready. It's my last job before we evacuate.'

He quickly inserted the urinary catheter into the semi-conscious Ben. Brendan assisted with the space blanket and they soon had Ben loaded onto the back of the ute, the stretcher wedged into place.

Huon put his hand on Bronte's shoulder. He had to hand it to her—she'd been working like a Trojan for the last hour. But he'd noticed the surreptitious intake of jellybeans. She needed a break. 'This will be a rough trip. I'll take over the bagging.'

She threw him a scalding look, her grey eyes flashing like glinting steel. 'I intubated him and I'm staying with him.'

'Fine.' Frustration threaded through the single word. Hell, he'd only been trying to help. He banged on the cab of the ute. 'Lachlan, let's get moving.'

'Right, Doc.' The ute moved forward, slowly negotiating the rutted road.

Huon breathed a sigh of relief when they arrived at the King Air. With skill born from years of practice, he and Brendan quickly loaded Ben safely into the plane, strapped him in securely and connected him to the ECG machine. Two minutes later they were airborne.

With Bronte caring for Ben, Huon entered the cockpit and radioed Flinders Medical Centre. He spoke with the burns registrar, giving a detailed history so the patient hand-over at the airport would be swift. Ben needed to be in Intensive Care with minimal delay.

He returned to the cabin and looked at Bronte. Her stethoscope framed her elfin face, and lines of exhaustion had etched themselves around her eyes.

Disappointment marched through him. This time Head Office had got it right. She was a real doctor, unlike 'Dr Disaster'. She was talented, good at her job and they worked well together. But already she looked dead on her feet. How would she be able to handle the workload Muttawindi demanded?

She leaned over Ben, adjusting his oxygen mask. Her skirt stretched tautly over her behind, outlining a delicious curve. His palm itched to touch it, his blood heating at the thought.

'How is he?' Focussing on their patient would surely make this unwanted desire go away.

'Stable.' Her grey eyes sought his. 'For now.'

He knew exactly what she meant. Burn victims could change in a heartbeat. Hell, it was good having a colleague to share those concerns.

'You worked well today.'

She looked at him incredulously, her eyes glinting. 'I'm a doctor. I did what I know.'

He sighed with frustration. 'Your competence isn't the issue. Muttawindi's needs and your pregnancy are the issues.'

'No, your stubbornness is the issue. I have a contract offering me a permanent position. Muttawindi needs another doctor, which is why I'm here.'

'Muttawindi needs a doctor who can cope with a punishing workload.'

Her eyes narrowed. 'I can do that. I've always worked long hours, they're not a problem to me.'

He sighed. 'Long hours might not have been a problem to you last month but right now you're grey with fatigue, you can't handle a day's travelling without vomiting and you've been mainlining jellybeans since we left the base.'

He ran his hands through his hair. 'How the hell will you cope? There's no one here to pick up the slack, unlike that big city hospital you've come from. And surely you'll want to be close to your family now you're pregnant.'

A slight tremor moved across her body but she remained silent, busying herself with checking Ben's observations. She recorded them on the chart.

Strained silence stretched between them but he knew the argument wasn't over. He could swear he could hear the cogs of her brain turning.

Suddenly, she reached into the medical kit and pulled out a mirror. She pushed it into his hand, her touch hot on his skin. 'Take a look at yourself. Those dark rings under your eyes speak volumes. You need a doctor to relieve some of your workload.'

Her voice was edged with steel. 'If you send me home now, you have no doctor. How long will it take you to get a replacement? Sounds like you've waited a long time already. I'm here, I'm ready to work and my contract's signed. You really can't stop me.'

Aggravation surged inside him and he ran his hand through his hair. Muttawindi deserved a good doctor and Bronte was that. But he needed real help himself. Not just a doctor for a few months.

He loved his job but being on call twenty-four hours a day, seven days a week was wearing him out. Life wasn't meant to be this hard. He'd lost Ellen. He at least deserved a break at getting work under control.

He had to see her make sense, make her see this wouldn't work. 'You realise you won't qualify for maternity leave?'

She nodded and bit her lip. 'I know that but I can promise you six months, perhaps a bit longer, and I can return to work when the baby is three months old.' She took in a deep breath, her small breasts straining against her crushed white blouse. 'Look, I didn't expect to be pregnant but you sending me away makes no sense. You need me.'

'Why are you so hell bent on staying?'

'Why are you so hell bent on sending me away?' Her gaze locked with his.

Because your smile does dangerous things to my heart.

Suddenly fatigue rocked through him. He was tired of doing this job on his own without the support of a colleague.

Bronte was here. Medically she knew her stuff. And the people of the district deserved the care of two doctors, no matter how short the time, no matter how disappointed they would be that yet another doctor wasn't staying for good.

He was over a barrel. She would have to stay even though it was a far from perfect situation. 'I can invoke the trial period clause.'

Her eye's widened in surprise. 'What's that?'

'Four weeks. You get to stay four weeks while I find a replacement.'

'Four weeks?' Bronte's tongue darted nervously along her lips, moistening them.

A deep longing crashed through him, heating his blood as he imagined her lips pressed against his own. He slammed the image out of his mind. 'It's my best offer.'

Bronte tossed her head defiantly. 'I'll be here longer than that.'

And the idea that she might terrified him.

CHAPTER THREE

BRONTE SAT ON the narrow, single bed in the sparsely decorated room at the Muttawindi pub. Flies and moths buzzed around the naked globe attracted to the feeble yellow light it emitted. Noise from the bar drifted up through the open window, which let in more insects than it did cool night air.

The red light from the cheap black digital clock read 11:00 p.m. Her first day in Muttawindi and she'd spent most of it traversing half of Australia. Ben was now safely in Adelaide. She and Huon had returned to Muttawindi only half an hour ago. With her belongings still in transit from Melbourne, Huon had insisted she stay at the pub.

The heat pressed in on her, making each breath an effort. She lay down, exhaustion permeating every fibre of her being. A slow trickle of tears slowly cooled her hot cheeks.

Pregnant.

She couldn't believe she was pregnant. Coming to Muttawindi was supposed to have been her new start. A time to put her past mistakes behind her, forget the pain of Damien, and to come out of the shadow of her sister. Establish herself as her own person. A baby had never been part of the plan.

Thoughts of babies had always been a long way in the future, coupled with the idea of a loving husband. What a joke that was. The conniving, duplicitous, horrible, biological father of this baby didn't know the meaning of love. He only knew self-interest.

The overhead fan turned slowly, moving the hot air across her skin. She rubbed her hand along her lower belly wondering at the life that existed there, growing daily.

One misguided mistake...

Now a new life was taking place.

She tried to get her head around that idea. She sniffed and shook her head against the pillow. Breathing slowly, she let her mind focus.

A baby would change her life. Well, she'd wanted change. Now she had it. More than she'd thought but change nonetheless.

Her baby.

Suddenly she knew her mistake had nothing to do with this baby. Her baby was innocent in all of this ugliness. It was a pure entity. One, she suddenly realised, she wanted. Desperately.

She'd come to Muttawindi to start again and to belong to a community. The baby, although unexpected, was an extension of that plan. Perhaps the baby would help? Babies crossed barriers that adults often couldn't. She'd always noticed how people spoke to pregnant women and new mothers, even if they didn't know them.

New place, new start, new life.

Going home to Melbourne jobless and pregnant wasn't an option. Her parents had been furious when she'd announced she was heading to the outback. They'd expected her to become part of Stephanie's entourage now she was touring as a sell-out singer.

Bronte blew her nose. She would *not* fail at her first real step away from her family's unrealistic expectations.

She had four weeks to prove to Huon she could combine pregnancy and working for the flying doctors of Muttawindi. Four weeks to show him and the town she belonged, that she was committed and needed. Then Huon would have no choice but to keep her.

She rubbed her tummy again. 'Hey, baby, let's show Huon how determined we can be.'

'Morning, Marg.' Huon walked into the dining room of the Muttawindi Pub. 'Can you rustle up some fruit, yoghurt and toast, please?'

'Right-oh, love. But it's not like you to pass up my bacon and eggs.' The publican gave him a rueful look.

Huon laughed. 'It's not for me, it's for Dr Hawkins. I'll have your full catastrophe breakfast, seeing my coronary arteries have had a week to recover from your yummy bacon.'

'That's my boy. I'll serve it outside. 'Might as well eat it there before the heat drives you inside for the rest of the day.' She disappeared into the kitchen.

Huon looked around at the familiar paintings and sporting teams' trophies. He'd been coming in to see Marg since he'd been a confused and troubled fourteen-year-old, newly arrived in Muttawindi. Marg's kitchen was a favourite haunt.

Comfort food.

Even though Claire and Ron, his Muttawindi foster-parents, had been wonderful to him, visiting Marg had been something he'd treasured. Marg was like the auntie he'd never had. An adult he could talk to about all sorts of stuff. The stuff you didn't tell your foster-parents.

He loved her and he loved this town.

When Ellen had died, the town had been the only thing that had got him through that dark year of first experiences without her loving presence. He pushed the thought away.

Today he'd come to collect Bronte. He'd telephoned her ten minutes ago and a sleepy voice had answered. He sighed inwardly. She'd still be exhausted from yesterday.

Hell, he was. He hadn't slept much last night. His dreams had been filled with a pale face, chestnut hair and eyes that could change colour from grey to deep sapphire blue.

He'd given up trying to sleep. At five a.m. he'd been out for a stint on his road bike, pumping his pedals around, pushing the images of Bronte Hawkins out of his mind.

Dr Hawkins was a business associate. A very *short-term*, business associate. He had no plans to get to know her.

Getting involved with any woman, let alone a pregnant woman, wasn't on his agenda. He'd loved once and lost. He never intended to live through that nightmare again.

Besides, Muttawindi needed him, they depended on him. He'd let them down badly, allowing 'Dr Disaster' to practice. His gut churned at the havoc one crazy person had wrought on the town. He hated talking about it. He just wanted to put it behind him but the court case was still pending, waiting to bring the horror back in vivid memories.

He would never let this town down again. Nothing would distract him from that. Not even a pair of fine grey eyes.

Bronte pushed the pub's dining-room door open. She saw Huon staring into a cabinet of sporting trophies, his sun-streaked blond hair gleaming in a shaft of light.

Her stomach flipped. Surely that was the baby and the nausea. She could *not* be attracted to this man.

Her naïvety had led her to total disaster with Damien and she was never going down that road again. She'd had enough pain and humiliation to last her a lifetime.

Besides, she had a baby to consider and hadn't she learned in lectures at uni that men were not attracted to women who were pregnant with another man's child?

She tossed her head and stood up a bit straighter. She would not allow herself to be sidetracked by a crazy adolescent lust thing or whatever it was she had. She was a grown woman and grown women used common sense and ignored shimmering sensations that heated their blood for men they hardly knew. Damien had at least taught her that.

No, she needed to concentrate on her baby and her job.

She gave her cheeks a quick rub, wishing she'd thought to put on some blusher. She ran her hands down her very crushed blouse and linen shorts, legacy of having been in a suitcase for two days. *Honestly, Bronte, you could take more pride in your appearance.* She stomped on her mother's voice.

Somehow she never really felt comfortable in her clothes and had decided long ago that clothes were just a necessary item to keep warm. Or, in Muttawindi's case, keep cool. She sighed as she tugged at her blouse, which seemed to hang off her angular body.

How she'd coveted Stephanie's curves when she'd been a teenager. She gave an ironic laugh. In a few months' time she'd have those curves but not quite the way her teenage self had imagined.

She took in a deep, steadying breath. 'Good morning, Huon.'

He turned and smiled, dimples appearing in his cheeks for the briefest of moments.

Bronte bit her lip against the wave of heat his smile sent through her.

'Morning, Bronte.' His voice was brisk and businesslike. 'I took a punt you wouldn't want a cooked breakfast, so Marg's bringing out fruit and toast.'

She gave him a wry smile. 'Gosh, how did you know?' The thought of anything else made her stomach heave.

'Lucky guess.' He opened the door to the outside dining area and ushered her through in front of him. The fresh scent of soap and peppermint tingled against her nostrils. She caught herself breathing in deeper, enjoying the crispness of his aftershave.

Concentrate!

She sat down, put a serviette on her knee and took a delicate nibble from the toast, willing her reluctant stomach to accept it. She deliberately avoided looking at Huon's eggs and bacon.

'So I'm up for a full day at the clinic.' She matched his businesslike tone.

'Given your state of health, I think a half-day would be plenty.'

She looked straight back at him, forcing herself to concentrate on her words and not his amazing blue eyes. 'Yesterday you told me that Muttawindi needs a doctor who can handle a punishing workload. I plan to prove that I can.'

His hands stilled on his knife and fork, and the yolk of the egg trailed yellow across the plate. 'Bronte, when I said those words I was angry. You'd just arrived, had unexpectedly vomited and I was still reeling from the fact you were pregnant.' He sighed. 'When we get unexpected news, we're not always rational. I'm sorry. I don't expect you to kill yourself on the job.'

'I don't plan to. But I intend to pull my weight like any other doctor. After all, this baby will have to get used to his mother working, so it can start now.' Her voice cracked and she gulped down some tea. A baby. The thought still overwhelmed her. She gripped the mug, needing to stay in control. Huon must not see how vulnerable she really felt.

'Do you need some time off to sort out things with the father of the baby?' His air of concern almost undid her.

'No!' The vehemence behind the word ricocheted around the garden courtyard.

His lips curved upwards. 'Right, well, I can see you're vacillating on that point.'

She forced a half-smile. 'Sorry, that was a bit of an overreaction. The father and I...it was all a mistake.'

His face became serious. 'You're still in shock right now but the time will come when you'll need to talk to him. When you do, let me know, and we'll arrange for you to have a couple of days' leave.'

He reached over and for the briefest moment his fingers touched her hand. Then almost as quickly he pulled his hand back, as if he'd been scalded. He plunged his fork into his bacon.

The featherlike caress of his fingers stayed on her skin, warming her. *Remember his impeccable manners.* Of course, Huon's good manners had driven him to show some sympathy. His touch hadn't meant anything more than that.

She pulled herself together. 'Thank you, I'll keep that in mind.'

'And when you need to talk about the pregnancy, I'm a good listener.' Concern swirled in his eyes with an overshadowing of hesitancy. It was as if he thought he should offer to be a confidant but he didn't really want her to take him up on the offer.

She dragged in a fortifying breath. 'There's really nothing to talk about. I made a mistake, I'm pregnant, end of story.' She tried to sound brisk, matter-of-fact. Right now she couldn't trust herself to talk about the pregnancy, it was all too raw. And somehow he knew that.

Huon stood up. 'I'll just pay for breakfast.'

Bronte reached for her purse. 'Please, I'll pay for my own breakfast.' She didn't want to be beholden to him.

His eyes twinkled. 'Actually it's the clinic who's paying. All part of expenses for settling in new staff.'

Heat flooded her face. God, how stupid could she be? Of course he wouldn't be buying her breakfast. He was her boss. Would only ever be her boss. 'Oh, right, thanks...'

She turned and walked outside towards the four-wheel drive. She was such a social klutz. *He wasn't Damien.* She had to remember that. Remember that he had no ulterior motive and no reason to charm her. His only need was for a doctor.

Although she worried about convincing Huon, she felt confident of winning over the locals. She loved being a doctor and she knew she was good at her job. Her peer reviews were always glowing. It was only her family who failed to recognise her skills.

They hadn't been very enthusiastic when she'd entered medicine. They'd never really accepted that their two daughters were so very different with different talents and interests. Stephanie had succeeded in the celebrity culture, first as a model and now as a singer.

Her parents' focus had always been Steph, first as doting parents and now as her managers. Bronte had accepted long ago that her own achievements would never be valued in the same way.

But she took great pleasure in the knowledge that her colleagues valued her. She was an excellent doctor and patients found her easy to talk to. She knew she'd be just fine in Muttawindi.

She looked along the street. The morning sun was reflecting a fiery orange off the decorative iron verandas, emphasising the glory of the Victorian buildings.

The grand buildings left standing in the main street were testament to the wealth that had once flowed out of the soil. This was going to be her main street now. Bronte took in a deep breath, breathing in the scent of her new home.

Huon's long stride sounded behind her. 'Right to go?'

She ignored the frisson of sensation that skittered across her skin at the sound of his deep voice. Instead she nodded and swung up into the vehicle.

Watching him vigorously move the gear lever into reverse, she realised that Huon Morrison did most things with intensity and single-mindedness.

He reversed out onto the road. 'We have assigned you a vehicle for use while you're here, but it won't be arriving for a few days.' His voice was businesslike and brisk. 'For the next couple of days you'll be with me, observing, and you won't need a car. I'll give you a couple of days before I throw you in at the deep end.' He gave her a grin.

A grin that exposed deep dimples in his rugged cheeks. Dimples that took away the worn and tired look that seemed so much a part of him. Dimples that sent a river of tingling through her.

But she couldn't focus on his dimples.

She focussed on his words.

Huon continued. 'Everyone thinks the flying doctors' service is for medical emergencies and we do handle those, but most of our work is clinic based. As a sub-branch of the Broken Hill base we're an important link in servicing the people who live in the six hundred and forty thousand square kilometres that make up our area.'

Bronte had trouble imagining such vast distances.

Huon looked at her and laughed. 'I know, it's hard to visualise, especially when you've grown up in the city. But it was John Flynn's vision to put a "mantle of safety" across Australia. And between the twenty-one bases across Australia, we're doing it. No Australian is more than ninety minutes away from medical help.'

'That's something to be really proud of.' The fact she was now part of this organisation, and hopefully part of Muttawindi, gave her immense satisfaction.

'It is. But remote communities are still under-serviced compared with their city counterparts. Muttawindi only has a doctor now because of the gas fields that have opened up to the north. Before that, there was only a twice-weekly clinic.'

Huon turned into the clinic car park and pulled on the handbrake. 'Here we are.' His blue eyes had an intense, questioning look. 'I'm assuming your pregnancy is not something you want to announce just yet. Your secret's safe with me.'

'Thanks.' Her throat tightened. His consideration threatened to undo her.

Huon opened the door. 'Let me know if you get too tired, OK?'

His genuine concern washed up against her, battering her resolve to keep all her feelings about the pregnancy to herself. She was petrified that once she opened up she'd fall to pieces and reinforce everything he thought about her working here and being pregnant.

She forced a smile. 'I'll be fine. I might demolish your dry biscuit and jellybean supply, but I'll be fine.'

Excitement at starting her job bubbled inside her. Combined with her nausea, it felt quite strange. She followed Huon into the building.

An older woman in her fifties crossed the waiting room, looking straight at Huon, her smile of loving tenderness for him alone.

Bronte's heart gave a lurch. She wondered what it would be like to be loved like that.

The woman spoke. 'Huon, Dad needs you to ring him before eleven this morning. He needs to know what size tubes you need for your new bike.'

Bronte realised with a start that this woman in a nurse's uniform was Huon's mother.

Huon grinned and shook his head. 'I told him to write it down. Right-oh, I'll give him a call.' He paused for a moment and then indicated Bronte with an outstretched arm. 'Claire, I'd like you to meet Bronte Hawkins. Bronte, Claire is the practice nurse and my mother.'

Claire gave her a welcoming smile. 'Sorry about the bike-tyre thing. We generally try to keep family stuff out of the office but my husband's off to Broken Hill today and, as you can see, he's a bit forgetful.' Claire seized Bronte's hand and pumped it hard. 'Welcome to Muttawindi. I'm so glad you're here. There's enough work in this district for three doctors.'

The warmth of Claire's welcome enveloped Bronte. 'Pleased to meet you, Claire. I've been pretty excited about coming out here, too.'

Claire beamed. 'That's wonderful because after last year we need a doctor who wants to be here. Outback life is very different from what you've been used to in Melbourne, isn't it, Huon?'

'And that's why Bronte's on a four-week trial. To see if she, Muttawindi and the workload all match up.' Huon picked up a pile of patient histories as if to say, *Subject closed.*

Claire's open and welcoming expression suddenly changed, and a frown creased her forehead.

Bronte wanted to stamp her foot and yell, *It was his idea, not mine.*

'Well, let's get started, then.' Claire swept her hand around the half-empty waiting room. 'I was expecting more people to have come in today to meet you, but after yesterday's emergency greeting I guess you'll be happy with a quiet day.'

Claire turned to Huon. 'You take Bronte to the examination room, and I'll send the first patient down to you.' She turned back to Bronte. 'I'll give you a detailed orientation of the clinic later. Right now you can observe and get a feel for the place.'

Bronte had a feeling Huon was well organised by Claire and wondered how he handled working so closely with his mother. She turned to follow him but the older woman put her hand on Bronte's to detain her.

Claire dropped her voice. 'He works too hard. Even as a child he was hard on himself. Since Ellen died he's been driving himself into the ground. Huon needs a doctor who is committed to stay. The town needs a doctor committed to staying. They've had a rough ride recently.'

Brown eyes filled with the protective look only a mother could have bored into Bronte's face. 'This four-week trial was his idea, wasn't it? Silly boy, he's still whipping himself about...' She paused for a moment, reconsidering her words. 'You *are* planning on staying, aren't you?'

Huon had obviously not said anything to Claire about her pregnancy. Could she use this to her advantage? She had precious few allies at this point. 'Yes, absolutely, I plan to stay.' *Well, it wasn't a lie.*

'Good, because I'm not sure how much longer he can continue with his workload and still stay standing.' Claire had the look of a lioness defending a cub. 'So I'll be holding you to that promise.'

Bronte wondered again at the love Claire had for her son. She couldn't imagine her own parents protecting her in that way. She thought of the baby growing inside her and realised that she wanted to shield it from harm, like Claire wanted to shield Huon from exhaustion. 'I'll keep my promise.'

'Thank you.' Claire's looked softened. 'Off you go, then, and start your day.'

Bronte had the distinct impression of having been dismissed by the mother superior. Claire's words played around in her head. *Since Ellen died.* Who was Ellen? A patient, a child, a lover? Huon didn't wear a wedding ring. Curiosity clawed at her. She was desperate to know but knew she really couldn't ask. Not yet anyway.

Jack, the first patient of the morning, arrived in the consulting room a moment after Bronte. He looked to be in his eighties with a weather-beaten face. His gnarled hands rotated a worn Akubra hat by the brim.

He sat on the exam couch and gave Bronte a long, hard, scrutinising look. 'Does the girlie have to be here? She don't look old enough to be a doctor.' His gravelly voice rasped around the room.

'Dr Hawkins is a qualified doctor, Jack.' Huon's tone was all business.

'You sure this time, are you?' The old man's rheumy eyes sparked at Huon. He then turned their gaze onto Bronte. 'From the city, are ya?'

Bronte could feel the waves of his animosity crashing into her. Honesty was the only way to play this. She smiled. 'Yes, I am, Jack. City girl, born and bred.'

'The last three doctors were from the city. City people never last out here.' Jack spoke with the finality of a man who had seen a lot of life.

Bronte opened her mouth to speak, to tell him she was going to be the exception to the rule, but he turned away from her and back to Huon, as if dismissing her presence.

'I came about me flu injection. Seeing you threatened to jab me at the pub, I thought I better head down here.'

'Good to see you're showing some sense. You don't want to spend this winter in hospital, like last year.' Huon gave him a knowing look. 'As well as the flu injection, you'll need to have the pneumococcal pneumonia vaccine.'

Jack grunted.

'I'll take that as a yes. Roll up your sleeve.'

Huon took Jack's blood pressure and then organised and administered the two injections.

Jack stood up, rubbing his arm. 'Right, then. I'll be off.' He walked from the room without looking at Bronte.

Bronte felt like she'd been hit by a piece of four by two. Jack had blatantly ignored her. Not a sign of welcome had crossed his face. It was as if he didn't want her there at all. So much for fitting in.

Her chest tightened. She tried to fight the rising tide of anxiety. This wasn't the best start and the four-week clock was counting down.

CHAPTER FOUR

BRONTE SIGHED, PUT three black jellybeans into her mouth and chased them down with some ginger tea. They'd just returned from an early clinic run at the gas fields and she was grabbing a quick five-minute break.

It was hard to believe her first week in Muttawindi was over. How could seven days seem like a month? Nausea plagued her and some days she felt like she was wading through mud as fatigue clung to her.

She was living on a diet of dry biscuits and had dropped so much weight that her work skirts and blouses hung off her. They were less flattering than usual and she knew she looked like a very bony scarecrow.

It's hard to believe Stephanie's your sister. It's like comparing a swan to a plucked chicken. Damien's sarcastic words skated across her mind, trying to take hold, trying to bulldoze the emotional fences she'd erected against him.

She pulled in a deep breath, banishing his voice, and sipped at her tea. Ginger helped control the nausea and she'd bought out the small supermarket's supply of ginger beer and ginger tea. The young cashier had looked at her as if she had two heads. Buying condoms would have drawn less attention.

Her hopes of winning over the people of Muttawindi in a few days had turned to dust. Although they seemed friendly enough when she met them out in the street, it didn't seem to transfer across into the clinic. She'd imagined a steady stream of patients, especially women, knocking at her door, seeking her medical services. But that hadn't eventuated.

'Doctors! I've got a frantic mother on the line,' Claire's worried voice called out.

'Come on.' Huon stuck his head through the door and beckoned Bronte towards the communications room. 'You can take this call. It'll be good practice for you, and I can see how you handle a remote consultation.' He gave her a reassuring smile. 'Just pretend I'm not here and you'll be fine.'

Bronte followed, her stomach churning. She needed to get runs on the board so that the people in town would start to trust her. So Huon had no reason at all to send her away at the end of her four-week trial.

When she saw the array of electronics in the room her nerves stretched so taut they almost snapped. Claire's brief explanation of all the buttons earlier in the week fled her mind.

Huon gestured to a chair in front of a computer terminal and other electrical equipment. 'Sit down and I'll switch the phone over so you can use the microphone.'

She sat down harder than she'd intended. The office-chair wheels skated out behind her, and she gripped the desk to steady herself from landing on the floor. *Great start.*

Claire stuck her head around the door. 'It's Jenny Henderson. I'll bring in the history in a moment.'

'Thanks, Claire.' Huon slid over the remote station medicine chest's list of contents, a notepad and a pen. Then he flicked a couple of switches on the console. 'You're on.'

Bronte gripped the microphone. Apprehension pooled in her belly. 'Dr Bronte Hawkins speaking. What's the problem, Mrs Henderson?'

'Where's Huon?' The woman's voice rose in agitation. 'I need to speak to Huon.'

Bronte squared her shoulders. 'I can help you, Mrs. Henderson.'

'No...I trust Huon.'

How could she be part of this community if the people wouldn't trust her? Wouldn't let her help them, even talk to them?

Huon pulled the microphone towards him. 'Jenny, it's Huon. Dr Hawkins is going to do this call.'

'But you're supervising her, right?' Jenny's panic played down the line.

The pointed words hit Bronte in the chest. She pushed them down inside her. She was an experienced doctor, and an expectant mother. She needed this place to live and she would prove to this town that she could handle whatever they threw at her, one case at a time.

She took in a deep breath. 'Mrs Henderson, I want to help. Please, tell me what the problem is.'

'My son Mark's been playing out in the shed. Now he's sounding a bit wheezy.' The anxiety of the woman's voice came down the line.

'Is he asthmatic?'

'No.'

'Is anyone in the family asthmatic?'

'His father's got mild asthma but it's under control.'

She wrote down 'Family history' on her pad. 'Could he have been exposed to any chemicals in the shed?'

There was a moment's silence. 'Only fertiliser.'

'Was he playing in it?' Bronte's mind raced forward, trying to work out what was happening. Not having the patient in front of her involved a certain amount of second-guessing.

Huon sat next to her with his arms across his chest, his body language saying, *This is your call, I'm not really here.* She had to handle this on her own.

Prove to both Huon and Jenny Henderson she could do it.

Jenny's voice rose in horror. 'Oh, God, he must have been. His clothes have a lot of white stuff on them.'

Claire handed Bronte the Henderson medical history. Bronte nodded her thanks.

'OK, Mrs Henderson—Jenny—take off all his clothes now.' If the child was having a reaction to the fertiliser, they needed to get him away from the particles.

She could hear the woman talking to her son. She drummed her fingers on the desk as she waited. Jenny's fear radiated down the line and the remoteness of outback life came home hard to Bronte. 'I've done that.' Jenny's voice trembled. 'But he's getting worse and he's gulping for air.'

'Get the spacer from the medical chest. It is a large plastic thing and it is number...' Bronte checked the soon-to-be familiar list in front of her.

'Doctor, I know the spacer. Now what?'

'Pick up the salbutamol blue puffer, number 107 in tray B. Puff one dose into the spacer. Then get Mark to put the spacer to his mouth and take four breaths. Repeat this three times until he has had four doses of the blue puffer.'

Bronte heard the phone clatter down as the terrified mother carried out the instructions. Bronte wasn't sure if she should wait and see if the boy improved, or put out a standby call for a pick-up. That sort of decision came with experience, and right now she felt very inexperienced. 'Huon, do I put in a standby call for a pick-up?'

'If I wasn't here, what would you do?'

'I'd put in a standby call.'

'Right, then ask Claire to do it.'

'I heard that. I'll contact Broken Hill now.' Claire's efficient voice trailed off as she walked from the room.

'Thanks, Claire.' Bronte turned her attention back to her patient. 'Jenny, is Mark's breathing getting easier?'

'Not really.' The mother's anxiety thundered down the phone to Bronte.

'OK.' Bronte tried to make her voice calm and soothing. 'We need to wait four minutes from the last puff and then we assess.'

She checked down the medical chest content's list and found the number for adrenaline. Mark might need an injection if he didn't respond to the bronchodilator.

Leaning forward, she gripped the microphone. 'Jenny, is Mark able to take deeper breaths now?'

'No! He's getting worse. His chest isn't taking in much air at all and his lips are purple.' Her voice rose in panic. 'What do I do?'

Bronte took a deep breath. 'You need to give Mark an injection. He's having a severe allergic reaction and we need to reverse that. I'll guide you through it step by step. How much does Mark weigh?'

'Um…about…twenty-five kilograms.'

Bronte did a quick calculation in her head. It was vital the correct amount of adrenaline was given.

'Take out the ampoule number 99. It will be in your fridge. Check the label says adrenaline.'

Bronte heard a rustling noise then Jenny's voice came down the line again. 'Got it.'

'Well done. Now, take the syringe out of the packet. Then snap the glass top off the adrenaline ampoule.'

As Jenny carried out the tasks, Bronte found the silence of the phone unnerving. She clamped her lips firmly, almost sucking them into her mouth, so she didn't talk again until Jenny came back on the line. It was important not to overwhelm the already panicked mother.

Once again the isolation of the rural community struck her. It wasn't just the patients who were on their own, the doctors were alone, too. Bronte was used to being in a large teaching hospital with colleagues to consult. Medically she knew what to do, but it was always reassuring to run ideas past someone. Huon didn't have that luxury.

She took a quick glance at him but his face was impassive. Impassive but exhausted. No wonder he looked worn out. It wasn't just the physical workload but the mental strain of doing this job all on your own.

The lines of fatigue were carved in deep around his eyes. Had some of the lines been added by grief for Ellen, whoever she was?

Jenny's voice came back on the line, sounding steadier. 'I've opened the syringe.'

'Great. Now push the plunger all the way into the syringe and take the cap off the needle.' She paused a moment to allow Jenny time to complete the task.

'Put the needle into the adrenaline and draw up the fluid until it gets to the marking of almost four.'

Again she paused. 'Ready?'

'Yes.' Jenny's voice wavered.

'Then hold the syringe up with the needle pointing to the ceiling. Gently push the plunger until the top of the black tip is level with three.' Hell, was that clear enough? Explaining something that she did every day without thinking was a big challenge.

'Doctor, I've got the stuff in at three. Now what?' Fear mixed with a stoic resignation in Jenny's voice.

'Swab Mark's tummy with the alcohol swab.' She heard Jenny's sharp intake of breath. 'Jenny, you can do this. Just remember that skin is tough so be quick and firm and the needle will glide in.'

Bronte rubbed her eyes. She wished she was right there with Jenny. Wished she could actually see Mark, hear his air entry.

Huon dealt with stuff like this every day. So could she. So *would* she.

A minute passed. 'Jenny are you there?'

'Yes, Doctor. I've given the injection but he's still having trouble breathing.'

'It will take a couple of minutes to work. Now repeat the puffer-in-the-spacer again. And then come back to me.' She turned to Claire. 'Mark needs to come to Broken Hill.'

'I'll patch you through to Base.' Claire turned to the radio to contact Broken Hill.

Another minute passed. 'Jenny, how is he doing now?'

'Oh, Doctor, he's breathing more easily.' Jenny's voice broke. 'I was so scared but the blueness around his lips has faded.'

Bronte let out a breath she hadn't known she'd been holding. She'd done it. She'd got through her first remote emergency. 'Well done, Jenny. Keep up the puffs.'

'Thanks, Doctor, I will. Now can I talk to Huon?'

Bronte's bubble of happiness burst. 'Yes, certainly.'

Huon leaned over in front of her towards the microphone, his hair almost tickling her face.

Bronte breathed in his mint-clean, wholesome, no-nonsense scent, which pretty much described the doctor beside her. She had an urge to run her hand through Huon's wavy hair.

Oh, God, what was happening to her? She was pregnant by another man, in a town that didn't trust her as a doctor, and attracted to her boss who didn't think she was physically able to handle the job. What would the psychologists make of that?

She pushed her chair back, putting much-needed space between her and Huon, and listened to him talk to Jenny.

'There's a plane at Wirriea Station, Jenny. They'll swing by and collect Mark in about twenty minutes. Ring us back if you're worried about Mark between now and then.'

'Thanks, Huon.' Jenny hung up the phone.

Huon flicked off the microphone and turned to Bronte. 'You did well.' The deep resonance of his voice vibrated around her, making her heart skip. 'Handling a remote emergency can be scary stuff, especially when you don't have a colleague to bounce ideas off. And out here that is the rule rather than the exception.' His smile radiated understanding and empathy.

She looked straight into Huon's face, and tried hard not to let herself sink into those blue eyes that sparkled with shades of dark and light. 'But she didn't trust me.'

A slight frown creased his forehead. 'She got a surprise that it wasn't me, that's all.' Huon closed the medical folder in front of him. 'Come on, time for lunch.'

She followed him into the lunchroom feeling like a child that hadn't been heard. 'But it wasn't just Jenny Henderson. Jack didn't want to have anything to do with me either. Most of the patients I've seen this week have been disappointed I wasn't you. I thought country people were supposed to be friendly.' She heard her voice catch, and cursed herself for starting to breakdown in front of him.

Huon's face looked pensive and he ran his hand through his hair.

She remembered the last few times she'd seen him do that. It was when he didn't want to do or say something. 'So?' She prodded him for an answer.

'Bronte, this community's had a lot of doctors come through and stay for only a short time.'

'You're the one insisting on a four-week trial. I want to stay for longer.' Her voice rose in frustration. 'I don't plan to go.'

His eyes flickered with resignation. 'Look, when you took this job you weren't pregnant. I'm doing you a favour with the four-week trial so you know exactly what you're letting yourself in for workwise. Then you can make a truly informed decision.'

Frustration threaded through her. How did she get through to such a stubborn man that she'd made her decision already? She and the baby were committed to Muttawindi.

'How many doctors have been in Muttawindi in the last year?' She needed as much information as she could get to try and understand the town, understand their lack of trust.

'Four.'

'Four permanent position doctors have all left?' She tried to hide the incredulity from her voice, not able to believe the high figure. No wonder the town was slow to warm to her.

'Three were locums so they hadn't committed to stay.' He ran his hand through his hair in an agitated manner. 'The fourth one had to return to Sydney.'

His words came out harshly, surprising her with their intensity. But before she could comment, an awful thought thudded into her. 'Do the patients know I'm on a four-week trial?'

Huon looked affronted. 'No, of course not.'

'OK, so they're not biased against me because of that. So, how much time do you think it will take until they trust me?' She tried to keep the worry out of her voice.

'Word will be out soon on how you handled Ben's burns and how you treated Mark Henderson. The grapevine will start, but you can't rush it. Things take time.'

And that's what worried her. Time wasn't something she had a lot of.

Bronte found a note on her desk in Huon's barely legible scrawl. "Clinical meeting at twelve p.m., my office."

She glanced at her watch—it was almost noon.

The note surprised her. She'd had two weeks in Muttawindi and had worked out the routine of clinic life. But perhaps these meetings occurred on a monthly basis?

A clinical meeting usually meant case review. It seemed odd that he hadn't given her more warning or asked her to pull particular patient files to present.

She knocked on Huon's door and walked in. 'You wanted to see me?'

He looked up from his writing and smiled, his dimples briefly weaving their magic. 'I did. Close the door and grab a seat.' He moved a pile of medical journals from one of the chairs. 'My TBR pile.'

'Sorry?'

He grinned again. 'My to-be-read pile.'

She laughed to hide the swirl of heat that flooded her when he smiled, when his eyes sparkled a brighter blue. 'I've got one of those as well. They have a habit of multiplying when you turn your back.'

He casually leaned back in his chair. 'Have you read the latest clinic statement on antenatal care?'

She nodded. 'Yes, I did. I thought it covered all the pertinent points.'

'Great, so did I. So, let's get your blood tests organised.'

'What?' Surprise mixed with anxiety. What did this have to do with case review?

'You need to have your first official antenatal check-up. You weren't planning on doing it yourself, were you?' His gaze homed in on her face, reading her expression closely.

'No.' Defiance filled her and she met his gaze head-on. 'But with getting everything else organised I hadn't got around to arranging to go to Broken Hill.'

He gave a half-smile. 'Which is why I'm suggesting I take some blood and do the usual tests.'

Her anxiety took flight at everything involved in an antenatal check-up. 'I appreciate your concern but I'm your colleague, not your patient.'

He leaned forward, understanding dawning. 'I'm not talking a complete check-up, just the history, blood tests, BP and weight. Claire can help you with the rest.'

'Oh, right, of course...' Heat filled her face at his thoughtfulness, which she'd misunderstood again.

'The outback has its drawbacks and this is one of them. There's no other doctor for three hundred and fifty kilometres. As professionals we have to learn to compartmentalise our lives.' Kindness filled his voice. 'For fifteen minutes I have to be your doctor, not your boss, for the baby's sake.'

For the baby's sake. Of course he was right. She was being silly. She needed this check-up. It wasn't that she didn't trust *him*. She didn't trust herself. Her irrational attraction to Huon hadn't gone away like she'd hoped.

In the last week she'd found herself watching him, watching how the tendons in his hands moved when he examined a patient, how his eyes crinkled when he smiled, and how his biceps bulged when he assisted Brendan in loading a patient onto the plane.

And now she'd have to watch and feel his hands on her as he took blood. She dragged in a steadying breath.

Huon reached over, pulled out a history form and started going through the questions. 'What was the date of the start of your last normal menstrual cycle?

At least the first question was easy. 'December fifteenth.'

He spun the dial on the gestation calculator. 'September...'

'Twenty-first. I'm ten weeks.' She shrugged at his glance. 'I worked that out the first night.' He nodded in understanding. 'So, a spring baby. It's a good time of year to have a baby. He or she will be three months old before the summer heat kicks in.'

She gave a high-pitched laugh. 'Well, if you're going to have an unplanned pregnancy it should be at a convenient time, right?' She heard the quaver in her voice.

His empathetic look only made her feel worse.

'Any family history of significance?'

'Not on my side, no.'

He glanced at her, his eyes scanning her face. 'On the father's side?'

'I don't really know.' She bit her lip and swallowed. A wave of emotion rolled in on her, threatening to swamp her. For two weeks she'd avoided talking about the pregnancy. Avoided talking about Damien.

Tears pricked at the backs of her eyes. The doctor in her knew that holding on to grief and pain only made it worse, but she'd held on to it because she didn't want Huon to know how stupid and naïve she'd been.

She didn't want anything to damage her chances of staying in Muttawindi. She only wanted him to see the competent doctor, the professional who was on top of things and in control. She wanted him to realise she was the doctor he could rely on to work with him in Muttawindi for a long time.

So she'd said nothing, kept her own counsel.

But his gentle, caring approach had brought all her feelings rushing to the surface, and she couldn't hold them in any longer.

Telling him meant exposing herself to his scrutiny, risking everything. But despite what he might think of her, despite the danger he might not think her worthy of staying, she had to take the risk of telling him the whole sordid story. She couldn't hold on to it any longer.

Huon watched the colour drain from Bronte's face. She looked as fragile as a porcelain doll, as if one knock would shatter her.

He must have pushed her too hard this morning at the busy gas fields' clinic. Damn. Guilt trailed through him at scheduling this meeting at lunchtime. He might be able to keep going but Bronte needed to have regular meals.

He pulled over a platter of sandwiches Claire had made for them. 'You look really pale—eat a sandwich.' He passed the platter of food towards her. 'Tuna's good for the baby.' He gave her a wry smile.

She failed to meet his gaze.

The guilt dug in deeper.

Bronte constantly looked like she was going to faint. *That* was the reason he knew she needed to be reassigned to another base. She didn't have the stamina for Muttawindi. Right now she was putting on a brave front, almost ignoring the pregnancy. But sooner rather than later, reality would hit her. Hopefully by then he would have a replacement doctor and she would be back in Melbourne with the father of her baby and her family.

He watched her nibble her sandwich. She'd lost weight since she'd arrived. The only thing plump about her was her lips. And images of those lush lips on his skin haunted his dreams every night.

And *that* was the most important reason she had to leave Muttawindi. If she weren't here, she wouldn't invade his thoughts. Couldn't unsettle the solo life he'd made for himself since Ellen had died.

He tried to call up the image of Ellen's face, but the shadowy likeness, now indistinct, hovered for a moment then faded. He'd adored Ellen. She'd been his first love. Now he could hardly picture her.

His heart contracted in a familiar pain. The pain some days he thought he controlled. Death had stolen Ellen's life, and he'd accepted that. But now time had stolen her image. He hated that.

The quietness of Bronte's voice sliced into him, dragging him back to the present. 'I only knew the father of the baby for a few short weeks.' Tension emanated from rigid shoulders. She put the sandwich down and clenched her hands into tight balls. Her whole demeanour spoke of a person at battle with herself.

'Some people might call it a brief affair. I don't know if it even qualifies as an affair. I foolishly thought it was love and the beginning of a future together.'

'Love can blind us.' Huon's words sounded trite against the pain in her voice.

Bronte shuddered. 'Well, it sure did that to me. I made a monumental mistake. I was really, really stupid.' Her voice quavered for a moment before becoming firm. 'My sister is Stephanie Hawkins.' Her gaze met his directly, as if expecting some kind of reaction.

The name rang a distant bell. 'Is she the actress that's now a singer? Sorry, I'm not that up with celebrity gossip.'

She gave him an ironic look. 'That's one of the things I love about Muttawindi. It's a long way from the high life.'

'Hey, we've got the B and S balls.' His eyes twinkled in mock defence. 'But you're right, it's a far cry from the Crown Ballroom.'

She dragged in a deep breath. 'Yes, Stephanie is the singer and her latest album just went platinum. She's also the face of Maybar make-up.'

So that was where he knew the name. 'I think I've seen her in one of Claire's magazines. That's pretty big in the celebrity stakes.'

She nodded. 'It is. And Steph's worked really hard to get where she is.'

'As have you. Passing your medical exams is no walk in the park.' He gave her a smile, hoping it would relax her. The doctor in him knew she needed to talk. She'd effectively avoided it for two weeks.

But the man in him didn't want to be her confessor. The less he knew about her the better. But he couldn't stand to see her upset.

'Thanks, but in the eyes of my parents it fades compared with stardom.' She bit her lip. 'My parents expected the whole family to be part of Steph's business, and up to a point I'd gone along with that.'

'Family's a strong pull.' Huon focussed on reflecting her thoughts back to her, counselling style. A counsellor was objective. A counsellor didn't get involved. A counsellor didn't see the person on the other side of the table as a beautiful woman with eyes that made his body throb.

'It is, but I'm twenty-eight and it's time for me to carve out my own life. I met Damien at the time I was convincing my parents I needed to leave the family firm and not be part of Steph's entourage.'

She gave a wry smile. 'He made me feel special. He did the full-on seduction thing. He'd text me at work, send me flowers, wine and dine me.' Her grey eyes suddenly flashed silver. 'And in a superb piece of acting that completely fooled me, he really seemed to understand where I was coming from and what was important to me.'

She sighed. 'But conmen work out your weaknesses, don't they? Unlike the family, he supported me in my plans. He even talked of coming to the outback with me. For the first time in my life I had an idea of what it must be like to be my sister.' She nibbled her bottom lip.

The unconscious action sent a wave of longing through Huon. A familiar longing. One that had arrived the day Bronte had. It would go when she left in a couple of weeks. It had to.

Right now he had to concentrate on being a counsellor. 'We all love to feel special. There's no crime in that.'

'No, there isn't, but when reality breaks through the fog of what you thought was love, the actions of the other person can seem like a crime.' Bitterness tinged her words. Her hands were still curled into tight fists.

He wanted to lean forward and touch her, comfort her. But he leaned back instead, needing all the space between them that he could get. 'So what did Damien do?'

Pain slashed her face, the muscles tightening as her memories came back. 'On the night of Steph's Maybar launch at the Crown Ballroom, Damien had left his laptop at my place. He rang, needing an advertising file for a client, and asked me to print it off for him and bring it to the ball.

'I found the file but I also found his screensaver. It was a raunchy picture of Stephanie. He also had an enormous folder filled with hundreds of photos and articles about her.'

Huon forced his thoughts onto Bronte's words rather than her. If he focussed on her pain, he'd lose his objectivity. 'That must have been a huge shock. What did you do?'

'I arrived at the ball ready to confront him, and saw him at the bar deep in conversation with a friend. They had no idea I'd arrived and I overheard Damien talking about "Operation Stephanie". Apparently his plans were coming along really well, even though he had to put up with spending time with the unattractive sister to get closer to Steph. Every dull minute spent with me would be worth it when he landed the famous Stephanie Hawkins in his bed.'

Anger curled in Huon's belly. He wanted to physically thump the guy that had caused Bronte so much anguish. But all he could do was try and make her feel a little better. 'Ouch. So this guy is a complete bastard?'

Her eyes filled with gratitude and she smiled, her strength radiating through her pain. 'Absolutely. I'm better off without him.' She tossed her head. 'I slapped him so hard he fell off the barstool. I hope his physio bills hurt him just as much as his bruised coccyx.'

A wicked grin crossed her face as she met his gaze, her eyes taking on a smoky hue. A flare of heat ripped through him, blasting its way into the deepest spaces of his body. Defrosting the cold that had seeped into him since Ellen's death.

Scaring him.

The counsellor kicked back in, taking control. 'Does Damien know about the baby?'

The smoky hue in her eyes disappeared instantly, replaced by glinting slate. 'No. We used contraception so it's going to be a shock.' A frown creased her forehead. 'I'll tell him when I'm ready to deal with communicating with him. I don't want anything to do with him but he deserves to know a baby exists.'

He admired her attitude. Telling him wouldn't be easy. 'What about your parents?'

Her mouth tightened and she stared him down. 'When I'm settled in Muttawindi, when my job here is confirmed and I'm further along in the pregnancy, then I'll tell them. That way it's all a *fait accompli* and they have *no choice* but to respect my decision. If I told my parents now, they'd just try and organise me and take over.'

He needed to be devil's advocate, that's what a counsellor did. 'Grandparents usually want their grandchildren close by.'

She breathed in deeply. 'Haven't you heard what I've been saying? I have to make a break from my family. Their brand of love comes with many conditions and it is suffocating. It took me twenty-eight years to work out that no matter how hard I worked I would never be as special as my sister. I am *not* subjecting my child to that.'

Huon ached inside for this baby who would be denied a family. He'd been there and it hurt like hell. All kids needed a family.

'But—'

Her voice cut across his. 'I plan to bring the baby up by myself. I want this baby to be raised surrounded by love, not disappointment.'

Her point rammed home. He knew only too well that a kid needed unconditional love to grow and flourish. Muttawindi had given it to him when he'd arrived homeless and alone. 'It's not going to be easy for you, raising this child alone.'

'No. But then again, most things worth doing aren't easy.' She gave him a tired smile.

A smile that sent a jolt of desire through him. Electric and dangerous.

Every nerve ending screamed for him not to become involved. She should leave. He needed her to leave.

But Bronte's determination swam around him, dragging him along. She wouldn't waver in the face of his arguments. She planned to carve out a life for herself and her baby in a town far away from her own home town.

Should he be forcing her away if she really didn't have anywhere to go? If her family didn't value her? If their love for the child came with conditions? An image of a lonely boy desperate for love flooded his mind.

No, he couldn't send her back. Couldn't send her and her baby back to a place where they weren't valued or loved. No one deserved that. Everyone deserved a place to call home. And Muttawindi loved a stray. He knew that only too well. As soon as they realised what a great doctor she was they'd embrace her and the baby. Could he deny her and her child what the town had given him?

But the thought of her staying scared the hell out of him. In two weeks she'd caused him to experience sensations he'd forgotten he could ever feel. Sensations he knew would only lead to more pain. Life had taught him that.

But he couldn't send her back and still have a clear conscience. He sighed, giving up all hope of having a doctor who could carry the heavy load of Muttawindi, giving up all hope of the distance *he* desperately needed from this woman who invaded his thoughts and dreams.

He ran his hand through his hair in resignation. 'You're determined to stay, so go ahead.'

Disbelief raced across her face, quickly followed by relief. 'You won't regret this decision.'

But he already did.

CHAPTER FIVE

BRONTE SQUEEZED A Muttawindi-grown lemon into a glass of cool, spring water. She drank it quickly, quenching a thirst generated by two hours of non-stop talking on the radio clinic.

It had been three weeks since Huon had dropped the issue of a trial period and she'd thrown herself into work. She'd been putting in long days, needing to prove to Huon that he'd made the right decision. And she'd been trying to connect with Muttawindi.

It had taken a *lot* of convincing but he'd finally taken a Saturday morning off, leaving her in charge. It seemed strange to be alone. Part of her missed seeing his rugged, tanned face, the determined set of his jaw and the blond cowlick that refused to be tamed.

The sensible part of her knew a day away from him would give her much-needed breathing space from her growing attraction.

But even though he wasn't in the clinic, his presence seemed everywhere. Visions of his sparkling eyes, crinkling at the edges when he smiled, filled her mind. She could hear his deep, melodious laugh when she closed her eyes and see his passion for his town and patients.

Everyone in the town adored him. It hadn't taken long to work that out. Everyone spoke of him in glowing terms. But no one had mentioned Ellen. She desperately wanted to know who she was but knew she had no right to ask. Yet.

Work. She needed to think about work.

Work was what she needed. Work kept her focus off Huon.

She rubbed her tummy. 'We did OK this morning, you and me. People are starting to warm to us.' She'd taken up chatting to the baby—it sort of helped the whole pregnancy thing seem more real.

But she wanted to be much more than second best to Huon. She bit into a dry biscuit. He tended to hover over her like a mother hen, double-checking everything. It didn't help the town get to know her and she needed time alone with this community as a doctor. Bonding time.

She was certain the more they saw her in action, the more they would accept her. And this morning's clinic had been a building block. Although the town wasn't throwing a ticker-tape parade for her, this morning had been a solid start.

The radio sounded. Bronte pressed the microphone to 'on'. 'Dr Hawkins at Muttawindi, Mary. Over.'

'Dr Hawkins, we've had a call from Greg Tigani, the manager of the citrus orchard out on the Kintawalla Road. He's bringing in his two-year-old son by car. ETA five minutes. Over.'

'Any information? Over.'

'Sorry, Bronte. Greg's mobile went out of range.'

'OK. I'll be on standby. Over and out.' She walked over to the treatment room and checked the oxygen and suction. Claire kept everything in working order but it was always good to check.

The toddler probably had a high temperature. The current viral illness going around had kids spiking high fevers all over town.

Well, she could reassure the dad, and hopefully send away another happy customer who would spread the word that Bronte Hawkins was OK. Every case helped her cause.

She heard the wire door slam and she ran down the corridor. A very worried-looking man in workboots, shorts and T-shirt cradled a toddler in his arms.

'I need to see the doc.' The man's voice wavered.

'I'm the doctor, the new doctor—Bronte Hawkins.' She gave the man what she hoped was a reassuring smile. 'Please, bring the little guy down here.' She walked down the corridor and ushered the man into the treatment room.

'What's his name?' Bronte indicated a chair for the man to sit down.

'Tom. He's Tom and I'm Greg. Greg Tigani.'

'Pleased to meet you, Greg. What's been happening with Tom?' Bronte looked at the pale little boy who was snuggled into his dad's chest.

'He hasn't been quite himself the last day or so.'

'Has he had a temperature?'

'Maybe, but not really high. We haven't actually taken it. But he got worse on the trip in. I think he's been having some sort of fit. He can't seem to swallow properly or open his mouth. Can you help him?'

'I'll certainly do my best.' The history medical of illness was confusing, with nothing really specific to go on. Kids with fevers were prone to febrile convulsions so perhaps he'd fitted in the car.

Except he was cool now. 'Greg, I need to examine Tom, so if you lay him on the examination couch you can sit next to him and hold his hand.'

The little boy's pale face was almost whiter than the sheet underneath him. The child was awake, not drowsy. If he'd fitted in the car, he should have been drowsy.

'Doc, I thought you'd have finished for the day. I was that worried I wouldn't be able to find you.'

Bronte looked at the troubled father's face. 'Running late has its advantages.' She put her hand on his arm for a moment to support him. 'I'm glad I'm here.'

'Me, too, Doc. Me, too.' Greg's heartfelt words gave Bronte a buzz of happiness.

She bobbed down so she was at the same level as Tom and gave him a smile. 'Hi, Tom, my name's Bronte and I'm going to have a look at you and try and make you better.'

Tom gripped his dad's hand and whimpered.

As Bronte reached for her stethoscope she heard the wire door slam with its usual bang, and footsteps sounded in the corridor.

'Hello, Greg, Bronte.' Huon walked through the door, nodding to both of them.

Surprise raced through Bronte. What on earth was he doing here on his day off? Couldn't the man stay away from the clinic for one full day?

'Huon, Tom's crook. Can you have a look at him?' Greg's voice cut across Bronte's thoughts.

What? A wave of resentment mixed with disappointment surged inside her. A moment ago she'd been Tom's doctor. Now, with Huon here, Greg seemed to be dismissing her. What was Huon trying to do to her? Undermine her?

'Dr Hawkins is examining him, Greg, but I can stay if you like.' Huon came over to Tom and tousled his hair.

Bronte tamped down her anger. Huon wasn't taking over. He'd acknowledged her as the primary doctor, but his arrival meant Greg would naturally turn to the doctor he'd known the longest.

Bronte pulled her mind back to her patient. Tom needed her complete attention. Placing the stethoscope on Tom's chest, she listened carefully. The toddler's heart rate was slightly elevated, but air entry to his lungs was clear.

'Greg, you said that Tom had been unwell for a couple of days?' Bronte asked her question to Greg's back as he was looking at Huon.

'Sort of, but not really. Last night he didn't want to eat dinner. He's had times when he cries like he's in pain. And at breakfast Nancy tried to get him to eat and he wouldn't. It's like he wants to talk but sometimes he can't.' Greg's large frame seemed to slump with worry. 'Huon, what do you think is wrong with him?'

'That's what Dr Hawkins and I are going to work out.' Huon turned to Bronte, his face worried.

He had a right to be worried. So far Tom's symptoms were so vague she didn't have a clue what was wrong, but the child looked seriously unwell. 'Has he been sick in the last couple of weeks and then got better?'

'No.' Greg shook his head. 'The other kids got summer colds but he's been fit as a flea. Can't keep him inside—he's always off climbing something.'

'Can you open your mouth wide like this, Tom?' Bronte made a large O with her mouth.

The little boy copied her.

'Oh, mate, you didn't do that for Mum at breakfast.' Greg turned to Huon. 'He wasn't able to do that in the car either. I don't understand.'

Huon ran his hand across his jaw. 'When he couldn't open his mouth, was his body rigid, like a spasm?'

'Yeah.' Greg nodded. 'Like his muscles all went tight.'

Bronte looked at Huon and a thread of understanding ran between them. She quickly and closely examined Tom's arms and legs. On the base of Tom's foot she found a sticky plaster.

'When did Tom cut his foot, Greg?' Bronte couldn't disguise the urgency in her voice.

'Not sure. A week ago probably.' Greg turned to Huon, deliberately blocking Bronte. 'Look, I didn't come here about a small cut on the foot.'

Bronte quickly pulled on the beige edges of the dressing, removing it to expose a small cut with a moderate amount of pus.

'Huon.' Bronte pointed to Tom's foot.

She watched Huon's eyes darken with frustration and resignation on seeing the cut. She sensed an amazing connection with him. It was like they shared a network link. They'd built on each other's knowledge and had come to the same diagnosis. 'Greg, are Tom's immunisations up to date?'

'Immunisations?' Greg looked confused for a moment.

'His vaccinations for tetanus, diphtheria and whooping cough—are they up to date?'

Greg's face cleared. 'Nancy read an article about brain damage, so we decided not to get him jabbed.' He turned away from Bronte. 'Huon, you know how we feel about this. Can you just focus on Tom rather than asking me stuff that's got nothing to do with him being sick?'

Huon spoke, his voice tightly controlled. 'Greg, this is the very reason I've pushed for you to immunise the kids.'

The lights flickered and a spasm contorted Tom's body. The little boy's jaw went rigid and the muscles of his face pulled up, giving him a grinning expression.

'Hell—trismus.' Huon grabbed the intravenous set. 'Get the magnesium sulphate, Bronte. We'll run it in through an IV to manage the spasms.' He turned to Greg. 'Tom's got tetanus. When he has a spasm he can't open his mouth. Lockjaw is an early sign.'

Greg put his head in his hands. 'Tetanus! But how can he...?'

Bronte wrapped the tourniquet around Tom's arm and found a vein for the IV. 'Greg, tetanus spores are found in manured soil and they will grow in any wound. It can be a clean wound or a deep, mucky wound. The spores are happy in either. Tom loves being outside and like most kids he probably runs around in bare feet.'

Greg raised his head, desperation clawing at his face. He looked at them both. 'Is he going to be all right?'

Bronte shared a fleeting look with Huon. Neither of them knew. 'He needs to go to Adelaide. He needs to have human tetanus immunoglobulin, which is only available in major cities. He'll be nursed in Intensive Care and he might need to be ventilated—have a machine breathe for him—if the spasms get really severe.'

Huon placed a clear paediatric mask on Tom's small face to give him extra oxygen. 'Bronte's right. Tom needs to go to Adelaide. Right now we're going to sedate him to help reduce the spasms, along with the other medication we're giving him.'

'Can Nancy or I go with him?'

Huon put his hand on Greg's shoulder. 'Of course you can, but time-wise it will probably be you. Ring Nancy from the phone at Reception.'

Greg stood up slowly, kissed Tom on the forehead and headed towards the door.

Huon turned to follow. 'I'll call Base and organise the flight.'

Bronte nodded and glanced down at Tom, watching the rise and fall of his chest. He was spasm free now, but for how long? It was the first case of tetanus she'd ever seen and she had no idea exactly how the disease would play out.

He was a desperately ill little boy and she couldn't wait to get him to Adelaide. The trip could be a nightmare as Tom could fit again at any moment. She and the flight nurse would have to be vigilant in their observations.

Huon walked back into the room, his expression less dark than when he'd left. 'We're in luck. Brendan can be here in five minutes.'

'Thank goodness something's working out for Tom. Who's the flight nurse?'

'It should be Hayley, which is great as she's got loads of paediatric experience. Mind you, none of us have much experience with tetanus. This is only the second case I've ever seen.'

He tilted his head and the sunlight glinted off his blond hair in a halo effect. He smiled. 'You did well to diagnose it. I'm impressed.'

'Thank you.' Warmth rushed through her at his compliment. Warmth combined with the deep longing that his smile always evoked. A smile that always made her feel so very special.

Which was ridiculous because he smiled at everyone that way. She had no reason to feel more special than anyone else.

Bronte pulled her mind back to her patient. She adjusted Tom's IV. 'I'll be happier when he's in Intensive Care.'

'Me, too.'

Greg walked back into the room. 'I just heard the plane. Nancy won't make it in but she's organising to come to Adelaide on a flight out of Broken Hill tonight. She's getting onto her mum to mind the other kids.'

'Right. Well, she can ring Bronte for regular updates.' Huon scooped up Tom. 'Grab the IV, Bronte.'

Bronte disengaged the IV from the pole and they slowly walked out to the airstrip with Greg in tow.

Brendan had left the plane's engines running while he opened the plane door. As Huon's foot hit the bottom step he yelled out to Bronte, 'Give the IV to Greg, it will be faster that way.'

'What?' She could hardly hear her own voice over the engine noise. She had no idea what Huon was talking about.

'I'll give you an update when we get to Adelaide.' Huon nodded to Greg. 'Come on.'

Bronte's brain stalled. Tom was *her* patient. She should be on that plane with Tom and Greg, not Huon. What the hell was he doing?

Greg took the IV from her hands. 'Thanks, Doc.'

The noise of the plane deafened her. Confusion swirled with anger, making her speechless. As much as she wanted to hurl words at Huon, she couldn't argue with him in front of a patient.

The two men disappeared into the plane. Brendan closed the doors and a minute later the plane taxied down the airstrip.

Furious, Bronte watched the plane disappear into the blue sky. She wanted to scream at the plane. Scream at Huon. How could he have done that? He'd totally taken over without discussing anything with her. He'd literally stolen her patient.

He'd never done anything like that before. Sure, he'd hovered but had never completely taken over.

She did a quick calculation in her head. Huon would be back in six hours. When he stepped off the plane she'd be waiting for him. He had a hell of a lot of explaining to do.

Bronte stifled a yawn and looked at the clinic clock. Exhaustion clawed at her but she wasn't leaving until she'd spoken to Huon. She'd rehearsed ten times what she was going to say, hoping she could stay calm but really she was ready to throttle him.

She pictured her hands on his neck. But instead of life-threatening pressure she found the image more sensual, with her hands skimming across his skin up into the tendrils of hair that caressed his collar.

'Arrgh!' Her yell broke the silence of the clinic.

What was wrong with her? This man was her colleague. And right now he'd crossed an ethical boundary by accompanying *her* patient to Adelaide.

She needed to stay focussed. Not get sidelined by her attraction to him. An attraction she blamed totally on her pregnancy hormones.

But you can't just blame the pregnancy. She hated it when her rational self kicked in. Pregnant or not, Huon would have fascinated her, drawn her in like a moth to a flame.

He seemed to have no idea that his combination of rugged good looks, athleticism and caring approach sent her pulses pounding.

And it had to stay that way.

By the end of the night they would have established some working rules. Rules that would prevent this confusion from happening again. Rules that would help her keep her feelings for Huon in check. Rules that would reinforce that he was a fellow doctor, nothing else.

Hours later the buzz of the King Air sounded. She suppressed an urge to race outside and accost him. No, she would stay inside. Let him come to her.

She went into the clinic's kitchen and put the kettle on. She plonked cutlery on the table, the sound of metal colliding with wood representative of her skittering thoughts.

She pulled out a platter of cold chicken and salad from the fridge, which Marg had sent over. Huon probably hadn't had a chance to eat.

The outside fly-wire door slammed shut, its thud reverberating down the corridor. Huon was back.

She hauled in a deep breath. *Stay calm, don't get angry, take it all slowly.*

'Bronte?' His deeply timbered voice called out her name.

'I'm in the kitchen.' *Stay calm.*

His firm and decisive footsteps sounded on the linoleum floor and he walked into the room. All six feet of him, looking handsome but exhausted.

Bronte squashed the flare of concern his fatigue always elicited. 'How's Tom?'

'Ventilated but stable, thank goodness.' He dropped into the chair and stretched his legs out in front of him. 'This looks great, thanks.' He picked up a drumstick and bit down into it.

'Marg sent it over.' She sat opposite him and spooned some potato salad, chicken and green salad onto her plate.

'Marg's a great cook and she's always wanted to feed me.' Huon grinned. 'Of course I don't object.' He loaded his plate with food. 'You're here late. I was worried there might have been another emergency, so I came in to check.'

She could feel her face tighten. 'Thought you'd come and take over another one of my patients, did you?'

'Sorry?' Confusion swam across his face. 'I came in to see if everything was all right.' He looked straight into her face, his blue eyes darkening slightly. 'I'm worried you're working too hard. I came in to see if you needed a hand. You look tired and you know that only makes you extra-nauseous.'

The genuine concern in his voice disarmed her. She wanted to sink into that concern. But she couldn't. It wasn't personal concern, just professional.

Huon glanced around. 'Why are you here at seven o'clock on a Saturday night?'

'I'm here because I needed to talk to you about Tom.'

He poured them both a mug of tea. 'I would have rung you to let you know how he was.'

'I know. That's not the reason I'm here.'

He paused, his mug halfway to his mouth. He set it down and focussed his attention onto Bronte. 'OK,' He elongated the K.

Her words came out in a rush. 'I expected to be on that plane accompanying *my* patient to Adelaide.'

His brow creased for a moment in surprise. 'Oh. I guess as I've known Tom since he was born I just assumed I'd go with him.'

'If you apply that logic, I'll never do an evacuation with anyone except strangers to Muttawindi!' She blew out a breath, trying to keep calm, frustrated he thought this was no big deal. 'Today was your day off. You shouldn't have been here. I was the doctor in attendance. Why did you feel the need to check up on me?'

'Check up on you?' An expression of disbelief crossed his face. 'Hell, Bronte, you're a wonderful doctor. I totally trust you. I wouldn't have taken the day off if I didn't.'

'But that's the point. You didn't take the day off.'

'Of course I took the day off. I wasn't here this morning.'

'But you arrived at lunchtime! Why did you come in then?' She bit her lip to stop her voice rising.

'I just thought I'd call by and see how your radio clinic went.'

She crossed her arms. 'But I could have told you how it went at report meeting on Monday. You know, that day that follows the weekend, the weekend being those two days a lot of people don't come into work.'

He raised his brows. 'Sarcasm doesn't suit you. What do you really want to say?'

'How can I become an accepted part of this community if you keep turning up when you're rostered off and taking over? You know everyone in this town better than me. How can I get to know anyone if you won't share your patients?'

'Now you're being silly. Of course I share the patients.' He gave her a condescending smile. 'You can't rush this, Bronte. All you need is time and you'll get to know everyone.'

His expression and tone of voice flamed her frustration. 'No, I won't. Not if you won't let me. I don't think you're able to share this town with me. You can't stay away from the clinic, and you take over when you're here.' She rushed on, driven by his lack of understanding. 'In fact, I think the other doctors left because you wouldn't let them into the hallowed halls of Muttawindi.'

Huon's face tightened as anger and regret wove across his face. He spoke quietly. 'Your predecessor wasn't a doctor.'

'What?' She must have misheard.

He ran his hand roughly through his hair. 'He wasn't a doctor. He had fake qualifications and posed as a doctor. I was exhausted when he arrived so I took a week off. In that time he managed to cause iatrogenic illnesses with medication and misdiagnose appendicitis. Lisa McQuilly's lucky to be alive.'

Oh my God. That was why the town was so wary of her. That was why Huon hovered over her.

He nodded. 'I blame myself.'

'But you weren't to know. Head Office would have hired him in good faith. You're not the first doctor to have something like this happen—it happened in Melbourne last year.'

'But I should have observed him. The town trusted me so they trusted him. I have to make it up to them. I owe them good medical care.'

Frustration whizzed through her. How did she counter irrational blame? 'You give them excellent medical care and so do I. That nightmare is over. You know I'm competent so now you can step back and relax.'

'It's not as simple as that. They depend on me.'

She heard her voice rise. 'And they can learn to depend on me. You need to let go. I need you to let go so I can get to know the town and have a chance of belonging. So the baby and I can be part of Muttawindi.' She had to make him understand. 'Hell, how can I compete with you, the local boy made good, the doctor who's second to God, their very own son, if you won't share the load and share the patients?'

Huon's face drained of colour. 'I'm not their son.'

She pushed her plate away. 'Oh, please, Huon. They idolise you. You're one of them, not an outsider like me.'

'I didn't arrive here until I was fourteen.'

Something in his voice made her look more closely at him. His eyes reflected an emotion she couldn't exactly pin down but part of her experienced a moment of pain.

'But I thought you were born here?'

'I was born in Adelaide.'

'Oh.' Surprise filled her. 'But your family originally came from here, right? They returned when you were a teenager?'

'No.' The word came out on a sigh.

Bronte noticed a slight shudder go through him. Something was going on here, something big. Whatever it was, Huon wasn't really offering it up. And she sensed that this story wouldn't be comfortable for him to tell.

But she also had a growing feeling it was important for her to hear it. 'Are you saying you were an outsider like me?' She tried to keep her voice light and not sound like an interrogator.

'I was. I arrived here an angry and belligerent teenager.'

She smiled. 'Most fourteen-year-olds don't want to move and leave their friends to come to a new place with their parents.' Bronte knew that feeling well.

'I didn't come with my parents.'

Questions raced across her mind but she stopped her tongue from asking them. Instead, she chose silence, hoping it would encourage him to tell his story.

Tension radiated from him. The usually rugged yet gentle planes of his face became sharp and pinched. 'My parents died when I was nine and I went into a group home.'

His words hit Bronte, winding her. Instinctively, she reached out her hand and covered his. 'Oh, God, I'm sorry.'

His blue eyes bored into her, hooded with pain. 'Yeah, it wasn't good.'

All her preconceived ideas about Huon crumbled. She'd been so certain he had a loving family, who featured largely in his life, especially when he'd been so adamant her child needed a family.

Huon's hand moved, his thumb caressing hers. A shiver of longing swept through her. 'How did you end up here in Muttawindi?'

He let go of her hand and sat back in his chair, silent for a moment. 'By a long, tortuous road.' His hurt was audible. 'I lived in the group home then with a few foster-families in Adelaide. By fourteen I was jack of the whole thing. I got in with a car-stealing gang and I landed up in front of a magistrate. He gave me a choice. Two years in a youth training centre or come out here.'

'And you chose here?' Bronte looked into his sky-blue eyes, now darkened with painful memories, and wished she could absorb some of his distress.

'I did. Best decision I've ever made. Ron and Claire took me in, made sure I was fed and clothed, made sure I went to school, and loved me.'

He gave a wry smile. 'Thank goodness they saw through my bravado, my tough-kid act. Between them and the town's people, like Marg, they showed me I could do a lot better in life than steal cars. They taught me I could do anything if I put my mind to it.'

Huon's words whizzed around Bronte's brain. He'd been dealt a lousy hand as a kid and yet he'd turned himself around completely. 'And Claire convinced you to do medicine?'

'She encouraged me. Muttawindi had never had a doctor. Claire was the remote area nurse in charge of the bush hospital. As I grew up, the town grew, too. With the gas fields opening, it seemed a logical choice to come back here as a doctor. Give back to the town that took me in. And Ellen agreed.'

'Ellen?' She tried to voice the word casually despite her desperation to know.

'My wife.' He sighed and swallowed hard. 'She died a couple of years ago.' His voice rasped out the words. 'The town had to rescue me a second time.'

His grief tore at her. No one deserved to lose their parents and their partner. 'I'm so very sorry.' Her words sounded hollow and useless against the pain in his voice. 'Life can be pretty unfair sometimes.'

An emotion she couldn't identify flickered behind his eyes. 'Yeah, some wonderful lives get cut short for no reason.'

Bronte watched his fingers trace the handle of his tea mug, trying to absorb his story. From street kid to husband, on to respected doctor and then widower. It was a hell of a roller-coaster journey in a short time. No wonder Huon had an incredibly strong connection to Muttawindi.

Suddenly everything fell into place. Huon thought he owed the town everything. The town had cared for him during his darkest days and now he cared for the town. That's why he'd gone with Tom. It had nothing to do with not letting her be involved.

It was everything to do with Huon needing to be there for the town. His family.

He leaned in towards her. 'This town is a pretty amazing place.' He picked up her hand. 'I promise to let you get on with your job and I'll try not to step on your toes. You're needed here.'

His fingers on her hand set off mini-explosions inside her. She leaned towards him as if propelled by the force of his penetrating eyes. His scent of soap and dust enveloped her, and she breathed it in, searing it onto her memory.

He needed her. He wanted to kiss her.

Flames of longing danced in his eyes. The same fire that burned inside her. Did he feel the same attraction she did?

His head moved closer, his breath stroked her skin.

Stroked beneath her skin, stirring the simmering warmth which exploded into a raging heat that licked at every part of her.

Time stilled. Her heart pounded loudly against her ribs, the sound filling her ears. The air around her pressed in on her, hot, close, in anticipation of his kiss. A kiss which part of her wanted and part of her feared. An uncontrollable force edged her forward.

Huon tilted his head even closer, his hair brushing her face, his lips parting with a slight tremble.

Bronte closed her eyes, giving in to the inevitable moment, giving up the battle to fight the burning desire deep inside her. She longed for the soft pressure of his lips against hers. She ached to taste him and have him fill her throbbing need, a need that had grown from the moment she'd met him.

Abruptly Huon pulled back.

Her eyes flew open, seeking his. But his eyes now shuttered from any discernible emotion gave her no clues.

'Muttawindi really needs a doctor like you.' He dropped her hand.

Her skin chilled at the loss of his touch. Disappointment flooded her, dousing the heat.

Of course, the town. Huon saw everything in terms of Muttawindi. She understood that now. Huon needed her to stay because the town needed a second doctor. And he lived to care for the town. There was no room in his life for anyone else.

She'd misread all the signs again, just like with Damien. How had she been so stupid to let herself think Huon wanted her, even for a moment?

CHAPTER SIX

AN HOUR LATER, Huon pushed open his front door and dumped his keys on the hallstand. He headed down the long hall towards the kitchen, his footsteps echoing on the Baltic pine floorboards.

Pulling open the fridge, he reached for a stubby, twisted the cap, and raised it to his lips. The amber fluid, cold in his throat, felt good. It might be nine o'clock at night, but the heat hadn't lessened.

He slumped onto the couch, flicked on the TV and channel-surfed for a few moments. Satellite access, a myriad of channels and still nothing worth watching.

Damn. He tossed the remote onto the coffee-table. The silence of the house pressed in on him. Not even the cicadas were singing tonight. Loneliness surrounded him, squeezing him, making his chest tight.

His first official day off in a long time had come to an end. Except he'd taken Tom to Adelaide.

And opened the door to his past. Hell, he hated talking about it. Thankfully he didn't have to very often because everyone in town already knew his story.

And Bronte's initial look had been the same look of sadness and sympathy he always got which was why he avoided telling people. He didn't want to look back—his past belonged exactly there.

But after the sympathy in Bronte's huge grey eyes had faded, he'd glimpsed a tantalising fire of wanting.

Images of her long, slender neck flooded his mind. He longed to touch her cascading hair, plunge his face into it, and breathe in her intoxicating scent. And those round ruby lips...

His groin tightened at the thought. This woman was turning him inside out. He'd never reacted like this to a woman before.

Not even Ellen. He'd loved her dearly, but it had been a love that had evolved from adolescence. He'd met Ellen on his first day at uni, and she'd become his best mate. Marriage had been a natural extension of that loving friendship. A friendship that had turned into a deep, abiding love.

But Bronte had a magnetic effect that drew him in. Hell, he'd almost kissed her tonight. Her soft bottom lip had trembled, urging him to kiss her, to take what she was offering.

And he'd wanted to. God, how he wanted to.

But he couldn't. He wouldn't.

Bronte was pregnant, confused, and he wouldn't take advantage of her vulnerability. He didn't want to risk hurting her.

Hurting himself. He could never go through losing someone again. He'd managed to climb out of the black hole of grief when his parents had died, and then after Ellen. The thought of heading down there again terrified him.

No, he wouldn't put himself out there for that.

The town gave him care and friendship and that was all he needed.

All he had to do was think of Bronte as his colleague. His pregnant colleague. His job was to monitor the pregnancy and her workload. She tended to push herself to the limit and someone had to make sure she didn't overdo things.

Hell, he could do that.

So what if he wanted to caress and smooth out the worry lines on her forehead, if his fingers itched to tuck her hair behind her ear, and her laugh sent rivers of longing through him? He was a professional. He could lock down his feelings and be her colleague and her friend.

How hard could it be?

Huon pulled up in front of Bronte's house. The summer heat had given way to glorious autumn days. It was still warm but not stifling.

He'd taken to calling by, checking that everything was working well.

Her old corrugated-iron cottage, Muttawindi's solution to termites, needed a few repairs. He enjoyed getting out his tools and seeing his handiwork improve things.

Huon picked up the picnic hamper Marg had packed for him. Bronte had mentioned she was going to paint this Sunday and, knowing Bronte, she wouldn't think to stop for lunch. She'd work until she dropped.

It was hard to believe how much energy she had these days compared to the exhausted doctor who had arrived in town. But he didn't want her getting tired and sick. So he'd organised lunch. He'd drop it off and head straight out to Kintawalla and have a swim.

A quick visit. Nothing else. He wasn't staying. This was all part of antenatal care. *Yeah, right.* He was just making sure she was taking care of herself and the baby.

He walked around to the back door of her house, pulled open the fly-wire door and walked into the kitchen. 'Bronte? It's Huon.'

Footsteps sounded down the hall and Bronte appeared in the kitchen, holding a paintbrush. She'd piled her long hair on top of her head and held it back from her face with a scarf. A short, tight T-shirt hugged her breasts and over the top of it she wore a giant pair of overalls. They hung baggily from her shoulders, allowing for her growing pregnancy and some. Bare feet peeked out from under the rolled-up khaki fabric.

Her face glowed in a way only a pregnant woman's could. No longer gaunt from fatigue and nausea, but rounded and radiant, with a hint of justified pride.

And her patrician nose wore pale green paint.

Desire thundered through him. Bronte in old painting clothes was a far sexier woman than Bronte in her buttoned-up workclothes. He grabbed a steadying breath.

'Hi, Huon.' Surprise mixed with pleasure crossed her face. 'What brings you here?'

'I've brought you lunch.' Huon held up the basket.

'Oh, that's kind but you didn't have to. I could have rustled something up.'

'Really?' Huon walked over and opened her fridge. 'Would you have been having the mouldy cheese or the brown banana?'

'You're exaggerating. It isn't as dismal as that.'

Half indignant, half laughing, Bronte walked up behind him and peeked over his shoulder into the fridge.

He felt her closeness, her warmth radiating into him, her spicy scent encircling him, tempting his senses. His blood heated and his heart pounded. He wanted to move away, get some distance, but he was caught between Bronte and the fridge.

At least the fridge was cold.

'Look.' She pointed to the freezer. 'I have bread in there.'

'And not much to put on it.' He turned to face her, resisting the temptation to touch her, resisting the longing that pulled at him to wrap his arms around her and hold her close. That would be a disaster.

He sighed. 'You have to eat properly. You tell your patients that, and you need to take your own advice.'

For a moment she looked sheepish. 'You're right. Sorry, I got distracted by the nursery.' She waved her paintbrush in the direction of the hall. 'Come and look at it. I'm really pleased with how it's coming along and—'

'You need to stop for half an hour to eat.'

'Oh, all right. I can see I'm not going to win this round.' She laughed, put the paintbrush down and sat at the table, leaning back in the chair. She swung her feet up onto another chair and swung her arms out wide, her breasts straining against her T-shirt.

She gave him a wicked grin. 'I'm ready, so feed me.'

His breath stalled in his chest. This woman had no idea what her teasing did him. No idea of the effect she had on him. No idea of her sexuality.

And it had to stay that way.

Huon opened the basket, unloaded the contents onto plates and then picked the basket up again. 'Make sure you sit for half an hour.'

'Aren't you going to stay?' A brief streak of disappointment crossed her face. 'You can't just drop in lunch like meals-on-wheels and go. You have to eat too. Can't you spare twenty minutes?'

'No, I really need to—'

'Hey, if you can tell me I have to stop and take a break, I can tell you the same thing.' She pushed the second chair out with her foot and crossed her arms. 'Sit.'

In a reflex action to the tone of her voice Huon sat before he'd realised he had.

'Good.' Bronte raised her brows. 'See, it wasn't that hard, was it?'

Huon picked up a salad roll. 'I had no idea you were so bossy.'

'I learned it from you.' Bronte laughed and then poured a glass of water from the jug. 'You're really sweet, dropping around with lunch. I could get used to being looked after.' A wistful tone entered her voice.

Then she almost seemed to shake herself. She sat up straight and reached for the baguette filled with salad and tuna. 'I'm starving.' She bit down into the crunchy bread.

Her actions tore at him. He hated glimpsing the vulnerable Bronte. He didn't want to think about that, it was dangerous territory. It was much easier to think about the determined, focussed Bronte. The Bronte who worked hard, and who was totally centred on creating a lifestyle for herself and her baby. Mother and child united.

'Have you made your ultrasound appointment? You're eighteen weeks now so you need to get it done, plus you need to see John Phillips, the obstetrician at Broken Hill.'

She rolled her eyes. 'Yes, Doctor. I'll make the appointments on Monday if I have time.' She pursed her lips like an old-fashioned schoolmarm. 'But you're not on duty now so eat your lunch.'

He raised his brows at her avoidance tactic. 'I'll remind you on Monday.'

She poked her tongue out at him and grinned, looking like a cheeky sixteen-year-old.

The wildfire in his veins blazed again and he gulped down a glass of water. Time to change the topic. 'So I'm guessing you've got some paint on the wall and not just on you?'

She looked down at herself and laughed. 'I had a bit of fun with the roller. Oh, well, it doesn't matter, I never look good anyway, so maybe some paint might give me the allure I lack.'

'You look pretty good to me.' The words came out low and husky.

For a brief moment Bronte stilled. A flare of something sparked in her eyes then died. 'Yeah, right. I'm in the oldest, most ill-fitting clothes I own.'

'Yes, but you wear them with style. I actually like you more in this outfit than in your navy blue skirt and white high-neck blouse.' He spoke the words before his brain censored them.

She raised her brows. 'Well, then, you'll be pleased to hear the days of the skirt are over. I can't do up the zip.'

He'd committed himself to a dangerous road so he may as well continue. 'Great. Give it to the op-shop.'

'Huon!' Her eyes sparked in indignation.

'No, I'm serious. It's a skirt that should be worn by a fifty-year-old matron, not an adventurer like you.'

'I'm hardly an adventurer.'

'You've left behind the life you knew and come out here to start again. I'd call that adventurous.'

Bronte tilted her head and looked at him. 'I suppose when you put it like that, I could, at a stretch, be called adventurous. But it really doesn't matter what I wear, I never look any good.'

Huon remembered the first morning Bronte had spent in Muttawindi. He'd been struck by the fact that she wore clothes that were too old-fashioned for her, clothes that didn't flatter her. He'd realised she didn't seem to know she was beautiful. At the time he'd put it down to fatigue and nausea. No one felt gorgeous when they were about to throw up.

But now he wondered if there was more to it. 'You think you never look any good?' He tried to keep the disbelief out of his voice.

'I was once compared to a plucked chicken.'

'Well, you can forget what that creep told you, he only wanted to hurt you.' He tried to keep the anger that simmered inside him whenever he thought of Damien out of his voice.

'My mother and sister have always been keen to point out to me that I could look better.' She spoke lightly but with a trace of bitterness.

'Really?'

'Yes. Steph was the gorgeous girl. She loved the party clothes, the dress-ups, the accessories and make-up. And then there was me. Mum tried to dress me like Steph but I always felt wrong, overdressed, too tizzy.'

Images of Bronte's wardrobe flashed in front of him. Always sedate, always plain, almost puritanlike clothes.

'So you eventually rebelled against that and gave up all the tizz?'

Her face registered surprise. 'I suppose I did.' She fiddled with the edge of her plate. 'Look, clothes are a necessary evil to keep me warm or protect me from the sun. As long as they're functional, it really doesn't matter.'

'Ah, but that's where you're wrong. Mark Twain had it right when he said, "Clothes maketh the man."'

'Yeah, well, they don't maketh this woman.' A warning edge entered her voice.

Huon pushed on. 'Maybe you just haven't tried the right clothes.'

'What is this? When did you become a fashion guru?'

Huon laughed. 'I can't say that I'm one of those new "metrosexuals". But haven't you ever had a favourite outfit? One that when you wore it, you felt special?'

Bronte downed her water and refilled her glass, the only sound in the room the ice clinking against the tumbler.

Huon watched her tight expression as she dredged her memory against her better judgement.

'I had a pair of jeans once that I loved. Whenever I wore them as a kid I felt free and able to do anything. But Mum always insisted on dresses or skirts so the jeans went by the wayside.'

That was it. Bronte didn't relax in her clothes. That was the difference today. She was relaxed and at ease in her old overalls and her way-too-tight T-shirt. And her radiance shone through.

For some reason he needed her to recognise her own beauty. She needed to know she was gorgeous as well as a talented doctor. Maybe getting her to find her own style was the first step towards making her realise she was beautiful. 'None of your clothes are going to fit any more, are they?'

Bronte shook her head. 'No, and I dread having to buy a new wardrobe. I hate shopping for clothes.'

'Don't, then.'

'What?'

'Today you look sensational in old painting gear.'

Warring emotions played across her face. 'Huon, there is no way I can possibly look sensational.'

'Bronte, believe me, you look great and you're comfy, right?'

'Yes, but I can't wear these clothes to work!'

'Maybe not the T-shirt.' He gave her a grin. 'Although it might be the way to get old Jack onside.'

He laughed at her blush.

'If you feel comfortable, that's half the battle. Tune in to the adventurer in you. An adventurer needs new clothes. You loved the freedom those jeans offered you, so go for clothes that give you the same feeling.'

'But it's too hot for jeans.' Her voice sounded strained, filled with a mixture of old hurt and apprehension.

'Choose shorts, then. Think outside the square. Instead of replacing your wardrobe with maternity-type clones, go for the adventurer-out-back look. You might just surprise yourself.'

Bronte pushed her now empty plate away in an almost defiant action. 'Huon, I think you need to stick to medicine—you're good at that. But fashion advice, I don't think so.'

He looked at her sceptical face and sighed. How did you convince someone they were beautiful when they couldn't see it? She deserved to know that; she deserved to see herself as she really was. Brave and beautiful.

He had no idea how he was going to open her eyes to her own beauty but he'd give it a go. After all, that's what colleagues did—they looked out for each other, right?

Bronte waved Huon goodbye and wandered back to her painting. She dipped the brush into the tin, ran the bristles against the edge to drain the excess paint and started to cut in around the door.

Huon had taken to dropping in. He usually arrived to fix something or to give her something. It had started a few weeks ago with her blood-test results. Today it had been lunch. Whatever it was, he never stayed long. He'd only stayed today because she'd bulldozed him into it.

Since the night she'd challenged him on not being able to share the patients, the night he'd opened up about his past, the night she'd so stupidly thought he would kiss her, his behaviour had lurched between being her colleague and doctor, and being a friend.

It was like he couldn't make up his mind. She had the feeling he regretted opening up to her. But if he did want to keep things strictly professional and only work-related contact, why was he dropping in to fix her hot-water service, fix the drooping curtain rail or remind her about appointments she should make?

It was a friendship that was tearing her apart.

She wanted so much more.

But he was still grieving for his wife.

You look pretty good to me. Huon's low, husky voice kept replaying in her mind. Why would he have said that? Did friends say stuff like that? No one had ever really told her she looked good, except for Damien's lies, which didn't count. Compliments about her appearance had been so few and far between she couldn't really remember hearing any. As a child she had constantly been compared to Steph, and found to be sadly lacking.

And for Huon to give her a compliment when she was covered in paint, she couldn't work it out. Bronte placed her paintbrush down on the drop sheet and walked over to the cheval mirror. Her image looked back at her. Plain and paint-splattered.

She knew Huon hadn't been teasing her, so why would he have said what he had? She looked again. Her face was more round now, giving her a softer look. Her hair had grown since she'd arrived in Muttawindi and curled gently around her face. Her breasts had definitely grown. For the first time ever, she had some.

She ran her hand over her stomach and cupped the small bulge that had popped out in the last few weeks. 'Hey, baby, you're making some changes. I wouldn't say I'm pretty, but maybe I'm not quite as plain.'

Suddenly she thought of the catalogue that Claire had given her last week. At the time she'd shoved it in her bag, not really wanting to look at it.

Bronte rummaged through the pile of reading on her desk and found it. She turned the pages and looked at the maternity clothing, wondering if Huon's fashion advice had any merit. Towards the back of the catalogue she found a pair of maternity cargo shorts and a contrasting sleeveless white shirt, decorated with large, bold, indigo flowers.

She could see herself wearing something like that.

Her mother and Stephanie's fashion instructions boomed in her head. She tossed the catalogue aside. She wasn't one to give in to flights of fancy. The paint fumes must have got to Huon, making him say things he didn't mean.

She looked like a pregnant woman. Nothing more, nothing less. Nothing to write home about. She was reading more into a silly conversation than she should.

Bronte picked up her paintbrush and then turned up the CD really loud, hoping to blast all the voices out her head, especially Huon's.

But the catalogue kept drawing her attention.

Maybe she could order one thing, just to try it out?
She'd think about it tomorrow.

Bronte struggled to tie up the X-ray gown and eventually pulled a second one on to hide the split back. She didn't fancy her bottom being on public display when she walked into the ultrasound room.

Dignity got parked at the door in hospitals, and Broken Hill Base was no different. She'd come in to Broken Hill for her twenty-two-week ultrasound, sharing the plane with Huon who had a meeting with the hospital's chief medical officer.

Actually, Huon had harangued her into coming. He'd pointed out in no uncertain terms that the ultrasound should have been at eighteen weeks. He'd gone ahead and made the appointment for her and booked her on the flight. She hadn't been able to put it off any longer.

Going to an ultrasound on her own wasn't something she was putting her hand up for. There was something about the routine ultrasound that screamed 'happy expectant couples'. It was one of those pregnancy things you did with the father of your baby.

But Huon was right—she couldn't avoid it any longer, no matter how much she might wish her situation were different. So here she was, waiting. Alone. Butterflies batted in her stomach. It seemed silly to be nervous but she was about to meet her baby 'on screen'.

'Dr Hawkins.' The young female radiographer called her name.

Clutching her gown close to her, she walked into the room and clambered up onto the examination table.

'Would you like me to video the ultrasound so you can take it home to your partner?' She bustled about, warming the gel and checking the transducer.

Bronte swallowed against the lump in her throat that rose every time she thought about the fact she was doing this pregnancy and parenthood gig all on her own. 'A photo will be just fine, thanks.'

The lights dimmed, the warm gel hit her belly and the transducer pressed down on her skin. The machine blipped and pinged and suddenly a white shape appeared on a black background. Floating on its back like a film star in a luxury swimming pool was her baby, nonchalantly sucking its thumb.

She gasped as a tidal wave of emotion swept through her. Joy, happiness and apprehension, all wrapped up together, exploded inside her. Tears pricked the backs of her eyes as wonder took over.

She tried to listen attentively to the radiographer as she called out the crown-rump length and the biparietal circumference measurements of the baby. Tried to be a doctor. But her gaze was riveted to the picture on the screen.

My baby.

The door opened and a shaft of light dazzled her, silhouetting the tall figure in a doctor's coat. The door closed behind him.

'I thought you might like some company.' Huon's deep voice warmed her as he sat down on the swivel stool next to her.

Gratitude filled her, mixed fleetingly with something she couldn't name. She blinked back tears. He'd known what a momentous occasion this was and he hadn't wanted her to be alone. 'Thanks.'

'Pretty cute kid.' He grinned at her, a grin full of pure delight as his gaze took in the somersaulting foetus.

He'd come to the ultrasound. 'Takes after me.' The quip hid the roller-coaster of feelings surging inside her. His grin always undid her, but combined with his thoughtfulness and caring she didn't know if she wanted to laugh, cry or sing.

'You're just in time to hear the baby's heartbeat, Doctor.' The radiographer positioned the transducer and suddenly the room filled with the sound of racing horses' hooves.

New life.

'One hundred and twenty-six beats per minute.' The radiographer's voice sounded over the boom of the heartbeat.

'Perfect.' Huon breathed out the word.

He squeezed Bronte's hand, his heat racing through her veins. Words jumbled in her brain and jammed in her throat. He was here, sharing this moment. Feeling the same awe and wonder.

Her heart beat faster. He wanted to be here with her. With her and the baby. She held his hand tighter.

Suddenly, Huon dropped her hand and stood up, moving closer to the screen. 'Is the placenta high on the uterine wall?' His tone was brisk and businesslike as he faced the radiographer, his back to Bronte.

'No sign of placenta praevia. No sign of anything untoward. The baby looks great and everything lines up with a twenty-two-week gestation.' The radiographer indicated all the measurements on the side of the screen.

'Excellent. Make sure I get a copy of that report.'

He looked at his watch. 'Bronte, I'll see you back at Reception. I just have to catch up with the orthopaedic registrar about a hip replacement.'

He gave a quick wave, the door swung open and slammed shut. Her doctor had left the building.

Her doctor.

It was a surreal moment. For one brief minute, when Huon had squeezed her hand, her fantasy of sharing her pregnancy with him had seemed real.

Now it was vapour.

Disappointment crept through her, oozing into deep crevices, taking hold.

He'd been doing his job. Just like he always did his job. He always treated his patients as people, never as numbers. He'd been extending that same care and courtesy to her because she was his patient.

And she knew that. Why was she lapsing into a fantasy world? Why did she let herself think she was any more special than any other of his patients?

She wasn't. But she wished so much that she was.

The letter in Huon's hand weighed less than twenty grams but it sat heavy against his palm. He'd collected the mail from Head Office while Bronte had been seeing the obstetrician.

Now she sat opposite him in the plane, her eyes closed, her face relaxed and at peace, enjoying a rare moment of not having to do anything or be anywhere. He could sit and watch her for the entire journey.

Did he want to break that moment and let reality intrude? The image of her radiant face shining with the miracle of seeing her baby *in utero* had been on constant replay in his mind for the last two hours.

What had he been thinking when he'd gone into the ultrasound room? He'd been monitoring her pregnancy for three months and he'd thought he could be the doctor and stay detached. But seeing Bronte's baby doing backstroke across the screen had ripped open feelings he'd put aside a long time ago. He and Ellen had talked about children but that hope was lost to him now.

The baby and Bronte belonged together as a unit. She was still sorting her life out, and had her own issues to grapple with. She wasn't emotionally ready for a relationship.

And he sure as hell wasn't.

He turned the letter through his fingers. It was addressed to Bronte. The return address read, 'Damien Cartwright, Melbourne.' Bronte must have written to him like she'd said she would.

He shouldn't care what was in the letter. It was nothing to do with him. But what if the father of the baby wanted a role in Bronte's life? He didn't want to think about that.

Bronte was a woman with a lot of guts and determination. She'd cope with whatever Damien had written. But he had an overwhelming urge to want to protect her. Keep her in Muttawindi. Keep her safe from any more hurt.

But he couldn't.

'Did the mail come?' Bronte stretched and leaned forward, her eyes sparkling in anticipation. 'I'm expecting a package.'

'No, packages, just this letter.'

She took it from his outstretched hand, turned it over and stilled. Her eyes sought his. 'It's from Damien.'

'I know.'

He'd expected apprehension in her eyes. But he saw surprise quickly followed by resignation. 'You'll want to open it when you're alone.'

She shook her head. 'You know the whole story so I'd rather deal with it now.' With a slight tremble in her hand she peeled open the envelope.

He watched her closely, looking for a hint of reaction, fearing the contents would change the course she had chosen for her life. Fearing they would affect him.

She dropped the letter in her lap and smiled up at him. 'He doesn't want any contact.'

'He's not marching into town?' He tried to sound flippant, to hide his relief that Damien Cartwright wanted no part in Bronte's life.

'He's given me the address of his lawyer for the future "should the child wish to make contact when he is older".' She shoved the letter back into the envelope. 'Thank goodness that's over. I doubted he'd want any involvement but knowing for certain is a huge relief.'

Her grey eyes sparkled as she looked at him and smiled. The wariness and worry that had tagged her since her arrival in Muttawindi had fallen away, replaced by expectation and hope. 'Now I can really start to live here, and in a month or so when the house is painted I'll tell Mum and Dad about the baby.'

It was as if she'd had an emotional make-over.

Passion and zeal shone through, making his own carefully constructed life look grey and listless.

But he'd spent two years crafting his life. It was what he wanted, what he needed.

Wasn't it?

CHAPTER SEVEN

IT HAD BEEN a busy few weeks and today's full day clinic was no exception. The late afternoon sun bore down hot and strong under the veranda at Marmambool Station. Bronte could feel the sweat trickling down her back. So much for an outback winter. The seasons seemed to have forgotten to move along.

The baby kicked her from under her new sleeveless shirt. After her initial hesitation she'd found she really enjoyed shopping by catalogue. 'Yeah, I know, it's been a long day. Almost home time.' She rubbed her belly where the foot had pummelled her. She longed to collapse on the couch at home. Although only at the beginning of her third trimester, she was starting to tire more easily.

She glanced over at Huon and was struck by the sight of his blond hair, in stark contrast to the tight black curls of the Aboriginal preschooler who sat on his lap. The little girl had his stethoscope in her ears and had stuck the end of it under Huon's shirt. He was pretending to be sad while she patted him on the arm.

She swallowed hard. The image of Huon and the child lanced her deeply. Her child would have no father. And no man would want to take on another man's child. The baby kicked again. Bronte blinked rapidly. She was *not* going to cry at work.

Right now just about anything set her off. Television commercials for overseas phone calls, fathers kissing babies' feet on nappy promotions, and a blond and blue-eyed doctor who had no idea the effect he had on her.

Wherever she went, she had people singing the praises of Huon. And rightly so. He was a wonderful, caring doctor. But, combined with her working with him so closely most days, it gave her precious little time to recover and armour up her heart for the next day. She needed the privacy of her own home to do that.

Her feelings for Huon had only grown and intensified. She longed for the glimpses of the Huon who had held her hand at the ultrasound, who had been awed by the sight of the baby. But he was back to being polite but distant.

'Are you all right, Bronte?' Claire's concerned voice broke into her thoughts. Claire had been mothering her ever since the pregnancy had shown itself.

She pulled her face into what she hoped was a smile. 'Fine, just a bit tired.'

But Claire had followed her line of vision. 'He'd make a great father.' She looked closely at Bronte. 'He and Ellen had planned to have children but, like all their plans, they got cut short.'

Bronte grabbed the opportunity she'd waited weeks for. 'What was Ellen like?'

'She was a warm and generous woman who loved the outdoors.' Claire sighed. 'She worked as an engineer out on the gas fields, doing a job she loved, but a gas leak and explosion took her from us.' Claire gave Bronte a knowing look. 'I don't suppose he's told you anything about her?'

'No...but I guess he finds it hard to talk about her.'

'It's time he was past grieving.'

The matter-of-fact tone in Claire's voice shocked her. 'I don't think there is a time limit on grief, is there?'

'I think there has to be. Ellen wouldn't have wanted him to live alone. As his foster-mother, it's hard watching him put his life on pause. It's time he pressed the play button and moved on.'

'I suppose he'll move on when he's ready.'

Claire's eyes bored into Bronte's face. 'I think he's ready, he just doesn't know it. He needs someone to show him he's ready.'

Claire's scrutiny had her cringing inside. Were her feelings for Huon so obvious?

Carving out a life in Muttawindi was hard enough, without the residents seeing her heart bleeding on her sleeve. Without them knowing that the plain doctor who had got herself knocked up had the hots for their doctor. Without them knowing that Huon never looked at her twice, no matter how much she wanted him to.

She wanted to run and hide in a dark place and be alone. But she couldn't do that. She had to squelch the hopeful look in Claire's eyes. She had to put this rumour or thought process or whatever it was to bed right now.

She had to lie through her teeth.

'Well, I wish him well. He obviously enjoyed being married and I hope he finds someone who will love him.' Bronte avoided looking at Claire and turned to walk away.

'Bronte!' The command in Huon's voice carried down the veranda, making her turn sharply. He only used a tone like that when he was worried. She knew the moment she heard his voice that going home had just got delayed.

Craig Bennett, the young roustabout she had examined earlier in the day, stood next to Huon, his face streaked with fear. Huon had his hand on the youth's shoulder.

'Bring the resus kit, we've got a man down.'

She nodded, grabbed her medical boxes and ran down the veranda steps towards the two men. 'What's happened?'

Craig's voice wobbled. 'We were loading cattle onto the truck and Reg got jammed between the truck and the rail. Cattle stood on him.' His face paled to alabaster white. 'Doc, his bone's sticking out of his leg.' Craig twitched and then dropped in a dead faint.

'Claire!' Bronte's and Huon's voices merged.

Claire rushed over. 'I'll look after him. You two go and attend to Reg and I'll radio Broken Hill.'

Bronte stowed the medical kits in the ute and jumped into the cabin. The moment her bottom touched the seat Huon gunned the engine. She raised her brows as a plume of dust enveloped them

He gave her a grin. 'Sorry. The only excuse I get to drive fast is in an emergency.' He slowed down a fraction in deference to the gravel road as he drove towards the mustering area.

'Over there.' Bronte pointed to the cattle yard and the circle of men who had their hats in their hands.

Bronte ran over to the group, her medical case jolting her knees and the baby doing somersaults. She was worried about what she would find. On the short journey she'd been thinking through the worst case scenario. What if the cattle had trampled more than his leg?

A man who looked to be in his fifties lay on the ground, his face contorted with pain. Bronte dropped to her knees.

'Reg, I'm Bronte Hawkins. I'm a doctor.' She put her fingers to his carotid pulse, which pumped thinly under her fingers. She'd expected a thready pulse so no surprise there. The shocked man was bleeding but was it only into his leg?

'Reg, I know this sounds a dumb question, but where does it hurt?'

'Me leg doesn't tickle, Doc.' He gave her a look of incredulity.

'Anywhere else?' She whipped up his shirt and examined his chest, noting his breathing wasn't laboured. She gently palpated his abdomen, feeling his liver and spleen. 'Did you get trampled anywhere else?'

'Nah, Craig managed to pull me out. I'll have to thank him for that.'

'How is he?' Huon put down a larger medical kit next to the resuscitation gear Bronte had carried. 'Any abdominal injuries?'

'Looks like he was really lucky that way. No sign of flail chest, no abdominal tenderness.'

Huon knelt down next to her, his shirtsleeve brushing her arm in an unconscious caress. 'Do you want to do the IV or the leg?'

She turned to her patient. 'Any preferences, Reg?' She was slowly undoing the damage of 'Dr Disaster' by giving people choices.

'Me leg's bloody sore. I reckon a woman's touch wouldn't go astray there.'

Bronte smiled and resisted the temptation to hug the injured man.

Huon gave a mock look of indignation. 'Hey, I can be gentle.'

'Doc, I've still got the bruises from the last examination you gave me.' The stockman's brave front faded as a spasm of pain hit him.

Huon put his hand on Reg's arm in a reassuring gesture. 'Lie still and a bit less cheek. Let us do the work.'

Bronte reached into the medical kit and grabbed the scissors. 'Sorry, Reg, but I'm going to have to cut your moleskins so I can treat your leg.'

'It's the least of me worries, Doc.'

The cut fabric folded back to expose part of his femur protruding from a jagged gash. Bronte's stomach plummeted. She'd hoped the injury would be to the tibia. This sort of injury was both life and leg threatening.

She looked at her watch. Time was vital. He needed to be in Theatre within three hours or he had a high risk of losing his leg.

'BP ninety on sixty-five.' The worry in Huon's voice matched her own.

They needed to stop the bleeding and bring up Reg's blood pressure. 'As soon as I've doused this wound with Betadine, I'll put on a pressure bandage. Do you have Haemaccel?'

Huon nodded. 'I'm putting in two lines. One of Hartmann's, and one of Haemaccel. It's his best option until he can have a blood transfusion.'

She poured the antiseptic wash over the wound, the brown liquid spilling down Reg's leg into the red soil. Having a cattle hoof inside your leg wasn't going to make it a clean wound. It would be debrided in Theatre but meanwhile she could help minimise the damage of bacteria going wild.

Little Tom Tigani flashed through her mind. 'When did you last have a tetanus shot, Reg?'

'Last year, when I was fencing over at Blaketon.'

'Great.' One thing ticked off the list. But the worry about gangrene was ever present. He needed a bolus dose of penicillin.

'Are you allergic to penicillin?' Huon's voice mirrored her thoughts. This happened all the time. In emergencies their minds worked in unison. It was a shame some of that *simpatico* couldn't be translated to other parts of her life.

'No, Doc, not allergic to anything I know of.'

Bronte applied a gauze dressing and the pressure bandage to the wound. Then she pressed her fingers into Reg's foot, trying to find a pedal pulse. Fractures like this could cut off the blood supply to the lower leg. She felt around his ankle, gently probing. Nothing.

She felt again, taking her time, being thorough. Still nothing.

She swore silently. This wasn't good for Reg. 'Can you feel my hands on your foot?'

'Sort of. It's a kinda fuzzy feeling.' His stoic look wavered for a moment. 'Me leg's gunna be all right, isn't it?'

Bronte didn't want to lie to him. She looked towards Huon in the slight hope she'd been overreacting. But deep furrows of concern brought his brows together in an uncharacteristic way. When Huon looked like that, things were bad.

This was no ordinary, straightforward fracture. Reg had no blood supply to his leg and now it looked like nerve damage, too. 'It's a nasty break, Reg. We're doing everything we can to save your leg.'

He gasped in shock and pain. 'Do you mean I might lose it?'

'Not if we can help it. But you're going to need surgery, a rod inserted into your leg, and traction. You'll be out of action for a long time.'

She tried to put some spin on the situation. 'Luckily, Gerald Robertson, the orthopaedic surgeon from Sydney, is in Broken Hill for a week, doing hip replacements. So we have an expert right here, and you won't have to go to Adelaide.' Considering the time factor, that could mean the difference between saving and losing the leg.

Reg groaned and closed his eyes for a moment.

He needed pain relief. 'Do you take any prescription medication?'

Reg shook his head.

'Do you have asthma or other lung problems, liver problems?'

'No, Doc, I'm generally pretty fit and well.'

She gave him a wan smile. 'Well, that's a plus at least. Right now we need to improve the blood supply up to your leg. I'm going to put a Donway splint on it to get the bone aligned. But before I do that I'll give you a morphine injection for pain relief. It will make you feel a bit sleepy.'

Huon finished taping the IV against Reg's arm and then called one of the station hands over. 'Reece, can you hold this bag of fluid nice and high for me?'

The man stepped forward, eager to help. 'Sure, Doc, no worries.'

Bronte drew up the morphine. 'Huon, ten milligrams of morphine.' She tapped the air bubbles out of the syringe.

She saw Huon's nod of acknowledgement. Dangerous drugs had to be accounted for at all times. She plunged the needle quickly and deeply into Reg's thigh.

Huon gently touched her arm. 'Would you like a hand with the splint?'

His eyes looked straight into her soul. She knew he could see how worried she was about Reg's leg. If the splint couldn't restore the blood supply, Reg faced amputation. Huon, in his usual way of caring for everyone, had made sure he was available to help her if she wanted it.

And she did want his help. Trauma medicine was all about teamwork. 'Yes, please.' She prepared the splint by adjusting the length to match Reg's leg length.

'Ready when you are.' Huon gave her a reassuring smile and a bolt of longing streaked through her. To him it was just a smile. To her it represented everything she wanted and knew she couldn't have.

She focussed on the splint application. 'I'll strap the ankle, you do the upper thigh.' She turned to Reg. 'The great thing about this splint is that we don't have to lift your leg, but it might hurt as I position your foot.'

'Just do what you have to do, Doc.' He spoke the words bravely, trying to mask his fear.

She gently placed his foot against the backboard of the splint and crossed the webbing around his foot, keeping it flexed upward.

The stockman's face blanched and he gripped Reece's ankle.

'Almost there, Reg. Huon, are your straps in position?'

'Yes, you can inflate the pump now.'

She activated the pump. With the pneumatic traction in place, she checked for pulses again. She prayed the splint would have aligned the bone and removed the pressure from the arteries.

Her fingers detected a faint pulse. Relief rushed through her and she wanted to high five Huon. 'Pulses present, thready but present.'

His grin said it all. 'Great! We're ready to roll. Where's Brendan?'

'Right behind you, Huon.' The pilot's baritone voice startled Bronte.

She laughed in surprise. 'That was perfect timing. Right, Reg, we're going to lift you up onto the stretcher. With the splint on and the morphine, you shouldn't feel too much discomfort.'

Brendan and Huon moved forward to lift Reg. Bronte didn't protest. She'd accepted that pregnancy and heavy lifting didn't go together.

Bronte looked at her watch. 'Brendan, can we be in Broken Hill within two hours?'

'Weather's clear. We should make it.'

That should mean the leg could be saved. But with a crush injury like that, she couldn't rule out a fat embolism. The next seventy-two hours would be crucial.

'Let's get going, then.'

* * *

Four hours later Bronte was back in Muttawindi. Brendan had made the trip in one hour, forty-five minutes, giving the orthopaedic surgeon some room to manoeuvre in Theatre and hopefully save Reg's leg.

She'd ring the hospital in a few hours. But right now exhaustion dragged at her, and all she wanted to do was go home. She picked up her bag to walk home, planning to collapse onto her couch the moment she stepped through the door. And close the door firmly on another emotionally exhausting day, working with a man who had no idea she was a woman as well as a colleague.

She had eight desperately needed Huon-free hours to get ready for another day.

Well, eight hours when he was physically not in her space. She knew her dreams would be filled with images of his dimples, unruly cowlick and a smile that melted her every time she experienced its rays. And recently a baby had entered the dreams, snuggled in Huon's strong, tanned arms.

She rubbed her temples, which throbbed at the thought.

'You need an early night.' Huon walked towards her, his car keys in his hand.

He had no idea that he was the cause of her restless nights. Him and the baby, who usually took up gymnastics at three a.m.

His eyes zeroed in on her walking shoes. 'Come on, I'll drive you home.'

'Thanks, Huon, but the walk will be good.'

'It's dark outside and you're dead on your feet. I'm driving you home.'

She didn't have the energy to argue. She could handle another five minutes with Huon. After all, what was five minutes after a full day?

He opened the car door for her and then walked around to the driver's side. 'So, did you get Graeme Elliot over to look at that wiring in the kitchen I was worried about?'

A stab of guilt pierced her. Huon had been doing a pretty good impression of Mr Fixit, helping out with handyman-type things. He'd reminded her once already about the electrician. 'It's on my to do list. I got sidetracked with organising the nursery.'

Concern creased his forehead. 'I'll ring him if you like.'

Part of her wanted to say yes, but she had to stand on her own two feet. She was big girl and soon to be a mother. And Huon's brand of task-oriented friendship was increasingly hard to deal with when she wanted so much more. 'That's kind of you, but I'll do it tomorrow.'

She rested her head on the headrest and closed her eyes, mostly because she knew Huon wouldn't press her with her eyes shut. She felt the car turn twice and knew she was almost home. Almost home free, Huon free.

Coloured lights flashed against her eyelids as the four-wheel-drive stopped abruptly. Bronte opened her eyes.

'What's happened?' A fire engine blocked the short street.

'Don't know, but we need to find out. I'll grab my bag in case we need it.' He hopped out of the car.

She opened her door and the acrid smell of burning wood and melting plastic stung her nostrils. She jogged to join Huon.

They walked quickly around the front of the fire engine. A wall of heat forced them back.

Bronte gasped and gripped Huon's arm. Flames leapt out of her beloved 'tinny' house. Exploding glass shattered into the night and the corrugated-iron walls that resisted the termites so well buckled in the extreme heat.

An almighty roar rent the air as the crackling sound of the fire combined with a deafening crash and the roof caved in.

'Oh, my God!' She couldn't bear to look.

She felt Huon's arm around her as she buried her face in his shoulder. Great sobs racked her chest.

She had no house and no possessions. Desolation speared her heart. Now she and the baby were truly alone.

Huon looked on in horror as Bronte's house exploded in front of his eyes. The volunteer firefighters had no hope against such an inferno.

Bronte slumped against him. He had to get her away, get her somewhere safe. 'Come on, Bronte, I'll take you home.'

She looked at him, her eyes wide and uncomprehending, her feet not moving.

In a reflex action he picked her up, cradling her in his arms, and carried her to the car. Her warmth flooded him, his arms tingling where they touched curves and hollows as he held her tightly against him.

He gently put her in the passenger seat, fastened her seat belt and then started the car. Bronte remained silent, staring straight ahead.

He kept glancing at her, worry eating into him as he drove the short distance to his house, holding her hand between gear changes.

She started to shake. Shock settled in.

'We're here.'

She sat unable to move yet her body shook on its own accord.

He lifted her out of the car and took her inside, laying her on the couch. He ran into his bedroom, whipped the cotton blanket off his bed and headed back to the lounge room.

'Here.' He tucked the blanket around her, wrapping it around her shoulders. 'I just want to check you and the baby, OK?'

She nodded silently.

He took her blood pressure. 'That's fine, but I want to listen to the foetal heart.'

Again the silent nod, followed by an almost automatic action of pulling up her blouse. The sleeveless blouse with bold blue flowers on it that he'd been admiring all day.

He did a quick abdominal examination to find the lie of the baby and, using the Pinard, he lent his ear to the trumpet stethoscope. He heard the rapid heartbeat, like horses' hooves racing against turf.

Thank God.

Relief moved through him but was quickly overtaken by something else. The feelings that had stirred when he'd been at the ultrasound grew. The memory of wanting to be a father, a longing to create a family.

He sat up and stowed the Pinard away, hoping to stow the feelings away as well. They didn't belong in his new life. 'You and the baby are fine. All you need is a strong, hot cup of tea with a truckload of sugar.'

Still she shook, eyes bleak with despair seeking his. 'The baby and I have nothing.'

Her desolation lashed him. This beautiful, brave woman was falling apart in front of him. He couldn't let her do that.

He sat down next to her and picked up her hand, which was cool to his touch. He covered it with his other hand. 'The important thing is that you weren't in the house tonight when the fire started.'

'I should have called the electrician. You kept reminding me, I—'

'Shh, it might not have been the wiring. It happened and it's over. You're safe, the baby's safe. We can replace the house and the possessions.'

'I...I don't even have any clothes.' The reality of the situation was slowly sinking in.

'It's a shame all of those great new clothes went up in flames. Still, now you have the perfect excuse for a totally new wardrobe.' He gave her a grin.

She looked up at him through thick brown lashes. 'I just didn't think I would be starting motherhood in a small room in a country pub.'

His world tilted. 'You can't stay at the pub.' The words shot out before he had a chance to think.

He couldn't let her live in the pub. Not when the station workers drove into town and whooped it up until the early hours of Sunday morning.

He ran his hands through his hair. He didn't want to offer his house but he had no choice. Bronte would have to live with him. Sweat broke out on his forehead. Sharing a house with her scared the hell out of him. Seeing her every day at work was hard enough, but now it would be out of hours as well.

'You can stay here.' His chest tightened. Her scent would be in the bathroom. She'd be sleeping in the spare bedroom next to his and eating breakfast with him in the mornings.

He'd just lost his buffer zone.

'Are you sure about this, Huon?' Her eyes sought his.

Hell, no. He was only sure it was a bad idea, but it was the only option open to him. He reached out and gave her a reassuring pat, forcing his voice to be light. 'Hey, what are friends for?'

Suddenly she was reaching for him, her arms going around his neck, her fingers lacing against his skin, her breasts pressing against his chest.

Her perfume, which reminded him of hot, tropical nights, sent a white bolt of heat through him. He buried his face in her hair and breathed deeply.

Her fingers unlaced and trailed along his jaw, driving showers of sensation into every part of him. 'Thank you.'

Two words whispered in a husky voice drove every rational thought from his mind.

She leaned forward, her ruby lips capturing his in a gentle but searing caress.

She tasted of salt and tears, heat and spice. Her lips opened slightly and he extended the kiss, delving deeper, exploring the world she offered to him.

She sighed against his mouth and fire exploded inside him. He pulled her closer, feeling all of her against him, wanting to feel her skin against his, wanting her heat to mix with his.

The baby kicked him.

Sanity returned.

He needed distance.

He had to get off this couch, out of this room. He stood up abruptly. 'Sorry, you're exhausted and you need to sleep. I'll get your room organised.'

Sleep. That was the last thing Bronte could think about. She watched him hurriedly leave the room. She struggled to get her breathing under control. Huon's kiss had been like sweet nectar flowing in her veins.

He'd tasted of sunshine and fresh air. She'd longed for his kiss, and it had exceeded her fantasies. His mouth, hot and welcoming, had probed her own, unlocking quivering waves of sensations she hadn't known she could experience.

And then he'd abruptly pulled away.

The look of horror on his face stayed with her, etched on her mind. Sympathy had for a moment spiralled out of control. And he'd quickly realised his mistake. She was his colleague, a friend perhaps, but nothing more.

Reality crushed her. She'd kissed him. It had all come from her. Huon didn't desire her. He was still grieving for his wife.

In her heart she'd always known it. Now she had the evidence. He'd pulled away so fast it had been as if she'd been toxic.

She breathed in hard and deep to steady herself. She had a baby to provide for. She could do this. So her house had burnt down and she didn't even have a change of undies. But she had a job. She could buy new undies.

A hysterical laugh bubbled up inside her but she squashed it. She couldn't fall apart now. The thread of determination inside her tightened.

She'd been thrown a curve ball but she wouldn't let it faze her. Muttawindi kept throwing her challenges. She could rise to them. But sharing a house with Huon might be the hardest challenge she'd ever had.

CHAPTER EIGHT

HUON CONCENTRATED ON making breakfast. *Eggs, bacon, tea, Vegemite, butter.* He ran the ingredients through his head as he walked into the pantry. He knew reciting lists in his head wasn't a good sign. But any distraction techniques to keep his mind off the curvy, chestnut-haired woman sleeping two rooms away were worth trying.

Last night's kiss had been playing in his mind half the night. He could still feel the touch of her skin against his and the heat of her mouth as he'd drunk in her taste.

He needed to forget all the desires that kiss had sparked. He didn't want to crave that sort of intimacy. It wasn't safe. And yet last night, when sleep had finally claimed him, it had come from knowing she and the baby were safe and sheltered in his house.

But he wasn't thinking about that. No, he was focussing on the facts. Yesterday he had lived alone. Today he had a housemate. A very temporary housemate, hopefully. After breakfast he'd ring Head Office, get the details of the insurance company and get the ball rolling.

All plans needed to lead to Bronte being moved into her new place before the baby was born. She needed her own space to lead the life she so desperately wanted for her and her baby.

And the idea of a mother and child in your house scares you to your marrow.

He picked up the food and dumped it on the kitchen table. *Eggs, cheese, herbs, hummus.* He cracked the eggs into the bowl, focussing on the procedure of mixing up an omelette. Forcing the image of his lips on hers out of his head.

He lit the gas and greased the pan. The beaten eggs sizzled as the mixture hit the heated surface. He reduced the heat.

'Good morning, Huon.'

He looked up and his chest tightened. Bronte stood in his kitchen, her hair cascading in a mass of curls around her shoulders. She wore one of his blue chambray casual shirts, which flowed across her rounded stomach but barely fell to mid-thigh.

She tugged self-consciously at the hem of the shirt.

'I can't seem to find my clothes.'

His gaze caught the action and travelled the length of her long, shapely legs and he imagined the soft mound at the top that was barely hidden underneath his shirt. His hand gripped the spatula.

'Huon?'

Her voice penetrated his fog of desire and he remembered the frying-pan. The omelette had just become scrambled eggs. 'Clothes, right. Sorry.' His brain had scrambled as well. 'I washed them for you and they're drying.'

Appreciation flashed through her eyes. 'Thanks.'

'No problem, I thought you'd feel more comfortable in your own clothes.' He grinned. 'Not that you don't look cute in my shirt.'

She tugged at the shirt again as if the action would lengthen it. Then she gave him a look of hurt mixed with disbelief. 'I feel ridiculous, and never in my life have I been cute.'

He wanted to shake his head in disbelief. How could she not know how gorgeous she was? She had no idea that she made his blood run so hot it almost boiled. That his fingers itched to touch her silky skin and explore the few areas the shirt actually covered.

He pulled out a chair. 'Here, everything will seem better after breakfast. I've made eggs.' He buttered toast, dished up the food, poured her tea, and sat down opposite her at the long red-gum table.

She leaned back in her chair with a devilish smile on her face.

'What?'

She waved her arm out in front of her across the top of the food. 'All of this from a man who eats at the pub most of the time.'

He laughed. 'Surprised I can cook? I used to cook a lot before Ellen died. But cooking for one isn't the same.'

'I agree, it's always easier to cook for more than one. Thanks for cooking for us.' She patted her tummy and smiled.

His stomach lurched. Since hearing the baby's heartbeat he could no longer just think of Bronte alone. It was now Bronte and the baby, inextricably entwined.

See, you enjoy cooking for them. The voice in his head nagged and he tried to ignore it. She was a very temporary housemate.

Bronte started to eat then paused and fixed him with a long look. 'Living by yourself when you've been used to sharing a house can be really lonely. I imagine you've had some tough times.'

He thought of the long, quiet evenings, the nights he'd gone to the clinic or to the pub just to escape the stifling silence of the house. He nodded. 'The crazy thing is, when Ellen was alive she was often away on site at the gas fields. I didn't find the house quiet and oppressive then.'

'Because you knew she was coming home eventually.'

'Probably.'

'It's a funny thing, silence. It can be comforting. But when it's forced onto you, it can be scary, even soul-destroying.' She smiled a warm smile of understanding.

In a few short sentences she'd described exactly what it was like, living in his house. Why he'd left a lot of the house untouched and mainly lived in the kitchen area.

'Maybe you should get a dog. Pets are a great presence in a house.'

Huon almost choked on his eggs. 'What sort of pathetic message does that send? My wife dies and I get a dog.'

She tilted her head and looked straight at him. 'Ellen died two years ago, Huon.' Her matter-of-fact voice differed from what he was used to hearing when people spoke of Ellen.

Even so, he knew where this conversation was heading and he didn't want to go there. He got it often enough from Claire. 'Don't even think about telling me to move on. I'm quite happy with my life the way it is, and I have *no* plans to change it. Despite what most people think, not everyone in this world needs a partner.' The words rushed out in a forceful blast, stronger than he'd intended.

An understanding look crossed her face. 'I wouldn't presume to tell you it was time to get a partner, especially as my qualifications at couple-dom are a dismal failure. But, Huon, it's not a crime to be lonely. Healthy human beings crave company. If you're not ready for a relationship, no one in this town would think less of you for getting a dog.'

He didn't want to hear this. Didn't want her understanding. Didn't want her knowing that the idea of loving someone else scared him to death. Didn't want her knowing he was lonely. Didn't want her know-ing that last night, having her in the house had meant he'd slept well for the first time in months. 'I thought we were supposed to be organising you today, not me.'

She raised her brows and went back to eating her eggs.

His stomach suddenly didn't feel like food. He picked his plate up and walked to the sink. He didn't need to be analysed over breakfast. He was happy with his life the way it was and there was no way that he was put-ting himself out there again to be hurt. When you loved, you lost. He couldn't lose anyone again.

No, he didn't need to be analysed at all. Especially not by a glowing, pregnant woman. A woman with eyes that caressed him with concern, while wearing only his shirt.

Sexuality and sympathy. A potent mixture he had no idea how to handle.

He'd barely survived breakfast. The sooner he contacted the insur-ance company and Bronte was in her own house, the better. He wanted his quiet, unquestioning, non-probing house back.

Bronte ate the rest of her breakfast in silence. Perhaps she'd pushed Huon a bit far. Perhaps Claire's take on the situation wasn't accurate? His reac-tion when he'd thought she was going to tell him to move forward with his life had been very strong. Maybe he wasn't done grieving?

Ellen's touch was still very much part of the house unless Huon was into throw cushions and pastel furnishings. It didn't look like he'd changed much in two years. Except for the large kitchen. She could see Huon's stamp here.

It was a mish-mash of comfy furniture with state-of-the-art cook-ware. The large wooden table cried out for a crowd of people to gather around it, for children to crawl underneath it, and for food to make its surface groan.

But she wasn't sure Huon could recognise that just yet. She wished he could. Wished he could see that moving on was exactly what he did need. He would be happier if he did.

Women's voices sounded near the back door.

'Yoo-hoo, Huon.'

'In the kitchen.' Huon stowed the plate in the dishwasher.

Jenny Henderson walked in, carrying a large box, followed by Nancy Tigani, who clutched a bassinet, and Claire, who pushed a pram.

Claire gave Huon a motherly kiss. 'There's a load of stuff outside. Bring it in for us will you, dear?'

Huon raised his brows at being ordered about by his mother and gave her a mock salute. 'I'm on the job.'

As the wire door slammed behind him, the women put their load down on the table, looked at Bronte and all started to speak at the same time.

'Bronte, how are you? You poor thing.'

'What an awful thing to have happen to you.'

'At least you and the baby are all right. You are all right, aren't you?'

The concern in their voices swirled around her. 'Yes, the baby and I are fine. Homeless, but fine.'

Jenny gave her a hug. 'We know you lost everything. So last night after we heard the news we got on the blower and today we've got you some gear.' She pointed to some of the boxes. 'Baby clothes, pots and pans and we've also got some furniture.'

Bronte didn't know what to say. Words died on her tongue as a surge of emotion tightened her throat. 'That's so kind. I—'

'Nonsense, it's what we do when someone is having a hard time. After all, you've been looking after our families for the past few months, now it's our turn to look after you.' Jenny smiled and her voice filled with emotion. 'You kept me calm when Mark couldn't breathe. I'll never forget that.'

Tears stung the backs of Bronte's eyes. She went to speak, but Nancy sat down next to her and spoke first.

'And my Tom owes his life to you.' She squeezed Bronte's hand. 'We've got some clothes for you. We're sorry they're not as trendy as those new maternity clothes you've been wearing just recently.' She looked over at Claire. 'Didn't she look just gorgeous in that vivid green dress that buttoned up the front? I loved it.'

Claire smiled. 'Actually, my favourite outfit was the striped cargo pants teamed with the ruched camisole top.'

Bronte had the weirdest feeling. It was very strange being discussed when she was present in the room. Kind of like an out-of-body experience.

Nancy turned back to Bronte and sighed. 'I always looked such a frump when I was pregnant. I wish I had your style.'

Bronte almost choked with shock. 'My style? I don't have any style. Now my sister, she got all the looks and style.'

Claire rolled her eyes. 'Bronte, believe me, you've got style and the looks. Since you got over your morning sickness and filled out, you've been glowing. And those vivid prints you chose work really well for you. Much better than that dull Melbourne-black-suit look you had when you arrived. You've created your own style and you look gorgeous. You just needed to come to Muttawindi to do it.'

Bronte looked at the women all nodding in agreement and wondered. No one had ever told her she was gorgeous. *You look pretty good to me.* A small voice whispered what Huon had said. But she hadn't listened.

Nancy smiled. 'Claire's right. And even though I couldn't wear these clothes with flair, I know you will.' A flicker of understanding crossed her face. 'I know it will feel very strange, wearing someone else's clothes, but it will only be for a week or so until you get can to Broken Hill or order up from Adelaide.'

Jenny got up and plugged in the kettle. 'And feel free to alter anything. I'm pretty handy with a needle so I'd be happy to do that for you. Nancy isn't going to need the clothes again, not since Greg's had the snip.'

Nancy giggled. 'Not unless I play up.'

The women laughed and Bronte sensed their strong bond of friendship. They had just extended part of that friendship to her.

Her heart soared. She may have lost her house, she may be wearing someone else's clothes for a bit, but these women cared about her situation enough to rally round her.

For the first time since coming to Muttawindi she had a glimpse of how it would be. Part of a town, part of a community. A doctor and a friend.

A box on legs staggered into the room. 'Hell, Mum, you've got enough stuff out there to fill the front room.' Huon wiped the sweat off his brow. He turned round and tripped over the pram.

'Ouch.' He pushed it out of the way with a shove and rubbed his shin.

Claire gave him a sanguine smile. 'Yes, well, you have plenty of room here so you won't notice it. I've told people to drop anything they have directly here. They can leave it on the veranda. Make sure you offer them a cup of tea if you're home.'

Bronte saw the look of horror on Huon's face at the realisation that his house was about to be filled with baby and house furniture. He was clearly regretting he'd asked her to stay. 'Claire, really, what you have brought here today is plenty...' Her voice trailed off as Claire fixed her with a steely look.

'This town looks after its own. You wouldn't want to offend anyone, would you?'

'No, I... No, certainly not.'

Claire smiled. 'Good, that's settled. Ron and I will be over later with another load.' She picked up her bag. 'Come on, ladies, we've got work to do.'

Jenny and Nancy gave Bronte a quick hug goodbye and one minute later the house was silent after the whirlwind.

Huon gave her a wry grin. 'I think you just got what you wanted. That was Muttawindi in action, the Muttawindi I knew you would eventually discover. They love nothing more than looking after someone who needs a hand.'

He picked up a box, his pants stretching taut across his behind. 'I'll move this into the front room. Then we'll ring Head Office and find you a new house.'

A chill sliced through the warm glow the women had brought her. She gave herself a shake. For so long she'd craved the acceptance of the town and now she had it.

So why did she have an empty space inside her? Suddenly she knew the love of the town was no longer enough. She wanted to be loved by a man. To be loved by a blue-eyed, blond-headed doctor who couldn't wait to move her out of his home.

The aching, empty space widened, and coldness seeped into every part of her.

'You need to take the medication every day, Mrs Chung.' Bronte tried hard not to let the frustration she felt show in her voice.

'I feel well. I fit, I take herbs.' The older Chinese woman spoke in a forthright manner.

'I understand that, but high blood pressure is called the silent killer for just that reason. You can feel well and then, wham, you have a stroke.' Bronte resorted to emotional blackmail. 'Look at Elsie Davis.'

'Ah. Very sad.' Mrs Chung's face softened. 'I miss her.'

'Everyone does.' Bronte covered Mrs Chung's work-worn hand. 'Keep exercising, keep taking your herbs but take your blood pressure medication as well, OK? I want you to be around and well enough to keep bringing me that sensational wonton soup.'

The older woman beamed. 'You need feeding. You want healthy baby. I put ginger in soup, helps digestion. Warm for baby. Baby close now.'

Bronte laughed. 'No, Mrs Chung, I still have quite a few weeks left to go.'

The old lady put her hand on Bronte's stomach and tilted her head to the side and grunted as if to say, *young girls know nothing*.

Bronte wrote up her notes after Mrs Chung had left. The town had thawed towards her so much that she now had to deal with many patients wanting to know how the pregnancy was going. This included them asking if they could feel her tummy.

There was something about pregnancy and the rest of the human race. No matter how bad things were, people's spirits seemed to be lifted by a pregnancy and the thought of a new life.

A few of the older patients had initially tut-tutted about the lack of a husband, but most people seemed to be accepting of her as a sole parent. This baby was going to have an entire town of honorary aunts and uncles.

Bronte stretched and rubbed her back.

'Knock, knock. Got a minute?'

She turned towards the door. Huon stood in the doorway, holding two steaming mugs. He looked like a grown-up version of a rough-and-tum-ble boy with his blond hair curling up on his collar, his cowlick spring-ing forward, resisting all efforts to be flattened, and his clothes looking like they'd been thrown on.

Given that he'd been out to an early morning emergency, they prob-ably had been. She'd heard his footsteps on the Baltic pine floorboards at about five a.m.

'Sure, what's up?'

'Lewis Barkly's in Coronary Care at Broken Hill. Apparently he'd stopped taking his beta blocker medication and now he has unstable angina.' Huon sighed. 'These old miners think they're as tough as old boots. I just wish they'd listen to me more.'

'I just had Mrs Chung in with failure to comply as well. I think I need to start a group for these elderly patients. They can get together and I can give a quick chat about general health, answer questions about medica-tion, and then they can have a chinwag for the rest of the time.'

Huon laughed a deep rumbling laugh and his eyes twinkled. 'Great idea, but you're just doing it because you know Mavis Petrie will ar-rive with one of her triple sponge cakes, and Mrs Chung will bring you more soup.'

'Absolutely! You know me too well.' Bronte forced herself to ignore the flare of longing that rocked her body whenever Huon smiled at her. She had to ignore it or she would fall apart. 'Actually, I was planning on that soup being my contribution to dinner tonight.'

He laughed. 'Copping out on cooking again?'

'Not at all.' She tried to look affronted, without success.

Sharing the evening meal with Huon had become the highlight of her day. Technically they took it in turns to cook, but she'd noticed he often arrived home before her and started the meal. He would urge her to lie on the couch and chat to him while he cooked. The conversation would start off as patient debriefs, but would soon range over a broad range of subjects.

She so enjoyed this time and she knew life would be lonely when she finally moved into her house.

Huon's voice broke into her thoughts. 'But, seriously, a group for the elderly is a good idea. Perhaps you could start it before you go on maternity leave and I can run it while you're away?'

'I can start the group and manage it while I'm on leave.'

'Just wait and see how you go, OK?'

His concern wrapped around her and she wanted to sink into it, but there was no point. He was a kind, considerate boss, a caring friend, but nothing more. She had to learn to be content with friendship. Had he felt more than friendship for her, he wouldn't be harassing the insurance company so much to get her moved out of his house.

Huon pulled a printed piece of card out of his shirt pocket and turned it over a few times in his hand. Then he slapped it on his thigh.

Bronte looked from his face to the card and back again. A range of emotions played over his ruggedly, handsome face. Then he ran his hand through his hair.

'What do you need to tell me?' Bronte gave him a direct look.

Huon looked sheepish. 'Why do you think I need to tell you something?'

Bronte smiled. 'The hand-through-the-hair thing.'

'What?'

'Whenever you're worried about something or needing to do something you don't want to do, you run your hand through your hair.'

He looked at her surprised. 'Really? Do I? I had no idea.'

She laughed at his baffled expression. 'Well, you do, so spill the beans.'

'You know how our organization has to do a lot of fundraising to keep our planes in the air?'

'Yes. Claire gave me a run-down the other day when we were in Broken Hill. She also introduced me to the very formidable Catherine Berry. Within ten minutes she had me buying and posting a soft toy plane to every child I knew.' Bronte giggled at the memory.

'We need more Catherines.' Huon grinned. 'If it makes you feel any better, she has me organised every year with an ever-increasing number of Christmas cards. Unfortunately she doesn't offer to write and send them for me, so most are in my bottom drawer at home.

'Anyway, our region has a huge fundraising effort each year, culminating in the Outback Ball. People fly in from all over New South Wales and southern Queensland. It's a sensational weekend, loads of fun.'

Bronte grimaced. 'I guess it is, if you enjoy that sort of thing. Even before the debacle of Damien, I never enjoyed the glittering social scene.'

He gave her a sympathetic smile. 'I know the full-catastrophe social occasion is not your thing, especially after your experience at your last ball, but this will be different and you'll have a great time.'

Bronte's mouth went dry at the thought of a crowd, a ball and dancing. 'No, I won't have a great time. I left Melbourne to get away from all of that stuff. Besides, someone has to stay behind to attend any emergencies and that suits me. You go and I'll man the fort.'

'Sorry, Bronte. You have to come. The community will expect it. It's all part of the job.'

She crossed her arms across her chest. 'No, my job is to be their doctor, not their social butterfly. I'm sorry, Huon, but the community will have to accept that I can't be there. I do much better meeting people one on one.'

'It's part of your job description.'

His words numbed her. 'What?'

'As a Muttawindi flying doctor, you're expected to take part in fundraising activities. This goes with the territory.'

Oh, God. Panic started to rise in her chest. She had no choice. Just like with her family. Duty.

Her voice croaked on the words. 'When is it?'

'Tomorrow.'

'Tomorrow!' Her head spun. 'I can't go. I don't have a dress. I'm seven months pregnant, for heaven's sake, and even Broken Hill wouldn't have the sort of dress I'd need.'

A shaft of rational thought pierced her panic. She narrowed her frantic gaze at Huon. 'How long have you known about this?'

Colour stained his cheeks. 'Six weeks.'

'Six weeks!' Her voice rose hysterically. 'Why didn't you tell me?'

'Because I knew you'd react like this. Because your house burnt down. But mostly because the last ball you went to wasn't a good experience for you.' He put his hand on hers. 'But this is work, Bronte. Remember that. Plus the people of the district here value you. You know that now.'

The heat of his hand seeped into her. Her head spun, her chest tightened. A ball. Dear God, she couldn't do it. Couldn't walk into the crowd pregnant, dowdy and alone.

But before she could speak, Huon stood up and walked out into the corridor. A moment later he returned, carrying a large box with a well-known designer's logo printed on the top.

He placed it down in front of her. 'The dress problem is solved. I ordered this for you and it came in on yesterday's mail plane.' His eyes crinkled at the edges.

Bronte sat stunned. A million thoughts raced across her brain, going in all directions, never stopping long enough to form.

Huon put his hand on her shoulder. 'I'll be there with you the whole time. It'll be OK, Bronte, I promise.'

She looked up into his face. His expression was of concern mixed with expectation. She faced defeat. No matter how much she wanted to, she couldn't wriggle out of this. She sighed. 'Where's the ball?'

'This year it's at the Lundgreens' Station, which is an hour's flight away. We'll head off after morning clinic tomorrow and stay the night at the station.' He stood up and smiled down at her, his dimples carving deep into his face, giving him a devilish look. 'Remember to pack the dress.'

He walked out of the office.

A kernel of anger flared inside Bronte. How could he have withheld the information about the ball from her? The whole town had left her out of the loop, as if they had all conspired against her to get her there.

She felt powerless, and she hated that. Huon had organised everything and she was expected to just tag along. Just like at home. Just like her parents.

She dumped the dress box onto the floor without opening it. She wanted to kick something. She wanted to hit something.

She wanted to cry.

Except this situation wasn't quite the same as with her parents. She glanced down at the dress box. This large rectangular box represented a wonderfully kind man. A man who had not only listened to her but had taken on board what she had said all those weeks ago.

Curiosity overcame her. She leaned over, opened the lid and gingerly pulled back the layers of pale blue tissue paper.

She gasped. Her fingers touched silver-grey silk. The bodice was covered in tiny grey, blue and white beads. She pulled the dress out of the box and held it up against her. Full length and sleeveless, with a short fitted bodice and masses of flowing silk to cascade over the baby, it was the most elegant gown she'd ever owned. But she wouldn't be able to do justice to the dress. Beautiful women wore dresses like this. Not her.

I'll be there with you the whole time. It will be OK, Bronte, I promise. Huon's words echoed in her head.

Yes, he'd be there as her boss and her friend, just like he always was. Dealing with that when she wanted so much more was harder than the thought of the ball itself.

She rubbed her stomach. 'Well, baby, looks like we're going to a ball. Let's hope the plane holds up better than the pumpkin.'

CHAPTER NINE

HER HEART POUNDED, her fingers trembled and a wave of stress-induced heat swamped her. Bronte dragged in a deep, calming breath. There was no way she was going to sweat on this gorgeous dress. She slipped her feet into delicate silver sandals, brushed on some pearly pink lipstick and spritzed her favourite perfume onto her neck and wrists.

The day had seemed interminable. She'd stretched out morning clinic as long as possible, until Huon had pulled rank and ordered her onto the plane. Normally she loved to sit and gaze out of the plane window at the expanse of red dust and grey scrub, taking advantage of a trip that wasn't a medical emergency. But today the landscape had passed in a blur.

In stark contrast to the entire district, she was the only person not caught up in the excitement of the event. At the clinic, all her elderly patients had excitedly asked her about the ball and said how much she must be looking forward to it. They had insisted she give them a blow-by-blow description next week.

Mrs Nikvolski had given her a knowing look and in her fractured English had said, 'Dr Morrison, he look good in a tuxedo, yes.'

Bronte knew he would look more than good. Part of her ached to see him, another part didn't want that painful frustration. Wanting so much more than friendship and knowing it wasn't on offer, cut her deeper every day.

The whole occasion filled her with dread. Snatches of the last ball she'd attended kept rolling across her brain. Damien's voice snarled in her head, *There wasn't anything left in the looks department for you after Stephanie took it all.*

She gave herself a shake to try and rid herself of the negative thoughts that plagued her. She was here. Huon was with her. She would get through this.

The room the Lundgreens had given her to dress in had a full-length mirror. Up until then she'd avoided looking at herself in the dress, but it was crunch time. Any minute Huon would collect her to walk her down to the ballroom.

The baby somersaulted inside her. 'OK kid, I'm going to open my eyes any second and look.'

She'd never taken so long over make-up, never spent this amount of time on her hair. But the dress demanded perfection and although she knew she fell a long way short of that, she didn't want to look like a pregnant whale either.

'Five, four, three...'

The baby kicked her.

'Oh, all right.' Bronte went to open her eyes as a knock sounded on the door. She spun away from the mirror, her heart beating out an erratic rhythm. Huon had arrived.

She pulled the door open. Her breath stalled. He stood in front of her, all six feet of him, clothed in an immaculate black tuxedo that fitted him like a glove.

The pin-tucks on his white shirt lay crisp and sharp against his solid chest and flat stomach. Perfection from head to toe, except for his bow-tie, which lay untied around his neck. A grey piece of silk, dark against the whiteness of his shirt.

She wanted to savour this moment before words intruded, before she lost him to the other women at the ball. She wanted to memorise the image of this handsome man. The way his blond hair curled, how his bluest-of-blue eyes twinkled with easy humour, and how his tanned face, now free of the shadows of fatigue, relaxed into a deep dimpled smile that took her breath away. And had done from the very first moment she'd met him.

'Bronte.' Huon's deep voice broke into her concentration. 'You look amazing.'

She glanced down at her dress and back at him, disbelief and uncertainty filling her. He was only being polite. She sighed. 'You don't have to say that.'

Frustration crossed his face. 'What are you talking about? Haven't you seen yourself in the mirror?'

She dropped her gaze from his probing look. He knew her too well.

'Damn it, Bronte, you haven't looked, have you?'

'I was about to when you—'

Without waiting for her to finish her sentence, he grabbed her hand, swung her out behind him and then frog-marched her back into the room and over to the mirror.

'Look, damn it.' His hand held hers firmly.

'You're as bad as the baby,' she mumbled under her breath.

'What?' Confusion underlined his frustration.

'Nothing. I'm looking, I'm looking.' Her heart pounded so hard she was sure he must hear it.

She slowly raised her gaze to the mirror. And blinked. Twice. She hardly recognised herself. The silver-grey of the dress made her eyes large and luminous. The flowing material flattered her pregnancy and for the first time ever the bodice hinted at a cleavage.

Huon spoke softly. 'You look stunning. Surely you can see that?' He gripped her hand securely. 'And men like Damien are not worth thinking about.' He looked at her, his eyes willing her to really listen. 'Forget him, he's not worth your concern. People like him wouldn't know true beauty if it kicked them.'

She wanted to believe him but still the voices of her family filled her head.

His voice deepened. 'You've always been gorgeous, you just didn't recognise it.'

His words called up other words. *I wish I had your style.* Nancy Tigani's voice sounded in her head, along with that of Jenny Henderson and some of her other patients. Bronte looked in the mirror again.

A new thought slowly emerged, putting down tentative roots. Perhaps she did have style? It was certainly a different style from Stephanie's and her mother's, but it was *her* style. The thoughts fired up. And her style looked pretty good. Lightness flooded her. She was an attractive woman in her own right. Stephanie had classic good looks, but beauty came in different packages.

And Huon had seen it. Her heart turned over. He'd recognised her style when he'd chosen this dress. Her heart ached with gratitude. He'd seen something in her that she'd never seen before. And he cared enough to want her to see it.

She suddenly realised he'd been edging her gently towards this moment. He'd seen what she'd been blind to all her life.

This amazing man who held her hand had opened her eyes, infusing her with self-confidence. He'd given her a gift no one else had, and she loved him for it.

She loved him.

She raised her eyes to his reflection as the realisation hit her. She loved him. For too long she'd tried to tell herself it was a crush, a silly infatuation. But she knew it was much more than that. This wonderful man was her closest friend, her confidant and her mentor. He was the first person she thought of in the morning and the last person she thought of at night. He filled her thoughts and dreams.

But he didn't love her.

And he couldn't know how she felt. Somehow she had to keep the knowledge of her love for him to herself. Tonight, tomorrow and for ever.

Huon studied Bronte's expression anxiously. She'd been silent for a few moments and had schooled her emotions into a blank mask. He couldn't tell what she was thinking about the dress, herself, anything.

Suddenly she smiled, smoothed the silk over the baby and turned towards him. 'Thanks for the dress, Huon. You're right, it's just my style.'

Relief flooded him. 'It's my very great pleasure.'

The dress had been a big leap but worth it. He'd been racking his brain for weeks about how to open Bronte's eyes to her own loveliness.

He didn't know why it had become so important to him that she see this in herself. And he didn't want to examine those feelings too closely. Now was the time to enjoy the evening with a beautiful woman on his arm.

He let go of her hand and crooked his arm out towards her. 'Shall we go to the ball?'

'I don't think so.'

His stomach dropped and he scanned her face. 'What's the problem?'

Her eyes flashed with devilment. 'This dress and I deserve an escort who is fully dressed.'

Relief filled him and he laughed. 'Bow-ties and I don't go together very well.'

She rolled her eyes. 'So you can manage tiny stitches when little Julie Mondale cut her eye, but you can't tie a bow-tie.'

'Guilty as charged.' He grinned ruefully.

'I'll do it for you.' She stepped forward and picked up the ends of the bow-tie. Her hair brushed his face and her spicy perfume enveloped him as her fingers gently brushed his neck.

Her head down bent, her focus completely on the job in hand, she had no idea what she was doing to him. Like a flame to fireworks, her touch set off explosions of longing deep inside him. His groin tightened.

This bow-tying was a bad idea.

He'd spent a lot of time in the last few weeks avoiding being alone with Bronte in his house. To avoid this sort of closeness. The sort of closeness that battered him and tossed his emotions around like a dinghy on the ocean.

But he'd promised Bronte he'd escort her to the ball and make sure she had a good time. And that was what he was going to do, no matter how tough he found it to stay detached. She deserved this night. A night where, for the first time, she could walk into a room with confidence in herself and shine.

'There you go, that was easy.' She stood back and cool air raced between them, filling the space that had a moment ago glowed white with heat. She smiled up expectantly at him. 'The hard bit's over. Now we can go to the ball.'

But the hardest part of the evening was just beginning.

Bronte was having the most wonderful time. She'd never been to a ball quite like it and she'd danced until she was breathless. The night sky glowed with a canopy of stars that only the outback could offer. The dance floor, half inside the marquee and half outside, gave a romance to the night no big city venue could match.

Fresh seafood had been flown in for the occasion, piled high on ice, and Bronte realised there was *one* thing she did miss about Melbourne.

She'd danced with Brendan, Greg, and even with Ben, who, complete with pressure bandages on his burns, had made his first outing since coming home from Adelaide.

She sipped her lemonade. She belonged to this fantastic community. They valued her and welcomed her. Life was good.

But her gaze kept straying to Huon. Across the room she saw him dancing with Hayley Gaylard. A stab of jealousy ripped through her.

Huon saw her and waved, his grin melting her bones.

He had no idea the pain his *bonhomie* caused her. He'd been attentive all evening, making sure she had a drink, that she wasn't too tired. Being the friend he had always been. Nothing more, nothing less.

And why should she expect anything else? She might love him but he'd made it clear he wasn't ready for a partner. He, too, had fears he was fighting.

Even if he overcame those fears, would he want her? She didn't know. But she did know one thing. Tonight she felt beautiful. Tonight she glowed, and Huon had seen that.

'Ladies and gentlemen, take your partners for the final dance set.' The master of ceremony's voice boomed out of the large black speakers.

'May I have this dance?' Huon appeared beside her, his face mock serious, his hand extended.

She laughed and bowed. 'My card has one vacancy.'

'Glad to hear it! You've been a hard woman to catch.' His eyes danced with fun.

'That's what happens when you do a *Pygmalion* number on a girl.'

His eyes went serious for a moment. 'You did that all on your own. A dress is just window-dressing. When you glow from the inside, people warm to that.'

Everyone but you.

'Come on, they're playing our song.' He pulled her out on the dance floor and spun her around to the well-known 1970s tune.

Laughter and elation filled her as her body moved to the music, swaying to the beat. As she spun, she glimpsed Huon's warm, smiling face, his cheeky grin and look of relaxed happiness. It was a far cry from the exhausted man who'd met her at Broken Hill six months ago. Had she been part of that change?

Just when she thought she would never catch her breath, the beat changed.

Huon drew her in tenderly, as if in slow motion. His arm circling her waist, gently pressing her ever closer to him until her belly touched him. His chest pressed against hers. His heart beat against her breast hard and fast, just like her own.

The familiar heat from his touch surged inside her. Time slowed down. Every moment extended. Every moment intensified. The music wrapped around her, drawing her closer to Huon. Narrowing her world, this time, this moment to Huon and nothing else.

His fingers tightened on hers. His head moved nearer, his smooth cheek brushing hers in a soft caress.

Tiny sparks erupted, racing through her, touching all parts of her. She swayed towards him, as if pulled by a gossamer thread. Any space between them was too big.

The length of his body moved against hers, moulding into her curves, around the baby, as if he was designed to fit to her. As if together they had found their rightful places.

His heat transferred into her body, tantalising her with longing, yet confirming that they belonged together.

This was different to anything she'd ever experienced. This time she knew with a clarity that stunned her. This was her man and she wanted him.

Her gaze sought his. The shutters he normally kept tightly battened on his emotions rose for a moment and she glimpsed wanting, longing and desire.

Wanting, longing and desire for her.

Her heart soared. He wanted her. Sure, he was fighting wanting her, but he did have real feelings that matched her own.

Wordlessly they danced out under the night sky, their eyes never breaking contact, messages of need shifting between them, powerful and primal.

The other couples receded into the background. Bronte was only aware of Huon, the touch of his breath on her face, the heat of his body against her, the caress of his hand on her back and the driving need to feel him even more closely.

She needed to show him he could love again. That he didn't need to fear the longing. That it was OK to go with the overwhelming attraction and give in to the desire. Show him that his fears belonged in the past.

Tonight she was beautiful. Tonight she could do this.

Her foot pivoted on the edge of the dance floor. The house was only metres away. 'Come on.' She whispered the words as she gently pulled him towards the house.

He hesitated for a moment. 'Bronte, this isn't a good idea. I—'

She put her finger to his lips. 'Shh. Stop thinking, just go with the flow.'

His eyes darkened with desire, but flickered with a kernel of restraint.

The restraint worried her. She leaned towards him and ran her tongue slowly along his bottom lip, imprinting herself onto him. Branding him, making him hers.

The restraint in his eyes withered as desire flared. He groaned and followed her to the house. They slowly made their way to the bedroom, closing the door firmly behind them. Worry etched his brow. 'Bronte, you're killing me. Are you *really* sure about this?'

'I'm very sure.' She stepped into his arms, wrapping them around her. 'This is meant to be. We've fought it long enough. Take a chance, take a chance at happiness.'

He stood still, looking at her, his deep blue gaze penetrating her soul. A war of emotions swirled in his eyes—yearning, self-control, fear and lust.

She couldn't breathe. What if he rejected her? What if he threw away this chance?

He sighed a long shuddering breath, as if all the restraint he'd placed on his emotions had suddenly broken loose. He lowered his head and captured her lips with his.

Elation surged through her. He tasted of champagne, strawberries and wonder. She welcomed him, knowing that he belonged to her, sealing him to her with her own heat and taste.

His hands released her hair and he buried his face in it, a small moan escaping his lips.

She gloried that she could do this to him. She ran her hand through his curls and down along his neck, releasing the bow-tie she'd so carefully tied a few short hours ago. She longed to have his skin against hers, to touch his solid chest and taste the saltiness of his body.

His lips found her neck and she arched back, giving him free access to explore, taste and tantalise.

With one hand he eased the zip of her frock, which fell to the floor. For a brief moment panic flared that he would not like what he saw. But he stood before her, his eyes full of awe, marvelling at the pregnant swell of her body.

He reverently rested his hand on her belly. 'If you're worried, we don't have to...' His voice trailed off.

She cupped her hand around his face, in awe of the thoughtfulness of this amazing man, who put her needs ahead of his. 'The baby and I are just fine. We want you.'

She slid off his shirt and pressed her lips to his chest, flicking her tongue across his nipples.

He groaned and pulled her gently down onto the bed. 'I think it's my turn to do some exploring.'

And he did. Using his tongue in ways she never thought possible, he traversed her body. He caressed her nipples, sending ribbons of pleasure rocking through her. He trailed his lips across her belly, igniting a path of wanting, winding lower and lower until she was a quivering mess, urgent with need, clamouring for release.

But still he wouldn't let her go.

'We're doing this together, sweetheart.' His gentleness brought tears to her eyes as he eased inside her, the ultimate transfer of heat.

She moaned with the wonder of feeling him in the truest sense, nothing between them but white-hot desire overlaid with loving.

Slowly, gently and with reverence he stroked her, building her need, taking her with him, climbing to the place where they belonged. Joy, pure and wondrous, surged inside her as together they flew.

Later, Bronte lay in Huon's arms sated and secure, knowing she belonged here. She revelled in the comfort and protection of his strong arms and the sense of finally coming to a true home.

She'd found her true love and the knowledge filled her with a bliss she'd never thought a person could know.

Huon felt the regular swoosh of Bronte's breath against his chest. He lay and watched her sleep. Her long lashes caressed her cheeks, and her plump, ruby lips, which had so recently caused him so much pleasure, were slightly parted.

He let himself just watch her, releasing his mind to wander in a euphoric daze, flitting from thought to thought.

It had been so long since he'd lain with a woman and his body still tingled in awe at the sensations she had elicited.

He had never imagined that tonight he would make love to Bronte. He'd been alone for too long. For months he'd fought his attraction to this sexy, courageous woman. Tonight, when she'd so generously given herself to him, he'd given in to desire and taken what she offered.

His plan of keeping some distance hadn't worked. He thought he'd be safe if he danced with the nurses, the mothers and the grandmothers, but he'd always known exactly where Bronte had been in the marquee.

Every time he'd seen her dancing in another man's arms he'd wanted to cut in. Whenever she'd laughed, smiled and unconsciously twirled a lose strand of hair around her finger as she'd talked to the young station hands, he'd wanted to storm over and claim her as his.

And finally when he'd held her in his arms on the dance floor and she'd looked up at him with her large eyes, darkened with desire, he'd fallen into their depths. He'd tried to hold onto his resolve, but hell, didn't he deserve to be in the arms of a gorgeous woman if she wanted him?

Happiness and contentment permeated every cell of his body. *Take a chance at happiness.* Bronte's words played across his mind. Perhaps she was right.

Bronte, the baby and me. The thought swirled in his head. A house, kids in the yard, a wife, colleague and lover all rolled into one. Other people lived the dream, and he could, too. Why had he fought it for so long?

Bronte snuggled into him, a sigh escaping her lips, her hand splayed against his chest in a proprietorial way.

The euphoric haze vaporised.

Reality cascaded over him like a bucket of icy water.

Panic made him rigid. Dear God, what had he done? He'd made love to Bronte. Pregnant Bronte, colleague Bronte, dear friend Bronte. A woman who'd been so hurt before she would only have given herself to him because she loved him.

He couldn't be that man.

He couldn't be anyone's partner ever again.

He'd barely survived losing his parents and Ellen. And Bronte came with a baby. A child who would wrap itself around his heart like vines in a jungle. Tight, unconditional, unyielding.

He'd opened his heart as a youth to Ellen and had lost part of it when she'd died. Now he was all grown up and knew the danger of loving. Losing Bronte and her child would be double the pain and he would go under. Grief would consume him.

He had to walk away now. Walk away before he loved her. Walk away while it was still just lust. It was better to be alone than destroyed by grief. The last two years had taught him that.

He had the town to care for, and they cared for him. It was a safe life. It had to be enough.

CHAPTER TEN

BRONTE LAY NEXT to Huon, revelling in his warmth and comfort. They'd made love. She'd convinced him to take a chance at happiness, to put his fear aside. Now they could both move forward with their lives.

Move forward together. Together with a baby.

She snuggled in, wrapping her legs around his.

Huon suddenly stiffened against her.

She lessened the pressure against his leg. 'Sorry, did I hurt you?'

'No.' He moved away from her slightly.

Bronte squashed the jab of disappointment that edged in under her ribs.

The mattress moved and Huon swung his legs over the edge of the bed, sitting up with his back to her.

Cold swooped in, chilling her skin. Chilling her inside and out. She struggled to think clearly. Something was very wrong.

Huon cleared his throat. 'I think I'd better head back to my room. We wouldn't want to embarrass the Lundgreens.'

She sat up, pulling the sheet around her, suddenly self-conscious about her nakedness. She finally found her voice and spoke against the rising panic that threatened to choke her. 'I think the Lundgreens probably expected things like this to happen.'

Huon stood up and pulled on his trousers. 'We're the local doctors so we need to act with some decorum, don't you think?' The zip of his trousers sounded loud against the booming silence in the room.

'I think we need to talk about what's going on here.'

He bent to tie his shoes, deliberately not looking at her. 'Nothing is going on here. I have to work in the morning so I'm going to my room to get some sleep.'

Bile scalded her throat. Her heart beat so fast she thought she might faint. She gripped the sheet to her chin and frantically tried to stay on top of her world, which had suddenly tipped sideways. Huon was leaving her.

It had happened again. She'd been duped by a man. Used and discarded. She blinked back the tears that stung her eyes. She would not cry in front of him. She would hold onto her dignity.

No! A voice screamed in her head. This wasn't like Damien. She felt the difference but struggled to work out what is was.

Her thoughts raced around her head as she tried to absorb and make sense of Huon's rejection of her. A few short hours ago she'd believed he was finally over Ellen. Believed he was ready to take a risk and move on with his life, despite what he'd once said about living alone. And she'd pushed him to take that risk.

She'd fallen in love with a kind, generous, caring man. A man who, despite the personal losses in his life, still managed to care for others ahead of himself.

She bit her lip and breathed deeply. But was he caring for himself? Memories of a conversation with Claire flashed across her mind.

It's hard, watching him put his life on pause. He'd make a great father. He and Ellen had planned to have children. He needs someone to show him he's ready.

Suddenly she knew his rejection of her wasn't anything to do with her. It wasn't because she was a poor second to anyone. It had nothing to do with her looks.

It had everything to do with him putting his life on pause. Treading water. Not risking love again. He'd loved and lost his parents, he'd loved and lost Ellen. He was scared of losing her so he was sending her away.

Pain now, less pain later. Crazy thinking. How did she fight that? 'We've just made love. You can't deny how wonderful it was for both of us.'

His eyes, dull with resignation, sought hers. 'Bronte, I... Look...I'm sorry. I should never have given in to you. One of us should have been sensible. It should never have happened.'

'But it *did* happen.' *Because I love you.* She tried to keep her voice level. 'It happened because of an overwhelming attraction between two consenting adults. An attraction we've both fought for a long time.'

'We should have kept fighting it.' He ran his hand through his hair in a familiar gesture. 'We made a mistake.'

Frustration surged inside her. 'No, *we* didn't make a mistake. I know that *I* made the right decision.'

'OK, *I* made a mistake and, heaven knows, I'm truly sorry. But this isn't meant to be. You're not ready for this. Right now you need to be focussing on your baby.'

Disbelief rocked her. 'Don't presume to tell me what I am or am not ready for. Look at yourself. You're the one pushing me away. You're the one not ready.'

'I can't give you what you want.' His voice, ragged with guilt, sliced through her.

Her heart contracted in pain. 'What do you think I want?'

'You want someone to love you. You want a lover, a husband and a father for your child.'

The words, stark and harsh, pummelled her, shaking her resolve that she could fight his false belief. Lover, husband and father to her child were exactly what she wanted.

And that was exactly what he was running from.

Her face paled even more. 'Hell, Bronte, I didn't mean to hurt you.'

'It's a bit late for that now. The damage is done.' Her words, edged with steel, cut deep.

He wanted to make her pain less but he didn't know how. 'I tried being married once.' The words sounded trite.

'And by all accounts you had a happy marriage. You could have that again.'

'I had a short marriage. I can't do that again.'

'You're choosing not to do it again, Huon. You're choosing to put your life in neutral, commit to no one and deny yourself any chance of happiness.'

His heart twisted as her words struck deeply. 'You don't understand, no one really understands—'

She cut across his words. 'I think I *do* understand. No one can predict the future, Huon, but avoiding relationships just in case they don't work out, or get cut short, isn't living.'

'It's worked well for the last two years.' He held onto those words, ignoring the disbelieving voices in his head.

Bronte's derisive look screamed that he was a coward.

'What? Working yourself so hard so you can't even think or feel? Being on call to the town so you can kid yourself that their care and devotion is enough to sustain you emotionally?'

Her words bombarded him like shrapnel. He needed to cut this conversation off. Fast. 'I'm sorry I've hurt you, but as a couple and a family we were never going to work out.'

'That's right.' The bitterness in her voice ate at him like acid on paper. 'We wouldn't work out because you won't even try.'

She hauled in a deep breath. 'I'm not begging for your love, Huon. I deserve better than that. But you're throwing away a chance at happiness. A real chance to restart your life, a life lived to the full instead of this half-life you're clinging to now.'

She got up from the bed and grabbed her dressing-gown, pulling the sash tightly around her. 'As soon as I get back to Muttawindi, I'll move into the pub. I don't want to impose on you any longer.'

He sighed. 'Don't be ridiculous. Stay until your house is ready. We're both adults. Surely we can be civilised and share a house for a few more days.'

'That's right, we're adults.' She spoke firmly, with no trace of emotion. 'Just like you, I'm making a choice. And I'm choosing *not* to live in your house a moment longer than I have to.'

She marched to the door and hauled it open. 'I'm ready for you to leave now.' She looked at him, her head tilted to one side, her hair gently falling around her face. He experienced the ever-strengthening tug on his feelings, which he tried to stop.

He walked towards the door. His gut ached, his head pounded, and so did his heart. He'd done what he'd had to do. Bronte was under no illusions of a happy-ever-after. And he was getting his old life back.

So why did it feel so wrong?

'Landing in two minutes, Bronte.' Brendan's voice sounded in her headphones.

Rain pounded the plane windows and a wave of apprehension gripped her. She hoped the storm would pass quickly because rain could turn outback airstrips into quagmires in a very short time.

'Helen's symptoms sound very much like appendicitis. And with this weather, let's make it a quick evacuation. None of us fancy being stranded at Nandana, doing emergency surgery.' Claire voiced Bronte's thoughts.

She nodded in agreement and rubbed the slight dragging pain on her abdomen. The baby must be pressing on something. Probably ligament pain.

'You OK?' Claire had been trying to mother Bronte over the long seven days since the ball.

'Fine.' But she wasn't fine. She was physically exhausted and emotionally numb. Work had been frantic but she'd welcomed the diversion it had offered. During the day she had focus. It was the long, lonely, empty nights she hated.

She hadn't moved into the pub as the insur-ance company had come through with her house. Technically, she had moved into her new home. The boxes stacked high were testament to that. Claire and Nancy had fussed about, offering to unpack for her, but right now she couldn't face it. So she got up each morning, went to work, came home and went to bed.

She knew she needed to focus on the baby. Knew she needed to get her house ready, do some nesting. But she couldn't bring herself to start.

Each day she saw the worry in her patients' eyes. Worry for herself, worry that their town might lose one or both of their doctors. She knew she looked grey and gaunt. No one had really said anything specific, but people knew. Knew she loved Huon. Knew he didn't love her.

They squeezed her arm; they touched her hand and shook their heads. It took every ounce of energy she had to hold herself together.

She'd momentarily toyed with the idea of leaving. But she wasn't leaving. This was her town now. She'd worked too hard to run away. Worked too hard to prove to her parents she could stand on her own feet and live her own life. They'd finally accepted that and as a peace offering had sent her a cot for the baby.

The sun would rise and set each day, but her life would never be the same. But she would get through it. Somehow.

Huon had taken leave and gone to a conference in Sydney. She had seven days before she had to face him. A week to pull herself together. A week to learn how to turn the clock back, and be his colleague again instead of his lover.

A week to learn how to cope with loving a man who couldn't love her back.

The plane's undercarriage vibrated and the wheels touched the ground roughly. Not Brendan's usual smooth landing, so the strip conditions were already changing.

A frantic Barry Pappas met the plane, his rain jacket soaked through. 'Bronte, she's just collapsed.'

'Let's go!' Bronte jumped into the truck, her medical case banging her legs. The dull pain in her stomach turned sharp for a brief moment. She grimaced and gripped the handlebar above the window.

The pain faded.

Barry raced the truck through every pothole on the gravel track. The vehicle had barely stopped when Bronte opened the door. The rain slashed at her as she ran the short distance to the back door of the homestead.

'Doctor, she's in here.' Jane Pappas's terrified voice called from down the corridor. 'She keeps going to sleep on me.'

Bronte knelt down next to Helen. She gave Helen's shoulder a shake.

Helen groaned and her eyes fluttered open and then closed.

'Well done, Jane, for putting her in coma position.' Bronte gave the scared teenager a reassuring smile. Then she did the ABC of emergency care. Helen's airway was clear, but her breathing was too rapid.

Claire took Helen's blood pressure. 'Eighty over forty.'

Shock had lowered her blood pressure but was it due to a bleed or peritonitis? 'Tell me what Mum said about where it hurt.'

'She hadn't felt well for a few days. She had a pain but it moved about a bit. But she was gripping her tummy when she fell. She'd been vomiting this horrid brown stuff.' The young woman's face blanched at the description.

'Her temperature is 40.' The thermometer beeped in Claire's hand.

'Barry, is Helen allergic to penicillin?'

'No.' The farmer's face was white under his tan.

'I'll put in an IV. Claire, you draw up penicillin and then put in a second IV. We need to get a jump on this infection.'

Claire had already got out the antibiotics. Bronte appreciated her knowledge and experience. But she missed Huon. When Huon was with her, the load seemed shared.

Now everyone's expectations rested on her shoulders.

And she had a desperately sick woman spiralling into hypovolaemic shock.

'Bronte.' Brendan's deep voice, laced with urgency, made her turn.

'You've got five minutes or we won't be able to get out. The strip is turning into mud.'

'Right.' Hell, just what they didn't need. She wanted a stable patient before they were airborne, but if they were stuck at Nandana, Helen would die.

A jagged pain pierced her. Instinctively she put her hand on her lower belly, which felt hard under her fingers. She breathed out. The pain receded.

She focussed on Helen. Her veins had collapsed due to shock and finding a site for the IV was like looking for a needle in a haystack. She tightened the tourniquet. 'Claire, have you found a vein?'

'Still trying.' Unease made her voice quaver.

Bronte's finger's gently palpated Helen's skin.

'Three minutes, Bronte!'

Brendan's words hammered at her. She dragged in a calming breath. She would find a vein. *Must* find a vein. A small mound rose under her fingers. She flicked off the cannula cover and slid the needle home. 'Gotcha.'

'I've got a vein in her foot.' Claire inserted the needle and drew back blood. 'Thank goodness.' The relief in her voice echoed Bronte's.

'Brendan, we're ready. On my count.'

Barry and Brendan stepped forward and lifted Helen onto the stretcher.

Outside, rivers of red mud coursed along the track to the airstrip.

It was impossible to keep dry and everyone was soaked to the skin in moments.

As Claire and Barry loaded Helen onto the plane, Brendan touched Bronte on the shoulder. 'There are no guarantees. The strip is a mess. We might not be able to get out. This front is stronger than was forecast.'

'Helen needs surgery or she'll die.' The bald words hung in the air between them.

'I understand, but I have to consider six lives, not just one.'

Bronte bit her lip. The decision rested with Brendan, and he had to consider everyone's safety. She sent up a prayer that they could get out of Nandana and started to walk up the plane steps. Rain lashed her, her hair stuck to her face and a pervading sense of doom overtook her.

Red-hot, searing pain pierced her belly. She doubled over, gripping the handrail, unable to move.

The baby.

Fear rushed through her, invading every part of her. Somehow she managed the last three steps into the plane.

The pain hit again, strong, fierce and terrifying. This time she felt a warm, thick wetness between her legs. Blood.

No! A voice screamed in her head. No, this couldn't be happening. She still had six weeks before her due date. She instinctively crossed her legs.

But an antepartum haemorrhage didn't care about dates or prematurity. It didn't care that at thirty-four weeks gestation her baby's lungs might not be mature enough to work without assistance. Didn't care that she was one thousand kilometres from a neonatal nursery. That Huon was nowhere close by and she was the only doctor.

The isolation of the outback rammed home loud and clear.

Now three lives hung in the balance.

The rain thundered against the plane. Everything was in the lap of the gods.

CHAPTER ELEVEN

SYDNEY HARBOUR SPARKLED blue through the famous seafood restaurant's window. Not a grain of red dirt to be seen. Huon listened to his medical colleagues talking about the merits of discussing routine folate intake to all women of childbearing age.

But his mind kept wandering to Muttawindi. Had Jack's test results come back? Would the old devil have gone to see Bronte about them?

Bronte.

He ran his hand through his hair and suddenly stopped midway. *Whenever you're worried about something or needing to do something you don't want to do, you run your hand through your hair.*

Bronte's words rang in his head. She'd noticed things about him he hadn't even noticed himself. She knew things about him no one else did. But there was no point going there. He couldn't love her. Not in the way she wanted. He couldn't love anyone in that all-encompassing way ever again.

And given time, she would understand that. She would come to see that his decision was the right one. The only decision available to them.

His mobile phone vibrated. Claire's number came up on the display. He sighed inwardly. Claire was furious with him. He could understand that. He felt pretty lousy that he'd let things go so far with Bronte. He didn't need other people reminding him of his own shortcomings.

Claire had given him a verbal serve two nights ago. He loved his foster-mother dearly, but he really didn't want to have another conversation about Bronte. Not now anyway. He'd let the call go through to message bank.

He forced his concentration back to the discussion that surrounded him.

'Huon.' Jason Craig, a fellow doctor from Queensland, hailed him from across the room.

Huon walked towards him and shook his hand. 'Good to see you, Jason.'

'You, too. Listen, I've just been speaking to that gorgeous flight nurse of yours, Hayley Gaylard, on the phone. Muttawindi's trying to get hold of you. Hayley said something about a storm and a pregnant patient. Anyway, can you give her or Claire a ring now?'

A wave of concern rippled through Huon. 'Sure thing. Thanks, mate.' Perhaps Taylor Lewis had gone into labour. They probably couldn't find the file. He was certain it was on his desk.

He punched in Claire's number and waited for the phone to be answered.

'Huon, thank goodness.' Claire's usually firm and in-control voice, sounded fraught.

'What's up?' He was probably in trouble about the file that she'd wasted time looking for.

'It's Bronte.'

A chill traversed the length of his body, leaving a trail of dread. 'What about Bronte?'

Her voice trembled. 'She's had an antepartum haemorrhage.'

His stomach dropped to his knees and a roaring filled his ears. Not again. Surely life wasn't about to rip away another person he cared for? He gripped the phone tightly, his knuckles white. 'She's only thirty-four weeks pregnant.'

'I know that.' Claire paused. 'Huon, she's lost a lot of blood.'

His mouth went dry at the news. 'Where is she?'

'She's on her way to Adelaide.'

He heard the tears in Claire's voice and forced himself to concentrate on what he needed to know. 'What was the baby's condition when she left Broken Hill?'

'Distressed.'

'Hell, why didn't they do a Caesarean in Broken Hill?' He asked the question but he already knew the answer—he just didn't want to think about it. Bronte and the baby needed to be in a major hospital with intensive-care facilities. They could both die.

His heart twisted, sending immense pain into every corner of his body. His legs weakened. Bronte couldn't die. Bronte and the baby could not die. He wouldn't let that happen. He couldn't lose them.

He'd thought that if he pushed Bronte away he'd be immune to pain like this. God, how stupid had he been? He'd hurt her badly, pushed her away, and left her alone. Now she was fighting for her life. Alone.

His chest tightened. It hurt to breathe.

'Huon.' Claire spoke slowly, as if speaking to a person who didn't understand English. 'Listen to your mother. Get on a plane, *now*, and go to Adelaide.'

But he didn't need to be told that. Every part of him knew he had to be with Bronte. He had to be by her side. She needed him.

He needed her.

Why had he thought he could keep her at arm's length? His heart belonged to her. And to the baby. It always had.

His mind raced. He had to get to Adelaide as soon as possible. He looked around at the crowded reception room. Who did he know in this room who had a plane?

Two hours later he ran up the stairs to the birthing suite at Flinders Medical Centre. Thoughts of death skittered across his brain, and bleakness entered his soul. What if he'd arrived too late?

He hated himself. He should have been there. He should have been in Muttawindi, not bloody Sydney. It should have been him accompanying Bronte on the flight to Adelaide, not Hayley.

Guilt ate into him. Thank God she'd had Hayley. And Claire. But he should have been with her. She would have been distraught with fear. She knew the possible outcomes of a bleed in pregnancy. The loss of the baby.

And he'd forced her to cope with all this on her own.

He rounded the corner of the unit and called out to the nurse. 'I need to see Bronte Hawkins, she's a doctor, but she's pregnant and a patient and...' the incoherent words tumbled out, carrying his fear.

The young nurse looked at him with concern. 'Take a deep breath, sir. Are you a relative of Dr. Hawkins?'

'No, I'm not but—'

'I'm sorry, sir, but it's immediate family only.'

The nurse turned away.

'I don't think you understand, I'm a doctor too, Huon Morrison, and I work with her. I need to see her.'

The nurse turned back. 'I can take a message.'

Frustration surged inside him. He'd battled Sydney traffic, a raging electrical storm and a light plane trip to get here. No one was going to stop him from seeing her. 'You don't understand. I love her.'

He heard the words and recognised the truth. He realised he'd been fighting the truth from the moment he'd met her. His heart was inexorably entwined with hers.

'Pardon me?' Surprise lined the nurse's face.

'I said I love her. And I need to see her so I can tell her that.'

The nurse gently rested her hand on his arm. 'You might have to wait to tell her. Right now she's heavily sedated in Intensive Care.'

He gripped the reception desk. 'Is she all right?' The question sounded inane. By definition, people in Intensive Care were not all right.

'She's lost a lot of blood and they're worried about complications. The next forty-eight hours will be crucial, but you know that, Doctor.'

He bit his lip. Yeah, he knew that. A breath shuddered through his body. He was scared to ask the next question but knew he had to. 'And the baby?'

'The baby is in Neonatal Intensive Care.' The straightforward words simultaneously lessened and worsened his fears. 'Who would you like to see first?'

He desperately wanted to see Bronte. Hold her hand, tell her he loved her, but if he saw the baby first he could tell her about the baby. Give her a reason to fight. A reason to survive.

He turned and walked towards NICU. Autopilot took over as he struggled to function in the darkness that enveloped him. One foot followed the other.

Three hours ago he'd been so convinced that his life's plan of living alone was correct. Now he desperately wanted a wife and a baby so much that it hurt.

Now he might never have them.

The nurse walked him through to the baby. Huon rested his hands on the Perspex of the Humidicrib and stared at the tiny child.

Translucent. Fragile. Delicate.

It was hard to work out where the wires and drips stopped and the baby started.

'Dr Morrison?' A young intern put his hand out. 'I'm Kieran Hamilton, and I'm looking after Baby Hawkins.'

Huon dragged his eyes away from the baby. 'Resps are up.'

'Yes, they are. We're hoping with the oxygen that this little battler will find breathing less of a struggle. Due to the rapid delivery there wasn't time to administer anti-inflammatory drugs, but at thirty-four weeks we're not certain of how much value the lungs gain from them anyway.'

Kieran checked the oxygen levels. 'The next couple of hours will be crucial for your baby. We're hoping to see an improvement.'

Your baby. Huon didn't correct the intern. He wanted so much for this baby to be his. 'And if there's no improvement, you intubate and nurse in an open cot?'

'That's correct.' Kieran rested his hand on Huon's shoulder in a sympathetic gesture. 'Page me any time.'

Huon nodded his thanks and turned back to the baby. A desperate need to touch the tiny child filled him, bringing with it a rush of primal, gut-wrenching love.

He flattened his hands against the Humidicrib in a futile gesture to get closer. Tears pricked the backs of his eyes at the sheer miracle of a new life. A life that was struggling with every breath. He watched the tiny rib cage shudder up and down.

'Come on, little one. Your mummy loves you so much, and so do I.'

The nurse touched his arm. 'I'll take you to see Dr Hawkins now.'

He nodded, blew his nose, and walked to Intensive Care.

Huon was always amazed at how busy yet quiet Intensive Care was. The silence was punctuated only by the beeping machines and low voices.

Like the baby, Bronte lay with tubes and drips and wires attached to her. Her glorious hair, the hair he loved to bury his face in, rested like a dark veil against the white pillowslip.

Love and fear collided. His heart lurched. He sat down next to her and lifted her cool hand, cradling it between his own. 'Bronte, it's Huon.'

'She's sedated so you might not get much of a response at the moment.' The nurse smiled at him. 'But talk to her. Tell her what you told me, I'm sure she'll want to hear that.'

'It might be a bit late.' His voice trembled.

'She's stable at the moment, Doctor. We've passed the first hurdle.' The nurse tried to sound reassuring.

Huon sighed. 'What I mean is, she might not want to know. I've been a bit slow at realising it.'

She nodded in understanding. 'Love is one big risk, Doctor. But if you don't take the risk, you lose out on so much more.'

'I'm starting to realise that.'

'That's the first step. I'll leave the two of you alone.' She pulled the curtains closed behind her.

Where did he start? He rested his head on her hair and breathed in her scent. Somehow, even with all the surgical antiseptic and anaesthetic gases, her trade mark spicy scent lingered. He breathed deeper. He needed to be as close to her as possible.

He squeezed her hand. 'Bronte, you have a daughter. If she has half the fighting spirit of her mother, she'll pull through with flying colours.'

He watched the rise and fall of her chest and scanned her face for signs of recognition, but she slept soundly. He dragged in a breath. 'You've had me so scared I could hardly breathe. I thought I might lose you and the baby. I pulled in every favour I could and got here as fast as I could. I know it doesn't make up for me not being with you when you needed me most.'

His voice quavered. 'Please, wake up so I can tell you what a bloody idiot I've been. Please, wake up so I can tell you I love you.'

He leaned forward, his lips grazing hers. Willing her to wake up, willing her to respond to him. He needed her like he needed oxygen. But she slept on.

Pain. Sharp, hot, penetrating pain. Bronte stopped trying to move. Her mind struggled against the black fog, trying to make sense of what was happening. She remembered the flight, remembered her fear.

The baby.

She reached her hand down to her belly. Her fingertips touched flat-ness and a gauze dressing. Panic filled her. She tried to lift her head, use her voice.

'Bronte.'

She felt a hand over hers.

'It's all right. The baby's all right.'

Thank you. She whispered the words to herself. The baby was alive.

'She's a gorgeous little girl who's as beautiful as her mother.' The voice echoed in her head, trying to penetrate the thick fog that filled her brain.

Urgency filled her. 'I need to see her, hold her.' She tried to sit up but a spinning sensation pushed her backwards.

'You can, sweetheart. Very soon.' The deep timbre of the voice sounded clearer, familiar.

Huon's voice.

She fought the fog. It couldn't be Huon. He was in Sydney. She was in Adelaide. She turned her head and tried to force her leaden eyes to open. The lids were so heavy they dragged against her efforts. 'Huon?'

'Yes, darling, it's me.' His ragged voice rasped the words.

She tried again and opened her eyes. Her vision blurred at first, then started to clear.

Huon leaned close to her, his penetrating blue eyes filled with worry. Deep crevasses of lines criss-crossed the black rings under his eyes. His hair spiked up as if he'd run his hand through it a thousand times.

The fog swirled in her head. He couldn't be real. She must be imag-ining this. She put her hand out and touched his cheek, rough stubble grazing her fingertips.

'You're here.' She heard the croaking disbelief in her voice.

'I am. I've been here two days.' He ran his hand through his hair. 'I should have never been away from you. I'm so sorry.'

'Two days?' She couldn't believe she'd lost two days. 'And Helen?'

'She's doing well. Better than you. You've been pretty ill and wor-rying us sick.'

'Us?' She grappled to think clearly.

'Me, your parents, Claire and the entire town.'

'My parents?' She tried to make sense of his words.

'They flew here. They love you.' He picked up her hand. 'I love you, too.'

Had she heard right? The words hammered in her head and she struggled to focus on his face. 'You love me?' Disbelief coloured her words.

'I love you with every part of me.' He brought her hand up to his face, resting it against his cheek. 'I've been such a fool. I had a gift in front of me and I threw it away.

'I'm *so* sorry. You have no idea how sorry I am. If I could turn back the clock, I would. I hope to make it up to you for the rest of your life.'

Her heart beat faster at the sincerity of his words. Words she'd so wanted to hear. And with his words, hope seeped into her, but she forced her brain to concentrate. She needed to know why he'd changed his mind, needed to be sure he really had. 'But you told me you didn't love me, that you couldn't give me what I wanted.'

'I've been a complete fool.' He sighed a ragged breath. 'I thought I couldn't give you what you wanted. And you were right about me living a half-life. After Ellen died I didn't want to risk loving anyone again. I didn't want to risk loving you.'

A ray of optimism shone inside her. He'd worked it out. He'd recognised what he'd been doing. 'And you pushed me away to try and keep your heart safe?'

He stroked her face and nodded. 'I did. But I made the biggest mistake of my life that night at the ball. I was scared. I was too scared to commit to you and the baby. I thought if I held back, I could never feel the pain of losing someone again.'

He blinked furiously. 'And it happened anyway. Two nights ago I thought you might die. The pain was so strong, so intense that I knew there and then I loved you.' His voice cracked. 'And all I could think of was I hadn't told you.'

Her heart surged with joy. Huon really loved her. He'd been to hell and back while she'd lain in hospital. She wanted to hold him close to her, tell him it was all right, that she understood. But two IV drips and a monitor were in the way.

She squeezed his hand to reassure him. 'I'm here, Huon, and I'm fine.'

'And I'll give thanks for that every day of my life. I know I've hurt you. I know I've taken far too long to work this out, but I love you, Bronte. I think I've loved you from the moment I saw your cute behind sticking up in the air as you struggled with that worn-out case.'

She laughed, then gripped her belly where the stitches pulled. 'And to think I kicked that case when it had actually done me a big favour.'

He tucked her hair behind her ear. 'I love you with all my heart and I want to be part of your life. I want to be your lover, your husband and father to your gorgeous daughter. I can only hope you'll let me.'

She thought her chest would explode from happiness. He wanted to be with her. He'd put his fear aside and was looking to the future. A future with her and the baby.

She looked at his handsome face, etched with lines of worry and pain, and wanted so desperately to ease them away with loving hands. 'I'll let you love me and I'll love you straight back. I couldn't think of anything more wonderful than raising my daughter with you.'

'Will you marry me, Bronte?'

'Absolutely.' Elation filled her. Her life was just beginning. Muttawindi, Huon and a baby daughter. Bronte knew she'd finally found a true home.

EPILOGUE

MUTTAWINDI WAS DRESSED to party. Bunting hung in the streets, the band played and baby Georgina Claire, in a white lace dress, shrieked with delight when she saw her mother.

Bronte, radiant in a flowing ivory gown, smiled a smile of pure joy. The entire town and half the district had come for the wedding. An enormous white marquee lined the main street and the dance floor was, by request, half under cover, half under the stars.

It was hard to believe that four months ago everything had seemed so bleak. Today her new family surrounded her, as well as her old family and dear friends, who had all come to help her and Huon celebrate. Celebrate their love.

She looked over to her new husband of two hours. Looking drop-dead gorgeous in a tux, he was dancing with Mrs Nikvolski.

'Mrs Nikvolski always had a soft spot for Huon.' Claire's voice sounded in her ear.

Bronte laughed and turned towards Claire, who stood holding Georgina. 'Yes, she told me more than once how good he looked in a tux.'

'I doubt you have anything to worry about from that quarter. Huon's gazed seems permanently riveted to you.' Claire's face broke into a wide grin. 'And it shouldn't be any other way. Ron and I have to thank you for bringing Huon back into the real world. And for giving us a gorgeous granddaughter.'

Tears filmed Bronte's eyes. 'You raised a wonderful man, Claire. I should thank you.'

Claire sniffed. 'Off you go and dance with him, then. Georgie is fine with me, aren't you, sweetheart?'

Georgina blew a bubble, happy in her grandmother's arms.

Bronte gave a silent prayer of thanks for her good fortune. She had loving in-laws and a town that fought over the right to spend time with Georgina.

Georgie had shown a determined spirit from the start and had been able to come home to Muttawindi soon after she'd been born.

The joy of being a mother never ceased to amaze Bronte, the wonder of watching her daughter grow, the delight of holding her close and the extreme happiness of knowing that she had a loving father.

'Dr Morrison, are you ready to dance?' Huon's warm and loving hands snaked around her waist, pulling her back against him.

A surge of heat raced through her at his touch and she turned in his arms. 'I'm ready, Dr Morrison. Ready for a long, slow dance.'

His eyes darkened with desire and she thrilled that she could elicit this response from him.

He pulled her even closer, her body melding into his in a perfect fit. 'Did I ever get around to telling you how beautiful you are in that dress?'

She laughed. 'Only about ten times.'

He ducked his head and nuzzled her neck. 'I'm looking forward to telling you how beautiful you are out of that dress.'

His voice, husky with emotion, sent ripples of white-hot sensation through her, making her ache with delicious anticipation. 'I'll hold you to that.'

'And I'll hold you and Georgie close to my heart for the rest of my life.' His lips grazed hers in a loving kiss, sealing his commitment to her.

And she kissed him right back.

* * * * *

Lucy Clark is a husband-and-wife writing team. They enjoy taking holidays with their two children, during which they discuss and develop new ideas for their books using the fantastic Australian scenery. They use their daily walks to talk over characterisation and fine details of the wonderful stories they produce, and are avid movie buffs. They live on the edge of a popular wine district in South Australia, and enjoy spending family time together at weekends.

A Baby For The
Flying Doctor

Lucy Clark

To Vikki—
thanks for your generosity in sharing your
experience and knowledge about Down's.
It was greatly appreciated.

Eph 2:10

CHAPTER ONE

EUPHEMIA GRAINGER MADE her way along the corridor of the old refurbished train, measuring her steps in time with the sway of the carriage. It was quite exciting. She'd never been on a train before, well, not this sort. This was a long-distance train that cut its way from west to east across the wide brown land of Australia. She'd boarded the train at the Didja station, but there were still another two full days of train travel before she arrived in Sydney.

Phemie smiled, pleased she'd finally decided to do something for herself...well, sort of for herself. Anthony had been a big part of her decision to travel by train and she was definitely the sort of person who put others first.

Being raised with a disabled brother—a brother she loved dearly— had taught her that her needs generally came second. Sometimes, when she'd been growing up, she'd been jealous of the attention Anthony received but had known it was necessary. After she'd experienced those moments of envy, she would be swamped immediately by guilt. It was hardly Anthony's fault he'd been born with Down's syndrome.

She was excited to see him on Friday morning when he and his friends would join the train journey for the last day of adventure. Her smile widened as she thought about Anthony. It had been three weeks since she'd last seen her brother and the excitement started to bubble because she knew just how much he'd enjoy train trav—

'Excuse me,' a deep, rich English voice said from behind her, and Phemie immediately turned, looking up at whoever had spoken.

'Sorry.' She moved to the side of the small train aisle so he could pass and glanced up, craning her neck because of his height. 'I didn't realise I was blocking the corridor— Professor Fitzwilliam!'

The words were out of her mouth before she could stop them.

Gilbert Fitzwilliam was startled as he looked down at the petite blonde woman before him, her large blue eyes looking up into his own brown ones. How could she possibly know who he was...unless she was connected with the medical community in some way? It was the only answer and even though she looked about twenty years old, she could still be a conscientious medical student, nurse, dietician or perhaps an intern.

She put out her hand and he automatically took it. He'd been shaking hand after hand for the past eleven months. Soon, though, it would all be over. One more conference in Sydney and his travelling fellowship would technically be over. Once he returned to the UK and completed the paperwork, he'd be officially unemployed. What he would do next, he had no idea. At the moment, though, he needed to keep busy.

'I've read your papers.' The pretty blonde nodded enthusiastically. 'Amazing stuff.'

Stuff? She was still shaking his hand, her slim fingers warm and inviting. When she'd initially looked at him, she'd had the most engaging smile on her lips and he'd been instantly captivated by her, by this...stranger. This stranger who knew who he was and had found his scientific papers to be amazing 'stuff'. 'Uh...well...' He cleared his throat and raised an eyebrow before looking pointedly at their hands.

'Oh. Sorry.' She immediately let go. 'I guess I hadn't expected to find you here. On the train, I mean. Last place in the world. Going to Sydney on a train, across Australia. Who would have thought?' Good heavens. She was babbling. She never babbled. Well, not unless she was nervous. Was she nervous? If so, why was she nervous? What on earth did she have to be nervous about? The fact that the man before her was one of the world's leading experts on emergency medicine—her particular forte—couldn't possibly have anything to do with it!

'I'm pleased you found them so informative.' Gil looked into her upturned face, once again struck by her beauty. The afternoon light coming through the window beside them gave her an ethereal glow that made her blonde locks radiant, her blue eyes sparkling with a pleasure he'd never thought his medical writing could promote.

They stood staring at each other, captured in a strange bubble in the middle of an aisle in a train carriage. Phemie couldn't believe how distinguished and handsome Professor Fitzwilliam was in real life. She'd seen several stock photographs of him as she'd waded her way through medical journals and articles he'd written and even though she'd known she would be seeing him at the conference in Sydney, given he was the guest of honour, she hadn't expected to come this close to him. Not like this. Not in a personal rather than a professional capacity.

His brown hair was cut short even though she was certain that if he were to let it grow a little longer, it would have a definite curl to the ends. Flecks of grey peppered the sides but instead of making him look old, they gave him a distinguished air of authority.

It was his eyes, however, that had her staring, forgetting all her manners. The rich deep brown irises were flecked with golden swirls, making her feel both wild and yet safe at the same time. It was an interesting sensation and one she'd never experienced before, but it wasn't every day she stood gazing at a man she classified as medical royalty.

The train lurched, breaking the moment, bringing them both back to reality with a jolt. Phemie lost her balance, putting a hand to the wall to stop herself from falling but instead of finding hard wood panelling, she found hard muscular arms coming around her as Professor Fitzwilliam steadied her.

'Easy there.' He stood firm as the train continued to bounce around. The first thing that assailed his senses was her sweet yet subtle scent. He'd never known someone could smell like sunshine before but this young woman did. The second thing he noticed was the way his arm seemed to mould naturally to her shape. Her hand was resting on his shoulder, his hand at her waist.

As they wobbled back and forth, Phemie somehow managed to steady her feet, bending her knees slightly so she swayed better with the rhythm of the train. Now that she had herself back on track, she should really let go of him, although it appeared she was having trouble sending the signals from her brain to her limbs.

All she'd been able to concentrate on was the feel of his warm skin beneath his thin cotton shirt and how, due to her lack of height, her eyes rested at his chest level. Where his tie would ordinarily reside, there was now an open shirt, revealing a smattering of dark brown hair. She breathed in and tried not to crumple further into his arms as her senses were assailed with a light spicy cologne that she'd always loved.

He looked at her, momentarily surprised to find just how close they'd become. The train jolted again and he increased his grip. His gaze flicked from her lips to her eyes and back again and the urge to actually kiss this woman, this complete stranger, was utterly overwhelming.

How ridiculous. He didn't *do* instant attractions. He didn't *do* romance. He didn't *do* relationships. He'd been there, done that and his world had ended in despair. Work was the only thing that interested him. He could lose himself in work. He could write articles, develop new techniques. He could lecture and pass on information because work never let him down. It occupied his every waking moment and kept his mind busy. At least, that's the way things had been until a few minutes ago...before he'd had his arms around the beautiful blonde.

The train levelled out but it took Phemie a moment or two to process this fact. Her mind was too busy trying to decipher whether Professor Fitzwilliam had actually just looked as though he intended to kiss her! Or had that been her own imagination? She was already half in love with the man's mind. He was so brilliant, so insightful and now that she'd come face to face with him, so...incredibly gorgeous. She did her best not to sigh out loud.

'Uh...' Phemie licked her lips and edged backwards, almost flattening herself against the wall. 'Thanks.'

'For what?' He'd let her go. He was no longer touching her and yet his body still tingled and buzzed from the powerful electric jolt he'd received when holding this delightful young woman in his arms. The fact that she was the first woman to have elicited such a response since his wife was something he didn't really want to think about.

'For...uh...' Oh, come on, Euphemia. Get that intelligent brain of yours working, she silently scolded herself. 'Stopping me from falling.'

He nodded once. 'Yes. Right. Good. Well you're...uh, welcome,

Miss...' He fished for her name because deep down inside he simply *had* to know who she was.

'Grainger. Dr Euphemia Grainger.' She was about to shake his hand again but caught the impulse in time. No. No more touching of the muscular and well-toned English professor.

His eyebrow went up again in surprise at her name. Doctor, eh? So she was obviously older than he'd initially thought. It certainly helped explain how she'd known his identity.

'As I've already mentioned, I've read all of your papers.' Her smooth tones washed over him and he found her Australian twang rather delightful.

'I remember.' His lips twitched into a smile. 'Apparently they were amazing...stuff.'

She wrinkled her nose at the way he said the word, then a bright smile spread across her face, lighting her eyes. The overall effect made Gil suck in a breath. 'Sorry. That's my younger brother's influence rubbing off on me. He uses the word like water.'

Older sibling. Doctor. Stunning. Good taste in reading material. Gil filed away these points. 'So...Euphemia.' He rolled her name around on his tongue. 'That's a rather different name.'

'Family one, I'm afraid.'

'You don't like it?'

She shrugged. 'I guess you could say I'm used to it. I also like the aunt I was named after so I guess that helps.' Phemie glanced behind him and saw someone else was heading in their direction in the already overcrowded narrow, swaying corridor. She gestured to the person coming through and both she and Professor Fitzwilliam flattened themselves against the walls. She was highly conscious of where he was standing, trying to avoid being pushed into him, but the train lurched once more, causing her to press right up against the one man she was trying to avoid.

The heat was instant. The pressure, the awareness she had of him. It was starting to become too much for her. The person passing them stumbled as the train wobbled and Phemie held firmly onto the professor. She couldn't move until the other man had passed them by.

'Very squashy,' she whispered as her body pressed up against his. She didn't want to breathe in his scent. She didn't want to be aware of how incredible his body felt beneath her hands.

Gil worked hard at keeping his hands by his side, determined not to hold her again. Her chest was pressed against his body and the effort to ignore all sensations called on all his inner strength. Humour. Humour would be the only way to diffuse this situation. He grinned down at her. 'I don't know about squashy. I find this sort of situation helps you get to know complete strangers rather quickly.'

Euphemia was amazed at how a simple thing like a smile could transform someone's face. Small laughter lines appeared around his eyes and those rich brown irises made her think of melting chocolate. His mouth was curved, showing a tiny glimpse of white teeth, and she realised the whole awareness thing she was feeling with him was ridiculous and extremely temporary. Making light of the situation did seem the best option. She would follow his lead.

Returning his smile, the warmth of his body was still flowing against hers, all the way to her toes, but she did her best to ignore it. 'It most certainly does.' She looked down the aisle and was astonished and embarrassed to find the elderly man had passed them and was almost through the door at the other end of the carriage, leaving them both room to move.

Phemie shifted back immediately and straightened her light cotton jacket. Twice she'd been up against him, meaning she had twice the amount of wild awareness coursing through her body, yet somehow she had to ignore it. He was Professor Fitzwilliam, for goodness' sake. Her superior not only in qualifications but in experience. She looked at him, desperate to think of something to say that would make her sound intelligent and yet get her away from him as soon as possible.

'I'd best get back to my cabin.' She even pointed to where it was. Way to go, Phemie, she silently congratulated herself. No doubt the next Nobel Peace Prize candidate.

He nodded but when she didn't immediately move, he cleared his throat and put a bit of distance between them. It was strange. They were no longer near each other, she was about to leave, and Gil was struck with a burning desire to prolong their contact. He was intrigued by this young woman and he quickly decided that as long as he kept things businesslike, there was no reason why he couldn't chat with her. Perhaps he could assist her in a medical capacity? Help her to choose the area she might want to specialise in? Act as a sort of sounding board for any ideas she might have? After all, they still had a few days to go before arriving in Sydney and it would be foolish to completely ignore her...not after holding her so firmly in his arms.

'Look, Dr Grainger.' Yes. It was much better when he thought of her like that rather than as a desirable woman who had been in his arms twice in the past five minutes. 'I hope you won't think me too impertinent if I invite you to join me for a cup of tea in the lounge car. We could...discuss my papers or talk about the most recent breakthroughs in medical science.' Business. He needed to keep everything on a professional level.

His smooth deep tones washed over her and his rounded English vowels made her knees quiver. 'Oh.' One-on-one time with Professor Fitzwilliam! Her first instinct was to immediately accept but she'd learned long ago to temper those first instincts because responsibility always came first. She was the older sibling, the carer, the reliable friend who put other people's needs before those of her own.

'Think it over,' Gil said when it seemed she was having difficulty replying. 'It's a long journey and we'll no doubt "bump" into each other again.' And for some reason, he secretly hoped it was literally as well as figuratively. With that, he turned and headed back the way he'd come, but before he could reach the door, she spoke.

'I'd love to sit and chat with you.'

He looked over his shoulder, pleased with her answer. 'Great.'

'Especially about your latest journal article or your research developments. However...' she shrugged apologetically '...it's just that...um...I need to get my head around my conference presentation.'

'You're going to the conference?' Gil's eyebrows hit his hairline. Not an intern, then. Fully qualified specialist? Dr Grainger's age kept increasing in his mind. His lips twitched at the thought. Poor woman. She was becoming older and older the more he discovered about her.

'It's my first time presenting,' she confided with a laugh that ended in a sigh. 'I'm rather nervous, though.' She spread her hands wide. 'I guess that must sound silly to someone like you who can get up and give brilliant keynote speeches with ease and clarity. Still, I'm looking forward to it.' She didn't want the man to think she was incompetent.

'Don't let the fact that I've done many speeches fool you. I still get a little nervous.'

'You do?'

'Of course.' He didn't want to talk about himself, he wanted to learn more about her. 'I must say, Euphemia, it's very impressive you've had a paper accepted.' He knew the quality of the presenters at the conference and realised Dr Grainger must indeed be an exceptional doctor if her paper had been chosen. 'And you're going all the way to Sydney by train?'

'Yes. More time to finalise things, at least that's what I keep telling myself. I just want everything to be perfect.'

'And that's your cabin?' He pointed to the one she'd indicated previously.

'Yes. Well…until we get to Adelaide. Then I'll be sitting up in the day-night seaters.'

'What? Why? You can't sleep in those things and then present at the conference on Monday.' He had a rather large cabin which had two beds. Perhaps Dr Grainger might like to— He stopped his thoughts before they continued. It wasn't his place to solve the problems of the world, let alone the problems of petite and pretty Dr Grainger. He'd tried several times to take the world on his shoulders and had only ended up suffering from bouts of depression. No. It wasn't up to him to solve Euphemia's problems. Problems of a medical nature, problems where he could figure out a solution—that was completely different. It was one of the reasons he'd accepted the travelling fellowship because he'd needed to continue moving, doing something, *anything* so he didn't have to face his past.

'The seats aren't so bad,' Euphemia was saying, and Gil realised he'd zoned out for a moment. 'No worse than economy class in an aeroplane besides, I have friends joining me when the train stops in Adelaide so that way we can all be together.'

It wasn't his problem where she sat or why, he told himself again. 'Fair enough.' He nodded politely, deciding now was a good time to escape her unnerving presence. 'Well, I hope you'll be able to join me for a cup of tea at some point over the next few days. It's a long train journey and I'd relish the opportunity to sit and chat with you.'

'I'd like that. Uh…from a medical point of view, I mean,' she added quickly, just in case he thought she might want to chat about other things. 'Uh…not that talking to you about more general topics wouldn't be appreciated but—' She cut herself off and closed her eyes for a split second, wondering if she could make this moment any more difficult. She doubted it.

'I understand.' Gil held out his hand, being the ever-polite professor, and then wished he hadn't. He was still simmering deep down inside from the last time they'd touched. Why had he instigated another? He cleared his throat and called on all the professionalism he could muster. 'It was nice to meet you, Dr Grainger.'

'You too, Professor Fitzwilliam.'

'Gil.'

A shy smile touched her lips. 'Gil.' Once again they seemed caught up in time, their hands clasped, their gazes locked. She breathed in his name and tried not to sigh. 'Uh…er…' She shrugged, feeling a little self-conscious. 'My friends call me Phemie.'

'Phemie.' Gil nodded, still enchanted to find such an unusual name for such an unusual woman. He gave her hand an extra little squeeze before releasing it. 'I sincerely hope to see you around, Phemie Grainger.'

'Likewise, Gil Fitzwilliam.' With one more smile, he turned and walked away. She stood there like a gormless twit and watched him open the carriage door, heading through that one and then through to the previous carriage. There was no way she could help the deep, satisfied sigh that escaped her.

She'd just met Professor Fitzwilliam. *The* Professor Fitzwilliam. A man she'd admired for…well, since she'd been a medical student. He'd been writing medical articles for the *Journal of Emergency Medicine* for years and whenever her copy had arrived, his were the first articles she'd read.

Phemie returned to her cabin and sank into the chair. She looked at the notes for her presentation but found she simply couldn't concentrate. She was restless now and there was nowhere to prowl in the small cabin.

She'd met Professor Fitzwilliam…*and* he'd invited her to call him Gil. Honestly, she was behaving like a schoolgirl meeting a film star for the first time. Awe-struck and completely irrational. She needed help. Back-up. She reached for her mobile phone and was pleased to discover there was coverage. She pressed the buttons for the pre-set number.

'Dr Clarkson.'

'Melissa? It's Phemie.'

'Bored already? Didn't we just put you on the train about an hour ago?' her good friend Melissa Clarkson asked. Melissa was an OB/GYN working at the clinic and hospital in the small outback town of Didjabrindagrogalon which covered the district and community Phemie and her colleagues serviced through the Royal Flying Doctor Service. The two women had been friends since Melissa had come to search for her brother, Dex, but had instead fallen in love with her brother's best friend, Joss. Now happily married, Melissa was well and truly settled in the outback and this only served to strengthen the friendship they shared.

'He's here.'

'Who's where?'

'Gil...uh, I mean Professor Fitzwilliam.'

'He's on the train?'

'Yes.'

'Going to the conference in Sydney?'

'Yes. I guess so.'

'Why is he on the train? I know he had a two-day stopover in Perth because Dex went and caught up with him there. I wonder why he didn't fly to Sydney?'

'Dex knows him? Like as a friend?' Phemie asked with mounting incredulity.

Melissa chuckled. 'Yes. The two of them worked together years ago on the Pacific island of Tarparnii. From what Dex said, Gil was quite involved with Pacific Medical Aid for a while.'

'Why didn't Dex tell me he knew Gil...uh, I mean Professor Fitzwilliam?' Phemie closed her eyes, unable to believe she was already starting to *think* of him in a more personal way. That wouldn't do. It wouldn't do at all. She had no room in her life for any new...people. She was full to bursting and Gil, uh, Professor Fitzwilliam would just have to remain on the outer rim.

'You know Dex. He's hardly the name-dropping type. Besides, he's been too busy falling in love with Iris. You should see the two of them. Ugh. I hope Joss and I didn't look that gushy when we first got together.'

Iris was the new paediatrician who had come to Didja for only six months but now that she and Dex had sorted out their differences and also because Iris had recently become guardian to the most gorgeous baby girl, the Didja clinic had scored itself a permanent paediatrician. Phemie sighed, thinking how nice it was that her friends were all finding their perfect mates, and that deep gnawing sensation of loneliness she worked hard to ignore started to raise its ugly head again.

'You did. Trust me. It was nauseating,' Phemie teased, needing to get her thoughts back on track.

'Oh. Well. Can't be helped,' Melissa brushed Phemie's teasing aside. 'So, tell me, why is it a big deal that Gil's on the train?'

'He asked me if I wanted to join him for a cup of tea,' she murmured.

'What? The fiend. How dare he? Oh, the impertinence of the English,' Melissa joked. 'Tea! Who would have thought?'

Phemie chuckled, already starting to feel less rattled. 'Stop.'

'So when are you joining him for this tea-drinking ritual? In the dead of night? Early morning? Oh, I know—at afternoon teatime? Seems perfect for the tea-drinking to be performed.'

'I don't know.' Phemie shook her head. 'It was just sort of an open-ended invitation. I don't know what to do. Do I accept? Do I ignore it?'

'He's rattled you,' Melissa stated. 'The unrattleable Phemie has been rattled.'

'Well…I…I…er…'

'You're stammering. You never stammer. Not unless you're well and truly rattled. Good grief, Pheme. What happened when you two met?'

'We sort of…bumped into each other. Literally.'

'Ooh.' Delight dripped from Melissa's tone. 'Do tell, girlfriend.'

Phemie gave Melissa a quick recount of the past fifteen minutes. 'I'm supposed to be concentrating on my paper, on getting everything sorted out in my head so I don't make a fool of myself when I get up in front of thousands of people on Monday to do my presentation.'

'And now you can't concentrate because of *him*?'

'Of course I can concentrate. That's why I called you. If I talk it all out, then I can put it aside and focus.'

'Oh, piffle. You have hours and hours of doing nothing on that train.'

'Anthony's getting on—'

'On Friday morning. It's Wednesday, Phemie,' Melissa pointed out. 'Look, there's more than enough time for you to go over the presentation, spend time with Anthony *and* have the occasional cup of tea with a medical genius. It's a three-day journey from Perth and perhaps Professor Fitz-yummy is looking for a bit of company. Professional and platonic, of course. He is a gentleman after all.'

'Yes.'

'A gentleman who has already held you in his arms—twice!'

Even though Melissa couldn't see her, Phemie coloured a little at her friend's words. 'It was the train. It was lurching,' she said defensively.

'You believe that if you need to. Phemie?'

'Yes?'

'Go and have a cup of tea with him. Talk about the latest medical breakthroughs or whatever it is that you find interesting but for goodness' sake, relax a little. Let yourself go. Step outside that very comfortable comfort zone you've locked yourself inside. It's all too easy to stay put.' Melissa's tone said she knew what she was talking about.

'I've taken steps outside my zone,' Phemie felt compelled to say, even though she knew her friend was right. 'I'm working in the middle of nowhere, for goodness' sake. I left Perth. I'm out in the wide brown land... well, ochre land at any rate, and I'm meeting new people. I think that qualifies as stepping outside my comfort zone.'

'Or perhaps it's simply doing the same moves inside a different shape. You're the nurturing type as well as a workaholic. Going to Sydney on the train should force you to do one thing—slow down. You're still taking care of everyone else's needs except your own.'

'And you think having a cup of tea with Professor Fitzwilliam will take care of my needs?'

'It might.'

'Must be pretty powerful tea, then.'

Melissa laughed. 'Just promise me you'll try and be open to new experiences.'

'Such as joining an esteemed English professor for tea?'

'Exactly.'

* * *

An hour later, Melissa's words still ringing in her ears, Phemie gave up on the pretence of reading and searched for her shoes. All passengers had been warned by the train stewards to always wear closed shoes when walking about the train—especially between carriages.

As she left her cabin, she realised the train was really rocking now and she wondered whether the drivers were trying to make up time. She made it to the next carriage, trying to ignore the blast of cool air as she'd stood on the gangplank that connected the two cars together. In just under a month, winter would be here. Not that that mattered much where she lived, about fifty kilometres outside Didja's town centre at the RFDS base. Even in winter, the weather was still rather warm.

She walked through the next carriage, then heaved open the heavy door at the end, crossing into another carriage which she realised was the lounge car. Several people were seated here and there, some talking quietly, some reading or doing work on their computers. She headed through, wanting to get to the dining carriage to at least get a warm drink, hoping that might help her to relax.

'It's full.' A deep English accent washed over her and she turned to find Professor Gilbert Fitzwilliam sitting at one of the corner lounges, a Thermos on the table in front of him.

'Oh, hi.' Why had her heart-rate picked up the instant she'd seen him? 'Pardon?'

'The dining carriage. It's completely filled with people.'

'Oh.' Euphemia frowned, then shrugged. 'Oh, well. I guess I'll have to wait until the rush is over for a warm drink.'

'Not necessarily.' Gil indicated his Thermos. 'Would you care to join me?' When she hesitated for a moment, he continued, 'After all, I *do* remember inviting you to join me at some point. That point could be now.'

Phemie smiled. 'Yes. Yes it could.' She remembered Melissa's encouraging words about taking a step outside her comfort zone. Besides, it wasn't as though Gil was a complete stranger. She already felt as though she knew him, thanks to his brilliant articles and textbooks, and Dex knew him so that gave her a personal connection of sorts and a reason to trust him a little sooner than she would have trusted the average stranger.

Not that she was implying that he was average because, just by looking at him, she could tell he was more than above avera— She stopped her thoughts when she realised he was still waiting for an answer. 'Uh... well...all right, then, Professor. Let's do this now.' Phemie flicked the end of her blonde ponytail down her back and sat down opposite him.

'Excellent.' Gil opened the lid of his Thermos and poured out a cup. 'I'm sorry if you take tea with milk or sugar. We could probably rustle some up from somewhere but I'm afraid I drink it black.'

'All the better to infuse your mouth with flavours?' she asked.

Gil chuckled and the warmth of the sound washed over her. 'Something like that.'

'Black is fine.' Phemie took a sip and tried not to make a face. 'What sort of tea is this?' She'd been expecting plain black, not slightly flavoured.

'Earl Grey. Don't like it?'

'It tastes like dishwater.'

'Is that so? Well, as I am not a connoisseur of dishwater, I can't cast a vote on your assessment. Do you drink it often? Dishwater, I mean.'

Phemie laughed. 'Can't say that I do, although where I live, running water is considered a luxury so if anything gets into our water tanks, it can taste pretty gross.'

'So you don't infuse your mouth with the flavours from the washing-up water?'

She shook her head and laughed again. He was handsome. He was polite and now he was bringing out humour. Lethal combination.

'Tell me, then, Dr Grainger, what sort of tea do you usually drink?'

'Australian, of course. It's rich, full bodied and there's plenty of it.'

The light in Gil's eyes twinkled as their gazes held. Was she not only describing the essence of Australia but the essence of Euphemia Grainger? 'I'm intrigued. Sounds like something I should experience whilst I'm in your country.'

'I think you should.' Why did she get the feeling they were having two completely different conversations? There was a light in his eyes, one that made her heart rate instantly increase.

'It's settled, then.'

'What is?' Confusion creased her brow.

'That you'll meet me in the conference hotel lobby at the end of the first day's sessions to treat me to a rich, full-bodied Australian experience.'

Was he still talking about tea? 'In Sydney?'

'They don't drink tea in Sydney?'

'Yes. Of course they do. Sorry.' She was still coming to terms with the fact that Gil was more than happy to spend time with her at the conference...in a personal capacity. 'I'm not sure I remember where a good tea house is in Sydney. It's been a while since I was there.'

The train jolted a little and Gil rocked forward towards her but there he stayed, his face close, his words a little more intimate than before. 'Then we shall have to explore together.'

Phemie held her breath, her gaze flicking to his mouth, then back to his eyes, a strange warmth settling over her. The moment grew more intense when Gil visually caressed her lips. Her heart started pounding wildly in her chest, not from fright or uncertainty but from pure attraction—such as she'd never felt before.

Her lips parted to allow the pent-up air to escape. On a personal level, she knew next to nothing about this man and he knew next to nothing about her, yet there seemed to be something new, something exciting brewing between them...and it wasn't the dishwater-tasting tea.

'Euphemia.' Her name was a caress on his lips and for one heart-stopping second she thought he might continue his journey towards her and actually kiss her. She closed her eyes, trying to control her thoughts, her breathing, but all she could think about was how, at this second in time, she wanted to be free, to let go, to break all the rules and regulations she'd previously set down for her life.

She *wanted* him to kiss her. *Wanted* to know what it would be like. *Wanted* to feel the touch of his mouth against hers. It was ludicrous. It was impossible. It was what she wanted.

The next thing she knew, there was a loud screeching noise and she was thrown to the floor, landing hard with a heavy thud. She could feel firm hands on her upper arms and then she was somehow hauled against firm male chest as they started to slide along the floor of the carriage.

The train was stopping—and it was stopping at a rapid rate.

CHAPTER TWO

PEOPLE WERE SCREAMING, yelling. The scent of panic was in the air. A baby cried. The screeching noise continued. As the train came to a halt, all Phemie was conscious of was Gil and the way he'd automatically protected her, his body taking the brunt of the impact as they slid into the bolted-down lounge chairs opposite to where they'd previously been sitting.

When they finally stopped, it took a second for rational thought to return.

'Are you all right?' His voice was soft near her ear but full of concern.

'Hmm?' She opened her eyes, looking into those gorgeous brown depths which had hypnotised her earlier. She was lying in his arms, their bodies so close together she was positive he could hear her heart pounding wildly against her chest. The main question was whether it was pounding so badly due to the surprise of the train stopping or because she was in his arms?

'Euphemia!' His voice became louder and she saw the worried look in his eyes.

'Yes?'

'Are you hurt? Bruised? Can you stand?' As he spoke, he felt her head and down her arms. How could she—a trained medical professional—be more concerned with her reaction to this perfect stranger than the train accident? What was wrong with her?

'I'm fine.' And she wasn't sure she liked him touching her, simply because it caused a mass of tingles to flood her entire body and explode like fireworks. She shifted but it appeared he wasn't ready to move away just yet. 'I'm fine,' she reiterated. 'I'm OK. You? You hit that lounge pretty hard.'

Phemie touched his shoulder but on feeling the firm muscle realised her touch was anything but medical. Bad. It was bad. He was *Professor Gilbert Fitzwilliam*! She wasn't supposed to have an instant attraction to this man. He was a medical genius. He was a research phenomenon and he lived on the other side of the world. Apart from that, Phemie was most certainly not looking for any sort of romantic relationship. Not now. Not ever.

'I'll live.' Gil carefully stood, holding out a hand to help Phemie up. The sooner he put some distance between them the better. Having that gorgeous, petite body of hers pressed hard against his was something he hadn't expected to experience but now he had, he couldn't help his mounting intrigue for this woman.

Once she was on her feet, he let her go. Distance. He needed distance from her. He was so intent on moving away he almost stood on his Thermos, which had rolled to the floor. He quickly picked it up and placed it on a chair. 'Someone's pulled the emergency stop handle.'

'Agreed.' Phemie brushed herself down, straightening her clothes, pleased there was now space between them. She dragged in a few breaths to focus herself. 'Emergency stop means—'

'Something has gone wrong. No doubt medical assistance will be required.' He headed for the carriage door. 'I'll find a steward then hopefully we'll know what's going on. Stay here and ensure everyone in this carriage is all right.' With that, he opened the weighted door. Phemie watched him go, liking the way he walked—sure and firm and with purpose.

As soon as he was out of sight, her brain clicked immediately into medical mode and she went to help the other lounge-car passengers. There were a few bumps, a few bruises and scratches but for the most part everyone seemed fine, just very shaken. One man was more concerned about his computer than anything else. Everyone had questions but Phemie didn't have any answers.

She had just finished checking the pulse of a three-year-old boy, snuggled into his mother's arms, his cries having settled somewhat, when Gil strode back into the carriage, two stewards and a guard following him. One of the stewards carried a large medical kit.

'Dr Grainger. You're needed. This way.' His tone was as brisk as his strides and realising she was seeing the *Professor* in all his professional glory, Phemie excused herself from the young mother and followed the men.

'Apparently, there's been an incident a few carriages down.' Gil spoke softly yet clearly as they made their way through the empty dining carriage towards the rear of the twenty-two-car-long train. 'One of the passengers had an accident walking between two of the carriages. His mate was behind him, saw it happen and ran back to pull the emergency stop.'

'Do we have any idea what sort of injury?'

Her voice was calm, clear and in control. Gil was pleased. It appeared he had a doctor who was more than happy to assist in this emergency. He'd realised years ago that emergency medicine didn't suit every type of medical professional, but for him it provided variety and unique challenges and was something he thrived on...especially since June and Caitie. Gil shook his head. Now was definitely not the time to even think about his past.

'Lots of blood has been the main report.' Gil indicated to one of the stewards as they walked through to the next carriage and nodded, indicating the man should start his debrief now.

'Uh...yeah...right, Doc. We uh...just got a message through our radios...' he indicated the two-way communication device '...saying a man had hurt himself and there was a lot of blood.'

Phemie nodded, thinking through possible scenarios, but there were simply too many. 'Has anyone contacted the authorities? Sent for medical support?'

'Uh...I think the driver has notified the rail authority but I don't know about anything else.'

Phemie reached into the pocket of her jeans and pulled out her phone.

'It won't work here,' the guard said. 'We're in the middle of nowhere.'

'We're only about four hours out of Didja and *this* is no ordinary phone.' She punched in a number and a moment later was connected. 'Hi, it's Phemie.' She paused. 'I *am* having a break, I promise, but there's been an accident on the train.' The guard was able to give her their exact co-ordinates and she passed this information on. 'Get the plane in the air. I'll forward more details when I have them. Over.' She replaced the phone in her pocket.

'Over?' A quizzical smile tipped Gil's lips as they continued their way through the train. 'Do you always end your phone calls like that?'

'Oh. Yeah. Bad habit. I'm used to talking on a UHF radio.'

'Really?' Gil continued to be intrigued by this woman. 'Who did you just call?'

'RFDS.' At his blank look, she remembered he was from overseas and quickly explained. 'Royal Flying Doctor Service. We're based just outside Didja.'

'Didja?'

'Didjabrindagrogalon. It's the outback town where I boarded the train.'

'You work at the RFDS?'

'Yes.'

Gil digested this information as they finally arrived at the carriage with the injured passenger. As they'd walked, the stewards and guard had been stopped several times by people wanting to know what was happening. Some people were crying, others were visibly shaken, some had slept through the entire thing. Gil, however, was busy processing the information about Phemie. If she worked for the RFDS, which he presumed provided emergency medical support to the farthest reaches of this vast country, it surely meant she was an experienced doctor with several years of training behind her. Yet she looked so young.

Harlan, the steward carrying the medical kit, walked behind them. 'It's just down here...' He pointed as the end of the carriage came into view. There were lots of people standing around, blocking the way.

'Excuse me.' Gil's voice carried the authority necessary to make people obey. They shuffled by the crowd to find one man slumped to the floor, his eyes wide, his hands tinged with blood, his body shaking, staring blankly.

Beside him were another two stewards, leaning over a man in his early twenties. One was at his head, talking to him, trying to keep him calm. The other was at the man's feet. The patient's right leg was elevated, a blood-soaked towel around the foot.

'I'm Dr Fitzwilliam. What's happened?' Again, Gil's voice was clear and smooth. Phemie watched an expression of relief cross the steward's face. The cavalry was there and they were more than happy to back away.

'His toe's come off. His big toe!' The steward holding the towel was the first to speak, the words said with utter disbelief. 'He wasn't wearing closed shoes. He went between the carriages, the train lurched, his toe got caught and...and...saying this out loud makes me feel sick.'

'We tell the passengers,' Harlan said sternly, 'we tell them no flip-flops. No bare feet. We tell them all the time.'

'Yes.' Gil took the first-aid kit from Harlan, holding it open so Phemie could extract gloves. 'Thank you. Now isn't the time for chastisement or laying blame. The legalities can wait until later. The first priority is for the patient to be assessed. Harlan, you need to find the missing digit.'

'His toe's really come off?' Phemie had managed to manoeuvre herself around so she could take over from the young steward who was holding the towel. 'We need to find it.'

'Find the toe?' Now the young steward turned a nasty shade of pale.

'Believe it or not.' Harlan's voice was strong and sure. 'This isn't the first time something like this has happened. Of course, the last time was almost twenty years ago and even though we found the missing toe, it was too late to reattach it.' He seemed to be the one with the strongest constitution amongst the railway staff present and Phemie knew Gil had been right to put him in charge of the search. 'I'll get that organised immediately.' He turned to the guard and started discussing exactly where they had stopped and how far back they would need to begin looking.

Gil crouched down near the friend who was against the wall but kept glancing to where Phemie was busy assessing the foot in question. He put the first-aid kit down where she could reach it, then focused on the injured man's friend. 'What's your name?'

'Paolo.'

'I'm Gil. What happened? Can you remember?'

'We were just walking between the carriages. We were heading to the dining hall and Kiefer stumbled. I don't know. The train just lurched and then Kiefer was screaming and there was blood everywhere around his foot and the...the...I was right near the door and then I saw the emergency stop handle and I just...I just pulled it. I...' Paolo shook his head. 'There was blood and...' He clamped a hand over his mouth.

'It's OK,' Gil reassured him. 'You did the right thing. Any delay in stopping the train means we may not find the toe.'

'Oh—' Paolo went as white as a sheet, looking like he was going to faint.

Gil urged the man's head forward and motioned for Harlan to come over. 'Get someone to stay with Paolo, please. I need to assist Dr Grainger.'

'She's a doctor?' Harlan was stunned. 'She looks so young.'

As he made his way to Kiefer, Gil was pleased he wasn't the only one who'd thought Phemie to be a lot younger than she looked. 'Hey, there, Kiefer,' he said to their patient. 'I'm Gil and this is Phemie. Are you allergic to anything?'

'No. No.' Kiefer shook his head. Gil searched in the first-aid kit, pleased to find a penlight torch. He checked Kiefer's pupils. 'Been drinking tonight? Taking any substances?' He checked the man's pupils.

Kiefer shook his head again.

'I need to know. I don't care what it is but I need to know otherwise it makes it more difficult for us to treat you.' Gil could smell the faint remnants of beer on the breath of both Paolo and his mate but he needed to hear it.

'Beer. Just beer.'

'How many?'

'Three. Maybe four. Not that many. We'd just got started. We got hungry.' Kiefer was in so much pain Gil was surprised he hadn't passed out but the alcohol would have been enough to take the edge off the trauma.

'All right. Good.' The first-aid kit was well stocked but unfortunately there was nothing stronger than over-the-counter pain medication. It would have to do for now. Gil sent a steward to get a cup of water.

'How does it look?' he asked quietly as he watched Phemie. She'd placed the foot onto a clean towel and was trying to clean and wash the wound site to afford them a better look.

'From what I can see, it's been cleanly severed. There is sufficient skin to enable reattachment. He's a good candidate. I've asked for some ice-packs and also for a container of ice for when we find the missing digit.'

'Optimism. I like that.'

'Good, because I have it in abundance.'

'Really?'

Their gazes met, his brown eyes rich and almost teasing. For a split second it was as though they were back in the lounge carriage. Just the two of them, their minds having one conversation, their bodies having another. Tension. Awareness. Questions. They were all there and as Phemie looked away, she made the attempt to clarify her statement. 'Well, where my patients are concerned, at any rate.'

'Like all good doctors should,' he returned. Why had she felt the need to clarify? Was she not usually optimistic in other areas of her life? Her personal life? If that was the case, it only piqued his curiosity further. In fact, ever since he'd first seen Euphemia Grainger his thoughts had been more captivated by her than anything else. This was definitely something new for him to ponder, given that his thoughts were always about his research, his next lot of speeches and presentations. Thinking about a woman? Having a woman occupy his thoughts? No. That was wrong.

The steward returned with the cup of water and Gil administered two analgesic painkillers, knowing the previously consumed alcohol in Kiefer's system wouldn't react to the pills. Until help arrived, there wasn't much else he or Phemie could do except make their patient as comfortable as possible and find that toe.

Gil performed Kiefer's observations and reported the findings to Phemie. 'He's as stable as we can get him.'

'Good. I'm ready to bandage this foot up now. Did you want to look before I do so?' she asked, shifting slightly to make room where there wasn't any. Now that she'd said the words, she wasn't sure she wanted him to come any closer. If he did, it would only bring them into tight contact with each other, given the walkways were barely big enough to fit two people through side by side let alone hip to hip with a patient lying on the floor before them.

Gil tried to shift through but short of moving Kiefer's body to the side, getting anywhere near the foot in question was going to have to wait. He shook his head. 'I can't get through. Just show me from there. I have good eyesight.'

Phemie unwrapped the foot from the clean towel she'd draped over it and angled it slightly so Gil could see. He was, after all, Professor Gilbert Fitzwilliam, the British surgeon who had basically written the manual for emergency medical procedures. Whilst he perused Kiefer's foot, Phemie perused him. To say he wasn't at all what she'd expected was a bit of an understatement. He was more down to earth, more…natural than she'd thought, but, then, she'd never really thought about him as a person in his own right.

'You've done well at debriding. Bandage away. The healthier we keep the area, the better the chance of successful reattachment.' At that, he turned to Harlan, remembering to check on the status. The steward was the lynchpin in this whole retrieval operation and he'd done a good job. Whilst Gil and Phemie had been tending to the patient, Harlan's communication radio had been working overtime. Staff were out searching for the digit, other stewards were attempting to keep passengers as calm as possible and Gil knew it was Harlan who had given the train manager the right words to say over the loudspeaker to inform the passengers of the situation.

'Ice-packs are on their way,' Harlan informed them. 'Sorry it's taken so long.'

'No need to apologise,' Gil replied. 'We wholeheartedly appreciate the assistance you've provided and thank you. You've been most obliging.'

'Very good, sir.' Harlan almost made a little bow.

Phemie couldn't help but smile as she expertly finished off Kiefer's bandage. Gil really sounded like the professor when he spoke like that, all British with pomp and ceremony. She liked it and hoped it would serve as a reminder of who he really was. That way, she at least had a hope of keeping herself under better control.

Gil checked on Paolo and found him to be improving and more in possession of his faculties. Phemie began asking Kiefer the same basic questions again and whilst she knew he hadn't hit his head, the amount of shock his body was experiencing was extreme.

She pulled off her gloves and put them into a small rubbish bag Harlan handed her. 'I might give my people another call. See where they're up to.' She pulled her phone from her pocket.

'The bat phone again?'

Phemie's lips twitched at Gil's words. 'It's more effective than shining a big bright light in the sky.' The professor was not only gorgeous, affecting her in ways she didn't want to contemplate, but also had a won-

derful sense of humour. He was just the type of man she should keep
her distance from, starting with not agreeing to have tea with him in
Sydney. She dialled the number of the Didja RFDS base and thankfully,
Ben answered immediately.

'It's me. The emergency is a spontaneous amputation of the big toe.
Right foot. We have people out looking for the toe. Patient is stable but
requires analgesics. If you could contact Perth hospital, I think it's best
if Sardi takes the patient directly rather than going through Didja.' She
paused. 'Three hours. That's our window and we've already used half an
hour.' Phemie listened. 'I'm fine. I have help. No, another doctor. Yes.'
She turned her head, her gaze encompassing Gil. 'It was rather fortu-
nate. Right, that's about it for now. Thanks, Ben.'

She finished the call and put her phone away. 'They should be here in
about an hour, maybe less.'

'We're going to need more people searching for the toe.' Harlan had
heard what she'd said and he called through to the train manager to inform him of the situation.

'The most obvious place would actually be on the tracks themselves,'
Phemie said then shrugged. 'But who really knows. I've never had to
look for a missing digit before.'

'First time for everything?' Gil asked as he started to perform Kiefer's observations.

'Have you had anything like this happen to you before?'

'On a train travelling across Australia?' he asked with a hint of mischief. 'No.'

Phemie simply smiled and checked on Paolo. The other man didn't
want to leave his friend but Phemie managed to convince him to go and
pack their things and get ready to leave the train. 'Kiefer's going to need
your help. Your reassurance. Your support. Are you from Perth?' Paolo
nodded and she continued, trying to get Paolo's thoughts into a position
where he'd be more of a help than a hindrance. 'Then at least you'll have
somewhere to stay.'

'So I need to pack our things?'

'The better prepared we are when the plane arrives, the better it will
be for Kiefer,' she encouraged. Thankfully, Paolo now had a lot more

colour in his face and was able to stand and walk quite easily back to his carriage to get things organised.

When he'd gone, Phemie looked at Gil. 'How's Kiefer doing?'

'Stable. Tell me, will the plane be able to land close to the train? I mean, there's no airstrip nearby, is there?'

Phemie smiled. 'For a start, we're on the tip of the Nullarbor Plains. There's *nothing* but the odd shrub here and there, and, secondly, we're alongside the main road. I was just about to ask Harlan to arrange for any traffic to be stopped so the plane can land.'

'That would be beneficial.' Gil nodded.

'Oh, you'd better believe it. There's nothing like making an emergency landing on a road when there are cars heading straight towards you, neither of you knowing which way to swerve.'

'Really?' Gil's eyes widened and Phemie's smile increased. 'Are you being serious, Dr Grainger?'

Harlan chuckled at her words and again lifted his radio to issue more orders. He certainly was 'point-man' and Phemie was exceptionally pleased they'd managed to get someone who was as good at his job as Harlan had proved to be.

'Excuse me, Doctors,' the steward said a few moments later. 'I'm receiving lots of reports of other people with injuries and problems due to the train stopping. I was wondering if—'

'Set up the lounge carriage as a treatment area.' Gil's tone was firm. 'Dr Grainger and I will see whoever has a complaint. If it's possible to find any other medical personnel on the train, their assistance would be invaluable.' Gil then pointed to their patient. 'Kiefer will need to be moved as well so we can continue to monitor him until the RFDS arrive.'

'Very good, Doctor,' Harlan replied, and again turned to talk into his radio, issuing orders.

'Ready for the next round of injuries?' Gil asked.

Phemie nodded, a smile in her voice as she spoke. 'Nothing like doing an emergency clinic on a stationary train in the middle of the outback.'

'I'd have thought you would be used to it. Doing clinics and providing treatment to people who are too far away from medical care.' Gil was intrigued, not only with her job but with the woman herself. He was looking forward to really seeing her in action, doing what she did best.

'I am, but I usually have a team I know and trust as well as quite a few more medical supplies than we have here.'

'Up for the challenge?' His dark eyes were alive with excitement.

Phemie watched him closely. 'You're enjoying this.'

'Not the fact that people are hurt,' Gil quickly pointed out. 'Never that, but the chance to do some real outback medicine? Yes.'

'You like new challenges,' she stated, pleased with her insight.

'What doctor doesn't?' he quipped, but she had the feeling he was playing down his delight at doing something different. As Kiefer was transferred to the stretcher and an announcement made asking for any trained medical personnel to report to the lounge carriage, Phemie continued to think about Gil and his excitement. She guessed that after travelling the world for a year, giving lectures and demonstrations, this sort of medicine *would* be different and challenging for him.

When they arrived at the lounge carriage, she once more performed Kiefer's observations and was pleased the man was still stable. There had been no report yet that they'd found the toe and she hoped sincerely it was indeed found before the plane was ready to transfer Kiefer to Perth.

'I have some medical helpers for you,' Harlan announced, and indicated the three people standing behind him. First, he introduced Gil and Phemie then pointed to a man in his forties. 'This is Julian, he's a registered nurse.' Julian shook hands with both Gil and Phemie.

'I usually work in geriatrics,' he informed them, 'but whatever you need, I'm more than willing to provide.'

'And I'm Wilma,' said a woman in her late sixties. 'I've been a retired triage sister for quite some time but that doesn't mean I've forgotten anything.'

'I don't doubt it.' Gil smiled at her.

'And this is my granddaughter Debbie.' Wilma indicated the young twenty-year-old next to her. 'She's a dental assistant and I thought she might be useful to help with any administration and minor bandaging.'

'I'm first-aid trained as well,' Debbie spoke up.

'Thank you for your offer of help.' Gil's smile was warm at all three. 'I've no idea how this is going to play out but we no doubt have a very long train filled with confused and scared people. Debbie, as your grandmother has suggested, if you're happy to organise the files and keep everyone happy, that would be very helpful. Wilma, you do triage? Anyone requiring immediate attention goes either directly to Phemie or myself. Julian, you take care of the patching-up jobs, Wilma helping you as and when you need it. If anyone has any concerns, please don't be afraid to ask. We're all strangers but we need to work as a team, to put people's minds at ease and to ensure their needs are met. I've asked Harlan to have his stewards bring those passengers who are asking for medical attention right to us rather than announcing we have a makeshift A and E set up.'

'That would just cause panic,' Phemie agreed. 'Debbie, you're going to have your hands full but everyone's details must be recorded before they're seen by any of us. I also believe a tea trolley is being organised in case people need fluids.'

'Remember,' Gil said as the door to the carriage opened, 'if you're not sure, ask questions. That way, we can attempt to avoid any unnecessary errors.' Three elderly patients were ushered through the door and Gil nodded. 'Let's get to work.'

For the next few minutes, the lounge car seemed to fill up quite quickly. Now that there was somewhere to bring people who were complaining of injury or stress, the stewards seemed to be sending the entire passenger manifest. Phemie made sure she kept a close eye on Kiefer, but his observations remained stable.

As they all treated patients, some with minor injuries, some requiring suturing, Phemie couldn't help but watch Gil, watch his techniques, the way his clever hands seemed to heal his patients simply by touch. He also had a wonderful bedside manner, making people of all ages feel completely at ease. He really was quite a man and it was an absolute honour to have the opportunity to really see him in action.

The other volunteer helpers, Julian, Wilma and Debbie, were doing a marvellous job. The majority of people presented with cuts and bruises, most needing bandaging and reassurance.

Phemie was treating a heavily pregnant woman who had confessed she was travelling on the train because she was not permitted to fly.

'I just want you to check the baby. I fell quite hard when the train stopped and I don't know if everything—' She broke off, unable to finish her sentence. Phemie's heart went out to her. 'I know it's probably nothing but I just need to know the baby's all right.'

'Of course I'll check the baby. Besides, knowing the baby is fine may actually help you get some rest and that's what you really need to be doing. Off your feet, and resting. You have relaxing scenery to watch and you may find that you even doze off.'

Gil listened nearby as Phemie talked reassuringly to the pregnant mother. She certainly exhibited a natural caring ability, not only for this woman but for all the patients he'd seen her treat.

He wondered what the RFDS set-up was like, what situations and scenarios they dealt with on a regular basis. He was completely intrigued by it all.

Phemie was busy treating an elderly man for bruises and abrasions when she tilted her head to one side and listened, before calling to Gil, 'Here they are.'

'What?' Gil strained, listening so hard he thought his eardrums might burst. 'I can't hear anything.'

'The drone of the plane.'

He listened again. 'No. No drone.'

She shrugged. 'Guess I'm used to it.'

It was a whole two minutes later that he was able to hear the plane. 'I'll go greet the guys. You stay here,' she said as she stood, then stopped and put her hand across her mouth. 'Oh. Sorry. I keep forgetting who you are. Is that all right? Do you mind—?'

Gil smiled at her, a smile which had the ability to turn her legs to mush, and she instinctively put a hand to the wall to support her. 'It's fine, Phemie. I understand. This is your job. Just go.' The way she'd confessed to treating him like any other colleague was great. She wasn't fawning over him, she wasn't bowing and scraping to his every whim, as had happened during the past year that he'd been travelling.

He had his own support staff, including a secretary, events manager and personal aide. They all made sure he was where he was supposed to be and on time. Thankfully, they hadn't accompanied him on this train ride, instead preferring to fly across to Sydney to ensure everything was set up and ready for his arrival on Saturday.

Gil had no idea what this long delay would do to their overall timing but an emergency was an emergency. He would contact his staff when they stopped in Adelaide—the next city on their route. Until then, he was more than content to simply be a colleague of the delightful Euphemia Grainger. In fact, he wondered if he could somehow wangle an invitation to come and visit her Flying Doctor base once the conference was over.

He had a whole week set aside as 'vacation' time. His staff wanted to lounge about on Australia's famous golden beaches with little umbrella drinks in their hands. That wasn't for him. Going to a Flying Doctor base, doing something completely different, sounded like heaven. The more he dwelt on the idea, the more he liked it. Now all he had to do was get Phemie to agree.

When she eventually returned, it was with her colleagues and they were able to give Kiefer stronger analgesics, before they transferred him to the stretcher and prepared him for the plane.

'Still no sign of the toe?' Madge, the outback nurse practitioner, asked as they loaded Kiefer into the plane. Valma, the other nurse, was making sure Paolo was seated and the luggage stored. Gil had left their volunteer helpers to monitor the rest of the patients. There was no one urgent for him to treat and, besides, he wasn't about to miss seeing the RFDS in action.

'I was positive they'd find it.' Phemie couldn't believe she'd been wrong but looking for a severed toe along a railway line in the middle of such an enormous country really was like trying to find a needle in a haystack.

'They'll find it.' Gil put his hands on Phemie's shoulders and gave them a little squeeze. She tried hard to ignore the shock waves coursing through her system. It was ridiculous that a man she'd just met could evoke such a reaction yet that was exactly what was happening. She schooled her thoughts and attempted to keep herself as aloof as possible even though he was still touching her. 'Keep that optimism alive, Dr Grainger.'

His voice was rich and deep and its magnificence passed from the top of her hair to the tips of her toes. She tried not to close her eyes at the way he was so intimately affecting her. 'B-but the plane's about to leave.'

'And they'll—'

'Gil! Phemie!' It was Harlan. He was running towards them, holding a plastic lunchbox in his hands. 'We've found it. We've found it!'

'There you go, Phemie. See? Your optimism was right.' Gil gave her shoulders the briefest of squeezes before he dropped his hands and raced over to meet Harlan. He checked inside the container and found the severed digit on ice. 'Ready for transplant,' he announced triumphantly as he handed it to one of the RFDS nurses.

'Let's get in the air,' Sardi ordered as she headed for the cockpit.

'Knock 'em into a pile of dead bones at the conference,' Sardi called over her shoulder to Phemie.

'She means knock 'em dead,' Phemie explained to Gil as she watched her colleagues prepare for take-off. She herself had done it a thousand times before, ensuring the patient was stable, closing the doors, making sure everything was locked and in place. 'Sardi sometimes gets her English phrases mixed up.'

'A female pilot?' Gil was impressed.

'Sardi's the best.'

'Good to hear. Are there any males working at your base?'

'Ben does a lot of the administration. He's a nurse as well but so far he's the only bloke.'

'Lucky Ben. Surrounded by beautiful women all day long.'

Phemie could feel Gil's gaze on her and forced a nervous laugh. Surely he couldn't mean that *she* was beautiful? Sure, she knew she was OK looking but she'd hardly call herself beautiful. Small. Tiny. Petite even, but never beautiful.

They all moved right out of the way, waiting for the plane to taxi and take off. 'I don't think Ben sees it that way. I think he goes around the twist being surrounded by females all day long. Plus, he and his wife have three girls so there's really no hope for him.'

'Do you think Ben would like to have another man around next week?'

'I think he'd be delighted,' she said, thinking of the part-time medic position which had been advertised yet again. Trying to get doctors to come to the outback was nigh on impossible yet so desperately needed in a country the size of Australia. 'If there was another man around, poor Ben might finally be able to win the argument of whether or not the toilet seat remains up or down!'

'Then I accept.'

Phemie blinked twice then frowned, looking up at Gil. 'You accept what?'

'The position.'

'The position of what?' She was now totally perplexed. 'Gil, what are you talking about?' They turned and headed back towards the train.

'The position of visiting medical doctor for the week after the conference.'

CHAPTER THREE

'WHAT?'

Phemie was so startled by his words that she misjudged the depth of the uneven ground and came crashing down. Gil was by her side in an instant, helping her to her feet, even though she was trying to push him away at the same time.

'I'm fine. I'm fine.' She brushed herself down, knowing the reddish dust would never completely come out of her pale green top. Thankfully, her jeans were dark enough not to stain. She didn't want to feel his hands on her or his arms around her or to have his firm muscled chest anywhere near her own. His light spicy scent was addictive and the way the lightest touch of his hand on her body sent her insides spiralling out of control was something she'd rather not have to deal with right now.

She had a paper to present at the conference in Sydney. She had her brother and his friends joining her on the train when they reached Adelaide. She'd just had to watch her colleagues fly off without her and all of it combined was making her rather vulnerable. There was too much going on in her life right now and the last thing, the very last thing she needed was to hear Professor Gilbert Fitzwilliam declare he would be accompanying her back to the RFDS base for one week after the conference! No. It would not do.

Of course, on a medical level, everyone would be delighted to welcome him to their base. They'd be keen to have someone of his qualification and expertise helping out with the various emergencies and clinics.

But to have him simply declare his intention had knocked Phemie for six. Even now, as they walked back to the train, she was completely aware of him. She could feel him watching her every step lest she should stumble again.

She was not a damsel in distress. Far from it. She'd looked after herself for years, holding her family together as she and her parents had dealt with the differences and difficulties her younger brother Anthony experienced. Now Anthony was living independently in an assisted facility in Perth, travelling to Adelaide for holidays, and soon he would catch the train to take him to the opposite side of the country from where he'd lived. Her parents were enjoying their first holiday alone since their honeymoon. And Phemie? Phemie had left home, too. She'd moved to the middle of nowhere to work with the RFDS and had found the outback the most glorious place in the world.

No. She was not a damsel in distress, neither was she a fool. She refused Gil's help as they climbed back onto the train but even as she hoisted herself up, she knew she couldn't turn down Gil's other offer—that of visiting their base for a week after the conference.

She could certainly understand why he would want to view the whole RFDS set-up. He was from another country, one where they obviously didn't cover so much territory, given that England itself could fit nineteen times inside the State of Western Australia. The RFDS was unique and it was only right that an A and E specialist such as Professor Gilbert Fitzwilliam would want to see such a place in action.

Although, she pondered, it didn't necessarily have to be her own base where he spent his time. That thought sparked another and the idea grew.

That's what she would do. When she arrived in Sydney, she would call the Australian director of the RFDS and suggest that Professor Fitzwilliam be assigned to one or the other bases. The one stationed near Katherine in the Northern Territory might be good for Gil to observe, given they were certainly busy almost every day of the year. They covered a lot more territory than the Didja crew and he might even have the opportunity to visit her friends Sebastian and Dannyella at Dingo

Creek. Yes. He could go there. The real heart of the outback…which was far away from her.

'So? What do you think?' Gil asked as they headed back through the train, leaving Harlan to take care of the clean-up and other official duties. Harlan had also told them he'd need to have an accident report filled in but it could be done later.

'Think of what?' Phemie played for time, purposely ignoring him. Why was her heart thumping a little too fast against her chest? Was it due to Gil's nearness or because she was about to defy him? They made their way through the carriages, back towards the lounge car.

'Of me coming to the RFDS base?' Gil's eyes were alight with fun and excitement and for one brief, blinding moment Phemie *wanted* him to come back to the Didja Base with her. She didn't want to send him anywhere else, not when he looked at her like that.

She could well imagine the two of them, sitting on the front porch at the base, looking up at the stars as she pointed out the different constellations in the southern hemisphere. They would rock on the rocking chairs, they'd relax and chat after a busy day travelling either to a clinic or an emergency. He'd look at her with that gorgeous smile he was giving her now and she would capitulate and end up in his arms, his mouth pressed firmly to—

It was a bad idea. If her thoughts were this distracted by him after only a few hours in his presence, how on earth would she cope with him staying at the base, staying at *her* place, given that she lived at the base? No. It wouldn't do at all. The man had too much of a devastating effect on her equilibrium. Much better to see if he could go to Katherine for a visit. Much safer. He'd see more of the outback and he'd also be a three-day drive from where she was situated. Better.

His smile slipped a little, concern touching those deep brown eyes of his…eyes she could well and truly drown in. 'Are you all right, Euphemia?'

'Uh…I'm, er…I'm fine. Thanks.' She stammered quickly, fumbling over her words, not wanting him to guess the path her thoughts had taken. 'I have a lot on my mind. The conference, my paper, what's just happened with Kiefer. Uh…but with regard to you observing a—'

'Helping,' he interrupted. 'I don't plan to simply observe. I intend to be of service and work for my keep, so to speak.'

'Well…good. It does get busy and I'm sure your help would be greatly appreciated, but I'll need to see what I can organise. I'm not in a position to invite people back to the base to help out. There's a lot of paper work involved.'

'When isn't there?' he mumbled, but nodded as though he completely understood.

'I just can't make any promises. At this stage.' And that sounded to her own ears as though she was more than happy to have him around. Honestly, it seemed every time she opened her mouth, she just dug herself in deeper.

'That seems fair and I know you'll do your absolute best. You're a natural giver and carer, Phemie, and you go out of your way to help people. I know you'll put a lot of effort into doing all you can to assist me in my request.'

He wasn't being pompous, even though he might have sounded it. Phemie watched him as they headed back to their makeshift A and E and knew his words were sincere and from the heart. The brightness in his eyes also let her know he was serious and very interested in how the RFDS worked. She should be honoured that a man such as the professor would want to come all the way to the outback to not only see what they did but help out as well. Utilising someone with his skills and knowledge would be something she knew her boss wouldn't turn down, but on a personal note Phemie wasn't sure it was a good idea. Gil was just too…close for comfort.

When they returned to the lounge carriage, it was to find the number of waiting patients had dwindled.

'Most people were concerned about minor things and just wanted reassurance,' Wilma said as she made a cup of sweet tea for a patient. She handed over the tea and then pointed to where Julian was busy checking an elderly woman's pulse rate. 'Debbie's kept lists and files on everyone and has been highly effective in keeping people calm until they could receive treatment.' Wilma paused for breath. 'Kiefer and his friend are away, then?'

'On their way to Perth.' Gil confirmed. 'With the toe.'

'I'd heard it had been found. That's wonderful news.' The retired nurse beamed from ear to ear. 'Now, if the two of you would like to see those last few patients who have just come in, I think afterwards you should go and rest. Debbie and I can stay on here for the next few hours in case other people are brought in, and if we need you, we'll come and get you.'

Gil nodded but smiled at the other woman. 'Spoken like an experienced nursing sister who's used to bossing doctors around.'

Phemie chuckled as she'd been thinking the same thing. Not that she minded. Wilma had obviously been good at her job as today's organisation had shown and, besides, if she herself was able to escape to the confines of her cabin, to put some much-needed distance between herself and Gil, who was she to argue?

They treated the last few patients and as Phemie tidied up the rubbish and put it in the bin, she felt rather than saw Gil come to stand behind her. She turned to find he was wearing that delicious smile she liked and with it came the powerful effects. Phemie crossed her arms over her chest in an effort to give herself some sort of barrier against his natural magnetism. She was about to excuse herself when the loudspeaker above them crackled, startling Phemie a little.

'A little jumpy,' Gil noted. 'Are you usually so inclined?' He quirked an eyebrow, watching her with interest.

Phemie shrugged her shoulders then listened intently to what Harlan was announcing over the train's intercom.

'Would all passengers not presently receiving medical attention please return to their designated seats. Stewards will be around shortly to check on all guests.'

'Sounds as though we'll be getting under way soon enough.' Gil collected his Thermos from where it had been placed out of the way. 'I would be honoured if you allowed me to escort you back to your cabin.' He indicated the door not far from where they were standing and then made a small sweeping bow. 'After you, milady.'

Phemie couldn't help but smile. The man really was an odd mixture of old-world charm and dictatorial perfection. With the lift of an eyebrow he could either make someone shrink to the size of a peanut as he looked down that perfect nose of his or he could make a woman feel as though she were the most important person in the world, his eyes radiating his pleasure. Thankfully, she was experiencing the latter, those rich brown pools creating havoc within her.

Gil's smile increased when Phemie didn't move. She simply stood there, smiling up at him, her blue eyes bright with tired happiness. It was an unguarded moment, where her heart was there for him to see. He'd become quite good at reading people, especially with all the travelling he'd done that year, and as he looked into her eyes, he saw that there was a lot more to Phemie Grainger than he'd first thought.

He saw hardship, experiences, pain. He'd noticed it the first time he'd looked into her amazing eyes. They really were the window to her soul and he couldn't help but be intrigued by guessing what events had touched her life to make her look so tired yet so happy.

Life could be unkind. He knew all too well about that. He'd had a loving wife. He'd had a gorgeous child and both had been ripped from him. He'd known the pain of wanting what you couldn't have, what it was no longer humanly possible to have, and when he'd been unable to cope with the grief, with the agony of not being able to hold those he loved close to his heart, he'd locked himself away in the world of research and only recently had he actually started taking steps outside.

There was no way he wanted a romantic commitment ever again. He'd tried that once and he knew his heart wouldn't be able to take the pain and mortification in the event that something went wrong—again. Work had been his saving grace. Work had seen him through the dark nights and the depression, and now, after four years of constant work and concentration, he was starting to look outside those parameters.

Asking Euphemia to arrange for him to see a working RFDS base was still definitely within the bounds of his research, within the bounds of 'work', but it was something he wouldn't have asked a virtual stranger to do two years ago. He would have kept to his timetable. He wouldn't have deviated from the plan even for a second. Even taking the train from Perth across to Sydney had been his idea, not his handlers'.

This was the last stop on his world tour. He'd loved New Zealand and he'd been blown away by the few sights he'd seen when he'd spoken first in Brisbane, then in Darwin before making his way across to Perth. Still, apart from this train journey, he'd basically seen either the inside of a hotel room or a hospital operating suite where he'd lectured whilst performing surgery.

The train, which took three full days to snake its way across the wide brown land, had sounded like sheer luxury, especially when the rest of his team had declared they'd rather fly, something Gil preferred not to do, if at all possible. Too many planes. Too many flights. No. This time the train was a much better option. Three full days to simply be himself. To sit back, chat with the locals and absorb the quiet of a country half a world away from his own.

No one would know who he really was. No one would be pestering him to discuss his latest techniques. He'd just be a regular guy, travelling on a train, relaxing. Then he'd bumped into Phemie—literally. The fact that she'd recognised him almost instantly had been enough to burst his bubble but now he was sincerely pleased it had. He was having a much better time on this trip than even he'd been able to anticipate. Of course, attending to Kiefer and helping other passengers could, in no way, be classified as a good time, but watching Phemie work, observing her quick mind, assisting her—it had all been fantastic.

It was also fantastic to have her smiling at him as she was now. Why was it that whenever it was just the two of them, like this, time appeared to stand still? Scientifically he knew it was a complete impossibility but emotionally it was delightful. To be able to glimpse those emotions again. To be able to feel the warmth of a woman's interested gaze. To have a moment to feel as though he'd stepped into the sunshine.

It was safe. It was simply a bubble and bubbles popped, forcing him back into the reality where life was structured and full of problems ready to challenge his mind into solving them. It was why he could allow himself to enjoy the way he felt in her presence because he knew, ultimately, the bubble would burst when they arrived in Sydney. Euphemia Grainger was simply a diversion. Something with a little extra spark to get him through that final leg of his tour.

'Phemie?' The instant he spoke, Phemie's expression changed, the smile slipping from her face. They'd probably been standing there for only a few seconds but for some reason it felt like much longer—for both of them if her reaction was anything to go by.

What had she been thinking? The thought wouldn't remove itself as they said thank you to Wilma, Debbie and Julian then headed back through to the sleeping carriages. Had she been standing there wondering about how to pull some strings and get him onto her RFDS base? Had she been thinking about him in a professional capacity? What it might be like to have the 'famous' Professor Fitzwilliam at her small informal base? Would she worry about a thing like that? Or perhaps...just perhaps she'd been thinking about him in a more personal way?

Was she aware of the slight buzz which seemed to exist whenever they were alone together? He certainly was. He'd only met her a few short hours ago and on several occasions he'd found himself wondering what it might be like to capture her mouth with his, to hold her close and feel that soft petite body pressed against him.

It was wrong. It was ridiculous and it was something which would never happen. He was a man who not only prided himself on excellent self-control but who also knew that relationships were not for him. Add to everything that he and Phemie lived on opposites sides of the globe and there was a definite probability there would never be anything except professional courtesy or perhaps—at a stretch—friendship between them.

'This is me.'

Phemie stopped so suddenly Gil almost bumped into her. Just as well the train hadn't been moving or he would have once more found his arms sliding around her waist as he steadied them both. She was pointing at a cabin door.

'Ah...yes. I remember.'

Phemie smiled politely. 'Well...it's my cabin, at least for now.'

'And then the day/night seaters. You have friends joining you?'

'Uh...yes. My brother, actually. He and some friends are joining the train when we stop in Adelaide.'

'Your brother.' Now, why did he feel so pleased at that piece of information? 'The one who says the word "stuff" like water.'

'That's the one.' There was a small smile on her lips and she nodded. It was obvious she was very close to her brother and that was great. As Gil had been raised an only child, he'd often envied people who had close sibling and familial relationships.

'Well, I guess I should let you get to your own cabin. Here's hoping there are no other emergencies between here and Sydney.'

'Agreed.' He smiled and inclined his head politely. 'Goodnight, Euphemia. Sleep sweet.'

'Thank you.' He was so intent, so charming as he bade her farewell that she half expected him to gallantly raise her hand to his lips and kiss it. He didn't, however, and she opened her cabin door, slipping inside and leaning on it to ensure it closed properly.

What on earth was wrong with her?

Her heart was pounding against her chest. She was out of breath. Her knees were weak and her palms were perspiring. The man certainly had a killer smile and the way he smelt was utterly delicious and he was smart and handsome and had the most hypnotic eyes and deep, vibrating voice and she liked everything about him.

What on earth was wrong with her?

When the train finally pulled into Adelaide, Phemie was up, dressed and had already moved her bags to her appointed seat in the day-night section. She exited onto the platform, knowing they had a whole hour there before needing to board again.

She looked around at families greeting one another with hugs, kisses and tears of joy. There was no sign of Anthony and his friends. Phemie frowned, deciding to check inside the terminal in case they were waiting there, although she could have sworn they would have been waiting on the platform to see the train pull in. Slight alarm started to rise within her but she damped it down.

Inside the terminal, she walked the length of it, checking they weren't in the restaurant or in the little souvenir shop. No sign of them. Her mental alarm bells started to ring with more prominence. She pulled her mobile phone from her pocket and immediately hit the speed-dial for Liz's phone. While it rang, her gaze continued to search the terminal for any signs of Anthony or his friends. Had they been in an accident? Had someone gone missing?

As Liz's phone continued to ring, Phemie's intense alarm turned to panic.

'Good morning,' a deep voice said from behind her. She instantly recognised the British enunciation as Gil's and turned to look up at him. His eyes were still as powerful as ever. His voice was still as smooth. His nearness was still evoking a powerful reaction within her but everything was overshadowed by concern for her brother. 'I thought, if you're not busy, we might have breakfast—' He stopped when he saw the phone at her ear and the look of panic on her face. 'Good heavens, Phemie. Is everything all right?'

'I can't find my brother.'

'Oh. Where were you supposed to meet?'

'Here. On the platform or around it or...there was nothing firm but I'd expected him to be here when the train pulled in. He loves trains.' She was still looking around as she spoke, every muscle in her body tense, her voice strained.

Gil frowned a little. 'How old is he?'

'Twenty-four.'

Gil raised his eyebrows in surprise but quickly changed his expression back to neutral. If Phemie was older than her brother then she had to be either in her late twenties or early thirties. Good heavens, the woman certainly carried her age well.

'He's late. Anthony's never late.'

'I'm sure it's nothing to worry about.' Especially given her brother seemed old enough to look after himself. At twenty-four and travelling with friends, there was no telling where the young men might be and they were no doubt running behind schedule that morning due to late night partying.

'I can't get hold of Liz. Why isn't she answering her phone?' Phemie could hear her voice rising with mounting anxiety.

'Come. Sit down.' She was obviously agitated and he wanted to help in any way he could. He placed his hand beneath her elbow and was pleased when she allowed him to lead her to a chair by the door. She sat, cancelling the call she was making and trying another number.

'Why isn't he picking up?' She let it ring a few more times before hanging up. She clutched the phone between both her hands, her gaze intent on the door before it flicked around the terminal, desperate to have her brother miraculously appear before her.

'Maybe he forgot to charge his phone?' Gil offered the excuse in order to help. 'Batteries can go dead and usually when you're travelling you often forget to recharge them. I speak from experience on that point.'

'No doubt.' She wasn't really listening to him and he could see that not being able to find her brother was leading her into a greater state of anxiety. Gil was doing his best to try and calm her down.

'He'll be here.'

'He wanted to see the train pull in. He'll be so disappointed he missed it. He's been talking about it for months.'

Gil frowned. It was just a train, pulling into a station. There was nothing exciting about that. Well, perhaps to a young boy, maybe but not to a twenty-four-year-old. Then again, perhaps Anthony was a train enthusiast or was simply a young man who liked trains. Who was he to judge?

She flicked open her phone and pressed another few buttons before holding it to her ear. 'If I can just get hold of Liz and find out what's—' The terminal doors swooshed open and Phemie was instantly on her feet. 'Anthony!'

She snapped her phone back into place as her feet took flight. She ran across the room and threw her arms around a man of about five feet five inches, who was a little portly around the middle and had the distinctive facial features of a person with Down's syndrome.

As Gil watched, Phemie's previous agitation now made complete sense. It was clear to all and sundry that she cared and loved her brother very deeply and he found himself once more re-evaluating the way he viewed Euphemia Grainger.

She really was becoming the most intriguing woman he'd met in an extremely long time and that fact in itself was dangerous.

CHAPTER FOUR

GIL DIDN'T SEE either Phemie or her brother until that evening when he met them in the dining carriage. Euphemia had introduced him to Anthony in the train terminal and, of course, that meant he'd had to meet all of Anthony's friends and their carer—Liz.

Gil had been incredibly impressed that this group of adults, all with Down's syndrome, were travelling and exploring their own country. For people without a disability, sometimes the idea of stepping outside their comfort zone was something so terrifying they never even tried it and yet to see them openly embracing something new, something different and enjoying themselves really warmed his heart.

'I want to go to London one day and do lots of stuff,' Anthony had confessed when Phemie had explained that Gil was from England and that was why he 'talked funny', as Anthony had termed it. 'Mum and Dad have gone, haven't they, Phemie? They're doing heaps of cool stuff, aren't they, Phemie?'

'They are. They're cruising in Europe,' she supplied for Gil's sake.

'They send me postcards and stuff. I sent them postcards, too. I sent Phemie a postcard, too. I chose it all by myself and posted it in Adelaide.'

'Very clever,' Gil praised. 'I'm sure you picked just the right one for your big sister.'

'It had flowers on it and other pretty stuff. Phemie likes flowers, don't you, Phemie?'

'I do.' She'd kissed Anthony's cheek and smiled lovingly at him. Gil couldn't help the pang of envy that passed through him. He'd been raised by nannies and strict boarding-school masters, his parents more intent on their careers than on him.

He'd left them then, heading out of the station to stretch his legs whilst Phemie and Liz settled Anthony and his friends in for the next part of their journey. Gil was thankful he had the ability to be quite attentive to what was going on around him while indulging in a daydream. It wasn't something he'd done since his senior school days when he'd wished himself anywhere but at boarding school.

Today, however, he'd found himself thinking about Phemie. What type of woman worked in the outback of a vast country? What type of woman rearranged her schedule to accommodate her brother, even if it meant she ended up exhausted before presenting at a medical conference? What type of woman had the ability to look into his eyes and make him feel as though his life was simply a shell of an existence?

He knew he'd locked himself away when June and Caitie had been cruelly ripped from his life in that plane crash but he'd always thought he'd hid it well. Phemie would have no idea what had happened in his personal life yet she had the ability to look at him and make him want more.

That wasn't going to happen. He didn't do *more*. He'd tried to have a normal life. He'd met a woman, married her, settled down, become a father to a gorgeous baby girl and it had all been cruelly snatched from him. He'd tried it and it hadn't worked. No. He didn't do *more*.

Gil stopped by the dining table where Phemie was cutting food into smaller pieces.

'Phemie's doing my food,' Anthony said proudly. 'She does it the best. Mum does it next best and Dad does it bestest after that. Liz doesn't do it best at all.' The last was spoken in a sort of stage whisper yet Anthony's volume still radiated quite clearly.

'And what about you?' Phemie prompted. 'How good are you at preparing your own food?'

'I am the king at doing my food and lots of other stuff but I like it when Phemie does it because she does it best. It's good stuff.'

Gil smiled at the young man and watched as Phemie finished what she was doing. 'It does appear your big sister knows exactly how you like your food,' Gil commented, then looked around. 'Where are your friends, Anthony?'

'I was first,' Anthony replied with a mouth half-full, and received a scolding from his sister. 'Sorry, Phemie,' he replied, then swallowed. 'I was first,' he repeated.

'They're all on their way here,' she supplied, and pointed to the empty diners' counter. 'So if you want to order something to eat, now would be the best time to do it.'

'Good to know.' Still Gil didn't move. He also noticed that Phemie didn't have any food in front of her. 'Have you already eaten? Can I get you something?'

'I'm fine. I'm not that hungry.'

'I can get you a cup of tea,' he offered, and Phemie smiled politely. 'I'm sure they have a rich-bodied Australian tea.' He couldn't help but punctuate his words with a quick wink. The instant he'd done it, he silently scolded himself. What was he doing? Was he flirting with her? In front of her brother? In front of a carriage of other passengers? It was so unlike him yet the instant she smiled at him he felt as though he'd been rewarded. She'd allowed him to continue sharing their private joke.

'Thank you, Gil, but I'm fine.' She paused for a moment, teasing confusion peppering her brow. 'Don't tell me you've actually drunk the tea they serve here? I thought you were Thermos man with your Earl Grey?'

Gil's smile was bright and natural as he nodded. 'My dishwater, you mean.' He received a chuckle from her. 'You're absolutely right, Phemie. I am very particular about my tea. I do like it just—so.'

Gil glanced at Anthony and then looked back to Phemie, his tone dropping a notch. 'What about later this evening? We could meet in the lounge car again and this time try to make it through a conversation without anyone else pulling the emergency cord.'

'Never, never pull the emergency cord,' Anthony chimed in.

'Mouth full,' Phemie pointed out, and he quickly mumbled an apology before swallowing. 'Uh...I think I'm going to be rather busy tonight so I'll have to pass.'

Gil nodded. 'Then our date for tea at the end of the first day's session must stand.'

Phemie wasn't too sure how wise it would be to continue any sort of personal relationship with Gil once they disembarked. On the train, it was as though they were in some sort of stasis where the rest of the world and the rules that surrounded it didn't apply. They were simply doctors, doctors who had worked together to help people. They were two people who seemed to have some sort of crazy gravitational pull towards each other. They were equals—and she knew once they arrived in Sydney and went their separate ways, everything would change. As it should. He was Professor Gilbert Fitzwilliam and she was an outback emergency doctor.

He lived in London, in the middle of one of the world's busiest cities. She lived on an RFDS base in the middle of nowhere. It gave a whole new meaning to 'worlds apart'.

At the moment, however, she felt crowded, confused and conscious that Anthony was paying them a lot of attention. He might not completely understand what they were saying and why, but she'd learned of old not to underestimate him. The last thing she needed right now was to try and explain her relationship with Gil to her brother. The fact that *she* didn't understand her relationship with Gil only made the situation more puzzling.

'Sounds great,' she agreed—anything to get him to leave.

'Excellent.' The train carriage door opened and all of Anthony's friends came traipsing in, bringing noise with them.

'I was first,' Anthony called, this time remembering to swallow his mouthful of food before speaking. He looked at Phemie and received praise for his actions.

Gil looked from Phemie to Anthony to the plethora of people who had just entered the dining carriage and then back at Phemie. He nodded politely. 'I'll leave you to it, then.'

'Thanks. Have a good evening,' she said, unable to look away as he left the carriage. Gil smiled at Anthony's friends and nodded to Liz as he shuffled past them. Phemie's gaze travelled over his broad firm shoulders, his straight back, his muscled thighs and tried not to recall how incredible it had felt to have that gorgeous body pressed to her own. The sigh that escaped her lips was unintentional.

'Now, that's a sizzling look,' Liz pointed out, sitting next to Anthony.

'That man is pure sex on legs, Phemie. Why on earth aren't you follow-ing him out of here?'

'What's sex on legs?' Anthony asked and Phemie glared at Liz, who only laughed in return.

'All I'm saying is that I wouldn't kick him out if—'

'I get the picture.' Phemie held up her hands, indicating she wanted the present topic to end. She focused on her brother. 'Would you like something else to eat, love?' She needed normalcy, not ideas put in her head with regard to Gil Fitzwilliam. The man may indeed be sex on legs, as Liz had said, but that was beside the point.

No matter how sexy any man was, no matter how he might make her feel, no matter how her thoughts and body went haywire when he was around, it would all be meaningless in the end. Long-term relationships weren't for her. Marriage wasn't for her. Having her own children was something she could never do.

Whilst she loved and adored her brother completely, there was no way she was going to risk becoming pregnant and giving birth to a child with Down's syndrome. After Anthony had been born, her mother had looked further into Down's syndrome and discovered she was a carrier of the translocation trisomy 21 chromosome. This defective chromosome usu-ally related to children being born with Down's. Her parents had both been tested and so had Phemie. It wasn't until she had been older and in medical school that her parents had told her she, too, was a carrier of the defective chromosome. There was an increased risk Phemie would give birth to a child with Down's syndrome. No way was she going to subject an innocent child to a life like that and even though she hated to admit it, she couldn't be a parent to a child with a disability.

She'd lived that life. She'd watched her parents for years, their long-suffering patience almost running out on several occasions. The way they hadn't been able to pay the proper attention to her because of Anthony, the way they'd had to rely on her to take up the slack. Phemie felt as though she'd aged prematurely, especially throughout her teenage years when her mother had undergone treatment for ovarian cancer. Her fa-ther had almost fallen apart, his soul being slowly destroyed each time her mother had needed another dose of chemotherapy or a blood trans-fusion. Anthony's care had fallen to her and as such, she'd never experienced the normal teenage things. There had been no time for parties, no time for experimenting, no time for boyfriends. She'd been a surrogate mother to her sibling.

Thankfully, the chemotherapy had worked and her mother was now in very good health, but those years had taken their toll on Phemie. She loved her family, more than anything and if she'd had to do it all over again, she would, but there were still traces of resentment flowing through her veins. She'd vowed never to put a child of her own through what she'd been through and the only way to ensure that never happened was never to have children.

Caring for others was what she was good at and that was what she was busy doing. Working in the outback, caring for the community, helping others in any way she could. Those were the choices she'd made and she was determined to stick to them. The emotions Gil Fitzwilliam evoked deep within her could mean nothing to her.

Phemie helped Anthony and his friends for the rest of the evening, ensuring everyone was in the right seat and comfortable when it was time to turn out the lights and go to sleep.

She and Liz chatted quietly for a while, though fatigue claimed her friend and soon Phemie found herself sitting in a carriage full of sleeping people, yet she herself was wide awake…awake and, for some strange reason, unable to stop thinking about Gil.

Deciding she may as well stretch her legs as opposed to sitting there staring into the dark, she carefully left the carriage, heading towards the lounge car. It was now about one o'clock in the morning and she wondered whether Gil might be there, might be waiting for her, hoping she'd changed her mind.

Anticipatory delight coursed through her as she drew nearer to the lounge car. Would he be there? She wasn't sure exactly what it was about Gil Fitzwilliam—*Professor* Gilbert Fitzwilliam—she mentally corrected herself—that had her in such a tizz.

Of course she appreciated his medical genius. She'd read all his papers and agreed with what he'd written. She'd marvelled at the research he'd undertaken and the medical breakthroughs he'd made to date. She was definitely attracted to his intellect but, then, what doctor wouldn't be? The man was incredible.

And incredibly good-looking too, a little voice said.

There was no point in denying—especially to herself—the way she felt when she was in Gil's presence. There was something about him, something that seemed to affect her in a way she'd never been affected before. Was it his looks or was it more than that? Perhaps it was the way he made her feel as though *she* were the genius.

Of course, she admitted to herself, the reason she'd been unable to sleep had nothing at all to do with the seats and everything to do with Gil. So here she was. Pushing open the door to the lounge car, eager and nervous at the same time to see whether or not he was around.

Walking through, ensuring the door closed firmly behind her, Phemie headed into the carriage, checking the first small recess where three ladies were all sitting and talking about their travel experiences. Two other people had their laptops plugged in and were busy staring at the screens.

Phemie moved on to the next recess, her mouth now completely dry, her heart pounding in triple time against her chest. Would he be there? If he was, what would she say to him? Oh. She hadn't thought this through. What if he thought she was chasing him? Stalking him? Her step faltered and she thought about turning back but forced herself to go on.

Two more steps and she was at the next recess, her gaze eagerly scanning the area and the four people sitting there. Her heart fell and her shoulders sagged.

None of them were Gil.

He wasn't there.

She was stupid.

It was the mantra which had been on constant replay through her head since she'd returned to her seat and forced herself to close her eyes and at least pretend to sleep. Professor Gilbert Fitzwilliam wasn't interested in her. In the social circles he mixed in she was way, way down at the bottom of the ladder. Just a girl he'd met on a train. That's all she was and she wished the silly, wistful side of her would recognise that fact.

It wasn't that she was after any sort of romantic relationship but she had to admit it had been nice to have a man look intently at her the way

Gil had. He'd made her heart flutter, her stomach churn with anticipation and her knees go weak. That hadn't happened to her since high
school when Danny Ellingham, the boy she'd had a secret crush on, had
asked her to the school dance.

Of course, her parents had insisted she attend the dance, even though
her mother's health hadn't been too good. It was one night, a few hours,
she'd rationalised to herself as she'd dressed in the prettiest gown she'd
been able to afford. What could possibly happen in a few hours?

A lot, it had turned out, although not where her parents and Anthony
were concerned. They'd all made it through those hours yet for Phemie,
that night had been one that had changed her life for ever.

Everything went according to plan. Danny picked her up from her
home, chatted a few minutes with her father at the door. He was polite,
he held her hand and proudly walked into the dance with his arm around
her. She felt so happy and yet highly self-conscious. People were looking
at the two of them, whispering about them, and some girls even had a
hint of envy in their eyes. Danny was, after all, a good-looking guy. Joan
Glastonbury, however, glared daggers at her. Phemie knew the other girl
also liked Danny, but for tonight at least Danny had chosen *her*.

They danced, they talked and it seemed to be the night of her dreams.
She'd liked Danny for a long time, sitting beside him in maths, being his
lab partner in science, but she'd always thought he'd viewed her as nothing but a straight A student who could help him out from time to time.
When he'd asked her to the dance, she'd been stunned but of course had
said yes immediately. It wasn't until nearer the end of the night that she
realised she knew very little about him.

Tommy Spitzner, the smartest boy in the school, had brought his cousin
to the dance, a plump girl who had Down's syndrome.

'My parents made me bring her to the dance,' Tommy confessed when
they had both been getting drinks. 'I don't mind. Lerleen's great and
we get along fine.' Tommy laughed without humour. 'In fact, I think
Lerleen's the one who brought me to the dance. My parents knew I didn't
want to come but they keep telling me I'm too insular and said perhaps
I should think of someone other than myself, etcetera, and now here I
am at the stupid dance with my cousin.'

Both of them had looked over to where Lerleen was dancing by herself to the loud rock music. It was then that Phemie watched in horror as Danny and a few of his mates walked over to Lerleen and started teasing her. They pretended to ask her to dance then laughed and made rude comments when she eagerly accepted. Phemie's blood boiled over.

She'd marched over to Lerleen and stood next to the girl.

'Leave her alone.' She looked Danny square in the eyes, almost begging him to tell her it hadn't been his idea, that he'd been trying to stop the others, that he wasn't a part of it.

'We're just having a laugh,' Danny replied. 'It doesn't matter, Pheme. She doesn't go to this school and I don't think she even understands.'

'She may not, but I certainly do. Just because Lerleen has a disability doesn't make her any less of a person than you or I. She has feelings, she has rights and if you lot get excited by teasing and bullying people, especially ones who have a natural disposition to trust everyone they meet, then you're sadder than I thought.'

Tommy had come over and was guiding Lerleen away from the gathering crowd.

'You don't even know her,' Danny's friend pointed out.

'It doesn't matter. Picking on people is wrong and it most certainly isn't a means of fun, either.' She looked at Danny and shook her head. 'I can't believe you'd do something like this. You don't know what sort of damage you've caused that poor girl.'

'Why are you so defensive? Seriously, Phemie, how do you know what Tommy's half-wit cousin is feeling?'

'She's *not* a half-wit and I know what she's feeling because I understand Down's syndrome. My brother has it.'

'Down what?' one of the boys had asked.

She shook her head. 'We graduate in a few weeks from high school and you people have no idea about the world. You all live in your own little bubbles and don't care about anyone outside of them.'

'You have a brother like that girl?' Danny was almost aghast at the news. 'Why didn't I see him tonight? Are you ashamed of him? Hiding him away?'

'I'm not ashamed of him. He was in bed. He's younger than me and he goes to a different school.'

Danny then looked at his hands and wiped them on his jeans. 'I touched you. I held your hand. Eww. Did I catch it?'

'Nah, that only happens if you kissed her.' His mate sniggered.

Phemie shook her head in utter disgust. 'You people make me sick.' A teacher came over then and broken up the group. Phemie went to check on Tommy and Lerleen, pleased to find the girl was OK.

'Thanks,' Tommy said. 'I think I'll take her home now.'

Phemie nodded then turned to look at Danny, her hopes and dreams crushed. The tingles he'd evoked had turned to disgust but for a while there it had been nice. Nice to feel as though someone liked her.

Now, though, she wasn't in high school, she wasn't an adolescent and yet Gil had somehow awakened those feelings, those sensations which she'd thought totally dormant. Still, to have someone of the opposite sex interested in her, to look at her as though she were beautiful, to let her know she was still mildly attractive was indeed exciting. The fact he'd managed to evoke such a reaction made her wonder if she *was* looking for something more than she presently had—life in the outback, working with good friends and spending her evenings alone.

Growing up, there had always been Anthony to consider. Her parents had thought he would always be living at home, that he'd never reach the stage where he'd be capable of independent living. Phemie had intended to stay close to home to support her parents in any way she could.

Yet Anthony had surprised them all. Out of the two children in the Grainger family, he'd been the first one to move out of home into the assisted living facility where carers such as Liz were on hand to help them whenever required. He'd shown them all he was more than capable once his parameters had been set and now here he was, travelling across the country.

With Anthony not needing her as much, and her parents deciding this was their opportunity to travel overseas, Phemie had found herself floundering in a sea of confusion until an ex-colleague and friend from Royal Perth hospital, Dexter Crawford, had coaxed her to check out the RFDS.

It had been just what the doctor had ordered. Stepping outside her very comfortable comfort zone was something Phemie rarely did, mainly because she was needed in her comfort zone, needed by her parents and her brother, but with Anthony forging ahead on his own and her parents travelling, the RFDS had provided Phemie with the opportunity to do something for herself.

Granted, she was still helping people, as was her nature, and it hadn't taken her too long to settle down at the base where she'd been living for the past eight months. The staff she worked with, all of them, had been so extremely welcoming that she'd known she was in the right place.

Still, they were all married with families of their own and at times she felt the odd one out—the single one—which made her feel more isolated then the vast landscape of the outback.

Would it be so bad to have Gil come back to the base with her? It would only be for a week—seven days—and then he'd be gone. They'd experienced an instant connection—or, at least, she had. There was a good chance she was way off target but, still, having him around, knowing he could never stay…it might make her feel a little more normal for a while. She admired him as a professional and there was no denying she could certainly learn a lot from him in a professional capacity.

Just the thought of having him at the base made her skin prickle with anticipatory delight and her heart rate started to increase. No. She damped down those emotions. Attraction or not, she wasn't looking for a relationship.

'Phemie. I'm awake. Are you?'

A smile spread across her lips as she pushed her thoughts back into the box marked 'Do Not Open' and opened her eyes to look at her brother. 'I'm awake.'

'I'm really excited. I get to go to *Sydney*.'

He made it sound as though he'd travelled to the moon and just for a split second she wished she could see the world as Anthony did—a place of wonder and enjoyment simply waiting to be explored. 'I know, love.' She placed a hand on his cheek. 'How about you go and get changed out of your pyjamas and we'll head to the dining car so you can have something to eat.'

Childlike delight lit his features as he talked excitedly about what was on his 'list' of things to do today. He ticked them off on his fingers and Phemie listened patiently. It was part of Anthony. He needed to get everything sorted out clearly in his mind before he did anything

* * *

Phemie spent the rest of the morning helping Liz and passing the time until the train pulled into Sydney's central railway station. She didn't see Gil in the dining car or the lounge carriage or anywhere else for that matter and after they'd disembarked from the train and had collected their luggage, Phemie said goodbye to Anthony and his friends.

'Stay safe. Remember to only cross the road at traffic lights. Don't go out at night time. Listen to Liz. And call me. Every night.'

'To say goodnight to Phemie.' Anthony nodded, content to accept her instructions.

'Exactly.' She hugged him close. 'I love you.'

'I love you, Phemie,' he responded, and squeezed her tight just as a child would.

She watched him get onto the minibus that would take them to their lodgings, with promises from Liz that she'd make sure Anthony called every day. Phemie waved goodbye, blowing kisses until the minibus was out of sight.

Sighing, she looked around, bringing her thoughts back to her own life and the next obstacle that lay before her. She needed to hail a taxi and get to the conference hotel. There were no scheduled events until tomorrow morning's welcome breakfast, which was held for the presenters, the conference not really starting until Monday. Still, she was looking forward to having a proper shower, as opposed to the one she'd had on the train, swaying to and fro with a few drops of water landing on her skin, and hopefully managing to catch up on her sleep.

Looking up and down the street, she realised there wasn't a vacant taxi in sight. All the other train passengers had taken them whilst she'd been fussing over her brother. She pulled out her mobile phone and was about to punch in the number for the taxi service when a black car pulled to the kerb beside her. She was about to pick up her luggage and move to another spot when the rear passenger window slid smoothly down.

'May I be so bold as to offer you a lift?' The deep, accented tone she'd dreamt about washed over her.

Phemie glanced up from her phone to look directly into the brown, hypnotic eyes of the man she'd been hard-pressed to stop thinking about ever since they'd first met.

'Gil.'

He stepped from the car as the chauffeur came round and started to put Phemie's luggage in the boot. 'I'm presuming you're on your way to the conference hotel?'

'Yes.' She looked into his gorgeous face and tried not to sigh. He was so incredibly good-looking. There were no two ways about it.

'Then you must allow me to give you a lift.' He held the rear passenger door for her and as her luggage had already been stowed in the boot, she really had no option but to accept.

'Uh…thank you,' she replied as she climbed into the back seat.

'Hello, there.'

Phemie was momentarily startled at the other person sitting in the back of the car. She sat next to him and then found herself sandwiched between the two men as Gil climbed in beside her. Whilst there was more than enough room for the three of them, she was incredibly self-conscious of the warmth radiating from the professor.

'Euphemia Grainger, meet William Hartnell.'

'Pleased to meet you, Dr Grainger.' William shook her hand politely.

'William is my personal aide and right-hand man,' Gil explained.

'And his left hand too, sometimes. I also double as the gopher and bodyguard.' William leaned a little closer and said in a stage whisper, 'I'd even take a bullet for him.'

Phemie turned to look at Gil in horror and concern. 'You have people shooting at you?'

Gil laughed. 'No. William was merely joking. I apologise for his warped sense of humour. I guess as we've been travelling together for almost a year now, we're too used to each other's ways.'

'OK.' Phemie decided to simply clasp her hands in her lap and sit nice and still until the car arrived at the hotel. She needed to concentrate, to keep her mind firmly under control and not allow the sensation of being this close to Gil to affect her. Of course, they'd been much closer, given that she'd fallen on him when the train had made its emergency stop, but that touch had been accidental. She was also trying to fight the way his scent was winding itself around her, the warmth of his body radiating out to encompass her. She prayed for green lights all the way to the hotel because the sooner she could put a bit of distance between herself and Gil, the sooner she'd be able to start thinking coherently again.

'I take it Anthony's safely away?'

'Yes. Uh…thank you for asking.'

'When does the group fly back to Perth?'

'Wednesday.' The conversation felt stilted but she tried not to worry about it. Gil was the one who'd offered her the lift so as far as she was concerned he could make all the effort at conversation. Besides, she was too busy keeping her equilibrium under strict control.

'And when will *we* be leaving Sydney?'

'Sorry?' William chimed in before Phemie could answer. '*We*? What do you mean? Has something extra been added to your schedule?'

Gil shook his head. 'After this conference ends, I officially have one week's leave to do with as I see fit. Phemie, here, works for the Royal Flying Doctor Service. I'm going to spend a week in the outback with her.'

'You want to go to the outback instead of the beach?'

'Correct.'

'The rest of the team don't have to—?'

'No. You all have the right to choose what it is you want to do for that last week.'

'And you want to go to the outback?' William looked at Gil as though he'd grown an extra head.

Phemie felt as though she were at a ping-pong match. The two men were clearly friends but it was also clear that William didn't like being kept out of the loop, especially when it pertained to his boss.

She looked straight ahead. *Green lights. Please?*

'Phemie's going to try and pull some strings to see if I can return to the RFDS base with her instead of heading up to see the tropical coast.'

William pursed his lips for a moment before opening the folder that was on his lap. He took out a pen and made a notation. 'Dr Grainger, I'll be needing your cellphone number and a contact for the RFDS base.'

Phemie turned and looked at William, shaking her head in confusion. 'No. Um…this is all a bit premature. I haven't even spoken to my boss yet. Nothing is set in stone.' She was really starting to feel pressured and she didn't like it one bit. She liked things neat and organised and all hospital corners. Not higgledy-piggledy like this. If Gil wanted to come and see where she worked, she would talk to her boss but she wasn't going to be pushed around, having people making her life miserable.

'Which is why I need your contact details. So we can liaise and iron out travel plans,' William pointed out, pen poised.

Phemie looked at Gil and he could see she wasn't going to play ball—at least not William's way.

'Back off for the moment, William,' he remarked.

'Gil.' Phemie spoke clearly. 'I'll speak to my boss tonight and see what I can do. I need to find out if you can legally come and help but there will be a lot of red tape to get through. As I've already mentioned, I'm not sure I can promise anything. I'll let you know—both of you.' She turned to look at William, making sure he knew he wasn't being kept out of any loop. 'As soon as I have news. But until then this topic is off limits. I have to present a paper at the conference on Monday and I don't need any other interruptions. Understood?'

Gil could see the strain on her face and nodded. 'Understood, Phemie.'

She relaxed a little and was pleased when the car slowed down, hoping they'd finally arrived at the hotel. When she looked out the front windscreen it was to discover they were standing still in the middle of traffic. So much for green lights all the way.

'Problem?' Gil asked the chauffeur.

'Not sure, sir. Just a moment, I'll check to see if I can find out what the problem might be.'

'I hope it's not an accident,' William murmured as the chauffeur made a phone call. 'We're delayed enough as it is.'

'Sydney always has traffic jams.' Phemie tried not to shift around in her seat. She couldn't see much out the front window and moving to try and catch a glimpse of what might indeed be holding them up was only causing her to brush up even more against Gil.

'Good heavens,' Gil muttered, then, before she was aware of what he was doing, he'd unbuckled his seat belt and was opening his door.'

'Gil?' she called.

'What are you—? No don't,' William protested. 'Stay in the car. Gilbert?' But it was no use. The professor had disappeared. The chauffeur in the front seat was still making calls, trying to discover the reason for the delay.

'He's always like this,' William complained, and pulled his own phone from his pocket, pressing a button on his speed dial. A moment later he too was talking on his phone and Phemie wished on all the sanity she could muster that she'd had the presence of mind to decline Gil's offer of a lift and to find her own way of getting to the conference hotel. Even if it had meant she'd right now be sitting on board a bus stuck in the same traffic jam, at least she wouldn't have to be putting up with the prima donnas around her.

When the rear passenger door was wrenched open, she almost jumped out of her skin.

'Accident. Two cars, at least, from what I could see. It didn't happen that long ago. Emergency services have been called but we need to act now. Out.'

Phemie didn't need to be told twice and after he'd ordered the chauffeur to pop the car boot, Gil retrieved a small medical kit. 'It's all I've got.'

'It'll have to do. We can improvise wherever possible.' They started walking away from his town car, both of them ignoring William's protests.

'Improvise, eh?'

'Sure.' She grinned at him. 'If you want to survive a week in the outback, Professor, you'd best be a fast learner.'

A spark of interested delight flashed into his eyes, which left Phemie catching her breath with a wave of tingling anticipation. 'Oh, I am, Dr Grainger. Just you wait and see how fast I can learn.'

CHAPTER FIVE

As THEY WALKED past the parked cars, some impatiently honking their horns, others deciding to switch off their engines, Phemie was glad the accident hadn't happened in one of the tunnels. Thankfully, from what she could remember of Sydney, they weren't too far from Sydney General hospital, which meant that help would be on its way sooner rather than later. All she and Gil really needed to do was provide triage for the patients and provide whatever care they could.

'I thought there were only two cars involved.' Gil pointed to where there were two other cars, having slammed on their brakes and skidded into other cars.

'It looks like a backwards letter K,' Phemie remarked. There were three lanes of traffic, all of them now blocked by cars strewn across the lanes. Some of them had stopped perilously close to each other but had managed to avoid crashing. Of the others, they could see that some had only been hit in front, others were crumpled at both ends but the main car, right in the centre of the crush, appeared bashed from all sides.

'How do you want to play this?' Phemie asked, more than happy to defer to Gil.

'Take a look at the passengers in the surrounding cars. I'll check the main one to see whether there are any survivors.' There were two men out of their cars who were also trying to help and Gil walked up to them.

'My colleague and I are doctors. Have you any information on the situation?'

'Uh…we've called for emergency services—'

'I did that,' the younger man interjected, and Phemie realised he could be no more than twenty years old.

'Good thinking,' she praised. 'What's your name?'

'Connor. That's my dad, Jim.'

'I did twenty years in the army,' Jim remarked.

'Then you'll be able to keep a clear head.' Gil nodded. 'If you can keep traffic controlled and maybe find a way to clear a drivable path through for the emergency crews, that would be of great assistance. Take point where needed.'

'Yes, Doctor,' Jim replied, almost snapping a salute.

Gil turned to Phemie. 'Go check out those cars.' He pointed to the ones at the rear of the mess. 'Report back as soon as you can. I'll do the same.'

With that he headed off to the car in the centre as Jim and his son started taking control of the traffic. Phemie walked over to the end car and peered inside. Only one person.

'Hi. I'm Phemie. I'm a doctor. I'm here to help.' She'd said those words, or a variation of them, time and time again. It was true, too. She'd become a doctor so she could help people, patch them up and support them in their time of need.

This poor man required her attention now and she soon realised he was having difficulty remembering his name. After a brief examination, she could see a large bump already forming on his head. She needed him to keep as still as possible until the ambulance arrived. Phemie looked around his car in the hope that she could find something to keep his head supported.

She found a newspaper and a towel amongst his belongings in the back seat and was able to fashion a neck brace. All the while she worked, she continued talking to him, asking him questions, getting him to say the alphabet and count to twenty—anything to stop him from resting too much and falling asleep. Keeping his mind active was very important if he'd suffered a brain injury.

Carefully, she came from behind him and managed to manoeuvre the makeshift neck brace into place with little fuss. 'There. That should help but you must stay as still as possible,' she instructed. She looked around them outside and realised a few more people had left their cars and were wanting to help out.

She climbed from the car and called to a woman who was standing not too far away. 'Hi. What's your name?' Phemie asked.

'Nora.'

'Great. Nora, can you come and talk to this man? He's sustained a head injury and I need him to keep still but not to go to sleep.'

'OK. What's his name?'

'He can't remember at the moment. That's not important. Just ask him to say his times tables or count or spell words, things like that.'

'OK. I can do that.'

'Good.' Phemie took a deep breath, then headed towards the next car. Gil was striding purposefully towards her.

'How are you doing?'

She pointed. 'Patient in this car has an elevated pulse, sluggish pupils and a bad bump to the head. I've fashioned a neck brace to keep him stable and have a lady talking to him to keep him lucid.'

'You fashioned a neck brace?' Gil took a few steps closer and peered into the car, then turned back to Phemie and shook his head in wonderment. 'Good improvising.'

'Thank you. What's next?'

'Ground zero car is a mess. Both front passengers are dead. I think, but I'm not entirely sure, that there may be another person in the back of the car. Even if I'm right, it's all so mangled, I'm presuming they would have died on impact.'

Phemie shook her head and crossed her arms over her chest. 'Any idea what may have caused the accident?'

'I'm too busy right now to figure out the whys and wherefores. Let's just help as many people as we can.'

As they headed off to check on other vehicles, they both stopped for a moment when they heard the sounds of sirens heading in their direction.

'A welcome sound,' Gil murmured.

It wasn't long before they received help, the paramedics attending to Phemie's head injury patient and fire crews sorting through the wreckage. The police took over from Jim and his son, thanking them for their assistance, and soon a very slow parade of cars passed by as they continued to work.

Two women, both in their thirties, had escaped unharmed except for seat-belt bruises. 'We still need you to go to the hospital to be evaluated,' Phemie said firmly to one of the women who was eager just to go home and lie down. 'Sometimes, in situations such as this, your body can be in shock and other symptoms can present themselves a few hours after the initial accident. Please,' she urged. 'Go to the hospital, let them monitor you for the next few hours. It's a necessary precaution.'

'Dr Grainger is absolutely right.' Gil spoke from behind her, pulling off a pair of gloves. At the sound of his soothing English accent, Phemie felt a mass of tension leave her body. How was it he could have such a calming effect on her? Perhaps keeping him around at the Didja base for a week wasn't such a bad idea after all. They could do clinics, assist with house calls and emergencies then at the end of the day they could sit out on the verandah. Gil could talk to her in his normal easy-flowing tones and her body would instantly unwind. So rich, so deep, so…Gil.

'Wouldn't you agree, Dr Grainger?'

It was then Phemie realised she was standing there, staring up at him as though he'd just hung the moon. She gave herself a mental shake and nodded. 'Absolutely, Professor.' She honestly had no idea what she was agreeing to but if Gil had said it, it must be correct, right? When she turned to look back at the two women, Phemie realised that they, too, appeared to be under Gil's thrall.

Both women were looking at him as though he was the most perfect male specimen they'd ever come across and they would be more than willing to do as he'd suggested on the proviso that *he* was the doctor who looked after them during their time of investigation.

'You're a professor?' The first woman preened. 'English, handsome and a professor.'

'Are you married?' the second woman asked, fluttering her eyelashes at him.

Whilst Phemie thought the question gauche and impolite, it was only then that she realised that even *she* didn't know the answer to that question. All this time she'd been looking at him, mildly flirting with him, enjoying his company—as he had obviously been enjoying hers, given that a few times she'd been positive he'd wanted to kiss her—and yet she hadn't even considered the possibility that he might be married. It was so unlike her not to be sure. She planned everything. She was Miss Hospital Corners!

Even more surprisingly, she realised she was holding her breath, along with the other two women, as they waited for his answer.

'No,' he replied politely, but the firmness in his tone indicated there was a lot more to what he was not saying. His back had become more rigid, his shoulders were firmly squared and he was clenching the used gloves tightly in his hands. It was as though he was channelling all his frustration, his annoyance, his pain into the gloves in order to keep himself under control.

Pain? Gil glanced at Phemie and, yes, there it was. A deep, unabated pain in his eyes, and it only confirmed her feeling that there was a lot more going on. What had happened to him? Had he lost a loved one? Had some tragedy struck his life? Perhaps he had been married and it had ended in divorce? A bad marriage wasn't something anyone liked to talk about with random strangers. Was Gil's life in turmoil? Could that possibly be one of the reasons why he'd embarked on the travelling fellowship? Was he running away from his life?

'Let's get you ladies over to the ambulance.' Gil turned and called for one of the police officers to come and escort the women to the paramedics. 'Phemie,' Gil said when they were alone again, 'I was just talking to Kirk, the lead fireman, and he said there *is* someone in the back of the centre car.'

'Oh, no.' Phemie had looked at the wreckage and hadn't been able to see anyone but, then, the rear of the car had been so bent and pushed out of shape, it had been impossible to see everything.

'They have specialised equipment to pick up heat signatures, which tells them how many bodies—that sort of thing. They found a heat signature in the back.'

'Wait, but that would mean—'

'The person's still alive.'

'Oh, my gosh. All this time. If we'd known...' Compassionate pain filled her eyes and Gil marvelled at the woman before him. She'd handled herself so professional, so brilliantly with the emergency and even though he knew that working with the RFDS, she'd often be called to assist in all kinds of different and unique situations, to see her actually working her way methodically through what was required filled him with pride. It was an odd sensation, feeling proud of this woman he barely knew, but each different facet of her personality she allowed him to see only enhanced the gravitational pull he felt towards her.

'Is there anything we can do to help with the extraction?' Phemie started walking towards the centre car.

'Better leave it to the fire crews. They have the equipment to cut the person out. They've already peeled back the roof, which gives them better access.'

'To the people in the front,' she pointed out. 'But the rear of the car is so mangled it's going to take them a lot longer to get to that person. It might end up being too late.' Phemie stood back from the centre car, watching the emergency services team do their jobs.

They were in the process of shifting the two deceased bodies from the front of the car, hoping it would give them better access to the rear. The ground had already been sprayed with foam to ensure no leaking fuel ignited. This, however, made the area quite slippery, especially as she was only wearing a pair of flat boots beneath her jeans. Her light green shirt was covered by her navy jumper and Phemie was glad she'd dressed comfortably that morning. Then again, she'd anticipated already being at her hotel by now where she would have showered and changed into clothes more befitting a medical presenter at the conference.

Gil was dressed in a suit and had discarded his jacket before they'd left the car, his tie was now missing and she wondered whether he'd used it as an improvised tourniquet or whether it was rolled up in his trouser pocket. His crisp chambray shirt was no longer crisp, but was streaked with grime, blood and dirt.

It didn't matter. What they wore, how they looked, it didn't matter. What mattered was the trapped person and as Phemie looked on, she wondered if there wasn't a way to extract the patient from the rear of the car rather than going through the front.

'The only place that person could be is lying on the back seat floor of that car.' Phemie spoke clearly.

With the way the car seemed to have folded in on itself, she had a point. 'That's not a lot of room.'

'A child?'

'A teenager? I think we can safely surmise it's not a six-foot man.'

'Agreed. He simply wouldn't fit into such a tiny space. A woman?'

'That's more likely, but how did they get to the floor? With her seat belt on, it would have been an impossibility.'

'Maybe the seat belt snapped. Maybe they unbuckled it just for an instant to pick something up off the floor.'

'Too many scenarios and no need to puzzle our way through them. What we need to focus on is the best way to extract the person.'

'Or at least to get medical aid to them so that whilst the extraction process continues, they're at least getting analgesia and fluids.'

'If it was possible to...' He stopped and thought some more, trying to study the mess before them.

'Cut through the rear? That's what I was thinking but then the petrol tank poses a problem.'

'What about going in—?' Gil broke off and growled with impatience. 'The only way is what the crews are doing now. Removing the front passengers so we can get to the person in the back.'

'Frustrating.'

'I don't usually attend accident sites,' Gil murmured. 'Not in the last few years at any rate.'

'Prefer to stay in the hospital and wait for the patients to be brought to you?'

'Something like that.' Gil frowned at the slow, meticulous way the emergency crews were doing their best to get to the trapped person. It made him think about the plane accident that had taken the life of his wife and baby daughter. Had she panicked as the plane had plummeted? Had she felt any pain? Had she felt alone? Had she been thinking of him?

Gil hadn't thought about his wife's death in this much detail since the funeral. After he'd buried his family, he'd walked away, determined not to look back, determined to lock his heart up and never open himself up for so much pain ever again. He'd thrown himself into his work, wanting to make a difference with his research, with his developments. He'd lost weight, was hardly sleeping and, as William had termed it, was 'becoming a shadow of his former self'.

The travelling fellowship had seemed like a good idea. He could step outside his comfort zone whilst still remaining firmly in it. When you travelled, when you met new people every week, when you spoke in lecture theatre after lecture theatre on similar topics, you could still feel very alone.

That's what had happened to him. It was why he'd initially been looking forward to ending the tour and going back to London, even if it was only to attempt to have some sort of normal life. That was before he'd met the enchanting Euphemia Grainger.

She'd made him feel alive as he hadn't felt in years. She'd made him think about personal issues he'd wanted to leave boxed up in the far recesses of his mind. She'd made him realise he was become more attracted to her the more time they spent together.

Watching her now, watching the way she was empathising with their unknown patient, how she was as eager as he was to get in there and provide whatever medical care they could, it reminded him of himself. He had a need to be there for people, to give help, to solve problems. It appeared Phemie was cut from the same cloth.

'Dr Grainger, is it?' One of the firemen walked over to where she and Gil were standing, watching silently.

'Phemie, meet Kirk.' Gil quickly introduced them.

'Phemie, we need someone short enough to slide into the car and assess the patient as best you can. All of us...' Kirk indicated the police and fire staff '...are too tall.'

'Wait.' Gil held up his hand. 'You want Phemie to do what?' He wasn't sure he liked what he was hearing. All his English sensibilities started to bristle. Phemie was more than capable to doing what was asked, he had no doubt about that, but why her? So she was small. Surely there were other people who could do it. He would even volunteer to wedge himself into the small space but from Phemie's decisive look she was more than willing to do what was asked. His heart began to pound a concerned rhythm as he visualised her in that car.

'When we've finished clearing the front seats, we'll be needing someone, preferably with medical knowledge, to climb in and assess the patient. Dr Grainger seems the obvious choice. She's small enough and qualified.'

'That's fine.' Phemie nodded. 'How much room will I have?'

'You'll be able to get your arm through, possibly...' Kirk looked at Phemie's small hands. 'Both your hands.'

'Good. I'll go and talk to the paramedics and get set up.'

'Excellent.' Kirk headed back to his crew. As Phemie turned to head over to the ambulance, Gil reached out and stopped her.

'You can't climb into that car. It's not safe.' He left his hand on her arm, the warmth of his touch causing her body to flood with tingles.

'It's all right, Gil. It's not like I haven't done things like this before.'

'What?' His tone was incredulous. 'Are you completely insane? You're willingly and knowingly putting yourself in danger.' As he spoke the words, wanting desperately to change her mind, he also knew he had no right to ask, yet his protective urge towards her only seemed to be intensifying the more time they spent together.

It was insane. This wasn't like him at all. He knew Kirk had been right to ask Phemie. She had all the qualifications and she was small enough to fit into the space. He was also sure that if Kirk hadn't asked, Phemie would have volunteered. Still, the thought of Phemie climbing into that highly unstable vehicle made his stomach churn and his head whirl. But why?

'I'm helping someone in need and it's not *really* dangerous.' Why was he so concerned about this? He seemed almost adamant that she not be involved in this situation. Providing initial medical care was all well and good but when it turned serious, did Gil really expect her to pull back? 'I mean, I'm surrounded by emergency crew members who know what they're doing, the area has been doused with foam so there's little chance of the vehicle catching fire and, honestly, Gil, it's not the worst situation I've been in.'

Gil continued to hold her arm, not wanting to let her go. He took another step forward and then, to her surprise, placed his free hand on her cheek, caressing the soft skin there. Phemie froze, unable to move, unable to breathe, his soft, sweet touch creating havoc with her senses.

'I've seen how you work under pressure, Phemie. You're incredible. I'm not saying you're not capable of doing the work, just that...' He exhaled slowly and swallowed, his Adam's apple working up and down his magnificent throat. 'Be careful. Please. For me. Take extra care.'

Phemie was slightly puzzled at his soft, tender words, not sure why someone she hardly knew that well was so concerned for her well-being. Perhaps it was because he knew how much she was needed, especially after he'd met Anthony. Yes. That had to be it. Gil was merely showing this much concern because he was worried about Anthony. It was the only explanation she could come up with.

'I promise,' she remarked and tried not to nestle her cheek further into his palm. To feel him touching her like that, to be the recipient of such a caress, it made her mind jump all over the place and the last thing she needed right now was to lose her focus.

With strength she hadn't known she possessed, Phemie forced herself to step back, breaking all contact between them. Resolutely she squared her shoulders and lifted her chin. 'I need to focus.'

'Of course.' Gil also took a step back instantly berating himself for having shown her how much he'd come to care for her in such a short time. 'Do what you need to do.'

With a brief nod, Phemie walked over to the ambulance, trying to push the memory of his touch into the far recesses of her mind. Gil had touched her before, he'd held her firmly in his arms and been so close, they could easily have kissed. This time, though, his concern had been more personal rather than simply physical. It was dangerous.

CHAPTER SIX

GIL WATCHED AS Phemie was helped into the front passenger section of the car the fire crews had cleared. She crammed herself into place and was able to reach through a small gap to insert an IV line and check on the patient.

As she'd finished, the patient started to stir and Phemie managed to ascertain the woman's name was Mary and that she was twenty-one. Gil handed Phemie a syringe of analgesics, which she administered intravenously.

Apart from that, there wasn't much for Phemie to do except to stay in her cramped position whilst the crews continued their methodical removal of metal. Every ten minutes Phemie would listen to Mary's chest, managing to fit the stethoscope through the opening and then twisting around so her arm was almost fully extended in order to reach properly.

Gil was able to keep a close watch on the IV line, which was hanging on a makeshift rig above Phemie.

'How does it sound?' Mary asked, as Phemie carefully drew her arm back from listening to the heart.

'Like a heart should sound,' Phemie replied, a smile in her voice as she unhooked the instrument from her ears. 'So, you said you have a brother? Older or younger?' It was important for her to talk to Mary, to keep her as calm as possible whilst the extraction team worked all around her.

'Younger. He's only just turned thirteen.'

'Eight years. That's quite a gap. Any other siblings?'

'No. My parents had a lot of trouble conceiving. My mum was forty-two when she had Daniel.'

Phemie's neck began to prickle. 'That's rather late.' She hedged carefully, knowing full well that women who had babies later in life were more likely to have children with birth defects. 'Were there any problems with the baby? I mean, your brother is he…?' She paused, trying to think of a diplomatic way to ask without upsetting Mary.

'Daniel's gorgeous. Then again, I'm a little biased, although when people first meet him, they're a bit shocked to find he has Down's syndrome. I just don't see it any more. He's just…Daniel.'

Phemie nodded, even though Mary couldn't see her. It was what she'd been expecting Mary to say and in that moment she felt an instant connection with her patient. They were both older sisters to younger brothers with Down's. Mary would know exactly how Phemie felt about things without the need to explain or expand. The frustration, the guilt, the utter devotion. 'My brother has Down's, too,' she confessed.

'Really?' Mary sounded almost excited. 'Isn't that a strange coincidence. What's his name?'

'Anthony. He's four years younger than me.'

'So he's a grown up?'

'He is.'

'That's fantastic. What's he like?'

Phemie smiled as she talked of Anthony, pleased she'd found a topic that would keep her patient's mind occupied.

'I've often wondered what the future will hold for Daniel. Some people can be cruel and he's just so friendly to everyone he meets.'

Didn't she know that all too well. 'It's part of their nature,' Phemie murmured, thinking of all the times she and her parents had tried to instil the lesson of 'stranger danger' into Anthony. 'I think people are often afraid of what they don't understand.'

'They let their own ignorance blind them.'

'Exactly.' Phemie shook her head and smiled. 'It's so nice to talk to someone who really understands.'

'Me too.' There was a smile in Mary's voice. 'I used to love helping my mother look after him when he was little, and now that he's a teenager I guess I still worry about him. I love taking him out, going to the movies or out for pizza—that's his favourite food. We're really good friends even though there's such a huge age difference.'

'Friends?' Phemie was filled with envy. From the way Mary was talking, it was clear she'd had a *sibling* relationship with her brother, rather than being another carer, and that close brother-sister thing was what Phemie had always wanted.

'Sure. I guess I was so happy to finally have a baby brother that I've been a little possessive of him.'

'You spend a lot of time with him?' Phemie closed her eyes, not only feeling sick because she wasn't one hundred per cent sure Mary would be able to spend much time with him in the future but also feeling guilty that she'd never voluntarily spent time with Anthony. The times she'd taken him out had all been because she'd felt obliged to help her parents. Even though there was a bigger age difference between Mary and her brother than between herself and Anthony, it was the feelings in the heart that mattered most.

'I do. Or I did.' Mary's voice dropped to a whisper and she became silent.

'Mary?' No answer. Phemie looked up, checked the drip, glanced at Gil, who was standing by ready to give her anything she needed. She'd forgotten he was there, listening to her conversation. It didn't matter, though. Not now. Only Mary mattered. 'Mary?' She tried again, her tone a little more forceful. 'Mary, tell me what Daniel's favourite movie is. Anthony likes superhero movies. Mary?'

Phemie heard the sound of the other woman sniffing, as though she was quietly crying. 'Uh…he likes superheroes too. Don't most boys?'

She breathed a sigh of relief at Mary's reply. 'I guess they do.'

'My favourite is the one about the ice-skating princess. I even took up ice-skating because of that movie, wanting to glide and spin as gracefully as she does.'

'And can you?'

'I can. I don't skate in competitions or anything but it's where I go when I want to relax or when things aren't going right.' There was a pause. 'I keep imagining that's where I am right now. Skating around the rink, the breeze on my face, my arms out behind me as all the problems slide off and float away, leaving me free.'

A lump formed in Phemie's throat at Mary's words and she looked up at Gil. There was no need for either of them to say anything. Gil's gaze confirmed that he'd heard Mary and the look in Phemie's eyes said she wanted to find a place like that for herself, a place where all her stresses and worries could slide off and float away on the breeze. Gil's brown eyes encompassed her, making her feel safe and secure, letting her hope the place she might find that release was within his arms.

'Every year at Christmas,' Mary continued, 'my mum and I sit down and watch it together. It's like our tradition. I want to do that with my daughter. Or I did.' She fell silent for a moment and then Phemie could hear the sounds of crying again. When Mary spoke, it was with quiet acceptance. 'I'm not going to make it, am I?' It may have been spoken as a rhetorical question but Phemie decided to answer it.

'You have a very solid crew of workers who would beg to differ. I know it's hard to wait but everyone's doing everything they can. We're working as a team and we're going to get you out.' She was adamant about that.

'I'm scared, Phemie.'

'I know.' Phemie leaned forward, contorted herself through the wreckage again and found Mary's hand, holding it as reassuringly as she could. 'I know.' Her own tears slid down her cheeks and she closed her eyes, knowing she needed to be strong for Mary. They were getting closer to extraction with each passing minute. 'Um...' She sniffed and quickly schooled her voice to portray a confidence she didn't feel. 'What other types of sport do you like?'

Phemie successfully managed to distract Mary while Gil stood in silence, watching the strength that flowed through her. She was quite a woman.

The entire time Phemie was in the vehicle, his body was taut, his mind focused. It was as though he was on red-alert, watching carefully, working through differing scenarios just in case things went haywire. Phemie was putting herself in harm's way and whilst he understood her need to be helpful, he didn't like it.

Apart from that last searing look, she'd kept her focus on Mary, as it should be. Yet Gil had also noticed the way she'd not only physically but mentally removed herself from his touch when he'd caressed her cheek. Was she upset with him? Had he crossed a line? Had he gone too far, too fast? The fact that he had no idea why she affected him the way she did was a constant puzzle yet his need to feel that soft, sweet skin had been too powerful for him to resist.

Even if he did accept there was something of a more personal nature developing between them, the main question remained—what on earth could he do about it? He would be leaving her country within a very short period of time and returning to his own world of rules, regulations and red tape. Now, though, he wasn't sure he wanted to go. Was that why he was latching onto Phemie? She was like a breath of fresh air, one that had blown right into his neatly ordered life and completely disrupted it. Had he become so closed off, so insular that a beautiful and intelligent woman like Euphemia Grainger could just waltz in and shake him up? Maybe so.

After June and Caitie had died, Gil had locked himself into a world of work. He hadn't been able to help his wife and his baby girl but that hadn't meant there weren't other people who needed him. So he'd worked, he'd researched, he'd developed different means and methods for procedures and then he'd toured the world, telling all who would listen, hoping to make a difference somewhere, some place, some time.

However, had his self-enforced prison meant he'd completely lost touch with the real world—the world of beautiful and intelligent women? Sure, he had female colleagues and he respected them but never had one attract him the way Phemie did. He'd been more than content to remain alone, to remain in his own little world...until he'd met her.

Did he have to stay alone? Was there...could there be some possibility that his life *hadn't* ended when his family had been cruelly taken from him? It was a thought he'd never considered and he filed it away to take out later when he was in a less intense atmosphere.

The fire crews had made some progress but now they were getting to the stage that if they moved too much too soon, it could do more damage to Mary's already traumatised body.

'We're going to need to stabilise her as best we can before we move this last section,' Kirk was explaining. 'Unfortunately, we can't get the pat-slide in, the portable stretcher is too bulky so we're not exactly sure how best to keep Mary still while we continue to cut her out.'

Kirk was mainly talking to Gil as the two men surveyed the situation. From Phemie's vantage point she could see exactly what they were talking about. She'd just finished checking Mary's vitals.

'Are there some spare sheets or blankets in the ambulance?' she asked.

'I presume so,' Kirk answered,

'And rope? Do you have some rope?'

'Plenty of rope.' Kirk nodded.

'Then why not use the blanket and rope to fashion a sling? If Gil can manage to slide in around the side where you've already removed that back section and feed it through, hopefully I'll be able to reach in and pull it up this side of Mary, thereby—'

'Keeping her suspended in a sling whilst we lift the rest of the wreckage off her.' Kirk finished her sentence, nodding with excitement before racing off to get things organised.

'You really do think outside the box, don't you?' Gil remarked.

'Improvisation is a big part of outback medicine. You'll see that.' Phemie looked at him, the midday sun shining down on them. Thank goodness it was autumn rather than the height of summer otherwise they'd all be cooking in the Aussie heat and humidity by now. As she looked at Gil, the way the sun's rays were surrounding him almost gave him a sort of halo effect. It only served to enhance his good looks, his dark hair, his hypnotic eyes, his square chiselled jaw.

Phemie forced herself to look away. Staring at him wasn't the right way to keep herself under control. He was a colleague, possibly a friend. Nothing more. She started talking to Mary again, keeping the woman as alert as possible, given the circumstances. The last blood-pressure reading had shown they were currently replacing the fluids almost as fast as Mary was losing them. It wasn't a good sign. The internal or external bleeding—or both, depending on what they eventually found—needed to be stopped as soon as possible and once more Phemie experienced a high level of impatience, even though she knew everyone on the crew was doing everything they could as fast as they possibly could.

The paramedics had already called through to Sydney General and alerted A and E to the situation, giving as much of a breakdown of Mary's injuries as Phemie could presently ascertain. Things didn't look good but she wasn't going to let that deter her and pushed the negative thoughts to the back of her mind. She needed to keep talking to Mary, doing all she could to take the woman's mind off what was currently happening to her.

'Anthony loves tactile things,' she was telling Mary, the conversation having returned to the topic of their brothers. 'When he was younger, every time we walked into a new room, he'd have to touch the floor with his hand to feel the difference in the surface.'

'That's what Daniel does, too.'

'My mother, who is a total germaphobe, would carry around little wash cloths to wipe him down every time he'd run his hands all over the floor.' Phemie smiled at the memory. 'It doesn't seem so long ago and now, he's off travelling around Sydney somewhere with his friends.' She hoped to goodness he hadn't been caught in this traffic jam and made a mental note to call him when she arrived at the hotel.

'Really? He's travelling? He is so brave.'

'That's Anthony. Last year, he even moved away from home.'

'Now I know you're kidding.'

'Not in the slightest. He now resides in an independent living facility, specifically designed for adults with Down's, and he loves it.'

'It's so great to hear you talk like this, for me to know that Daniel's future isn't going to be so restricted by society.'

'On the contrary. I confess, I get a little jealous of him.'

'I know what you mean. Sometimes I wish I had Daniel's outlook on life. He's always so positive.'

Gil listened as he worked with the crews, pleased he had the opportunity to learn more about Phemie. He was highly intrigued by her and knowing more gave him a stronger feeling of control. Losing loved ones, especially his gorgeous baby girl, had left him more determined to control everything as closely as he could.

They all worked together and finally the makeshift sling was in place. Gil was ready with a neck brace to slip it around Mary's neck the instant he had access to her. Phemie had given Mary another dose of painkillers so her body wouldn't go into shock with what was about to happen. Having Mary lucid and able to follow instructions was going to be extremely helpful during the transfer process.

It would all happen quickly and everyone needed to be in position and on high alert. Phemie prepared Mary, talking her through what would happen so there were hopefully no surprises.

'I'm scared,' Mary said, and a lump lodged itself in Phemie's throat as she reached out and took Mary's hand in hers.

'I know you are. You have every right to be scared but also know we're all here for you, to help you, to get you out. OK.'

'I know.'

Phemie could tell the young woman was crying and she didn't blame her. Tears welled in her own eyes and she quickly blinked them away. She needed to be ready, to be alert, to be completely focused.

'Ready?' Kirk asked Phemie.

'Ready.' She nodded. Gil, who was standing opposite Phemie, could see the struggle she'd just gone through and once again, as he watched her pull herself together, as she pushed away the personal and pulled on the professional, he marvelled at that inner strength she seemed to exude.

'On three,' Kirk announced. 'One, two, *three*.'

It all happened so fast—the wreckage being shifted, the fire and police members pulling on the ropes to elevate Mary and then Gil and the paramedics transferring Mary to the waiting ambulance stretcher.

'Phemie!' Mary called, and Phemie was helped out of the car and over to the waiting ambulance. She climbed inside and reached for Mary's hand.

'There. You're out. You're ready to go. You've been amazing,' Phemie encouraged.

'I want you to call my parents and tell them about Anthony. Let them know that Daniel's going to have a great life.'

Tears welled up in Phemie's eyes at Mary's words, their hands gripped tightly together. 'I'll call.' Even now, Mary was thinking of others and Phemie couldn't help but love this woman she barely knew. 'You are a remarkable woman, Mary. You're strong. Keep being strong.'

'Thank you.' Mary's words were soft and silent tears slid down her dirty, blood-stained cheeks. 'For being my lifeline.'

Too choked up to speak, Phemie smiled through her tears and then let go of Mary's hand and exited the ambulance. She had no jurisdiction here. She was just a doctor who had happened to be passing by when the accident had happened and had stopped to lend a hand. She had no authority at the hospital, she didn't know any of the surgeons who would operate on Mary, and the lack of control left her feeling bereft as the ambulance pulled away.

'Are you all right?' Gil asked from behind her, and it was then she became conscious of the warmth of his body.

'No.' The tears wouldn't go away. She couldn't control them and the instant Gil put a hand on her shoulder, Phemie turned and almost crumbled into his waiting arms, her tension being released through her heartfelt sobs.

No one chided her for letting her feelings come to the surface. No one seemed concerned that she'd let her emotions get the better of her. No one said anything as Gil simply held her whilst she cried. The crews continued with their work, cleaning up the debris so the entire three lanes could once more be open again to the thick city traffic.

Gil tightened his hold on her, wanting to keep her close, pleased he could be there for her when she needed him. Closing his eyes, he savoured the feel of her, the touch of her hair against his cheek, the way that even after everything she'd just been through, her subtle sunshine scent still managed to drive him to distraction.

'She's not going to make it. I know. I can tell,' she murmured against his chest, and tenderly Gil stroked her back.

'We did everything we could. Now it's up to the surgeons and Mary.'

Phemie pulled back, her tears starting to dry up as quickly as they'd come. 'I'm sorry,' she instantly apologised. So much for trying to keep her distance from Gil. Here she was, standing literally in the middle of the road in a strange city with the man's arms firmly around her. Looking up into his eyes, she wasn't sure what she expected to see. Would he be annoyed? The fact that his arms were still holding her should be evidence enough that he wasn't annoyed. Maybe he was embarrassed, not only for himself but for her as well. Some professional she was, blubbering over a patient. Had he held her close because he'd wanted to hide her embarrassment? Confusion ripped through her and was followed closely by self-consciousness.

She splayed her hands against his chest, getting ready to ease back, but when she finally looked into his gorgeous brown eyes she faltered, her fingers becoming sensitised to the firm male torso beneath his cotton shirt. Her breath caught in her throat as she continued to stare up at him just as he was staring down at her.

'We should probably think about heading off now,' Gil murmured, his Adam's apple working up and down as he swallowed. His voice was deep, personal and filled with repressed desire. It was strange. It was wrong but it was happening. Both of them knew it but neither wanted to accept it.

'Yes.' It was all the answer she was capable of giving because her mind was too busy controlling her need to stand on tiptoe to press her lips against his. The heat that suffused her at the thought did nothing to help with her resolve to keep her distance.

'We should, uh…'

'Go,' Phemie finished, and it was another second before both of them seemed to drop their hands in unison. They quickly said goodbye to Kirk, who shook hands with Gil but then surprised Phemie by enveloping her in a hug.

'Good work, Phemie. Nice to have met you. Might even come out to that outback place for a visit.'

Phemie smiled tiredly at him. 'Didja is a sight to behold, Kirk. You'd be more than welcome.'

Gil couldn't help the mild stirring of…was that jealousy? He pushed it aside but possessively put his arm around Phemie's waist and guided her away from the crews back to where William had had their chauffeur park the car out of the way. He didn't *do* jealousy.

When she was once more seated in the back of the car, Phemie leaned her head back on the soft head-rest and closed her eyes.

'Are you feeling all right?' Gil asked quietly.

'Tired.' She didn't open her eyes and was sort of pleased when she felt his hand envelop her own. She knew she should have pulled away but the stress of being with Mary, of talking to her, of hearing Mary talk about her family and especially her brother…the whole situation was starting to catch up with her and Gil's support was more than welcome at the moment. She knew that once they arrived at the hotel, Gil would need to keep his distance. After all, he was the professor and, as such, needed to conduct himself in a highly professional manner. For now, though, she would take whatever he was offering.

Just this once, she wanted to imagine her life would turn out differently. She wanted to pretend that Gil was hers—the man of her dreams, just as she would be the woman of his. They would be heading to a conference together, as husband and wife. He would speak, give his views on various topics, and a few days later they'd return to the outback where their gaggle of three girls and two boys awaited them. Five, beautiful, healthy children.

The children would run around in the large open spaces surrounding the RFDS base whilst she and Gil sat on the verandah, sipping cool drinks as night-time fell. She would look at Gil and he would look at her, both of them with love in their hearts.

Phemie sighed with longing and let her mind continue to drift as Gil and William talked softly, their words blurring around her. She was surprised when Gil gently called her name, urging her to rouse, as they'd finally arrived at their hotel.

'What a journey,' William remarked as he checked a few things off on his folder. 'I thought we'd never get here.'

And now that they had, Phemie knew she had to let go of any sort of fantasy she might have entertained with regard to Gilbert Fitzwilliam. He was a stranger. Someone she'd met on a train. Someone who didn't factor into her plans for the future. Not now. Not ever.

'How are you feeling now?' he asked tenderly.

'Better.' Phemie smothered a yawn. 'I think I need to shower and change, though. No doubt that will improve the lethargy I'm currently experiencing.'

'And don't forget to give Anthony a call. He seems to live on pure energy. Maybe he can transmit some down the phone line.'

Phemie smiled tiredly at his words, realising he'd nailed Anthony on the head. Her brother was indeed always bright, always bubbly, always eager to see the good in absolutely everything. She wasn't quite sure whether that was due to the Down's syndrome or whether that was just Anthony's natural personality shining through. She liked to think it was a mixture of both as Anthony wouldn't be Anthony without the DS.

'Yes. Good thinking.'

'Then, perhaps later tonight, we could have dinner?' Gil's tone was polite yet intimate. 'Nothing fancy but perhaps a bit better than train food.'

William clicked his pen and made another notation in his file. 'I'll arrange dinner for two just down the road. Not that you dining together is any sort of secret, you understand, but I think it's best to—'

'Stop!' Phemie closed her eyes for a moment then shook her head. She looked at Gil as she spoke. 'I don't want to go to dinner tonight. I'm tired. I'm grubby. I'm uncomfortable. I've spent too long on a train, stressing about my brother and not getting much sleep.' The latter being all Gil's fault as she hadn't stopped thinking about him. 'And now with this accident and Mary and...' She trailed off and collected herself, calming her frantic tone.

'Thank you for the invitation, Gil, but this time I'll have to say, no, thanks. I think for the duration of the conference we need to keep everything strictly business. I'll let you know what happens with the RFDS request after I've spoken to my boss but apart from that—' Phemie held out her hand to him and tried not to gasp at the warmth that flooded through her as he slipped his hand into hers. 'Uh...thank you for the lift, thank you for an interesting train journey and uh...I hope you enjoy the conference and any sightseeing you get to do while you're in Sydney.'

The chauffeur had stopped the car and the hotel doorman was opening the passenger door. Gil didn't let go of Phemie's hand as he unbuckled both their seat belts, then climbed from the car, helping her out as he went.

He raised her hand gallantly to his lips and placed a sweet kiss on her skin. 'I'll have your luggage sent up to your room. Save you waiting around for it.'

'Uh...thank you.' Phemie tried not to blush, tried not to capitulate, tried not to throw herself into his arms and beg to have his mouth pressed to her lips rather than her hand. Why, when she was trying to keep things professional, when she was attempting to put some much-needed distance between them, did he go and do something like romantically kiss her hand? He was pure charm and when he aimed it in her direction, she was powerless to resist. However, she stilled the fluttering in her stomach and ordered her knees to stand firm, rather than collapsing into a heap right in front of him.

He let her hand go and it fell lifelessly back to her side. She needed to move. She needed to get out of there. Strong resolve. *Strong resolve!* It was what she must continue building if she was going to be spending more time with Gil once the conference was over. Strong resolve.

CHAPTER SEVEN

IT HAD BEEN an excessively long day and Phemie was pleased she'd followed through on her whim to soak in a bubble bath. To have that sort of luxury was rare in her life, especially as in the outback water was more precious than gold.

Afterwards, she'd slipped into her pyjamas and sat on the big comfortable bed, flicking through the television channels. She'd called Anthony as soon as she'd arrived in her room, knowing it would be nigh on impossible to truly relax unless she was sure her brother was all right.

He'd talked animatedly about his day and that he'd not only seen the Sydney Harbour Bridge but that their bus had driven across it. Next, they'd visited the Opera House and had had their photograph taken on the steps with the Opera House in the background.

Phemie felt a little jealous. He'd not only had a much better day than her but he'd seen some of the classic Sydney icons. The most she would get to see whilst she was there was probably the inside of this very hotel.

She continued changing channels with a despondent air until she found she was back at the beginning. 'Hopeless,' she murmured, and switched the television off. She should be tired. She should be utterly exhausted and she was, but at the moment she simply couldn't seem to settle down. Sleep, it seemed, was going to evade her once more.

Picking up her mobile phone, she called through to the Didja RFDS base and managed to catch Ben just before he left for the day.

'Don't tell me you're bored,' he joked.

'A little,' she confessed to her friend. 'But I'm also really tired.'

'Then either go to sleep or go out and see a bit of the city. You're going to be stuck in that hotel for the next three days so take the time to get out while you still can.'

'You make it sound like an asylum.'

'It's a hotel. It's a box. Give me wide open spaces and fresh air any day.'

Phemie sighed. 'I know what you mean.' She paused. 'Also, while I have you on the phone, can you give me an update on Kiefer?'

'Ah…I knew it. You rang to find out about a patient, rather than ringing because you've missed your ol' mate.'

'No. That's not true at all. I miss you. All of you.'

'Well, if you weren't such a brilliant doctor who wrote such a brilliant paper, you wouldn't have been chosen to present your findings along with all the other brilliant medics in the nation.'

'You are so long-winded. An update, please?'

'The reattachment operation went well, as you already know, and his post-operative recovery has been non-eventful.'

'Good. I needed some good news.'

'Bad day?'

Phemie was almost about to tell Ben about Mary and the car crash when there was a knock at her hotel door. 'Hang on, Ben. Won't be a moment.' Phemie went to the door and checked through the peephole to see who was standing outside the door, expecting it to be someone who had gone to the wrong room.

'Gil.' His name was a whisper, her eyes widening in surprise. What did he want? She'd received her luggage, so what more could the man want? He was standing patiently, hands behind his back, waiting for her to open the door.

She was trying desperately to make sure there was a professional distance between them and he was making that increasingly difficult when he kept bumping into her or offering a lift or coming to her hotel room to see her. Didn't the man understand she wasn't interested in any sort of relationship with him? Well, obviously, she wanted to keep on reading his articles and following his research breakthroughs but that was it. They were both doctors. He was more qualified, more experienced, more everything than her.

Being near him, having him standing close to her, looking into his eyes, remembering how it felt to be in his arms, the subtle spicy scent he wore drove her to distraction every time he was beside her. It was all becoming too much to fight but fight it she must.

There was no room in her life to have these feelings, these growing emotions for a man she would never be able to be with. She'd chosen her path, made her decision never to get married and have children, and she would stick with it. Helping people was what she did best and she'd proven that today when she'd helped Mary. And then Gil had helped her by supporting her when she'd broken down and cried.

Now he was waiting for her to open the door. The sooner she did, the sooner she could find out what he wanted and the sooner she could send him on his way. She could simply stand there at the door, he didn't even need to come into the room. Did he? No. He didn't.

Resolution made, she reached out her hand, pleased to find it firm and steady, and opened the weighted hotel door.

'Gil.' She didn't move out of the way, didn't invite him in.

'Euphemia.' His smile was warm and polite but this time it didn't meet his eyes. A niggling sensation started to rumble in her stomach as she stood there and watched him for another second.

'I'm on the phone,' she finally remarked when he didn't say anything more. Had he come all the way from the lofty heights of the suite he was staying in down to the fifth floor just to stand at her door and say her name?

'Sorry. I didn't mean to intrude.' Still he didn't move or walk away. 'May I come in?'

Why had he asked? She'd been doing such a good job of keeping her distance but now it would seem churlish to refuse. 'Sure.' Phemie moved aside, holding the door as he walked into her room. She lifted the mobile to her ear. 'I'll talk to you later, Ben. Bye.' She disconnected the call.

'I'm sorry to intrude, Phemie.' He looked at her bright print pyjamas, only then realising she was dressed for bed. When she'd opened the door, he'd been so captured by her hair, which she'd recently washed, as it bounced around her shoulders, the blonde tendrils curling a little at the ends. Her skin was fresh and clear of all make-up, and she'd never looked more beautiful. Phemie's beauty was natural, radiating from within, and he knew that was the main reason he was so captivated by her.

Still, he hadn't come simply to stare. That would be truly dangerous, as staring at Phemie only led him to want to touch her, and if he touched her then he'd want to kiss her, and whilst he'd thought about that quite a bit in the past couple of days, wondering how it would feel with his mouth pressed to hers, he knew following through on that whim would be foolish as well as downright mean to both of them. They lived worlds apart—literally.

'What do you want, Gil?' She was tired and she wasn't in the mood to play games, especially when it appeared he was just going to stand there, looking at her as though he was ready to devour her. She put her guard up, knowing she needed to keep a level head.

'Uh…yes. Sorry. There is a specific reason why I'm intruding on your evening. I'm afraid I have some bad news.'

Phemie's annoyance with him instantly disappeared and her breathing paused for a moment as her mind sorted through the reasons why Gil would come to her room bearing bad news. It didn't take too long to realise the answer. 'Mary.'

'Yes.' Gil shoved his hands into his pockets to stop himself from reaching for her. The look on her face was one of resigned acceptance, as though she'd known the odds hadn't been in Mary's favour. There was pain there, concern and also a look of defeat. It couldn't be the first patient she'd ever lost but he knew from experience that some people, despite how long you'd known them, could leave a lasting imprint on your life when they passed away. It appeared, for Phemie, Mary had been such a person.

'When?'

'The surgeon called me about ten minutes ago. She didn't make it through the operation.'

Phemie looked blankly at the light-coloured curtains, which she'd pulled closed earlier. The room was decorated in bland nondescript colours and that was how she felt right now. Bland and nondescript.

Gil could do nothing except watch her and wait. There was pain in her eyes. Those beautiful blue eyes which had been so vibrant in the past were now dull as they stared unseeingly past him.

'The surgeon called you?'

It hadn't been what he'd expected her to say but as she met his gaze, Gil nodded and took a hand from his pocket to rub it across the side of his temple. 'William tracked down the surgeon before he went into Theatre with Mary and told him I wanted to be kept informed of all progress.'

'I guess the name Professor Fitzwilliam carries more weight than I thought.'

Gil shrugged, not apologising for who he was. 'I knew you'd want to know, hence my intrusion.' He nodded politely, inclining his head so it was almost a bow. 'I'll leave you to your solitude now.' With that, he headed for the door but stopped when he heard her voice.

'I was probably the last person to just chat with Mary.' Phemie breathed deeply, unevenly, as though she was trying to control her emotions. 'It's ridiculous really. I hardly knew the woman and yet she's left a lasting impression on me. We talked. We chatted as though we were long-lost friends. There was no awkwardness. She was so open, so eager to tell me about her parents and Daniel. Two of her best friends had just died in that same crash and yet the way she spoke of them was with happiness and love.'

Phemie obviously needed to unwind, to say these things, to share Mary with someone else. Quietly, he walked back into the room and sat down, still keeping his distance. Being there to support her was one thing and he was more than happy to do that, but getting involved with her was quite out of the question.

She rubbed the back of her neck, massaging the area gently. 'I was only doing my job. I was talking to Mary to keep her lucid, to ensure she stayed awake, and yet she was having the last real conversation of her life.' Phemie swallowed over the sudden lump in her throat. 'I've come to realise how wrong I've been.'

'About?'

'Anthony. Listening to Mary talk about Daniel and how they were good friends...' Phemie stopped and shook her head. 'I've always wanted that, you see. I love Anthony but at the same time I've always yearned to have a real sibling relationship. Brother and sister. Arguing. Laughing.

Doing things together. I always felt cheated that I never had that and now Mary's made me realise it's my fault. I could have had that with Anthony if I'd only worked harder, seen him in a different light, not been so bothered about other "perfect" families and how they all interacted.' Tears dropped from her lashes and slid slowly down her cheeks.

'You are a *great* sister, Phemie,' Gil said. 'From what I heard of your conversations with Mary, and I don't want you to think I was eavesdropping, but her brother was much younger than her. That in itself makes a big difference. When you were telling her about Anthony, every time you mentioned his name, there was a deep, abiding love in your tone. You may not have had the relationship you *imagined* you wanted but you have a very solid relationship with him all the same. Sure, it may seem more like parent to child rather than sibling to sibling but that doesn't mean it's wrong or invalid. You shared yourself with Mary and I have to say, you're quite a woman. Not everyone can do that. You were open with her, telling her about your brother, your parents and about yourself, how you'd been afraid to leave your job at Perth hospital to move to Didja but that you're very glad you did. I heard you telling her how much you like helping people and that's when she thanked you for being there to help her.' Gil kept his words soft but firm, wanting to get cross to Phemie that she had not only listened to Mary, that she'd not only provided first-rate medical care, but that she'd also *given* that dying woman respect by treating her normally.

'The last thing Mary needed whilst she was trapped was to panic. You kept her sane, made her feel as though she was strong enough to pull through it.'

'But I knew she wasn't.' The words burst forth from Phemie like a rocket and she covered her face with her hands. 'I knew she wasn't going to make it. I just knew it yet I kept on giving her hope. False hope.'

'You're a doctor. You do what's in the best interests of your patient.'

Phemie dropped her hands and walked to the tissues, yanking one out and blowing her nose loudly. Where was the man who had held her so tenderly that afternoon? The one who had put his big strong arms around her, making her feel safe and secure? Where was he now? She needed him. Instead, she appeared to be faced with a doctor who was giving her clinical and logical answers about why she was so bereft at Mary's passing.

'Even lying to them in their last moments?'

'Yes.' Gil stood and strode towards her, clasping her arms with his hands. He wanted to give her a good shake but remained firm. 'This wasn't your fault. Mary's death wasn't your fault. You did everything you could and much, much more for her, and you need to accept that.'

'What if I can't?' She looked up at him. The desire to feel his arms about her, rather than firmly holding her at a distance, was what she wanted more than anything right now. She knew it wasn't right. She knew she shouldn't want him as much as she did but, having felt his arms around her before, she wanted that sensation, that feeling of being protected, of being cared for, to envelop her and wash away the pain.

'You have to. You're a professional.'

His words seemed harsh and she didn't want to hear them. 'She was my friend.'

'No. She was a patient. Someone who needed your help. She was a woman you met. A nice young woman who has had an impact on your life. You need to deal with it and move on.'

Phemie could feel her anger rising at his words. She was hurting, she was in pain and all he could do was spout platitudes about emotions he obviously knew nothing about. He may be a genius but it appeared he had no idea about feeling empathy for a person who had passed away. He was being cold and professional and the more he was like that, the angrier she became. She didn't like his rationalised reasoning. She knew the psychology but it didn't help the way she felt. She knew she needed to pull herself together, and she would—later—but right now she wanted to mourn for Mary and she'd foolishly hoped Gil would share her sentiments. Obviously, she'd been wrong.

With a quick move, she brought both her hands up between his and pushed them out to the side, effectively breaking his hold on her. 'I know what I need to do and I don't appreciate your attempts to psychoanalyse my emotions away. I'm upset, Gil. Someone I liked, someone I'm proud to call my friend, has just died and you're wanting me to be rational about this?

'Well, Professor, let me tell you that sometimes people need to be irrational. They need to do what's not expected. If I want to wallow, if I want to mope around and cry and be upset for a woman who at the age of twenty-one has had her life ripped from her, then I shall cry and be upset, despite how little I knew her. Our acquaintance may have been short but it was filled with special moments. Quality, not quantity. And she may have been just a patient in the beginning but by the end she was a woman I admired.'

'Phemie, I—'

She pushed past him and walked to the door, opening it, indicating he should leave. It was necessary that he go. Her yearning for his arms around her, her yearning for him to understand her emotions, her yearning for him to simply be there for her was becoming too much to deal with on top of everything else. She wanted to lean on him, to have him support her, but she also knew if she did that, if he offered that, it would only enhance the growing addiction she felt for him.

'Look, I understand you've had a very rough and long few days.'

'Yeah.' She laughed without humour. 'You've got that right, which is why you're leaving.'

'I didn't come here to upset you. I simply wanted to inform you—in person—about—'

'And I appreciate it. However, I'd also appreciate it if you'd just leave me alone.'

There was a certain look in her eyes as she said the words and Gil realised she wasn't just talking about the absent-minded way he'd handled himself in the past ten minutes. She was hurt, she was tired and he could see she really did want to be left alone. Not only that, he understood she also wanted him to keep his distance on a personal level. It was difficult, especially when she was wearing such cute pyjamas, making her look all snuggly and warm. Did she have any idea how alluring she was, how he was having such a difficult time keeping his hands to himself?

She was right, though. He should go. He should leave her alone. He wasn't quite sure why he continued to seek her out, why he continued to think of her so often, but he would endeavour to do as she now asked.

'Of course. My sincerest apologies, Euphemia.'

His clipped accented tones washed over her as he once more inclined his head in the polite way she'd come to equate with him before walking calmly through her open doorway. Out in the hallway once more, he turned before she could close the door.

'I do hope you manage to sleep well,' he murmured, before walking off towards the lifts and doing what she'd asked all along—leaving her alone.

Phemie was a little on edge the next morning. Although the conference didn't officially begin until Monday, Sunday had been set aside for conference speakers and presenters to not only get to know each other but also to be first in line to attend the Trade shows which would open later that afternoon to the rest of the conference delegates. As such, it was a full day's programme which began with a welcome breakfast in one of the smaller, more intimate conference rooms, where she came face to face with Gil.

'Good morning, Euphemia.'

'Professor.' She nodded politely as she scooped some strawberries onto her plate, ignoring the way her heart rate increased its usual rhythm.

'I trust you were able to sleep well?'

'Yes, thank you.'

With that, Phemie smiled, even though it didn't reach her eyes, and took her plate back to her seat. As she sat down, she made sure she didn't watch him to see what else he did or who else he spoke to.

'Do you know Professor Fitzwilliam?' Another presenter who was sitting at her table asked.

'Not really.' Which was true. What did she really know about Gil except that he was a brilliant specialist, was English and had the most hypnotic eyes she'd ever gazed into? The fact that he could set her heart racing with a simple look meant nothing. Or that he could make her knees weaken with the briefest of touches, or that being in the same room as him made her mind turn to mush. No. None of it meant a thing. Keeping her distance, protecting herself was the better thing to focus on.

She had almost finished her breakfast when the conference co-ordinator stood and tapped on the side of his glass for quiet. Soon everyone was paying attention.

'Welcome, presenters,' the female co-ordinator began, before launching into a rundown of the day's activities. 'First of all, though, I have the honour, nay, the pleasure…' she looked down at the front table where Gil sat and smiled brightly at him, almost *too* brightly, Phemie thought '…of introducing one of the world's leading experts in emergency medicine.' She continued by listing a long string of Gil's qualifications and achievements, before turning the podium over to him.

Amid a round of applause Gil took to the podium, dressed neatly in his three-piece pinstripe suit, where he looked every inch the revered professor he was. Phemie contrasted him to the man she'd met on the train and found they were vastly different. Even the way he spoke was different, his rich warm tones washing over her, his accent far more pronounced then in the quiet moments they'd shared together before Kiefer's accident.

Why did all of that—the journey on the train—seem so long ago? Why did it feel as though she *had* known Gil for more than a couple of days? Was it because she'd read so many of his articles she felt as though she really *did* know him? Or was it the frightening natural chemistry that seemed to exist between them?

Gil calmly scanned the room as he spoke. A smattering of laughter broke out and it was then Phemie realised she'd missed whatever little anecdote he'd just related. When his gaze settled on her she felt like a deer caught in the headlights of an oncoming car. Even across the room, it was as though his brown eyes devoured her and her breathing rapidly increased.

It was only a moment, just a brief flash of time, yet once again she felt completely encompassed by him. It was as though he'd been quietly searching the crowded room for her and her alone. Now that he'd found her, he couldn't be bothered paying anyone else attention.

Phemie looked down. Breaking the contact. Unable to endure the intense moment any longer. She forced herself to pick up her toast, to take a bite, to do something—anything—to get her mind off the man at the front of the room. When she realised her hand was trembling, she immediately put the toast back and clasped her hands in her lap, squeezing them together so tightly she thought she might snap a bone.

She wasn't able to look at Gil for the rest of his speech and at the first available opportunity she politely excused herself and made her way to the ladies room. Her heart was still pounding, her hands were still trembling and when she glanced at her reflection in the mirror, she was astonished at how wild and bright her eyes appeared.

Her blonde hair was pulled back into a chignon, she was wearing a navy skirt, white shirt and matching navy jacket. She looked every inch the professional yet she felt far from it. One look from Gil and she'd ended up a mass of schoolgirl tingles, unable to control her own body's reaction.

Deciding it was best to simply skip the rest of the welcome breakfast and return to her room until it was time for the trade show, Phemie exited the ladies room and headed for the bank of elevators. She didn't look back but instead focused on her escape from a man she simply couldn't stop thinking about.

When was she going to find some self-control? Relationships weren't for her. She knew that and it was a decision she herself had made years ago. Letting the way Gil made her feel rule her life would only mean she'd not only end up alone but miserable as well. If only he wasn't so attractive, so endearing, so…on her wavelength.

He was a doctor, which meant he understood the working hours she had to endure, he was great with his patients and most of all he'd been incredible with Anthony. She often judged people on how they treated her brother, especially given most new acquaintances were a little taken aback when they found out Anthony had a disability. Gil, however, had treated Anthony like a long-lost friend and the picture of the two of them sitting at the table on the train, laughing together, brought an instant smile to her face.

These facts only made Gil more dangerous, only made it even more necessary for her to avoid him wherever possible, especially during the next couple of days. When he returned with her to the Didja base, she would keep her distance and play the polite host to perfection. Gil might even want to go and spend a few days working with her good friend Dex. That would mean less time she had to tiptoe around the issue that she wanted nothing more than to hold him close and never let him go.

At that thought alone, Phemie closed her eyes, not wanting to think about him any more, about how he was affecting her and also about just how deep her feelings for him seemed to be developing. Even if she did, *could*, admit to herself that Gil might turn out to be someone special, someone she really wanted to spend time with, there was also the added complication of geography.

No. There wasn't any way that any sort of real relationship could prosper.

CHAPTER EIGHT

AT THE END of the day, Phemie flicked off her shoes and slumped down on to the bed, rubbing her feet. She was not used to wearing high heels and her toes were now starting to complain. She changed into more comfortable clothes, jeans and a burgundy knit top, before picking up the TV remote and lounging on the bed, luxuriating in the soft furnishings which she definitely didn't have back on the RFDS base.

The phone rang and she quickly switched the set off before answering the call. 'Dr Grainger.' Only after she'd picked up the receiver did she think it might be Gil, and a wild flutter filled her stomach whilst at the same time she dreaded knowing what she ought to say to him.

'Oh, yes…um…' The voice was female and hesitant. 'I'm sorry to bother you, Doctor. I'm, uh…Carren Milton. Mary's mother.'

Phemie gasped, pain rushing through her again, but she pushed it aside, knowing she needed to be strong, to pass on the information Mary had wanted her parents to know. 'Mrs Milton. Thank you for calling me.'

'I understand you were with Mary at the…the—'

'I was,' Phemie interrupted. 'She asked me to call you.'

'Oh.' Mrs Milton was close to tears and Phemie was having a difficult time controlling her own.

'She wanted me to tell you about my brother, Anthony.'

When the phone call ended, Phemie felt better about Mary and she started to feel the faint stirrings of peace. She looked around the small, impersonal hotel room and shook her head.

'No.' The walls felt as though they were about to close in. She was a woman who was used to wide open spaces and at the moment, feeling a little unnerved, she needed somewhere more open than this. Slipping on a pair of flat shoes and grabbing her room key, she headed down to the lobby.

'Better,' she murmured as she found an empty wing-backed chair in the hotel's French-themed café-bar. A waiter came over but she told him she wasn't ready to order anything just yet. He left her alone and she closed her eyes, finally starting to relax.

'Hello.'

At the rich, deep tones she recognised all too well, she opened her eyes and looked up to find Gil standing opposite her.

'Professor.' She tried to make her tone sound more tired as she shifted in the chair. 'I hope you haven't come to deliver more bad news?'

'Er...no.'

Phemie couldn't help allowing her gaze to wander over him and it was difficult not to be affected by his more casual attire of jeans and jumper—not that he didn't look incredibly handsome in a suit. He most certainly did but before her was the man she'd come to know on the train, rather than the medical genius. That thought alone relaxed her a little bit...but only a little. 'Is there something I can help you with?'

'I do believe we had a date to have tea together.'

Phemie stared at him for a moment, her fuzzy mind trying to comprehend his words. 'Oh, tea—drinking tea rather than eating tea. Yes. Oh, I'm sorry, Gil. I'd completely forgotten.' Her annoyance with him started to dissipate. Maybe it was his casual attire, maybe it was the calm look in his gorgeous eyes, maybe it was that she was just too tired to be defensive. 'I was going to find a tea house and I—' She stopped, sighing and pushing her hand through her loose blonde locks. 'I'm sorry.'

'You're exhausted.' She may not have invited him to sit down but at least she was back to calling him by his first name. He decided to take a chance and force his hand by sitting in the chair opposite. When she made no comment, he signalled the waiter.

'Two teas, please,' he ordered. The waiter nodded and went to walk away but Gil hadn't finished. 'I'd like Australian tea if you have it. Something rich in body and full in flavour, and if it's at all possible to get it in a pot with some proper bone china cups, I'd thoroughly appreciate it.'

'I'll see what I can do, sir,' the waiter replied, before leaving them.

When he looked over at Phemie, she was smiling and slowly shaking her head. 'Something wrong?' he asked.

'You're so…English,' she said with a chuckle, and he joined in.

'Thank you. I'll take that as a compliment.' He didn't care where they went to have a cup of tea together, at least he was finally going to get some one-on-one time with the woman who seemed to have invaded his thoughts. The area in which they sat wasn't overly crowded and he was pleased. He'd been in two minds whether to come and see her this evening, to force her hand in remembering their date, especially after what had happened last night and earlier this morning at the breakfast. It was clear she was tired but he really wanted to spend time with her, and after telling William he wasn't available for any tête-a-têtes this evening, he'd headed quietly from his suite and made his way to the lobby, surprised to have found her there.

While they waited for their drinks, they chatted about the conference sessions and she praised him for his speech, even though she hadn't really been paying attention to most of it, given she'd been too distracted by him.

'You mentioned when we first met that you would like me to have a look at your presentation. Is that still the case?' Gil asked after their tea had been delivered. He allowed it to brew before pouring two cups.

'I would but I don't—' She stopped and shook her head. 'You no doubt have better things to do. Besides, if you gave private lessons to every delegate, we'd never get through the conference!'

'Let me worry about my workload and you are not "every delegate", Phemie.' He looked into his cup for a moment before meeting her eyes. 'You're a friend.'

'Am I?' Phemie picked up her cup of tea and took a sip, needing to do something other than gaze into his eyes and lose all rational thought. She leaned her head into the side of the chair and closed her eyes, a furrow marring her brow. 'I'm so confused.'

'Mmm.' He couldn't agree more but decided not to voice his thoughts. It was true that he regarded her as a friend, as someone he wanted to care for, to spend time with, but confessing more than that wouldn't be wise, he felt.

She opened her eyes and stared at him. 'We hardly know each other, Gil.'

'Are we not trying to rectify that? We're sitting here, drinking tea and talking, finding out more about what makes the other one tick.' He sat forward in the chair and looked at her. 'I like hot Indian curries and the take-away shop makes them much better than I ever could. However, I prefer to cook my own roast dinner.'

'You cook?'

'I do and very well, thank you very much. What else can I tell you about me?' He thought for a second before a glint touched his eyes. 'I drive an old jalopy which was the very first car I bought when I was seventeen. I've lovingly restored it and enjoy keeping it in tip-top shape.' It was also the one place he'd found a bit of peace and happiness after the tragedy that robbed him of his family. He paused and sipped his tea, a far-off look in his eyes.

'You've missed your car?' Phemie's smile was one of surprise that Gil was displaying an emotional connection to an inanimate object. It was right. It grounded him. Made him seem more…normal.

He smiled longingly. 'I have. It's about all I'm looking forward to when I return to England.'

'Really? Your car? You can't do any better than that? Can't think of any other reasons why you want to go home after a year of travelling the globe?' She knew he was no doubt joking yet when she looked into his eyes it was to find them filled with sadness and regret.

'No.'

Phemie watched, waiting for him to expand his answer, but he remained silent. She put her cup down as her heart went out to him. 'Oh, Gil. Really? No family? Friends? Surely you have a great job waiting for you?'

'Not really. And friends…' He shrugged. 'I've made some great friends whilst travelling.'

'Like William?'

His smile was instant but it was nowhere near as bright or as relaxed as before. 'William and I have become friends, yes. It's difficult not to when spending so much time working together. That goes for the rest of the people who have assisted me on this fellowship.' He shook his head.

'In some ways it feels like yesterday the fellowship began but most of the time it feels like I've been travelling for ever.'

'Were you stuck in a rut? Is that why you decided on the fellowship?' Phemie put her hand up to stop him. 'Sorry. That was a little personal. You don't have to answer that. It was ru—'

'My wife died.' The words were out before he could stop them. He didn't talk to just anyone about his past yet somehow he had the instinctive feeling that Phemie was the right person. Ever since they'd met he'd felt such a natural yet deep connection with her. He'd read sadness in her eyes as well as struggle and hardship. Knowing she had a brother with a disability also meant her life had been filled with compromises... just as his had been.

Phemie gasped and put her hand over her mouth. 'Oh, no, Gil.'

'She died four years ago in a plane crash. It was one of those random things that happen. She was returning from Italy, after seeing her family, and the plane just...' Gil trailed off, his words spoken very matter-of-factly. It was as though if he put emotion into the words, it would make it more real. Instead, he related the information like a medical professional in order to distance himself from the pain. 'She died instantly, at least that's what they told me.' That had brought him little comfort because he could well imagine the panic she must have felt prior to the impact. It was also the reason he loathed flying. It was one of the hurdles he'd had to overcome when he'd accepted the fellowship and even though he'd been successful, he still preferred an alternative if possible. Hence he'd chosen to travel from Perth to Sydney via train.

Slowly, Phemie shook her head. 'Gil. No wonder you wanted to get away, to do the fellowship. How did you survive those initial years?'

'Work. Locked myself in and threw away the key. I started to realise it was time I reconnected properly with the human race and I couldn't do that trapped in an office behind a desk, researching and writing articles.'

'Ah.' Dawning realisation crossed Phemie's face. 'That's why you've been so prolific.'

'Exactly. Although I have to say that writing all those articles made it easier for me to not only secure the fellowship, it's also helped introduce me to a lot of very interesting people.' He looked pointedly at her and she smiled. 'People who I bump into on…oh, let's say trains, and they instantly recognise me.'

Phemie's smile increased and she shrugged. 'They were good articles. You have a natural flair for the written word and you explain new techniques with ease.'

'Says the woman who has such an impressive list of credentials she could be running a busy city hospital's A and E department yet is stationed with the RFDS in the Australian outback.' The look he gave her was one of admiration.

She started to defend her decision to move, not wanting him to know she'd gone to the outback as a way of trying desperately to find herself. She'd all but forced herself out of her very comfortable comfort zone and Didja was where she'd ended up. 'They need the help and it's difficult to get doctors in remote— Wait.' Realisation crossed her face. 'What do you mean "impressive list of credentials"? How do you know about my qualifications?'

Gil looked at his cup for a second before meeting Phemie's gaze. 'I…uh…have dossiers on all the conference presenters.'

'You do?'

'Yes. It's supposed to be a way of letting me know more about you so that when we meet and chat, I'm not completely in the dark. I guess, in a way, it makes me look good because everyone thinks I know what's going on.'

'And do you?'

He chuckled but there wasn't a lot of humour in it. In that instant Phemie had the inkling that he was more than done with this travelling fellowship. Too many countries, too many speeches, too many doctors to compliment and encourage. 'Not really.'

Gil put his cup down and leaned forward in his chair. 'I have to confess, though, that when I first received the dossiers, I sifted through them until I found yours.' He shrugged a shoulder. 'I just wanted to know more about you.'

'You did?' Her eyes widened at this and Gil stood, shifting his chair closer to hers.

'I've wanted to know more about you since the moment I bumped into you on the train.' The memory of her body close to his as people had passed them in those very narrow corridors came instantly to mind and a powerful heat spread through him.

'Oh.' She seemed to be saying that a lot tonight but she simply couldn't help herself. It wasn't only his declaration she was dealing with but the fact that he'd moved closer. Now his scent was winding itself around her, making her forget everything except the way he made her feel when he was close enough to touch. Heat was radiating out from his thigh, which wasn't too far from her leg, and she immediately shifted, crossing her legs beneath her and trying to edge back into the far corner of the huge chair.

'You've intrigued me from the first moment I met you, Euphemia Grainger.' His gaze was firm on hers as he leaned a little closer.

'Uh...hmm.' She kept her eyes trained on the top of his open-necked polo shirt, finding it increasingly difficult to meet his gaze. In the past few days his eyes had managed to have a hypnotic effect on her and right now, here, in this secluded corner of the hotel's café-bar, the two of them alone, she needed to hold onto every shred of sanity she could muster. 'Uh...and what have you...er...you know...discovered?'

'About you?'

'Yes.'

'For a start, you're one smart lady.'

'Oh. Thank you.' She swallowed, the tension within her mounting because she *felt* rather than *knew* something big was about to happen.

'Today's proceedings were all about the presenters having the opportunity to get to know each other and their keynote speaker before the conference really begins tomorrow.' His words were even, spoken in his normal tone, yet there was a definite undercurrent in the deep, resonant sound. 'I've had a day of talking, of relating, of smiling and making inconsequential remarks.'

'Mmm-hmm.' Phemie was watching his lips as he spoke, the tension in her still continuing to climb.

'Yet throughout it all, I kept thinking about one presenter in particular. One presenter who I haven't been able to stop thinking about.'

Phemie couldn't control the butterflies that were going crazy within her. His words were so soft, so gentle, so incredible to hear. Did he have any idea how wonderful his words made her feel? How special? Gil was admitting that he was thinking about her when he shouldn't be, that she had distracted him from his work, and whilst she felt a smidgen of guilt, her heart soared with elation.

'Uh...huh...I...um, know the feeling.' Why did her voice sound so husky? So intimate? So...not like her at all. Phemie glanced up at him, needing to exhale a little as her breathing was become more erratic with each passing second. 'Gil?'

'Yes?'

Phemie's smile was small but personal. Gil liked it—a lot. 'I think I'm getting to know the keynote speaker much better right now.'

'Yes.' It was then he saw it. That look of acceptance in her eyes. Previously, she'd been hard-pressed to even look him in the eyes, instead preferring to examine the top of his chest. 'Phemie?'

'Mmm?' Her heart was pounding so forcefully against her chest she was positive it was about to damage her ribs.

'Is this OK?'

'Huh?' What was he asking her? And how on earth did he expect her to be able to comprehend anything at the moment? Especially when he was looking at her as though he wanted to devour her.

'Me. Being here.'

'Here?' Her breathing was uneven and her gaze kept flicking between his eyes and his mouth, the intense awareness continuing to build and grow.

'With you.' He smiled and it was almost her undoing.

'It's, uh...' Her tongue snaked out to wet her lips as she sighed. 'It's fine. Whatever it is that I'm saying is fine because I can't think much right now,' she babbled.

'I know the feeling.' Gil reached out a hand and caressed her cheek, amazed at how perfectly soft her skin felt. 'You are incredibly beautiful.'

Her mouth formed a little 'O' but no sound came out. Instead, she licked her lips again, needing to wet them because of her heavier than normal breathing.

'I've wanted to kiss you for so long.' He cupped her cheek, Phemie's breath catching at his touch. He leaned in further, his breath fanning her face as he spoke, oh so softly. It was intoxicating having him this close!

'I've thought about it a lot,' he continued. 'About how your mouth would feel against mine. About how you would taste. About how, if I allow myself to follow through on such an impulsive action, I'd be open-ing Pandora's box.'

At hearing these words, words which were spoken with depth and emotion, Phemie started to tremble. He found her attractive? He wanted to kiss her? If he followed through on the action, what did it mean? What would happen next? She was so used to having her life all neatly mapped out before her and yet from the moment she'd met Gil, her schedule had been thrown into disarray.

Kissing him was what she wanted. It was what she'd thought about and she'd rationalised that it was OK, mainly because she hadn't expected him to be doing the same thing. She simply hadn't expected a man like Gil, with his knowledge of the world, with his experience, with his standing in the medical community, to want someone like her. Yet he'd just de-clared as much and there was truth in his looks.

'Gil.' His name was a caress on her lips and it was all he needed. That final moment of acceptance, that she was ready for this to happen. Was he, though? This would be the first woman he'd romantically kissed since his wife, June.

He looked at Phemie's lips. Parted, pink and ready for him. He was about to kiss another woman and it felt right. It felt *so* right.

Phemie's head was spinning. She was about to be kissed by a man, something that hadn't happened to her in a very long time. Something she wasn't sure she was ready for, but by the same token if he stopped now, she was sure she'd self-combust from anticipation alone.

'Phemie.' Her name was barely audible on his lips but as his mes-merising gaze dipped from her eyes to her mouth, she swallowed. She was ready. She was willing and she was more than able to fulfil her fan-tasy of kissing him.

Within the next second his mouth was on hers, and she slowly re-leased the breath she hadn't even been conscious of holding. Neither of them moved for that first incredible moment, wanting to absorb all the sensations surrounding them.

He cupped her cheek, angling her head towards him, holding her in place as he savoured her flavours. So sweet, so tender, so fresh. The woman was everything he'd imagined and more. As he parted her lips, he found her a willing participant, eager to go with him on this journey, to attempt to discover exactly what this thing was that existed between them.

Still, he knew he needed to keep his self-control completely in check. He wasn't ready for anything more than this and neither was she. This attraction between them had sprung up out of nowhere and whilst they were both acknowledging it, the fact remained that he didn't live in this country and he wasn't the type of man to use a woman for his own needs.

The sensations, the explosions of fireworks that seemed to fill the room as his mouth continued to explore hers were definitely unexpected. Although his touch was soft, delicate and to the point of being so light she could barely feel it at times, Phemie was too scared to move in case he stopped. She didn't want him to stop. The unhurried exploration of each other gave every emotion time to pass through her before exploding in a blaze of light. She felt as though she was floating, dizzy, giddy on the intoxication that was Gil.

The sensations were so refined, so minute, so intimate. His hand was warm at her cheek with only the slightest pressure to keep her close, and as she leaned into his touch, she heard him moan with repressed hunger.

Slowly, he edged back. The energy, the needs were intensifying and the fact that he was in a hotel, his mouth on hers, not even sure what his name was any more, was an indication that things had just become very complicated. Self-control. He needed to remain in control of the situation. If he remained in control of his faculties then he could cope with this mild flirtation—because that's all it could ever be. At least, that's what he needed to tell himself.

With one last taste, Gil eased back, his thumb rubbing almost imperceptibly across her cheek before he slowly removed his hand, unable to brush his fingers across her slightly swollen lips. She kept her eyes closed as her breathing returned to normal and as he sat there, looking at her, marvelling at just how beautiful she was, he was hard-pressed not to return his mouth to hers for a second kiss. The urge to throw caution to the wind was starting to overpower him.

He had to retreat before he risked causing them both pain.

He stood so abruptly he almost knocked the table over and moved away, striving to put distance between them whilst he regained control over his faculties. Phemie watched him, saw the look of determination on his face and came to the conclusion that Gil was now regretting what had just happened between them. Pain shot through her but she ignored it. Whilst she wanted him, and the kiss they'd just shared was total evidence of that, she had no room for him in her life.

Yes, they'd both been curious. Yes, they'd both thought about it and, yes, the attraction was still very much there, buzzing between them, but sharing a kiss changed nothing. At least, that's what she told herself in order to put barriers up between them.

'Um…' She searched her mind, forcing her brain to switch back into gear. 'We don't need to go over the presentation.' She shifted uncomfortably, before standing, shifting so she was behind the large winged-back chair. 'I'll be fine.'

'Of course you will. You're a smart, intelligent woman.' His tone was more normal, more brisk, more *professor-ish*. Good. Perhaps this meant they were back on a more even keel and could, therefore, move forward as though nothing had happened.

'Thank you.'

'And thank you for sharing tea with me. It had a lot of flavour and tasted nothing like dishwater.' His smile was polite but it didn't reach his eyes. Both of them were avoiding the topic, the one that would take them back to a place they'd best leave alone. Their easygoing camaraderie had vanished yet the memory of what had transpired was still uppermost in both their minds.

'You're more than welcome.' The awkwardness was so thick you could have sliced it with a scalpel.

Gil took a step towards the exit. 'I'd best go. You need to get back to your room and sleep.'

'As do you. You have a far busier schedule than I do.'

'True. Well.' He nodded politely to her. 'I'll see you tomorrow, Euphemia.'

'Thank you, Professor.'

At the use of his title, Gil raised one eyebrow but didn't make any other comment. 'Goodnight,' he added, before turning and walking towards the main hotel lobby.

Slowly, as he walked towards the bank of lifts, the realisation of what had just happened hit him with full force. He'd kissed another woman. A woman who wasn't his wife. A woman who wasn't June.

The pain of losing his wife and daughter had torn his heart to shreds. He'd locked himself away. He'd focused on work. He'd had one person after another telling him that in time he would move on. That in time his heart would heal and that he'd one day be able to love again.

He hadn't believed them.

Now, though…he was torn with a mixture of emotions. Part of him was proud that he'd managed to take that step. That after four years he was not only interested in another woman but had actually kissed her. Yet the other part felt as though he'd betrayed June. He'd kissed another woman. He'd moved on with his life and he'd left June behind. She didn't deserve that.

He took the lift back to his suite, where he kicked off his shoes and lay down on the bed, hands behind his head as he looked at the ceiling. It had taken him years to get over June's death and until the moment he'd pressed his mouth to Phemie's, he hadn't thought he had. He'd had some idea that sackcloth and ashes would be the normal way of his life and yet, without realising it, he'd moved on.

He'd somehow moved away from needing June lying beside him in the bed, hearing little Caitie breathing from the crib. He'd sold their house, he'd bought an apartment in Bath, not far from the hospital, and he'd locked himself and his memories away.

To find that at some point during the past four years he'd unconsciously moved on left him feeling more than a little guilty. That part of him felt hollow whilst the other part, the part that could still taste and smell Phemie in glorious Technicolor, felt free and elated.

It was all completely ridiculous. He simply didn't do personal relationships. Not any more. They caused far too much pain when things, beyond your control, went wrong. Perhaps it would be a bad idea to go back to the RFDS base where she worked. Being that close to the woman, working alongside her, without too many distractions, seeing her smile, or the way she brushed her blonde hair out of her eyes, or…

'No.' He stopped the thoughts. Personal relationships were out of the question but from a medical perspective he was highly intrigued with the RFDS set-up. To be able to experience it first hand might even assist with his research. Work. Work was what he needed to focus on, not the soft, supple lips of Dr Grainger, yet when he closed his eyes again, the vision of her face was all he could see.

CHAPTER NINE

PHEMIE KNEW THE only way she'd manage to get through the next few days was to focus on work. Thankfully, being at a medical conference, she was able to do just that. Discussing techniques with other doctors during lunch, looking at trade demonstrations and new products on the market, wishing the RFDS had unlimited funds to buy most of the new products. She filled her time with all those things but mostly she was one hundred per cent aware of avoiding Gil at all costs.

It wasn't hard, given she felt he was doing the same thing and as keynote speaker all of his time was scheduled down to the last second. If they had happened to be in the same place at the same time, they ignored the gravitational pull that existed between them and instead focused on niceties. He would ask how her nerves were holding up and she would praise him on his latest speech. He treated her the same way he treated all other delegates—with polite enthusiasm—and part of her was a little miffed at that reaction.

She *wasn't* the same as everyone else. She was the woman he'd kissed so tenderly and yet was treating like she was…just another person. Phemie knew her reaction was ludicrous. Of course Gil, professional that he was, wouldn't treat her any differently in front of other delegates simply because there might be the far-off possibility that he had an emotional attachment to her.

If he'd walked in, hauled her into his arms then dipped her backwards before planting a big smoochy kiss on her mouth, well…Phemie's breathing increased just thinking about it. She closed her eyes and worked at controlling herself before focussing on what was happening up on the podium.

It would be her turn soon. After the next break, she would be required to take the lead and present her work to the entire conference. Mentally she ran through her presentation again, hoping beyond hope that her computer didn't falter, that the laser pointer would work, that there wouldn't be a blackout.

Her anxiety rising, she quietly slipped out the side door of the convention room and dragged in a deep breath. She needed some air. Fresh air.

Sure steps took her towards the nearest balcony and within a minute she was breathing in the crisp yet polluted Sydney air. It had been raining but instead of the fresh, cleanness outback rain brought, here in the city the May shower had brought a certain mustiness. It didn't matter. Phemie gripped the edge of the balcony railing and closed her eyes, wishing she could breathe the fresh outback air. She was a long way from home and she knew it. Still, it wouldn't be long until she returned, back to the wide open spaces and her calm, contented life.

Gil would be coming back with her. She'd managed to arrange it all quite easily and now everything was settled. He would be there. With her. At her place. She knew that. Accepted it as fact. It was only for one week. She could cope. Then he would leave and she would put him from her mind and get on with what she did best—helping other people. He would be on the other side of the world and he would no doubt forget— No. She shouldn't be thinking of Gil right now. She focused hard, doing some mental gymnastics to get her mind back in order again.

'Phemie?'

She jumped almost sky high as she spun around, slipping on the slight wetness underfoot but managing to right herself almost immediately. Gil was by her side in an instant, his arms outstretched to her.

'Are you all right? I'm sorry. I didn't mean to startle you.'

'I'm fine.' She took a step away from him, needing the distance. 'What are you doing out here? You should be inside, listening to…' She stopped and shook her head. 'You know what? Do whatever you want. I need to go in now.' She stepped away, making sure her footing was sure and steadfast, given she wasn't used to wearing high-heeled shoes.

'Phemie. Wait.'

She turned and looked at him expectantly.

'Are you angry with me?'

'Angry? Why would I be angry?' There was veiled sarcasm in her tone. 'You say you're my friend, you kiss me and then you brush it aside as though it never happened.'

'I've been a little—'

'Busy. I know. It's fine. Listen, I need to go and calm myself down before my presentation.' Another step towards the door but this time he moved like lightning and was there before her, holding the door open.

'I didn't mean to add to your nervousness. I had to take a call so was already out of the convention room when I saw you leave. I simply wanted to ensure you were feeling all right. With regard to the matter of the other evening...' He paused and exhaled harshly, as though he was cross, but she got the feeling he was more cross with himself than with her. 'I would like to apologise if I've hurt or confused you in any way. That was never my intention.'

'It's fine, Gil. Really.' She walked back into the warmth of the convention centre.

'William tells me we're all set to go on Wednesday.'

'William's coming with you?' She was surprised at this news.

'No. By "we" I meant us.'

'Right. Yes. It's all been cleared for you to come back to the Didja base with me.' She made sure her words were calm, controlled and concise, not wanting to tell him how her boss had gushed at the thought of having such a prestigious doctor taking an interest in the RFDS. Gil's ego had been stroked more than enough during the conference. He didn't need more. 'We'll meet nice and early in the lobby. I think the flight is booked for six am. It'll be a long day of travelling so don't party too much.'

'I won't. I assure you.' His smile was equally as polite and Phemie nodded before turning away from him again. 'Uh...just one more thing.'

She turned, trying to remain calm. So much for getting her thoughts into gear. So much for focusing on the task at hand. All she was conscious of was Gil's light, spicy cologne, the warmth emanating from his gorgeous body and the way he made her knees turn to jelly when he looked at her the way he was doing right now.

'You'll do absolutely fine with your presentation.'

'How do you know? You haven't heard it.'

'I just know. Trust me on that and to combat the nerves, just do what I do.'

'What? Picture the audience in their underwear?'

'Heavens, no.' He gave a nervous chuckle at that idea. If he'd pictured Phemie in her underwear when he'd been speaking at the podium, he'd more than likely have had a stroke because she had an incredible body. In fact, he had to school his thoughts right now from picturing her in her underwear. 'Just before I'm about to stand up to speak, I bite my tongue, blink five times, squeeze my little fingers and snort.'

Phemie looked at him with utter incredulity before bursting out laughing. 'Do you really?'

'No, but having someone make me laugh does help. Usually I call on William but during the past year I've heard all his jokes and, believe me, they weren't that good to start with.'

Phemie's smile was bright and natural and Gil hadn't realised just how much he'd missed seeing it.

'Dr Grainger?' One of the conference organisers came over. 'We'll be ready for you soon. If you'd like to get your things and come this way?'

'OK.' Phemie took a few steps away but looked at Gil over her shoulder. 'Thanks.'

'You're welcome.' His smile was natural and gorgeous and she felt her knees starting to wobble again. 'Break a leg.'

'I guess you can feel quite safe saying that at a medical conference, but here in Australia we say "Chookas" instead.'

'Really?' The look he gave her said he wasn't sure whether or not she was pulling his leg. 'Well…in that case, er…chookas, Dr Grainger.' The smile on her face made her eyes sparkle and Gil felt the full effect, recalling just how intoxicating those lips of hers really were.

'Thank you, Professor.' As she turned and walked away, Phemie couldn't believe how much brighter she felt. Her nerves had all but disappeared and she was more than ready to stand in front of the delegates and give her presentation. And it was all thanks to Gil.

* * *

Phemie didn't see him again until Wednesday morning when they met in the hotel lobby before the sun had started to rise, in readiness for travelling to the airport to begin their journey to Didja.

'Good morning, Euphemia.' Gil greeted her with cheery politeness.

'How many cups of tea have you already had?' she asked, slumping down in the chair and pulling a face at his overly bright attitude.

'Only two cups of what you term "dishwater" this morning.'

Phemie sighed, a small smile touching her lips. 'Well, I've had no tea and no coffee either, so please stop being all sunshiny.'

Gil's lips twitched. 'Not a morning person, then?'

'More like a "don't disturb my sleep" sort of person.'

'Yet you're a doctor. That's a profession guaranteed to have high sleep deprivation.'

'Yet it rarely happens that we get called out to emergencies in the wee small hours of the morning.' She let her eyes drift shut but was more than aware of every move, every breath Gil took. How could she be so in tune with him? She'd known him for less than a week and this was the reaction she was having towards him. Imagine what she'd be like after the coming week in the outback…alone…together!

'You were the one who set the flight times,' he pointed out with complete logic. 'I'm sure we could have taken a later flight, thus giving you time to sleep.'

She opened her eyes. 'Actually, the morning flights are the only ones that go direct between the state capital cities. Other than that, we would have been flying from Sydney to Melbourne then to Adelaide then to Perth, where we would switch to the smaller aircraft to fly from Perth to Kalgoorlie and then drive to the base. The trip would have been completed when the sun had already set and as you mentioned that you don't necessarily like to fly…' She trailed off.

'Yes. Yes. I accept the early hour.' Gil shook his head, trying to remain positive in light of hearing her outline their travel plans. He knew it was going to be a long day, most of it spent in the confines of a plane, but for some reason, having Phemie Grainger sitting beside him was definitely taking the edge off the loathing he felt for flying.

Phemie yawned and closed her eyes. 'As it's going to be a long day's travelling, the sooner it's over, the better.' She sighed and relaxed further into the softness of the chair.

Gil watched her for a moment before calling over a hotel staff member. He spoke in hushed tones and then returned his full attention to the tired yet highly alluring woman before him. 'You don't like to travel?'

Phemie opened an eye for a second then closed it. 'Oh, I like travelling. I just prefer doing it to my own schedule. If the planes would run at exactly the times I wanted, I'd be more than happy. Perhaps even chipper.'

'You're a planner, eh?'

'A meticulous planner. My mother used to call me...' she yawned again, her eyes barely open '...Miss Hospital Corners when I was growing up.'

'Fairly apt, now, given you're a doctor.'

'That's what she thinks.' Phemie sat there, allowing her body a few more seconds of sleep. 'Oh.' She sat bolt upright and stared at Gil. 'Was I supposed to organise a taxi or have you alr—?'

'It's been taken care of.'

Phemie relaxed back in the chair again. 'Thank you.'

'Ah. Here we are,' Gil said, and this time Phemie really opened her eyes, smelling the delicious aroma of freshly brewed coffee. He waved his hands in a flourish. 'Ta-dah. This should help you.'

'Coffee?'

'Croissants and fruit, too,' he pointed out with a smile.

'Where? How?' Phemie watched as two staff members set the small coffee table between the lounge chairs with the food and drink Gil had somehow ordered.

'Here.' He poured her a cup of coffee. 'Milk? Sugar?'

'Black is fine.' She held out her hand and eagerly accepted his offering. 'Thank you. That was very thoughtful.' Why did he have to be that way? It only made him more endearing.

His gaze encompassed Phemie, his tone intimate and soft as he watched her sip the dark liquid. 'But remember, if you get sleepy today, feel free to rest your head on my shoulder.'

Phemie was pleased and surprised by his words. 'Uh...I'll keep that in mind.' Even the thought of doing that brought warmth to her body and a pale pink tinge to her cheeks.

'I hope you do.' There was a deep promise behind his eyes and it was one that told her he thought of her as more than just a friend. Yes, he'd declared they were friends and she'd agreed, but both of them were kidding themselves if they thought that's all it was between them. Still, for now, for the moment, friendship was good. She didn't need to run from him if it was just friendship, she didn't need to keep her guard up if it was just friendship, she didn't need to constantly be justifying her emotions to herself if it was just friendship.

Years ago, when she'd still dreamed of one day getting married and having children of her own, she had decided that her children would be the best of friends and the best of enemies. They would argue and laugh together. They would share and squabble. They would be normal siblings and she would be their loving mother who ensured they worked out all their differences so they could remain friends throughout adulthood.

She had no idea whether Gil had brothers or sisters and that just highlighted how little she really knew this man who was constantly in her thoughts. Seeing him with Anthony, how he'd treated her brother with respect and friendliness, had improved her opinion of him. Seeing him at the conference and the way he'd neatly fielded questions, spoken with enthusiasm and had given even the lowest in the medical hierarchy his undivided attention had improved her respect for him. Seeing how he was so thoughtful where she was concerned had improved her love for him.

Love!

Her eyes bugged wide open at that and she must have made a little sound as Gil immediately turned to look at her.

'Phemie? Are you all right?'

'Uh...' She looked away and swallowed. 'I'm fine.' She forced a smile. 'Coffee's still a little hot. Burnt my tongue,' she lied, whilst her mind completely rejected her previous thoughts. Love? No. She wasn't that insane. It would be ridiculous to fall in love with a man she barely knew who lived on the other side of the world...especially when falling in love wasn't in her plan. Not at all.

'Car's here,' Gil announced, and Phemie came back to earth with a thud, surprised to find her coffee finished and her plate empty. She looked at Gil to find him watching her.

'Are you sure you're feeling all right?' he asked again.

'Fine.' She smiled as though to prove it and stood, picking up her luggage.

'I can carry that,' he offered, reaching out for her suitcase, but she shook her head.

'I can manage. Besides, it's on wheels so it's no big drama.' She headed out the hotel's sliding glass doors and stopped short when she reached the kerb. 'A limousine?' Phemie looked quizzically at Gil. 'Is this...is this for us?'

'I thought it might be nice to travel to the airport in a bit of style and luxury,' Gil remarked as their luggage was loaded into the boot.

'I've never been in a limo before.'

'Really? Great. Then I'm glad I booked one.' When Phemie met his gaze, Gil shrugged. 'I thought you deserved a reward after your brilliant presentation. You were by far the best presenter at the conference.'

'Oh. Uh. Thanks.' Phemie felt self-conscious at his words as they climbed into the limo.

'Now,' Gil said, relaxing back, 'William has told me that I'd better not get bitten by any drop bears or hoop snakes. Oh, and I need to remember to check under the toilet seat for red-back spiders.'

Phemie laughed at Gil's words.

'What's so funny?' he asked.

'Who told William about drop bears and hoop snakes?' The smile lit her eyes and Gil tried not to stare too much. She was so incredibly beautiful.

'James Crosby. He's a colleague who lives here in Sydney. Why? Was he wrong?'

'Let's see...drop bears, aka killer koalas, drop from eucalyptus trees and attack you and, uh...hoop snakes bite their tails and then roll down the hill like a hula hoop before slithering over to bite you.'

'So it's true?'

'No. It's all...well, how should I put this...? Er...fictitious.'

Gil's eyebrows hit his hairline. 'Really?' Then he laughed. 'Wait until I tell William he was being teased. He thought Crosby was serious.' Gil paused. 'What about those red-back spiders?'

Phemie nodded, her expression serious. 'Oh, they're very real. Along with the brown snakes and the funnel web spiders.'

'Great. This country sure sounds like an adventure!' Gil eased back into the plush seats.

'Thank you for the limo ride,' Phemie said as she rubbed her hand back and forth over the cream-coloured upholstery. There were little lights in the roof and a fully stocked bar. 'It's fantastic. Anthony's been in a limo before and he took pictures but this...this is...' She looked at Gil, her eyes alive with pleasure. 'It was a lovely gesture.'

'I'm pleased you're enjoying it. It's also a way of thanking you for allowing me to come and stay at your base. I do appreciate everything you've done, the strings you've pulled to organise this, Phemie.'

'It wasn't difficult, Gil. Your name opens a lot of doors in the medical world.'

'At least it works somewhere,' he returned with a smile. It appeared that both of them were on their best behaviour today. After all, they would be spending a lot of time together as they travelled across the country.

Throughout the day, they talked on many topics, Gil even allowing her to read a rough draft of his next article. She was both honoured and flattered as well as being secretly delighted when he'd taken her constructive suggestions seriously.

Whilst they flew, she saw no outward signs of nervousness or anxiety on Gil's part except the way he talked non-stop during take-off and landing. She listened, she absorbed and she relaxed in his company. They were two friends, travelling together. That was all. Her earlier thought about being in love with him was obviously as ludicrous now as it had been when it had first popped into her head. She liked Gil. She admired him. Nothing more than friendship. That was how it had to be.

In Perth, they switched planes and boarded a small Cessna bound for Kalgoorlie. When they arrived in the large outback city, Phemie declared them to be in luck.

'I thought we'd have to drive from here to the base but look.' She pointed out across the two landing strips to where an RFDS plane stood. 'We can hitch a ride with Sardi.'

'Sardi's the pilot, correct?'

'Yes. Good memory.' When Phemie saw her friend again, the two hugged as a way of saying hello. 'I feel as though I've been gone for a year rather than a week,' she murmured as they boarded the aircraft. She watched Gil as he entered the even smaller space and sat in the seat she indicated. Once she was seated, she looked over at him.

'How are you doing?'

'Fine.'

'Liar.'

He turned and smiled at her. 'I'm sure Sardi's a most competent pilot and I also trust that you would never, knowingly, put me in danger.'

'No. I wouldn't.' He had faith in her. He trusted her. He accepted her. Phemie was overwhelmed at that and reached out to take his hand in hers, linking their fingers together. 'Not too much longer now.'

Gil looked at their entwined hands then back to gaze into her perfect blue eyes. The fact that she had been the one to initiate the contact spoke volumes and the elation he felt overshadowed his tension at flying.

He looked again at their hands, loving the feel of her smooth, soft skin against his. He'd only known her for a week. He'd held her in his arms, he'd talked to her, they'd worked together, he'd been immensely impressed with her on the medical front, he'd watched the way she'd cared for her brother…and not seventy-two hours ago he'd had his mouth pressed to hers in a most engaging and electrifying kiss.

She'd been a constant visitor to his dreams and when he was with her like this, the way her bright cheerful scent enveloped him only made him want to hold her, to be with her, to kiss her again and again. To say he'd reconnected with the world, that he'd been catapulted out of his comfort zone was almost an understatement. Throughout the entire tour he'd slowly withdrawn from his cave, meeting people, chatting, being sociable. He'd realised he *had* missed being connected with the world and whilst he knew he had to return to England, to the life he'd had before, he'd also been ready to stop moving from one hotel to the other. June and Caitie would always be a part of him, he knew that and felt that, but it was indeed time he moved on.

Then he'd met Phemie and she'd turned that level of 'normal' he'd thought he'd found upside down and inside out. She'd brought sunshine into places of his life he hadn't realised were dull and grey. She'd made him re-evaluate what he thought he knew. She'd accepted him as a person, a man in his own right as well as respecting him as a professional.

She'd opened his heart and awakened a passion which was addictive. He rubbed his thumb along her finger, relishing in the fact she'd given him permission to touch her, to be with her. The main problem was, he wanted more.

He swallowed the thought. They had a whole week together. Working alongside each other. Talking, having the ability to spend real time alone. He was looking forward to it and decided right there and then that he wasn't going to waste it. Life was for living. He hadn't been doing much of it prior to the fellowship and that meant he had lost ground to make up.

He tightened his grip on her fingers just for a moment and smiled. 'I'm glad you insisted we take the red-eye out of Sydney.'

'It has been a long day.' Why did her tone sound so husky? So intimate? She looked over at him and swallowed, her tongue coming out to wet her lips.

'But a good day.'

A small, inviting smile touched her lips as the tension between them continued to increase. 'Yes.' Phemie nodded and settled back in her seat, the heat from his hand suffusing her body, and she wanted, just this once, to enjoy the effect he had on her.

'So it was worth having your sleep disturbed?'

She looked at him with hooded eyes, trying not to subconsciously beg him to hurry up and press his mouth to hers. 'Indubitably.'

He smiled. 'You are so lovely,' he whispered as he caressed her cheek with his free hand and watched as her eyelids fluttered closed. Her breathing increased and then caught in a gasp when he rubbed his thumb over her lips.

'Gil.'

He heard the veiled hint of pleading and knew what he must do, what they both so desperately wanted. Cupping her chin, he lifted her head and in the next second had his mouth on hers.

Together, they leaned into the kiss, absorbing everything the other had to give, needing to feel, to recapture and expand on what they'd felt last time.

'This is insane,' she murmured against his mouth.

'I know but I can't help myself. You are so totally addictive.'

'We shouldn't be doing this.'

'Why not?'

'Because you live... And I...' Rational thought left her as he once more took her to heights she hadn't thought possible. Her breathing was erratic. His lips were tender and slow.

'We have all week to figure it out.' He spoke softly, desire in his tone.

'Fasten seat belts,' Sardi announced. The pilot's words were enough to bring them both back to reality. Phemie sat up straight and tried to pull her hand free from Gil's but found she couldn't. When she looked at him, his eyes were serious.

'I can't hide what I feel for you, Phemie, but I do want to understand it. To do that, we must do some research.' He kissed her again as the plane started to dip. 'And I have a feeling this is research we'll both enjoy.'

Pandora's Box was now definitely open wide and surprisingly he couldn't wait.

CHAPTER TEN

WHEN GIL HAD looked down through the window of the small plane to the land below, all he'd seen was what appeared to be a tin shed and two houses.

'That's it?' He was astounded. For some reason when Phemie had said the middle of nowhere, he'd thought she was joking.

'Home, sweet home,' she'd sighed.

'You don't live here, do you?'

'Of course I do.'

'I thought this was just where you worked.'

'It is. The house has sleeping quarters at the rear and the base office at the front.' She pointed. Now that they were getting closer the tin shed appeared much larger and he realised it was a hangar. The houses also came into focus and he realised there was only one official house. The other building was a very large garage where a number of cars were already parked.

She'd continued to hold his hand until Sardi landed the plane and then, almost reluctantly, had let go but only because she'd needed to open the doors. They retrieved their luggage and walked the short distance to Phemie's home.

'This will be your room,' she murmured, her body still tingling from the kisses. This time Gil hadn't pulled away, hadn't tried to keep his distance as he had the last time he'd pressed his mouth to hers. No, this time he seemed more than happy to continue what they'd both been fighting for the past week.

Phemie opened a door to show him a very basic room. A bed, a table and chair, a lamp, a small wardrobe, a clock and two framed pictures of Australian animals on the walls. That was it. The floor was polished wooden boards and a ceiling fan hung over the bed.

She'd already given Gil a tour of the front part of the house, which was where the RFDS office was situated. Ben had been diligently manning the UHF radio as well as the phones and had been very pleased to meet Professor Gilbert Fitzwilliam.

'Pheme's always reading your articles to me. Pointing things out. Personally, I think she's a little obsessed with you but there are worse things to obsess about, am I right? Besides, she thinks you're a total legend.'

Phemie had stared appalled at her colleague, unable to believe he'd said such embarrassing things. What must Gil think of her? That she was some gushing fan? Well, in a way she was but that had been before she'd come to know him on a more…intimate level. Now, to have Ben say she was obsessed with Gil only made things worse.

When Gil had looked at her, however, she'd quickly pasted on an over-bright smile and ignored the raised eyebrow that indicated he was very interested in what Ben was saying. Mortification still passed through her at the memory and she'd quickly moved Gil away from Ben, leading him to the bedrooms at the rear of the house.

'Sorry it's so basic. I had Ben air it out and remove the boxes I was storing in here. Apparently, he's even made the bed and put out some towels for you.' She pointed to the linen and felt like a right royal twit. Of course Gil could see the towels on the bed. She was nervous. That's all it was and she was starting to babble.

'I must remember to thank him,' Gil murmured, and then looked sheepish. 'I guess I didn't need to say that out loud. I'm used to saying things like that, having William make a note of it and then reminding me to do it later.' He put his suitcase down and took off his hat, waving it to create a small breeze around his face. 'Force of habit.'

'You're a busy man. You can't be expected to remember everything.'

'Yes, but here I'm not Professor Gilbert Fitzwilliam, Emergency Medicine Specialist Travelling Fellowship.'

'No. You're just…Gil.'

A broad smile crossed his face and his eyes lit with delight. Phemie tried not to be affected but still put a hand on the doorjamb for support. 'I like the sound of that. Just…Gil. I don't think I've been just Gil for quite some time.'

Why did the man have to be so incredibly good-looking? Why did he have to be here in her home? So close yet so far. The two of them all alone. She looked away and focused on a very interesting knot of wood in the floor boards.

'It's going to be great here. I can feel it now.' He walked further into the room and looked around. For all its sparseness, it was clean. The other reason he'd moved was because he needed to distance himself from Phemie. She was an incredible woman and one he was having a difficult time ignoring. The need to scoop her into his arms and carry her to bed was overwhelmingly powerful and he knew he needed to resist. At least, for now.

Gil smiled and the look in her eyes told him she was as aware of him as he was of her. A spark of desire had flared briefly behind her gorgeous blue eyes before she'd started studying the floor.

It appeared he wasn't the only one who was a little uncertain about the two of them being here alone and she had raised a good point on the plane. They lived on opposite sides of the globe. However, he did believe that during this week they'd find some way to work things out because what he felt for her was something that could no longer be ignored.

'Uh…' Phemie pointed up at the ceiling. 'Fan. A must in the outback.' She tapped the switch on the wall. 'Not rocket science. One is fast. Five is slow. The window.' She pointed. 'Try and ensure the screens are closed at all times. You may want to sleep with the window open, though. We get a nice breeze sweeping through most nights. Gives a bit of respite from the heat.'

'Pleased to hear that.' He walked over to where she stood and switched on the ceiling fan, its gentle whir the only sound in the room apart from their breathing. He was standing close to her and he could tell she was trying to resist the urge to take a step backwards, to put distance between them. 'Ahh…that should help cool me down.'

There was a thickness to his words that made Phemie wonder whether he was referring to the heat outside, which had hit them like a ten-tonne truck the instant they'd embarked from the aircraft, or the fact that they were in close proximity to each other.

She started to perspire, her body heat definitely continuing to rise, and as *she* was more accustomed to the dry heat, it had to be Gil's nearness causing the reaction. What she needed was a cold shower, rather than the breeze from the ceiling fan. Swallowing, she forced her legs to work, to move her away from him before she succumbed to the temptation to lean forward and press her mouth to his. He really was becoming utterly addictive.

'Bathroom.' The word came out as a breathless whisper and she quickly cleared her throat as she stepped into the hallway, her flat-heeled boots sounding on the floorboards. 'Bathroom is just opposite here. We'll be, uh…sharing the amenities…' again she couldn't meet his gaze '…so knocking whenever the doors are shut should be a good way to ensure we don't, uh…walk in on…each other.'

Her breathing continued its erratic increase and she realised she was behaving like a schoolgirl, aroused simply by thinking of Gil naked in the shower, that solid and firm body of his glistening with drops of water. Stop it! She shook her head and took a quick deep breath, hoping to get herself back under control.

'We're also under strict water restrictions so all showers are a matter of wetting yourself down, turning off the water, soaping, then turning the taps back on for rinsing and so on. On and off with the taps is the way to go. Every drop is precious. Uh…toilet is a septic tank so if it gets blocked, you'll be the one clearing it.'

'Fair enough.' There was a tinge of humour in his words and Phemie glanced up, her eyes now blazing with annoyance. She was trying so hard to control herself and obviously he found it amusing!

'This isn't a joking matter, Gil. Water is a precious and very valuable commodity out here. We're on tank water, which means it really only gets filled up when it rains. As it rarely rains, we have to use what we have sparingly.'

He sobered instantly. 'Agreed, and I wasn't joking about the water.'

'You were. You smiled when I mentioned the restrictions,' she remarked accusingly.

'No. I was amused at the way you were explaining about the septic tank. You blushed when you talked about a blocked toilet. I thought that was adorable.'

Phemie's annoyance disappeared instantly. 'Adorable?' She looked into his eyes and he immediately moved closer. 'Don't, Gil.' She put her hand up to stop him but it collided with his chest. He quickly covered her hand, holding it against his heart.

'This thing between us is only intensifying with every passing moment, Euphemia.' His words were soft, warm and filled with truth as he slipped his other hand around her waist. 'As I said before, we have a week to do some research, to figure out what this attraction really means.'

'Gil. It doesn't matter. I can't.'

'Can't what? Do you have any idea what it means for me to feel this way about you?' His words were soft, entrancing. 'These types of emotions don't come along every day. This isn't any ordinary attraction, Phemie. It's powerful and it's *real*.'

'I understand but I...' She trailed off as he brushed a kiss first to one cheek then the other, her eyelids fluttering closed as she relished the contact.

'I've been in a relationship, I've been married, I've loved and lost and I've been so incredibly alone. This fellowship has forced me to reconnect with the world but you've helped me to reconnect with my heart.'

Phemie was a little puzzled and swallowed over the dryness in her throat. 'What are you saying? That you l...?' She broke off, not sure she wanted to know the answer to that question.

'Like you?' Gil finished for her, and she opened her eyes to look into his mesmerising brown depths. 'Yes. I like you *a lot*.' The question remained as to what she felt for him. Was it lust? Was it like? Was it more?

'Everything's happening so fast,' she whispered. 'I'm not the marrying kind, Gil.'

He raised an eyebrow at that. 'A modern girl? Preferring to live together?' He was definitely surprised.

'No.' She shook her head. 'It's not that.' She dragged strength from somewhere deep down inside and forced herself to push away from him, to put distance between them both emotionally and physically.

'I'm confused.'

'I'm not the marrying kind, Gil, because I plan never to marry.'

'Not ever?' he asked with incredulity.

'Not ever,' she confirmed, and with that she turned on her heel and walked away from him, leaving him stunned.

Ten minutes later Ben, the RFDS administrator, came to look for him.

'Problem?' Gil asked as he looked up from the desk in his room where he'd been engrossed in some articles. He'd had a quick wash and changed his clothes yet after Phemie had dropped such a bombshell, especially since he'd confessed his interest in her, he'd retreated back into his work, needing to pull himself together in order to face her again.

'Callout. You right to go?' Ben asked, but Gil was already on his feet, reaching for his hat and sunglasses.

'Lead the way.' As he followed Ben to the front of the house, he found Phemie on the UHF radio.

'Is Rajene there, over?' she asked.

'Dad's gone to get her now, over,' a young man's voice replied.

'OK, Peter. We'll be there as soon as we can, over and out.' Phemie put the handset down and turned to face Gil, hoping her knees would continue to support her because when he was around, she often had trouble standing.

'What's happening?' Gil asked.

'Gemma Etherington's about to have her baby. We need to provide medical support until Sardi can pick up Melissa and Iris from the Didja clinic.'

'Melissa and Iris are...?' Gil waited.

'Melissa's an OB/GYN and Iris, Dex's fiancée, is a paediatrician.'

'Of course. I do recall him mentioning her now.' Gil nodded and Phemie was pleased to see he was in full professional mode. 'Where do we begin?'

'I'm going to quickly make a Thermos of coffee for me, tea for you, change my clothes, pack my medical bag and then we'll be ready to go.'

'So there's no rushing out the door in a wild flurry of excitement?'

Phemie couldn't help but smile as she headed into the kitchen. She filled the kettle from the water cooler before switching it on, knowing without turning around that Gil had followed her. Her ability to sense his presence was becoming acute. 'You've been watching too many movies, Professor. Whilst Sardi keeps the plane checked and ready to go, there are still a few last-minute flight details she needs to go over so we have about five to ten minutes before we'll be in the air.'

'Right. Good.' He pointed towards the bedrooms. 'You go change. I can make the drinks.'

'It's OK. I can do—'

'I'm here to help, remember.' He pinned her with a glare, his words calm. 'So let me help.'

Phemie shrugged and decided it was easier to retreat than argue.

'Pheme?' Ben called out. 'Will you be needing Madge at all? She's about twenty minutes away from the Etheringtons', having been out at the Prices', doing an immunisation clinic with Dex today.'

'I don't think so,' she called back. 'With Gil along, plus Rajene and knowing Melissa and Iris will be on their way, I think we'll have more help then we can poke a stick at.'

'Righto. Sardi will be ready in five,' Ben replied.

'Go.' Gil pointed in the direction of the bedrooms. Phemie did as she was told and when she returned, it was to find the drinks made and her medical bag packed. Gil and Ben were discussing the case.

'She already has six children?' Gil's eyes almost bugged out of his head at Ben's words.

'This is number seven,' Phemie added as she peered into the bag, quickly checking things through. 'Right, Gil. Grab the drinks and let's go.'

They headed out to the airstrip, where Sardi was in the cockpit going through her final checks. 'Back so soon?' she joked as they boarded. Phemie went through the routine of pulling up the steps and ensuring everything was locked down and secure.

'How are you doing?' she asked Gil.

'I've been better,' he said truthfully, and she didn't miss the different meaning of his words.

As she wasn't yet ready to discuss it any further she said, 'I mean with the flying.'

'I knew exactly what you meant, Euphemia. I chose to misinterpret. I'm fine with the flying. Thank you for your concern.' He was brisk and polite and she knew she really couldn't expect more. He'd all but laid himself on the line, telling her he was interested in her, and she'd pushed him away. It wasn't that she *wasn't* interested in him—quite the contrary—and that was the main problem. She *wanted* to see where this attraction might lead but if it lead anywhere towards marriage, towards children then she would end up hurting them both. No. She'd made her decision years ago and whilst the fleeting thought that she was already in the process of falling in love with Gil had passed through her mind, not acting on those emotions would no doubt save them both in the end. It was better that by the end of his week here that they part as friends, rather than enemies.

Phemie sat down and clipped herself into her seat. Moments later, they were in the air and when she looked across at Gil, it was to find him peering out the window. 'I'm sorry, Gil.'

'About?'

'What I said before. It was bad timing and I didn't mean any offence.'

'Is it true?'

'That I don't want to marry? Yes.'

'Then don't be sorry. At least you're honest. A man can't help but admire honesty in a woman even if she's saying things he doesn't want to hear.' He turned and continued to stare out the window.

Phemie tried to take his words at face value but her mind was in a whirl. Was he just saying that to be nice? As he'd been married once and it had ended in pain, she'd been quite surprised when he'd intimated marriage earlier on. Was that what he really wanted? Did he really plan to marry again? If he was willing to take such a risk again, surely that should indicate his feelings for her were indeed growing stronger with each passing day.

But what about the distance factor? They lived on opposite sides of the world. How could they possibly get married, or even begin to think along such lines when there was the huge obstacle of geographical location to consider?

It was probably just as well she'd admitted the truth to him. Telling him she planned never to marry was the right thing to do and now they could go back to their own lives at the end of this week, him in his country, she in hers.

It couldn't matter that she thought him the best man in the world. It couldn't matter that she wanted him to hold her hand, to be near her, to kiss her for the rest of her days. It couldn't matter that she had fallen in love with him because if she *did* let it matter, she would disappoint him in so many different ways. It simply wouldn't be fair to commit to a relationship, to marriage with Gil when she knew there was a risk of having a Down's syndrome child.

Then again, Gil had been wonderful with Anthony. He seemed to accept people for who they were, from whatever walks of life they had come. What would happen if they *did* get married, if they *did* have children and if one of those kids *had* Down's? She glanced over at Gil who was still peering out the window, excitement etched on his features. How would he react? She presumed, from what she knew of him, that he would embrace that child—any children they had—with the utmost love and conviction. When she thought of it like that, it certainly made a very appealing picture.

Gil was definitely challenging her, making her think of how different things could be. She'd always thought it would be safer not to risk having children, not to risk passing on the TT21 gene, but even the fact that she was now thinking about the possibility of an alternative life from the one she'd mapped out for herself illustrated just how much Gil was influencing her life.

For now, though, Phemie decided it was best to leave any other attempts at conversation and instead focused her mind on Gemma Etherington's possible needs.

When they were close to landing, Phemie ran through what would happen next so Gil wasn't floundering. 'As soon as we land, we'll be driven by ute to the homestead and then the real fun begins.'

'I completely comprehend the situation as it pertains to the medical emergency but I have to confess it's quite thrilling to be *flying* to someone's house to help them out.' He shook his head in wonderment. 'England is so small. Australia is so vast.' There was excitement in his tone and Phemie couldn't help but smile, pleased he seemed to have let go of their previous conversation. She knew it was by no means over but for now it was as though a medical truce had been called. They needed to be able to rely upon each other for the sake of their patient.

'I know how you feel.'

'You do?' He seemed surprised.

'Of course. We've all felt exactly the same way when we head off on our first call with the RFDS. Flying to a patient's home is different from driving there or having them come to you. It does become second nature to you after a while because it's a part of your everyday life. Although having you here, with your exuberance, helps us all to rekindle the love of what it is we do.'

'Good.' Gil nodded. 'Glad to be of help even before we've hit the ground.'

'Right…well, as Ben mentioned, Gemma's having her seventh child but back in January when she was about twenty weeks, she had a few problems. There were a few ante-partum bleeds but Melissa managed to sort everything out. Gemma, however, was put on complete bed rest for the duration of her pregnancy. Rajene, who's a retired midwife from Tarparnii, lives next door and has been performing daily checks on Gemma and the baby, giving the necessary steroid injections and any other treatments Melissa's prescribed.'

'A Tarparniian midwife, eh?' Gil was clearly impressed. 'I'm looking forward to meeting Rajene.'

'Of course. I keep forgetting you worked in Tarparnii and with Dex, no less.'

'You are correct. I went there not long after the death of my family.'

'Your *family*?' Phemie was stunned. 'You didn't say…' She stopped and waved away her words. 'I'm sorry, Gil. It's none of my—'

'Business?' He finished for her, his eyes dark and cloudy as he spoke. 'When I told you the other night that my wife had died in a plane crash, I left out the other detail, the one which still grips my heart every time I bring it up.'

'Gil. You don't have to—'

He held up his hand to stop her. 'I want you to know, Euphemia. With the way my feelings for you are intensifying, you have a right to know.'

'Gil—'

'Shh. You see, June, my wife, was travelling home, having taken our eight-month-old baby girl to see her family in Italy. My Caitie, my beautiful Caitie. June was holding her on her lap…' The rest of his sentence hung in the air and with both of them being emergency medicine specialists, they knew all too well the circumstances that would have followed.

'Oh, Gil.' Immediately, she reached across and took his hand in hers, her eyes filled with love. Her heart churned with the pain he must have felt, how he would have thought his world had been destroyed, how he would have questioned everything over and over again. Why? Why had it happened? Why had his family been taken from him? She'd heard before, from close friends, that it was possible, when you were really close, really connected with someone special, that you could feel their pain as though it were your own. That was how Phemie felt now, as though it was *her* pain, *her* family, *her* utter devastation. So strong was the bond she'd somehow forged with this man that she was deeply affected.

'How soul-destroying.'

Gil was overwhelmed at her response and put his hand over hers. He'd received sad looks, pitying looks, sympathy from everyone he'd worked with. Phemie's open and honest emotions were so very genuine, and he couldn't help but be touched.

'Almost there,' Sardi said, and both Phemie and Gil looked out the window as they flew over the Etheringtons' homestead. Neither of them spoke. Neither of them moved, their hands staying intertwined until they'd touched down, and even then it felt as though the only reason they were letting go was because they needed to work.

Every time she tried to distance herself from him, something happened to draw her closer again. Not that she hadn't wanted him to share his most soul-destroying past with her. She was honoured he trusted her and it did help her to understand him better. Why he'd locked himself away, why he'd written so many articles, conducted such a variety of research projects, why he'd accepted the travelling fellowship. Anything and everything to help him come to terms with what had happened to his family.

His family. Gil had been a father and there was no doubt, given the way he'd tenderly spoken his daughter's name, that he'd loved being a dad. That was another reason why there was absolutely no hope for them as a couple. Even if she entertained the idea that Gil might want her, might want to be with her, even marry her, they could never have children. It was too risky.

Gil's brightness returned as they climbed into Ron Etherington's four-door ute. Phemie decided to follow his example and be bright and happy but that didn't stop his revelation from playing over and over in the back of her mind. She climbed into the back seat, urging him into the front so he could get a close look at the 'outback'. Soon they were bumping over a dusty track, which Ron obviously thought was a well-defined road. Then again, maybe the man was taking a short cut as his wife was in labour.

'I dropped Rajene off at the house about ten minutes ago. I've gotta tell ya, Pheme, I'm mighty glad she lives close by. Gems was starting to pant and said the pains were getting worse every time she had a contraction.'

'Sounds as though things are moving along nicely.'

Ron laughed and took his hand off the wheel for a second. 'Look at me. I'm shaking. It's been like this every single time one of the kids has been born. I turn into a mess but this time...' He sobered a little. 'What with all the problems and everything...'

'Melissa has kept us apprised of Gemma's condition and as she's been taking it easy and resting and generally doing everything she's told, Gemma's given this baby the best chance in the world. Plus, she's carried it almost to term. Thirty-six weeks—that's excellent, Ron.'

'Good. Good. Almost there. Hang in there, my beautiful Gem,' he called with a whoop, even though there was no way his wife could hear him. 'The cavalry is coming.'

The makeshift road was less bumpy now and as Ron rounded a bend, the homestead came into view. It was just as Gil had pictured, having only seen the roof from up above. It was long, slightly raised off the ground and a wide verandah circled the entire building. The epitome of an outback homestead. He loved it.

'When we arrive,' Phemie said, and he angled himself in his seat so he could see her better, 'I'll take point. We stabilise, control the labour and do our best to keep everything and everyone calm until the experts get here.' She patted the medical bags on either side of her. One was the bag Ben had packed and the other was from the plane, containing the heavier equipment such as a portable sphygmomanometer and a portable foetal heart monitor.

'Right. Sounds straightforward.'

'Except that this is Gemma's seventh child and as a rule she should deliver quite quickly. We don't have the usual equipment hospitals have so improvisation is key.'

'Improvise. Right.' Gil nodded. He was serious, he was concentrating but the energetic buzz that emanated from him was almost overpowering. He was really enjoying this. She was about to ask how long it had been since he'd delivered a baby but didn't want to worry Ron in case Gil's answer wasn't what she wanted to hear. She simply hoped that Melissa and Iris would make it in time.

Finally, after what seemed like an eternity since they'd received the call back at the base, Gil and Phemie were rushing through the rear door of the homestead after Ron had practically parked on the back steps.

'They're in the bedroom,' Ron called, leading the way to his wife's side. The scene that met them on entering the room wasn't what Phemie had wanted to see. Gemma was lying on her back, propped up on her elbows, her feet pressed hard against the footboard of their bed. The bed had been stripped of its linen and was covered with a plastic protective sheet. Another protective sheet was on the floor and towels were draped over the polished wood at the base of the bed. Rajene was helping Gemma to breathe through a contraction.

Phemie took the equipment bag from Gil, who'd carried it in, and handed the portable sphygmo to him whilst she set up the foetal heart monitor. 'Gemma and Rajene, this is Gil. He's helping out for the week.'

Gemma, red faced and cheeks puffed, nodded but didn't miss a beat. Rajene gave a polite smile, which broadened when Gil greeted her in her native Tarparnese tongue.

'Report, please?' Phemie asked the midwife.

'She is almost to the full stage of dilatation.'

Phemie had a quick feel of the outside of Gemma's belly whilst Gil checked her blood pressure with the sphygmo. 'Very tight. Let's see what the heartbeat is doing.' The sound of the baby's heartbeat filled the air and brought a tired smile to Gemma's lips and a whoop of elation from Ron's. A second later Gemma braced herself against the foot board and moaned as she pushed.

'What? No. That can't be a push.' Phemie looked stunned.

'It was,' Gemma grunted through clenched teeth.

'But it's going to be another half an hour at least until Melissa and Iris get here.'

'Tell that to the baby,' Gemma remarked.

Phemie pulled on a pair of gloves and did an internal examination. 'You're fully dilated, Gem. I guess this baby's coming now despite knowing the specialists are on their way.'

'How long is it since either of you delivered a baby?' Gemma asked between pants, her question directed at both Phemie and Gil.

'Uh…a while.' It wasn't the fact of delivering a baby that had Phemie on edge but more the fact that Gemma's pregnancy hadn't been easy. What if something went wrong with the birth? What if there was something wrong with the baby? She silently wished for her colleagues—colleagues with years of experience in these matters—to hurry.

'A longer while,' came Gil's reply. He looked at Phemie and she could almost feel him reading her thoughts. If everything ran to course, they'd be fine. It was all the unknown variables that concerned them.

'OK, then. Well, as it's not been that long since I went through this,' she panted. 'I'll talk you both through each step.'

'No one's doubting your experience but I have to say there's nothing like having the experienced mother to talk the doctors through the procedure. I think I'm going to need to write this experience up in a medical journal otherwise no one will believe me,' Gil murmured, and received a laugh from Gemma.

'I like this one, Phemie. Good-looking and funny. Can we keep him?'

Phemie instantly raised her eyes to meet Gil's and found him watching her with equal intent. Could she? Could she keep him here with her? In the outback? Would he stay? She hadn't even thought of that before. Would he give up his life in England, his prestige and fame to become an outback doctor? If he stayed, though, what would that mean for her?

CHAPTER ELEVEN

WHILST GEMMA'S PREGNANCY had endured quite a few ups and downs, it appeared the delivery was going to be straightforward and for that alone Phemie was thankful. It also helped that Rajene, midwife extraordinaire, was there, guiding them in confused English. A few times, though, she would revert to Tarparnese when she couldn't think of the right description in English and Phemie was exceedingly grateful that Gil was there to converse easily with the woman in her native tongue.

'All right, Gemma.' Phemie positioned herself at the bottom of the bed, protective gown over her clothes, gloves on her hands and a prayer in her heart. 'Push when you're ready.'

Gemma grunted and groaned as another contraction hit and, straining against Rajene on one side and Ron on the other, she pushed her hardest.

'The head is crowning,' Phemie announced. 'That was great, Gemma,' she encouraged once the contraction had passed.

Rajene slipped a few pillows behind Gemma so she could rest between contractions and conserve as much energy as possible. Ron spoke words of encouragement and Phemie was peripherally conscious of the Etherington children hovering outside in the hallway. For the older ones, it wasn't the first time they'd seen the birth of one of their siblings. Gemma had delivered the last four of her brood here in this very room. However, Phemie was well aware that Melissa had organised to induce Gemma's pregnancy in two weeks' time to hopefully avoid any delivery and post-partum complications. That, it appeared, was not meant to be.

While waiting for Gemma's next contraction, Gil checked the baby's heartbeat and monitored Gemma's blood pressure. He was also in the process of setting up an area to receive the newborn baby. With confidence, he'd gone through Phemie's medical bag, pulling out what he needed and laying down blankets and freshly laundered towels on a small coffee table, which had been brought in for that purpose.

It was interesting to be sharing this experience with him—a man she barely knew. It was as though he'd waltzed into her life and changed it for ever.

He made her feel gooey inside and every time he looked at her it was all she could do not to catch her breath and sigh. He was so incredibly handsome, of that there was no doubt. She liked his thick brown hair and, even though he wore it short, she itched to run her fingers through it. She could look into his gorgeous and mesmerising eyes for ever and each time, she knew, they would turn her insides to mush. She wanted to touch his taut, firm body which, as he was now only wearing a polo shirt rather than the usual business shirt, showed off his gorgeous arm muscles.

Phemie remembered all too well what it had been like to have those arms around her, holding her close, keeping her safe. He'd protected her on the train when the emergency brake had been pulled. He'd offered comfort when she'd cried after Mary had left the crash site. He'd tenderly caressed when he'd been showering her with mind-melting kisses.

She felt safe with Gil. She knew he would never intentionally hurt her, just as she would never intentionally hurt him. She knew she could trust him, just as she hoped he found her worthy of that same quality. She not only admired his intellect but the way he used it and she'd felt unworthy of his praise when he'd called her smart.

He may have been through his own personal trauma with the death of his wife and baby but he had gone on with his life. He'd chosen to share his research and experiences with medics around the world and the fact he'd done all this whilst carrying such a personal hurt deep down inside only made her respect him even more.

'Sardi's just called through,' Peter, Gemma and Ron's oldest son, announced from the doorway. 'They've just left Didja.'

Phemie brought her thoughts back into focus as Gemma had another contraction. 'That's it. Push. Push. Keep pushing. The head is almost out. You're doing great.'

When the contraction ended, Gil once more performed the observations. 'Blood pressure is fine. Baby's heartbeat is still strong and healthy.'

Rajene and Ron were adding their words of praise, sponging the very hot and tired Gemma and giving her sips of water. Gil came around and knelt down next to Phemie, the warmth of his body so close it caused her skin to tingle. It was utterly ridiculous the way this man could affect her.

'I'm happy to take care of the baby once it's delivered but what if the baby requires oxygen? I know we brought the oxygen cylinder from the plane and I have a mask to give it to Gemma should she require it, but what about the baby? We don't have a humidicrib or an oxygen tent or any other pieces of equipment.'

Phemie nodded, understanding his concern. She kept her voice low but clear. 'This is outback medicine, Gil. If we don't have what we need, we improvise. You're a highly intelligent man, Professor Fitzwilliam. Think of a way to make what you need.'

As she watched, it was as though she saw his brilliant mind absorb her words and then click into action. He moved to the side of the room as Gemma had another contraction, this one so strong she was able to push the baby's head out.

Phemie knew there was no way Melissa and Iris were going to make it in time. Given that this was Gemma's seventh child, her body knew the cues, when to push, when not to push. Phemie checked to see if the cord was looped around the baby's neck but thankfully there was nothing there.

'The shoulders are rotating so when you're ready, some nice big pushes,' Phemie instructed.

'I thought you didn't know what you were doing?' Gemma quizzed, and Phemie smiled, pleased to see the mother's sense of humour was still intact. 'You're a big liar, Euphemia Graing—' Gemma pushed as the contraction hit.

When she was finished, Phemie looked at her friend. 'I didn't say I didn't know what I was doing. I merely said it had been a while since I'd delivered a baby.'

'Plus with all the problems Gem's had with this pregnancy,' Ron added. 'We don't know what—' He cut himself off and looked out the window, as though wishing the RFDS plane to instantly materialise.

'Whilst I think we'll all be happy when the cavalry arrives, we're all doing extremely well as it is.' Gil's voice was filled with reassurance and strength. 'Especially Gemma.' He smiled at the woman lying on the bed, panting between contractions, and Phemie couldn't believe how in that one instant any worry lines that had been etched on the labouring woman's brow lifted.

Not only was Gil a fantastic medical specialist, a great researcher and an excellent writer, he also had the ability to connect with his patients, to put them at ease and to leave everyone feeling as though everything would, indeed, be all right.

From then on a wave of determination filled the room. Phemie was conscious of Gil going over to speak to Peter, asking him for a few different things. When Peter returned, it was with his arms bundled with Gaffer tape, kitchen plastic wrap and a set of small plastic rods, which usually snapped together to form a platform to dry woollen jumpers.

Phemie wanted to watch whatever it was Gil was up to. She'd told him to improvise and it looked as though he was doing just that. However, Gemma and the baby required her attention and as Gemma continued to push, Phemie guided the small baby into the world.

Ron was there, watching the final moments of the birth, and finally was ready to announce in a loud booming voice that they had another daughter. Gemma laughed and collapsed back against the pillows, Rajene tending to the mother.

Gil had finished whatever it was he'd been doing and was by her side with a warmed towel to accept the newborn, his big hands forming a secure platform. Phemie retrieved two pairs of locking forceps from her bag and clamped the umbilical cord. Then she held out some scissors to Ron.

'Doing the honours, Dad?'

'Try and stop me.' Ron was elated and when it was done, Phemie looked at the baby, wiping her mouth and nose. A mild cry came out and Gemma sighed with relief.

'She's OK.'

Gil and Phemie waited as the little bundle started breathing, trying to find her rhythm. Phemie quickly administered an injection of vitamin K then frowned as she watched the rise and fall of the little chest more closely. 'Those breaths are a little fast.' When she looked at Gil, she realised he was counting the breaths.

'Ninety,' he said after a minute had passed.

'Rajene.' Phemie looked at the wise midwife. 'Would you mind helping Gemma with the last stage of labour, please?'

'What…what's wrong?' Ron asked, his gaze darting around the room, to his wife on the bed, to his other children in the hallway, to his new little daughter who was being closely watched by the two doctors.

'Peter, check on the plane,' Phemie called. 'If they're close, drive out to the airstrip to meet them.'

'Right.' The seventeen-year-old headed to do as he was told.

'What's going on?' Gemma asked, concern touching her voice.

'The baby's breathing a little too fast, trying to suck in as much air as possible,' Phemie said, taking the baby closer to Gemma. 'See? Her nostrils are flaring and you can see her ribs as her lungs try to work as hard as they can.'

'That's bad?'

'It's an indication of HMD—hyline membrane disease. We need to get her saturations stabilised.'

'Good call,' Gil said as he placed the baby down on the table he'd set up. There were heaters on either side so they could keep the baby warm and finally Phemie was able to see what it was he'd been constructing.

'An oxygen tent.' She shook her head in wonderment. 'Well done.'

'Her skin's pale and mottling.'

'Let's get her hooked up.' With Gil's improvised oxygen tent, they'd be able to apply the oxygen and improve the saturations in no time.

'Yolanda…' Ron was calling to his oldest daughter. 'Call through to the base so they can get a message to the plane that it's HMD.'

'Is she all right?' Gemma asked, her tone watery and scared. Rajene was busy delivering the afterbirth but was keeping a close eye on the mother.

'We're working on making sure she is.' Gil was the one to answer and again his words had a distinct ring of authority that would put even the most sceptical person at ease.

Gil turned the oxygen on and Phemie put the tent—a crude frame of plastic pipes held together with tape and then covered with plastic wrap—over the baby. The oxygen slowly filled the tent, Gil monitoring the saturation levels and both of them watching the baby's response.

'What are you going to call her?' Phemie asked, glancing over at Gemma, who was lying back with her eyes shut.

'We're letting the children choose her name,' Ron announced when Gemma didn't say anything.

Phemie smiled and glanced at the wide stares of the children in question peeping around the doorframe. 'Fantastic. So,' she addressed the children, 'what names have you come up with for a girl? Was it a unanimous decision?'

'It was,' Selena, the third eldest, announced.

'And what shall she be named?' Phemie asked.

The children all looked at each other then back at the doctors, their eyes bright with delight. 'We're going to call her Rajene Paris.'

Phemie turned to look at the midwife, whose eyes were wide with unexpected delight.

'You name babe after me?' Her tone was filled with complete awe.

'You've looked after Mum and the baby so well,' Selena continued, standing proudly as she spoke. 'We all decided it was the best name ever—if it was a girl,' she added with a little smile.

'Well,' Gil announced to all and sundry, 'I'm happy to report that Rajene Paris's colour is improving, her skin is becoming less mottled and her little lungs aren't having to work so hard to suck in air.'

'Oh. Oh!' Gemma said happily, and then promptly burst into tears. 'Oh, my darling baby is all right.'

The children all clapped, and the little ones, the youngest of whom could only be about three years old, jumped around excitedly. Suddenly, he stopped and looked up at Yolanda, who had come back.

'Can I play now, Landa?' he asked.

'Yes, Lee. All of you can go play. I think Mum and Rajene Paris need some quiet,' Yolanda announced. Once the younger ones had run off, she looked at the adults. 'Peter's just radioed through to say the plane has landed. Melissa and Iris are on their way.'

'That'd be right.' Ron chortled. 'Now that the drama's all over and every thing's as right as rain, they finally get here.'

Gil looked at Phemie and when he smiled she couldn't get over the way his gaze encompassed her. Together, they'd been able to care for mother and baby, which was their job. In that look, though, there was more. Gil's eyes radiated his happiness, his pride at what they'd done as a team.

Half an hour later, as they stood on the verandah looking at the land as dusk started to approach, Gil put his arm about her waist and drew her close. Phemie didn't stop him. She wanted to be held by him, to cap off this special day by being close to the man she was most certainly in love with. Seeing the way he'd cared for that baby, especially knowing how his own baby girl had been taken from him, her heart churned with love.

She loved him. She loved Gil and whilst she knew it was so incredibly wrong, that it could never be, she wanted this moment. Melissa and Iris were taking care of mother and baby, the Etherington children were helping to tidy up and make dinner and Rajene had been ordered to sit, relax and have a cup of tea. All seemed to be right with the world.

'We did it, Euphemia.'

'Yes, we did.' She snuggled back into him and sighed, covering his arms with her own. Gil dropped a kiss on the top of her head as they both simply stood and stared, absorbing the serenity. 'When I first heard the baby's cries, I thought everything was going to be fine. I thought, We've done it. And then she started...' Phemie stopped and shook her head slightly. 'And then I turned and you'd set up your makeshift oxygen tent. Genius, Gil. Pure genius.'

'I'm sure you would have come up with something even better. You're amazing at thinking outside the square box.'

She laughed without humour. 'I disagree. I don't see that in myself at all.'

Gil looked at her with a quizzical furrow on his brow. 'Well, then, I must disagree with your disagreement. On the train, for example, you were the one to get the RFDS organised.'

'I had a phone that would reach them.'

'And with Mary, in Sydney, you were the one who came up with the best way to move her.'

'Mary.' She sighed again, although this time it was one of remorse.

She pulled Gil's arms around her, needing to feel more secure. He was more than happy to oblige and dropped a kiss on her cheek.

'You are not to blame for her death.' Gil's words were adamant.

'I know. I'm sorry about that night, Gil. I didn't mean to take my frustrations out on you.' Phemie angled her head so she could see him better and couldn't help smiling when he dropped a kiss on the tip of her nose.

'No need to apologise. You shared an amazing time with Mary and I'm positive you'll never forget her. You are quite a woman, Euphemia Grainger. You care. You give. You put yourself on the line for everyone else. Isn't it time you did something for yourself? Accepted your reward?' He turned her in his arms and without waiting pressed his mouth to hers. Phemie kissed him back with all the love in her heart, wanting him to know, to feel, just how much she appreciated him, how much she needed him, how much she wanted him. 'I want to know everything about you,' he murmured against her mouth, punctuating his words with kisses. 'I want to spend my precious time here, chatting to you in every spare moment we have. I want to hold you, to kiss you, to simply be with you.'

'Sleep with me?' she asked, and he didn't miss that hint of hesitation in her tone.

A small smile touched his lips and he raised both eyebrows. 'I am a red-blooded male, Euphemia.' His voice was deep and filled with repressed desire. 'However, given the time constraints and other...geographical factors, I don't think such a course of action would be advisable.'

Phemie couldn't believe that she actually felt hurt by his words. She knew he was being honourable, that he was trying to do the right thing, but by the same token was she yet again to be rejected? When Danny Ellingham had rejected her, she'd thought it was because of Anthony, because of the Down's syndrome, but perhaps all those years ago she'd been wrong. Perhaps he'd simply been rejecting *her* and she hadn't realised it. 'You don't find me attr—'

Gil stopped her words by pressing his mouth to hers, showing her rather than telling her just how incredibly attracted he was. 'How could you even think that? From almost the first moment I saw you, I've yearned to have you in my arms, your body pressed to mine, my mouth worshipping you.' He looked intently into her eyes. 'You have come to mean so much to me in such a short time. You're special, Phemie. Very special, and very dear to me.'

'Gil. Listen I—'

'No. Please.' He pressed a finger to her lips. 'I heard what you said before, about never marrying.'

'I can't.'

'Why not?' He tightened his arms around her but pulled back, the pleading note in his voice showing he really wanted to understand. 'What I feel for you…' He stopped and shook his head. 'I didn't ask for it. I most certainly didn't expect it but Phemie, I've been in love before and this…what I feel for you…' He stopped again, trying to be diplomatic in his choice of words.

'Don't, Gil.' Phemie twisted out of his grasp and walked to the other corner of the verandah. As the sky was now changing colour, indicating the sun was indeed setting, she began to realise how tired she really was. She didn't have the strength to argue with him so instead she allowed his words, his sultry deep voice to wash over her.

'Phemie. You must allow me to tell you how I feel. To tell you how these feelings we're both experiencing don't come along every day.' He turned her to face him and took her hands in his. 'This is rare. So fast. So illogical but there it is. *You* feel it. *I* feel it. We were destined to meet.'

'Destined?' Phemie laughed without humour and pulled away from him again. 'No. There is no destiny, Gil. There is only shuffling around the cards we've been dealt, trying to find the best possible hand to play.'

'You've been hurt.' It was a statement. 'Did some man hurt you? Destroy your confidence? Break your heart? Is that why you came to the outback? To hide your light under a bushel?'

'No. You've got me all wrong, Gil. I wasn't hurt, or dumped or jilted. I came to the outback because I'm a coward.' She spread her arms wide. 'There. The unvarnished truth about the woman you think I am.'

'You are not a coward, Euphemia.'

'I am. I have been stuck in a rut my whole life. Doing what needed to be done and then being too scared to take a step into the unknown. Even Anthony had the guts to leave home long before I did. He's travelled and he's had adventures and I haven't done any of those things.' She hiccuped, unable to believe the level of emotion she was feeling saying these words out loud, especially to Gil.

'Anthony's "steps" into the world have all been orchestrated for him,' Gil replied calmly. 'Even his trip to Sydney was undertaken with the aid of a supervisor. Your parents would have prepared him for these eventualities so that—'

'But they never prepared me.' Phemie couldn't believe that tears were pressing firmly behind her eyes. She wiped them away with an angry hand. 'I love my parents, please don't misinterpret me, but for my whole life Anthony has been the main focus—for all three of us. He has *always* had to come first.' She looked down at her hands and was surprised to find them trembling. 'I love him, Gil. He's my brother but sometimes… sometimes I used to wish I was an only child, that I had that "normal" life the other girls at school had. I didn't want to be known as the girl with the Down's syndrome brother. That was my identity until I finished high school. I know none of this is Anthony's fault, or my parents'. They did the best with what they had but I didn't get to have an ordinary childhood and the scars of that still run very deep.'

'It's quite clear to all and sundry that you love him, Euphemia.' Gil came towards her again, holding out a pristine white handkerchief. 'But whilst you were growing up, you just wanted a bit of the attention. Correct?'

'Yes.'

'And then you felt guilty for wanting that?'

'Yes.' She nodded, unable to believe he understood. 'You have no idea what it felt like to grow up in that sort of…box. There was nowhere for me to go. No means of breaking out. My parameters were set.' She dabbed at her eyes and shook her head, giving him an ironic smile. 'And then, when I was in med school, my parents dropped another bombshell.'

'What?' Gil held his breath, completely unable to predict what she might say next.

'They told me I was a carrier. If I have children, there's a probability they'll have Down's syndrome.'

'Carrier?' Gil frowned. 'Down's is caused by a random event to the reproductive cells *before* conception.'

'Except if you're a carrier of a defective translocation trisomy 21 chromosome. Which I am and so is my mother. They had me tested when I was a teenager, although I had no idea what the tests were all about back then.'

And there it was. Gil almost sighed with relief as he realised that this was Phemie's road block. Now that he understood the problem, he could fix it. Fixing problems was what he did best and if he could help this most incredible woman, the woman who had helped him realise his heart didn't need to be locked away for the rest of his life, that it was strong enough to love again, then so be it.

'That is why you won't marry?'

'I will not subject my children to the life I've had. I know you can rationalise things and say that because I know all about Down's, that it's not as bad as other disabilities, I'll be better able to deal with it. I know I can point at Anthony and say look how well he's turned out. He's a stable and functioning member of society. He's independent and happy and now my parents are off having the holiday they never thought they'd have, but it was all still a very restrictive upbringing.'

'But you could overcome this, Phemie.' His words were clear, calm and very matter-of-fact. 'You would make the most wonderful mother and together—*together*—we would handle anything life threw at us, even if it was a child with Down's. You have your parents' experiences to guide you, plus your own experiences, and you would be such a perfect mother. I truly believe that, Phemie. There is no reason for you to be afraid. You are strong and powerful and incredibly independent.'

She heard what he'd said but still felt as though she had to make him understand where she was coming from. 'But you don't understand what my life was like. I ended up being so used to having my life ordered, structured down to the minutest detail, that when Anthony and my parents left, I had no idea who I was. I was a grown woman. I was a doctor. I worked at a hospital. I was good at caring for others but I was lousy at caring for myself.' Her breath caught on a hiccup. 'Do you have any idea what it feels like to look in the mirror and not recognise the person staring back at you?'

'Yes.' His reply was quiet and Phemie stopped her ranting to look at him more closely. 'Yes, I do, and it's terrifying.' He paused. 'When I received word of June's and Caitie's deaths, I shrank from the world. I *put* myself into the same sort of box you were raised in so, yes, I do understand. I understand the helplessness. I understand the isolation. I understand the way you rationalise things to keep yourself protected, safe.

'Then something happens and you're forced to take a step out of that boxed existence.'

'The fellowship?' she asked and he nodded.

'No doubt someone gave you the idea to come help in the outback.'

'It was Dex.'

'I should have guessed. He's a good guy and doesn't like to see obvious talent going to waste.' Gil came closer but made no effort to touch her. 'We're more alike than you realise, Phemie. Even though we were both stuck in a rut, even though we were no doubt extremely lonely, confused and wondering just how to get out—the fact is that we both did. We sucked in a deep breath and took the plunge—and look at what's happened?'

'We found each other,' Phemie whispered, then shook her head. 'But I can't have children, Gil. I just won't do that.'

'Understandable.'

'What?'

'I understand what you're saying, why you're saying it.'

'And you agree?'

'If you feel that strongly about it, then yes.'

Phemie frowned. 'Just like that?'

'You've made the decision, an informed decision, and I'm positive you've no doubt done a lot of research into this matter...' At Phemie's slight nod, he continued. 'But you shouldn't be punished by spending the rest of your life alone. Loneliness isn't for someone as beautiful as you. It would eat you up inside and you don't want that.' He wanted to caress her cheek, to touch her, to reiterate his words with actions, but he stood his ground, keeping the distance between them. He needed, more than anything, for Phemie to be the one to reach out to him. He'd come so far and he'd wait, no doubt impatiently, for her to come the rest of the way. If this was going to work between them, it needed to be a two-way street.

'But don't you want to have children? You've been a father once and I saw the look in your eyes when you held the baby earlier. You want children, Gil. I can see it.'

'I do, but there is more than one way to become a parent.' He closed his eyes for a moment then looked at her with an intensity that made her knees start to quiver. 'Phemie, I'm almost certain I'm falling in love with you. I also have an inkling that you may feel the same way.'

'Yes.' Why wasn't he making any attempt to take her back into his arms? Was he about to tell her that even though he felt that way, even though she'd just admitted to feeling the same way, they still couldn't be together? She held her breath.

'That's...' His smile was deep, encompassing and she breathed easily. 'That's wonderful to know.' Still, he stayed where he was. 'However, I think we need time,' he continued. 'We need to sit and talk and get to know each other more. There is still so much I don't know about you.'

'And I about you.'

'See? Let's take this week. Let's use it to our best advantage.'

'And then?'

'And then I need to return to England.'

Phemie's heart caught in her throat at his words and her eyes widened in pain. The thought of not having him there, not having him with her, made her feel ill. 'But— No!' She stepped forward and wrapped her arms about his waist, burying her face in his chest, her ear pressed to his heart so she could listen to it beat its comforting, steady rhythm.

'Shh.' He enveloped her, relieved she'd come to him. 'I'm not going to stay there. I know you can't leave Australia and I would never ask you to. You have your family and your much-needed work. Simply being here, in the outback, even for just half a day, has already shown me the importance of the Royal Flying Doctor Service.'

'You were a part of that team today.'

'And it was enlightening, exhilarating and utterly exciting. I have not felt so...thrilled with medicine since my time in Tarparnii working with Pacific Medical Aid. There, the medicine was even more raw than it is here and sometimes much more devastating than the car crash in Sydney, but being there, helping others, spending time with those poor orphaned children, becoming integrated into the community—it was that which saved my life. When I returned to England, life didn't seem so bad but I still had no idea exactly where I was supposed to fit any more. Even with the fellowship, I knew I was just putting off the inevitable.'

'Which is?'

'Finding out who I am and where I fit in the world.'

'And do you know that now?' She was gazing into his eyes as she asked the question and Gil smiled brightly before brushing a kiss across her lips.

'I'm starting to.'

She smiled and breathed him in, loving his scent, loving the feel of his body beneath her hands, loving everything about him. 'Good. So we use this week?'

'Yes.'

'Then you go back to England.'

'Yes.'

'And then?'

'And then I apply for a permanent job here.'

'Just like that?'

'Why not?'

'Is it really that simple?'

'My life in England…it's not there any more. It's here. With you.' He kissed her again. 'Simple as that.'

CHAPTER TWELVE

FOR THE NEXT WEEK, Phemie and Gil spent almost every moment together. They would eat breakfast, learning what each other preferred. Phemie was more than happy to eat cereal or toast but Gil preferred a cooked breakfast.

'Besides, it's cooler to cook in the mornings than the evenings,' he pointed out on his fourth day there.

They attended clinics, house calls and two emergencies. Each time Phemie watched Gil closely as they flew in the small aircraft but he either hid his loathing for flying very well or he was coming to terms with it, letting go of his past.

In the evenings, if they weren't called out, they'd take it in turns to cook and then either watch a movie or play cards or, Phemie's favourite thing, sit on the porch swing and look at the stars, talking softly and intimately.

When it was time for bed, Gil would kiss her softly, tell her that he loved her and then head to his own room. He insisted it was the right thing to do and Phemie realised that chivalry wasn't dead. As the end of his week drew closer, their time together became more intense.

'I don't want you to go,' she said at breakfast as she watched him finish cooking his bacon and eggs. She poured them both a cup of rich-bodied Australian tea, which just so happened to be Gil's new favourite drink.

'I don't want to go. I want to stay here with you, work with you, spend as much time with you as I can. However, I do need to tie up quite a few loose ends.'

'You'll call me after each leg of your journey?'

'I'll do my best. Just make sure you're somewhere that has good reception.'

Both of them were putting on a brave front for a goodbye they knew was going to be extremely difficult. 'We'll email and call,' he murmured, pulling her to his side. He switched off the frying pan, not feeling particularly hungry. Today he would make the trek from the base to Perth, then Adelaide and finally to Sydney. There, he'd meet up with William and the rest of his staff before they all flew back to England the next morning. 'I'll be back here before you know it.'

'Just as well you have such impressive credentials or else the RFDS might not have wanted to employ you. Ben even told me the word "over qualified" was bandied around,' she teased, needing to do anything to lighten the atmosphere.

'Just as well,' he replied, and caught her to him for a long, luxurious kiss. 'I love you, Phemie. I want to be with you. Always.'

'I know.' She also knew he wasn't looking forward to this flight. Tomorrow, especially, was almost a twenty-four-hour flight from Sydney to Heathrow. Gil's family had been taken from him before and she knew he was concerned that this time everything should go according to plan. 'Everything will be fine.' They both had to believe that, to keep focused.

Nothing more had been said about children but the fact that Gil accepted her reasons for not wanting to have her own had made Phemie relax. That he hadn't pushed her on the subject also meant he had a plan up his sleeve, that much she'd learned about him during this week. He was so incredibly smart and he would ponder and think things through quite thoroughly before voicing his thoughts. She would therefore trust him and in doing so she found she was finally able to let go of the enormous weight she'd been carrying around for far too long. Gil had helped her realise that her parents had done the best job they could to give her a good childhood. It may not have been the 'cookie-cutter' family home she'd thought a lot of other girls lived in but it had been solid. It couldn't have been at all easy for them yet they'd done what they'd had to do and

Phemie knew she was very much loved by them. Wasn't that all that really mattered?

When the time came for Sardi to fly Gil to Kalgoorlie so he could make the connecting flight to Perth, Phemie found her throat completely choked with emotion. Both of them were waiting until the last possible moment before he boarded the plane.

'I love you,' she whispered against his mouth as she kissed him, tears streaming down her face.

'Don't cry, love.' He held her tight, gripping his second chance at love, not wanting to ever let her go. He so desperately wanted her to go with him, to visit England, but he knew she couldn't leave, not at the moment. Her work here was precious and necessary and he respected that. Soon they would be running the base together. He'd have more time to write articles and he had a new scope of inspiration before him—adaptive emergency medicine. He would start by writing up how to make a humidicrib from nothing more than Gaffer tape, plastic pipes and kitchen sandwich wrap.

'I can't wait to get back,' he murmured, his eyes bright with love. 'I'd say keep the home fires burning but I think you'd best keep the fans whirring instead,' he joked, and was rewarded with a little laugh. With one last, heart-searing kiss, he boarded the plane, Madge pulling up the stairs behind him. All the RFDS staff had been welcoming and this past week had been one of the happiest he'd had in a very long time.

As the plane rose, Gil looked out the window at his beautiful Euphemia, standing next to the airstrip, waving. He watched until she disappeared from view.

'But *when* will the plane be here?'

Anthony's impatience was even worse than her own. Phemie walked into the front office and asked Ben to radio Sardi to check.

'I radioed her three minutes ago.' Ben was a rational man but he could quite understand Phemie's need to know everything about this flight. 'But I'll radio again.'

'Thank you, Benjamin.' She patted his shoulder and headed outside to where Anthony was peering up at the sky. She picked up his hat from the verandah and placed it on his head. 'Don't forget your hat, darling. The sun is super-hot here.'

'Yes, Phemie,' he responded, and she couldn't help but hug him close.

'I love you.' She was so proud of everything he'd achieved. He was her baby brother and, as such, was so vitally important to her. It wasn't too late, she realised, to achieve that sibling relationship with him. All she needed to do was to let go of the picture perfect family image she'd had in her head and move forward to what she had. Anthony was a great brother who loved her. What more could a sister ask?

'I love you, too, Phemie,' he replied in his normal voice, eyes still glued to the sky. 'I'm going to be the first one to find the plane. I'm good at that, and heaps of other stuff too.'

She laughed and danced around him, her excitement unable to be contained. 'I know you are.'

'I'm good at finding planes.'

'You're the best, and this plane is *my* kind of plane.' Gil was coming home. Home to her. To where he belonged. The past month had been the longest of her life but they'd spent the time talking and finding out more about each other.

Gil had turned down job offers, sold his apartment, made arrangements for his 'jalopy' to be transported to Australia and packed his belongings. The last time he'd moved had been when his family had died. Now he was moving *towards* his new family and he couldn't wait.

Gil's impatience was mounting. 'How much longer, Sardi?'

'Three minutes since you last asked me,' Sardi returned, but smiled, understanding his need.

Gil had been flying for, what felt like for ever, which he guessed it was, given that he'd simply been either in a plane or in an airport for the past couple of days, not wanting to stop over and spend the night anywhere, instead preferring to get to his Euphemia as soon as possible.

Finally, they were there, the hangar and the house getting larger and larger as they approached.

He looked out the window and saw Anthony jumping around excitedly, waving his arms about. What surprised him more was to see Phemie joining in with the jumping and the waving. He laughed, pleased she was excited he was back.

They'd talked so much on the phone and whilst he knew the separation had been good for both of them, giving them time to think things through, to be one hundred per cent sure this was what they both wanted, he had never been so glad to return to a place as he was right now.

'Wait until I land the plane first,' Sardi called jovially as Gil impatiently drummed his fingers. He'd been in this plane enough times to know how to operate the doors. The instant the wheels touched the runway, he unclipped his seat belt and checked his jeans pocket, patting the ring concealed there. Everything was ready.

Gil didn't know who was more impatient, himself or Euphemia, but the instant the plane door was open, she was in his arms, his mouth on hers, and they were reunited in a fire of passion and need.

'I love you,' she murmured against his mouth as she kissed him, tears of joy streaming down her face.

'Why are you crying, Phemie?' Anthony wanted to know.

'Because I'm happy,' she called over her shoulder, her arms still tight around Gil, never wanting to let him go. 'I'm so very happy.'

'I'll bet I can make you happier,' Gil said softly in her ear, and in the next instant, right there in the middle of the airstrip with the plane's engines still whirring behind them, he eased away and dropped down to one knee.

'Gil?' Phemie's eyes were wide as she looked at him.

'I didn't want to do this over the phone. I needed to be here, with you. To see your face, to watch your eyes light with amazement. Euphemia Grainger, you have no idea just what you do to me and I want you to keep doing it for the rest of my life.' He held her hand and to her utter astonishment he slipped on a diamond ring. 'Will you marry me?'

She gasped and covered her mouth with her free hand, a fresh bout of tears starting up. 'Oh. Oh.' This was it. She hadn't realised it until the moment was upon her but this was definitely it. Standing there, hearing Gil's words, safe in the love she could see reflected in his eyes, Phemie knew there was nothing more important in her life than achieving her own happiness, and Gil was the one who had not only helped her to realise it but was the one who was providing it.

All those years ago, when she'd cried herself to sleep, her mother stroking her hair, telling her that one day she would meet a man who'd love everything about her—well, that day was today and Gil was most definitely that man. Happy? She was more than happy. She was blissfully content, wrapped in his love and secure in the knowledge that whatever their life threw at them, whatever might or might not happen with regard to children, they would face their future as one.

'Oh, Gil,' she whispered again.

'What's the matter, Phemie?' Anthony wanted to know. 'More happy tears?'

'Yes. Oh, yes.'

'Was that answer to me or Anthony?' Gil asked.

'To you,' she said softly. 'You come first.'

Gil stood and swooped her up into his arms, spinning her round a few times as he kissed her.

'*We* come first,' he corrected. 'You and me. Together.'

'For ever.'

EPILOGUE

'WHEN WILL THE fireworks and stuff start, Phemie?' Anthony asked.

'Soon. Very soon,' she told her impatient brother. 'You keep watching the sky.' They were all gathered in the main street of Didja for the annual New Year's Eve fireworks and Phemie knew she'd never had a happier start to the coming year.

Last year, she'd preferred to stay at the RFDS Base, seeing the New Year in by going to bed early and waking up the next morning with a headache. This year, she thought as she hugged her husband close, would be so very different.

In a few weeks time, both she and Gil would head over to Tarparnii for three months to work with Pacific Medical Aid. The RFDS would send another doctor to the Base to cover them until their return...and when they returned their numbers would increase.

Gil had indeed had a plan brewing and when he'd talked about the amount of orphaned children in Tarparnii and the poor sanitation most villages experienced, Phemie's heart had turned over with need. The more he'd talked, the more Phemie had wanted to see these places for herself, to see those children and help in any way she could.

'When will the adoption be final?' Iris asked Phemie as they all stood together, waiting for the fireworks to start. Iris held her squirming daughter, Anya, in her arms and when the toddler saw Dex, she squealed with delight. Iris put her down and watched as the little girl ran over to her adoptive father.

'One month after we arrive in Tarparnii.'

'That's fantastic. Instant motherhood isn't easy,' Iris laughed. 'I should know having inherited Anya upon her parents' death but it's…' she sighed with happiness. 'Fantastic. You and Gil are going to love being parents.'

Phemie smiled up at her handsome husband who was busy talking to Joss and a very pregnant Melissa. 'I think we will.' She had a sparkle in her eyes and a glow which was perfectly radiant. She had some special news to share with her husband, news she was sure he wouldn't quite believe but she wanted to wait for the right moment. 'We have so much love to give, to share with our children.'

'Love does that,' Iris confirmed.

'When will the fireworks and stuff start, Phemie?' Anthony asked again and Phemie checked her watch.

'It's almost midnight, Anthony. One more minute.' Excitement coursed through Phemie as Gil tightened his arm about her waist.

'He's so excited,' he murmured, brushing a kiss to Phemie's lips. 'It's addictive.'

Gil had loved his first outback Christmas and now seemed to be intent on enjoying his first outback New Year. Phemie's parents and Anthony had been resplendent at their September wedding and had been more than happy to return to Didja to share in the newly weds' first Christmas. A few days later, the Graingers had left for another short holiday, Anthony wanting to stay on to experience New Year in Didja and who could blame him? The atmosphere was indeed electrifying.

'You're addictive,' Phemie returned and urged his head down for a more thorough kiss.

'Hey,' Melissa protested. 'You're supposed to wait until midnight actually strikes before the kissing starts.'

'You can talk,' Dex teased his big sister as he tickled Anya's tummy. 'Last year, you and Joss almost couldn't wait to lip-lock.'

Joss grinned at Melissa. 'Our first kiss and now—a year later—look where we all are.' He placed a hand protectively on his wife's belly, caressing the baby within.

'It's been quite a year,' Gil agreed, smiling at his Euphemia. He'd never thought he'd ever be this happy again and yet every day, his love grew for the woman at his side. He loved outback life, loved the vast, remoteness of it all and couldn't wait to fill their home with the children they both yearned for. Soon. It would all be happening soon.

'When will the fireworks and stuff start, Phemie?' Anthony asked and Phemie giggled as the ten second countdown began. Soon, she would tell her husband the good news, the most amazing news. When Melissa had confirmed Phemie's own suspicions, she hadn't believed it.

'Would you like me to do an amniocentesis to check for Down's?' Melissa had asked and Phemie had declined the offer. Gil had been right all those months ago. Together, with him by her side, she could do anything. She would make the most wonderful mother and he would be the most incredible father.

'Keep watching the sky,' she told her brother. 'It will light up your life.' She, however, wasn't watching the sky. Instead, she was looking as intently into Gil's eyes as he was into her own.

'You light up my life,' she murmured.

'Ditto,' he replied and kissed her passionately as the fireworks cracked and sparkled above them.

'By the way,' she murmured against his lips with utter happiness filling her heart. 'I'm pregnant and I've never been happier in my life.'

* * * * *

talk about it

Let's talk about books.

Join the conversation:

 on facebook.com/harlequinaustralia

 on Twitter @harlequinaus

www.harlequinbooks.com.au

If you love reading and want to know about our authors and titles, then let's talk about it.